DEATH TO CRENSHINIBON!

The fact that this drow was not a simple instrument of chaos and destruction, as were so many of the demon lords, or an easily duped human—perhaps the most redundant thought the artifact had ever considered—only made him more interesting.

They had a long way to go together, Crenshinibon believed.

The artifact would find its greatest level of power.

The world would suffer greatly.

R.A. SALVATORE

THE SELLSWORDS
Servant of the Shard
Promise of the Witch-King
Road of the Patriarch

THE LEGEND OF DRIZZT
Homeland
Exile
Sojourn
The Crystal Shard
Streams of Silver
The Halfling's Gem
The Legacy
Starless Night
Siege of Darkness
Passage to Dawn
The Silent Blade
The Spine of the World
Sea of Swords

THE HUNTER'S BLADES TRILOGY
The Thousand Orcs
The Lone Drow
The Two Swords

R.A. SALVATORE
SERVANT OF THE SHARD

THE SELLSWORDS

BOOK I

The Sellswords, Book I
Servant of the Shard

©2000 Wizards of the Coast, Inc.

Cover art by Todd Lockwood
Original Hardcover First Printing: October 2000
This Edition First Printing: June 2005
Library of Congress Catalog Card Number: 2004116898

9 8 7 6 5 4 3

ISBN-10: 0-7869-3950-8
ISBN-13: 978-0-7869-3950-3
620-95407000-001-EN

U.S., CANADA,
ASIA, PACIFIC, & LATIN AMERICA
Wizards of the Coast, Inc.
P.O. Box 707
Renton, WA 98057-0707
+1-800-324-6496

EUROPEAN HEADQUARTERS
Hasbro UK Ltd
Caswell Way
Newport, Gwent NP9 0YH
GREAT BRITAIN
Please keep this address for your records

Visit our web site at **www.wizards.com**

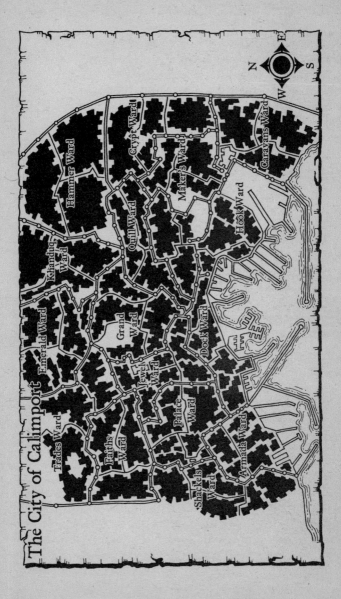

PROLOGUE

He glided through the noonday sunshine's oppressive heat, moving as if always cloaked in shadows, though the place had few, and as if even the ever-present dust could not touch him. The open market was crowded—it was always crowded—with yelling merchants and customers bargaining for every copper piece. Thieves were positioning themselves in all the best and busiest places, where they might cut a purse string without ever being noticed, or if they were discovered, where they could melt away into a swirling crowd of bright colors and flowing robes.

Artemis Entreri noted the thieves clearly. He could tell with a glance who was there to shop and who was there to steal, and he didn't avoid the latter group. He purposely set his course to bring him right by every thief he could find, and he'd pushed back one side of his dark cloak, revealing his ample purse—

—revealing, too, the jewel-decorated dagger that kept his purse and his person perfectly safe. The dagger was his trademark weapon, one of the most feared blades on all of Calimport's dangerous streets.

Entreri enjoyed the respect the young thieves offered him, and more than that, he demanded it. He had spent years earning his reputation as the finest assassin in Calimport, but he was getting older. He was losing, perhaps, that fine edge of brilliance. Thus, he

1

came out brazenly—more so than he ever would have in his younger days—daring them, any of them, to make a try for him.

He crossed the busy avenue, heading for a small outdoor tavern that had many round tables set under a great awning. The place was bustling, but Entreri immediately spotted his contact, the flamboyant Sha'lazzi Ozoule with his trademark bright yellow turban. Entreri moved straight for the table. Sha'lazzi wasn't sitting alone, though it was obvious to Entreri that the three men seated with him were not friends of his, were not known to him at all. The others held a private conversation, chattering and chuckling, while Sha'lazzi leaned back, glancing all around.

Entreri walked up to the table. Sha'lazzi gave a nervous and embarrassed shrug as the assassin looked questioningly at the three uninvited guests.

"You did not tell them that this table was reserved for our luncheon?" Entreri calmly asked.

The three men stopped their conversation and looked up at him curiously.

"I tried to explain . . ." Sha'lazzi started, wiping the sweat from his dark-skinned brow.

Entreri held up his hand to silence the man and fixed his imposing gaze on the three trespassers. "We have business," he said.

"And we have food and drink," one of them replied.

Entreri didn't reply, other than to stare hard at the man, to let his gaze lock with the other's.

The other two made a couple of remarks, but Entreri ignored them completely and just kept staring hard at the first challenger. On and on it went, and Entreri kept his focus, even tightened it, his gaze boring into the man, showing him the strength of will he now faced, the perfect determination and control.

"What is this about?" one of the others demanded, standing up right beside Entreri.

Sha'lazzi muttered the quick beginning of a common prayer.

"I asked you," the man pushed, and he reached out to shove Entreri's shoulder.

Up snapped the assassin's hand, catching the approaching hand by the thumb and spinning it over, then driving it down, locking the man in a painful hold.

All the while Entreri didn't blink, didn't glance away at all, just kept visually holding the first one, who was sitting directly across from him, in that awful glare.

The man standing at Entreri's side gave a little grunt as the assassin applied pressure, then brought his free hand to his belt, to the curved dagger he had secured there.

Sha'lazzi muttered another line of the prayer.

The man across the table, held fast by Entreri's deadly stare, motioned for his friend to hold calm and to keep his hand away from the blade.

Entreri nodded to him, then motioned for him to take his friends and be gone. He released the man at his side, who clutched at his sore thumb, eyeing Entreri threateningly. He didn't come at Entreri again, nor did either of his friends make any move, except to pick up their plates and sidle away. They hadn't recognized Entreri, yet he had shown them the truth of who he was without ever drawing his blade.

"I meant to do the same thing," Sha'lazzi remarked with a chuckle as the three departed and Entreri settled into the seat opposite him.

Entreri just stared at him, noting how out-of-sorts this one always appeared. Sha'lazzi had a huge head and a big round face, and that put on a body so skinny as to appear emaciated. Furthermore, that big round face was always, always smiling, with huge, square white teeth glimmering in contrast to his dark skin and black eyes.

Sha'lazzi cleared his throat again. "Surprised I am that you came out for this meeting," he said. "You have made many enemies in your rise with the Basadoni Guild. Do you not fear treachery, O powerful one?" he finished sarcastically and again with a chuckle.

Entreri only continued to stare. Indeed he had feared treachery, but he needed to speak with Sha'lazzi. Kimmuriel Oblodra, the drow psionicist working for Jarlaxle, had scoured Sha'lazzi's thoughts completely and had come to the conclusion that there was no conspiracy afoot.

Of course, considering the source of the information—a dark elf who held no love for Entreri—the assassin hadn't been completely comforted by the report.

"It can be a prison to the powerful, you understand," Sha'lazzi rambled on. "A prison to *be* powerful, you see? So many pashas dare not leave their homes without an entourage of a hundred guards."

"I am not a pasha."

"No, indeed, but Basadoni belongs to you and to Sharlotta," Sha'lazzi returned, referring to Sharlotta Vespers. The woman had used her wiles to become Pasha Basadoni's second and had survived the drow takeover to serve as figurehead of the guild. And the guild had suddenly become more powerful than anyone could imagine. "Everyone knows this." Sha'lazzi gave another of his annoying chuckles. "I always understood that you were good, my friend, but never this good!"

Entreri smiled back, but in truth his amusement came from a fantasy of sticking his dagger into Sha'lazzi's skinny throat, for no better reason than the fact that he simply couldn't stand this parasite.

Entreri had to admit that he needed Sha'lazzi, though—and that was exactly how the notorious informant managed to stay alive. Sha'lazzi had made a living, indeed an art, out of telling anybody anything he wanted to know—for a price—and so good was he at his craft, so connected to every pulse beat of Calimport's ruling families and street thugs alike, that he had made himself too valuable to the often-warring guilds to be murdered.

"So tell me of the power behind the throne of Basadoni," Sha'lazzi remarked, grinning widely. "For surely there is more, yes?"

Entreri worked hard to keep himself stone-faced, knowing that a responding grin would give too much away—and how he wanted to grin at Sha'lazzi's honest ignorance of the truth of the new Basadonis. Sha'lazzi would never know that a dark elf army had set up shop in Calimport, using the Basadoni Guild as its front.

"I thought we had agreed to discuss Dallabad Oasis?" Entreri asked in reply.

Sha'lazzi sighed and shrugged. "Many interesting things to speak of," he said. "Dallabad is not one of them, I fear."

"In your opinion."

"Nothing has changed there in twenty years," Sha'lazzi replied. "There is nothing there that I know that you do not, and have not, for nearly as many years."

"Kohrin Soulez still retains Charon's Claw?" Entreri asked.

Sha'lazzi nodded. "Of course," he said with a chuckle. "Still and forever. It has served him for four decades, and when Soulez is dead, one of his thirty sons will take it, no doubt, unless the indelicate Ahdania Soulez gets to it first. An ambitious one is the daughter of Kohrin Soulez! If you came to ask me if he will part with it, then you already know the answer. We should indeed speak of more interesting things, such as the Basadoni Guild."

Entreri's hard stare returned in a heartbeat.

"Why would old Soulez sell it now?" Sha'lazzi asked with a dramatic wave of his skinny arms—arms that looked so incongruous when lifted beside that huge head. "What is this, my friend, the third time you have tried to purchase that fine sword? Yes, yes! First, when you were a pup with a few hundred gold pieces—a gift of Basadoni, eh?—in your ragged pouch."

Entreri winced at that despite himself, despite his knowledge that Sha'lazzi, for all of his other faults, was the best in Calimport at reading gestures and expressions and deriving the truth behind them. Still, the memory, combined with more recent events, evoked the response from his heart. Pasha Basadoni had indeed given him the extra coin that long-ago day, an offering to his most promising lieutenant for no good reason but simply as a gift. When he thought about it, Entreri realized that Basadoni was perhaps the only man who had ever given him a gift without expecting something in return.

And Entreri had killed Basadoni, only a few months ago.

"Yes, yes," Sha'lazzi said, more to himself than to Entreri, "then you asked about the sword again soon after Pasha Pook's demise. Ah, but he fell hard, that one!"

Entreri just stared at the man. Sha'lazzi, apparently just then beginning to catch on that he might be pushing the dangerous assassin too far, cleared his throat, embarrassed.

"Then I told you that it was impossible," Sha'lazzi remarked. "Of course it is impossible."

"I have more coin now," Entreri said quietly.

"There is not enough coin in all of the world!" Sha'lazzi wailed.

Entreri didn't blink. "Do you know how much coin is in all the world, Sha'lazzi?" he asked calmly—too calmly. "Do you know how much coin is in the coffers of House Basadoni?"

"House Entreri, you mean," the man corrected.

Entreri didn't deny it, and Sha'lazzi's eyes widened. There it was, as clearly spelled out as the informant could ever have expected to hear it. Rumors had said that old Basadoni was dead, and that Sharlotta Vespers and the other acting guildmasters were no more than puppets for the one who clearly pulled the strings: Artemis Entreri.

"Charon's Claw," Sha'lazzi mused, a smile widening upon his face. "So, the power behind the throne is Entreri, and the power behind Entreri is . . . well, a mage, I would guess, since you so badly want that particular sword. A mage, yes, and one who is getting a bit dangerous, eh?"

"Keep guessing," said Entreri.

"And perhaps I will get it correct?"

"If you do, I will have to kill you," the assassin said, still in that awful, calm tone. "Speak with Sheik Soulez. Find his price."

"He has no price," Sha'lazzi insisted.

Entreri came forward quicker than any cat after a mouse. One hand slapped down on Sha'lazzi's shoulder, the other caught hold of that deadly jeweled dagger, and Entreri's face came within an inch of Sha'lazzi's.

"That would be most unfortunate," Entreri said. "For you."

The assassin pushed the informant back in his seat, then stood up straight and glanced around as if some inner hunger had just awakened within him and he was now seeking some prey with which to sate it. He looked back at Sha'lazzi only briefly, then walked out from under the awning, back into the tumult of the market area.

As he calmed down and considered the meeting, Entreri silently berated himself. His frustration was beginning to wear at the edges of perfection. He could not have been more obvious about the roots of his problem than to so eagerly ask about purchasing Charon's Claw. Above all else, that weapon and gauntlet combination had been designed to battle wizards.

And psionicists, perhaps?

For those were Entreri's tormentors, Rai-guy and Kimmuriel—Jarlaxle's Bregan D'aerthe lieutenants—one a wizard and one a psionicist. Entreri hated them both, and profoundly, but more importantly he knew that they hated him. To make things worse Entreri understood that his only armor against the dangerous pair was Jarlaxle himself. While to his surprise he had cautiously come to trust the mercenary dark elf, he doubted Jarlaxle's protection would hold forever.

Accidents did happen, after all.

Entreri needed protection, but he had to go about things with his customary patience and intelligence, twisting the trail beyond anyone's ability to follow, fighting the way he had perfected so many years before on Calimport's tough streets, using many subtle layers of information and misinformation and blending the two together so completely that neither his friends nor his foes could ever truly unravel them. When only he knew the truth, then he, and only he, would be in control.

In that sobering light, he took the less than perfect meeting with perceptive Sha'lazzi as a distinct warning, a reminder that he could survive his time with the dark elves only if he kept an absolute level of personal control. Indeed, Sha'lazzi had come close to figuring out his current plight, had gotten half of it, at least, correct. The pie-faced man would obviously offer that information to any who'd pay well enough for it. On Calimport's streets these days many were scrambling to figure out the enigma of the sudden and vicious rise of the Basadoni Guild.

Sha'lazzi had figured out half of it, and so all the usual suspects would be considered: a powerful arch-mage or various wizards' guilds.

Despite his dour mood, Entreri chuckled when he pictured Sha'lazzi's expression should the man ever learn the other half of that secret behind Basadoni's throne, that the dark elves had come to Calimport in force!

Of course, his threat to the man had not been an idle one. Should Sha'lazzi ever make such a connection, Entreri, or any one of a thousand of Jarlaxle's agents, would surely kill him.

⊕═══⊕

Sha'lazzi Ozoule sat at the little round table for a long, long time, replaying Entreri's every word and every gesture. He knew that his assumption concerning a wizard holding the true power behind the Basadoni rise was correct, but that was not really news. Given the expediency of the rise, and the level of devastation that had been enacted upon rival houses, common sense dictated that a wizard, or more likely many wizards, were involved.

What caught Sha'lazzi as a revelation, though, was Entreri's visceral reaction.

Artemis Entreri, the master of control, the shadow of death itself, had never before shown him such an inner turmoil—even fear, perhaps?—as that. When before had Artemis Entreri ever touched someone in threat? No, he had always looked at him with that awful gaze, let him know in no uncertain terms that he was walking the path to ultimate doom. If the offender persisted, there was no further threat, no grabbing or beating.

There was only quick death.

The uncharacteristic reaction surely intrigued Sha'lazzi. How he wanted to know what had so rattled Artemis Entreri as to facilitate such behavior—but at the same time, the assassin's demeanor also served as a clear and frightening warning. Sha'lazzi knew well that anything that could so unnerve Artemis Entreri could easily, so easily, destroy Sha'lazzi Ozoule.

It was an interesting situation, and one that scared Sha'lazzi profoundly.

PART 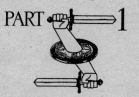 1

S T I C K I N G   T O   T H E   W E B

I *live in a world where there truly exists the embodiment of evil. I speak not of wicked men, nor of goblins—often of evil weal—nor even of my own people, the dark elves, wickeder still than the goblins. These are creatures—all of them—capable of great cruelty, but they are not, even in the very worst of cases, the true embodiment of evil. No, that title belongs to others, to the demons and devils often summoned by priests and mages. These creatures of the lower planes are the purest of evil, untainted vileness running unchecked. They are without possibility of redemption, without hope of accomplishing anything in their unfortunately nearly eternal existence that even borders on goodness.*

I have wondered if these creatures could exist without the darkness that lies within the hearts of the reasoning races. Are they a source of evil, as are many wicked men or drow, or are they the result, a physical manifestation of the rot that permeates the hearts of far too many?

The latter, I believe. It is not coincidental that demons and devils cannot walk the material plane of existence without being brought here by the actions of one of the reasoning beings. They are no more than a tool, I know, an instrument to carry out the wicked deeds in service to the truer source of that evil.

What then of Crenshinibon? It is an item, an artifact—albeit a sentient one—but it does not exist in the same state of intelligence as does a reasoning being. For the Crystal Shard cannot grow, cannot

13

change, cannot mend its ways. The only errors it can learn to correct are those of errant attempts at manipulation, as it seeks to better grab at the hearts of those around it. It cannot even consider, or reconsider, the end it desperately tries to achieve—no, its purpose is forever singular.

Is it truly evil, then?

No.

I would have thought differently not too long ago, even when I carried the dangerous artifact and came better to understand it. Only recently, upon reading a long and detailed message sent to me from High Priest Cadderly Bonaduce of the Spirit Soaring, have I come to see the truth of the Crystal Shard, have I come to understand that the item itself is an anomaly, a mistake, and that its never-ending hunger for power and glory, at whatever cost, is merely a perversion of the intent of its second maker, the eighth spirit that found its way into the very essence of the artifact.

The Crystal Shard was created originally by seven liches, so Cadderly has learned, who designed to fashion an item of the very greatest power. As a further insult to the races these undead kings intended to conquer, they made the artifact a draw against the sun itself, the giver of life. The liches were consumed at the completion of their joining magic. Despite what some sages believe, Cadderly insists that the conscious aspects of those vile creatures were not drawn into the power of the item, but were, rather, obliterated by its sunlike properties. Thus, their intended insult turned against them and left them as no more than ashes and absorbed pieces of their shattered spirits.

That much of the earliest history of the Crystal Shard is known by many, including the demons that so desperately crave the item. The second story, though, the one Cadderly uncovered, tells a more compli- cated tale, and shows the truth of Crenshinibon, the ultimate failure of the artifact as a perversion of goodly intentions.

Crenshinibon first came to the material world centuries ago in the far-off land of Zakhara. At the time, it was merely a wizard's tool, though a great and powerful one, an artifact that could throw fireballs and create great blazing walls of light so intense they could burn flesh from bone. Little was known of Crenshinibon's dark past until it fell to the hands of a sultan. This great leader, whose name has been lost to the ages, learned the truth of the Crystal Shard, and with the help of his many court wizards, decided that the work of the liches was incomplete. Thus came the "second creation" of Crenshinibon, the heightening of its power and its limited consciousness.

This sultan had no dreams of domination, only of peaceful existence with his many warlike neighbors. Thus, using the newest power of the artifact, he envisioned, then created, a line of crystalline towers. The towers stretched from his capital across the empty desert to his kingdom's second city, an oft-raided frontier city, in intervals equating to a single day's travel. He strung as many as a hundred of the crystalline towers, and nearly completed the mighty defensive line.

But alas, the sultan overreached the powers of Crenshinibon, and though he believed that the creation of each tower strengthened the artifact, he was, in fact, pulling the Crystal Shard and its manifestations too thin. Soon after, a great sandstorm came up, sweeping across the desert. It was a natural disaster that served as a prelude to an invasion by a neighboring sheikdom. So thin were the walls of those crystalline towers that they shattered under the force of the glass, taking with them the sultan's dream of security.

The hordes overran the kingdom and murdered the sultan's family while he helplessly looked on. Their merciless sheik would not kill the sultan, though—he wanted the painful memories to burn at the man—but Crenshinibon took the sultan, took a piece of his spirit, at least.

Little more of those early days is known, even to Cadderly, who counts demigods among his sources, but the young high priest of Deneir is convinced that this "second creation" of Crenshinibon is the one that remains key to the present hunger of the artifact. If only Crenshinibon could have held its highest level of power. If only the crystalline towers had remained strong. The hordes would have been turned away, and the sultan's family, his dear wife and beautiful children, would not have been murdered.

Now the artifact, imbued with the twisted aspects of seven dead liches and with the wounded and tormented spirit of the sultan, continues its desperate quest to attain and maintain its greatest level of power, whatever the cost.

There are many implications to the story. Cadderly hinted in his note to me, though he drew no definitive conclusions, that the creation of the crystalline towers actually served as the catalyst for the invasion, with the leaders of the neighboring sheikdom fearful that their borderlands would soon be overrun. Is the Crystal Shard, then, a great lesson to us? Does it show clearly the folly of overblown ambition, even though that particular ambition was rooted in good intentions? The sultan wanted strength for the defense of his peaceable kingdom, and yet he reached for too much power.

That was what consumed him, his family, and his kingdom.

What of Jarlaxle, then, who now holds the Crystal Shard? Should I go after him and try to take back the artifact, then deliver it to Cadderly for destruction? Surely the world would be a better place without this mighty and dangerous artifact.

Then again, there will always be another tool for those of evil weal, another embodiment of their evil, be it a demon, a devil, or a monstrous creation similar to Crenshinibon.

No, the embodiments are not the problem, for they cannot exist and prosper without the evil that is within the hearts of reasoning beings.

Beware, Jarlaxle. Beware.

—Drizzt Do'Urden

CHAPTER

1

Dwahvel Tiggerwillies tiptoed into the small, dimly lit room in the back of the lower end of her establishment, the Copper Ante. Dwahvel, that most competent of halfling females—good with her wiles, good with her daggers, and better with her wits—wasn't used to walking so gingerly in this place, though it was as secure a house as could be found in all of Calimport. This was Artemis Entreri, after all, and no place in all the world could truly be considered safe when the deadly assassin was about.

He was pacing when she entered, taking no obvious note of her arrival at all. Dwahvel looked at him curiously. She knew that Entreri had been on edge lately and was one of the very few outside of House Basadoni who knew the truth behind that edge. The dark elves had come and infiltrated Calimport's streets, and Entreri was serving as a front man for their operations. If Dwahvel held any preconceived notions of how terrible the drow truly could be, one look at Entreri surely confirmed those suspicions. He had never been a nervous one—Dwahvel wasn't sure that he was now—and had never been a man Dwahvel would have expected to find at odds with himself.

Even more curious, Entreri had invited her into his confidence. It just wasn't his way. Still, Dwahvel suspected no trap. This was, she knew, exactly as it seemed, as surprising as that might be. Entreri was speaking to himself as much as to her, as a way of clarifying his thoughts, and for some reason that Dwahvel didn't yet understand, he was letting her listen in.

She considered herself complimented in the highest way and also realized the potential danger that came along with that compliment. That unsettling thought in mind, the halfling guildmistress quietly settled into a chair and listened carefully, looking for clues and insights. Her first, and most surprising, came when she happened to glance at a chair set against the back wall of the room. Resting on it was a half-empty bottle of Moonshae whiskey.

"I see them at every corner on every street in the belly of this cursed city," Entreri was saying. "Braggarts wearing their scars and weapons like badges of honor, men and women so concerned about reputation that they have lost sight of what it is they truly wish to accomplish. They play for the status and the accolades, and with no better purpose."

His speech was not overly slurred, yet it was obvious to Dwahvel that Entreri had indeed tasted some of the whiskey.

"Since when does Artemis Entreri bother himself with the likes of street thieves?" Dwahvel asked.

Entreri stopped pacing and glanced at her, his face passive. "I see them and mark them carefully, because I am well aware that my own reputation precedes me. Because of that reputation, many on the street would love to sink a dagger into my heart," the assassin replied and began to pace again. "How great a reputation that killer might then find. They know that I am older now, and they think me slower—and in truth, their reasoning is sound. I cannot move as quickly as I did a decade ago."

Dwahvel's eyes narrowed at the surprising admission.

"But as the body ages and movements dull, the mind grows sharper," Entreri went on. "I, too, am concerned with reputation, but not as I used to be. It was my goal in life to be the absolute best at that which I do, at out-fighting and out-thinking my enemies. I desired to become the perfect warrior, and it took a dark elf whom I despise to show me the error of my ways. My unintended journey to Menzoberranzan as a 'guest' of Jarlaxle humbled me in my fanatical striving to be the best and showed me the futility of a world full of that who I most wanted to become. In Menzoberranzan, I saw reflections of myself at every turn, warriors who had become so callous to all around them, so enwrapped in the goal, that they could not begin to appreciate the process of attaining it."

"They are drow," Dwahvel said. "We cannot understand their true motivations."

"Their city is a beautiful place, my little friend," Entreri replied, "with power beyond anything you can imagine. Yet, for all for that, Menzoberranzan is a hollow and empty place, bereft of passion unless that passion is hate. I came back from that city of twenty thousand assassins changed indeed, questioning the very foundations of my existence. What is the point of it, after all?"

Dwahvel interlocked the fingers of her plump little hands and brought them up to her lips, studying the man intently. Was Entreri announcing his retirement? she wondered. Was he denying the life he had known, the glories to which he had climbed? She blew a quiet sigh, shook her head, and said, "We all answer that question for ourselves, don't we? The point is gold or respect or property or power . . ."

"Indeed," he said coldly. "I walk now with a better understanding of who I am and what challenges before me are truly important. I know not yet where I hope to go, what challenges are left before me, but I do understand now that the important thing is to enjoy the process of getting there.

"Do I care that my reputation remains strong?" Entreri asked suddenly, even as Dwahvel started to ask him if he had any idea at all of where his road might lead—important information, given the power of the Basadoni Guild. "Do I wish to continue to be upheld as the pinnacle of success among assassins within Calimport?

"Yes, to both, but not for the same reasons that those fools swagger about the street corners, not for the same reasons that many of them will make a try for me, only to wind up dead in the gutter. No, I care about reputation because it allows me to be so much more effective in that which I choose to do. I care for celebrity, but only because in that mantle my foes fear me more, fear me beyond rational thinking and beyond the bounds of proper caution. They are afraid, even as they come after me, but instead of a healthy respect, their fear is almost paralyzing, making them continuously second-guess their own every move. I can use that fear against them. With a simple bluff or feint, I can make the doubt lead them into a completely erroneous position. Because I can feign vulnerability and use perceived advantages against the careless, on those occasions when I am truly vulnerable the cautious will not aggressively strike."

He paused and nodded, and Dwahvel saw that his thoughts were indeed sorting out. "An enviable position, to be sure," she offered.

"Let the fools come after me, one after another, an endless line of eager assassins," Entreri said, and he nodded again. "With each kill, I grow wiser, and with added wisdom, I grow stronger."

He slapped his hat, that curious small-brimmed black bolero, against his thigh, spun it up his arm with a flick of his wrist so that it rolled right over his shoulder to settle on his head, complementing the fine haircut he had just received. Only then did Dwahvel notice that the man had trimmed his thick goatee as well, leaving only a fine mustache and a small patch of hair below his lower lip, running down to his chin and going to both sides like an inverted T.

Entreri looked at the halfling, gave a sly wink, and strode from the room.

What did it all mean? Dwahvel wondered. Surely she was glad to see that the man had cleaned up his look, for she had recognized his uncharacteristic slovenliness as a sure signal that he was losing control, and worse, losing his heart.

She sat there for a long time, bouncing her clasped hands absently against her puckered lower lip, wondering why she had been invited to such a spectacle, wondering why Artemis Entreri had felt the need to open up to her, to anyone—even to himself. The man had found some epiphany, Dwahvel realized, and she suddenly realized that she had, too.

Artemis Entreri was her friend.

CHAPTER

2

Faster! Faster, I say!" Jarlaxle howled. His arm flashed repeatedly, and a seemingly endless stream of daggers spewed forth at the dodging and rolling assassin.

Entreri worked his jeweled dagger and his sword—a drow-fashioned blade that he was not particularly enamored of—furiously, with in and out vertical rolls to catch the missiles and flip them aside. All the while he kept his feet moving, skittering about, looking for an opening in Jarlaxle's superb defensive posture—a stance made all the more powerful by the constant stream of spinning daggers.

"An opening!" the drow mercenary cried, letting fly one, two, three more daggers.

Entreri sent his sword back the other way but knew that his opponent's assessment was correct. He dived into a roll instead, tucking his head and his arms in tight to cover any vital areas.

"Oh, well done!" Jarlaxle congratulated as Entreri came to his feet after taking only a single hit, and that a dagger sticking into the trailing fold of his cloak instead of his skin.

Entreri felt the dagger swing in against the back of his leg as he stood up. Fearing that it might trip him, he tossed his own dagger into the air, then quickly pulled the cloak from his shoulders, and in the same fluid movement, started to toss it aside.

An idea came to him, though, and he didn't discard the cloak but rather caught his deadly dagger and set it between his teeth. He stalked a semicircle about the drow, waving his cloak, a drow *piwafwi*, slowly about as a shield against the missiles.

Jarlaxle smiled at him. "Improvisation," he said with obvious admiration. "The mark of a true warrior." Even as he finished, though, the drow's arm starting moving yet again. A quartet of daggers soared at the assassin.

Entreri bobbed and spun a complete circuit, but tossed his cloak as he did and caught it as he came back around. One dagger skidded across the floor, another passed over Entreri's head, narrowly missing, and the other two got caught in the fabric, along with the previous one.

Entreri continued to wave the cloak, but it wasn't flowing wide anymore, weighted as it was by the three daggers.

"Not so good a shield, perhaps," Jarlaxle commented.

"You talk better than you fight," Entreri countered. "A bad combination."

"I talk because I so enjoy the fight, my quick friend," Jarlaxle replied.

His arm went back again, but Entreri was already moving. The human held his arm out wide to keep the cloak from tripping him, and dived into a roll right toward the mercenary, closing the gap between them in the blink of an eye.

Jarlaxle did let fly one dagger. It skipped off Entreri's back, but the drow mercenary caught the next one sliding out of his magical bracer into his hand and snapped his wrist, speaking a command word. The dagger responded at once, elongating into a sword. As Entreri came over, his sword predictably angled up to gut Jarlaxle, the drow had the parry in place.

Entreri stayed low and skittered forward instead, swinging his cloak in a roundabout manner to wrap it behind Jarlaxle's legs. The mercenary quick-stepped and almost got out of the way, but one of the daggers hooked his boot and he fell over backward. Jarlaxle was as agile as any drow, but so too was Entreri. The human came up over the drow, sword thrusting.

Jarlaxle parried fast, his blade slapping against Entreri's. To the drow's surprise, the assassin's sword went flying away. Jarlaxle understood soon enough, though, for Entreri's now free hand came forward, clasping Jarlaxle's forearm and holding the drow's weapon out wide.

And there loomed the assassin's other hand, holding again that deadly jeweled dagger.

Entreri had the opening and had the strike, and Jarlaxle couldn't block it or begin to move away from it. A wave of such despair, an overwhelming barrage of complete and utter hopelessness, washed over Entreri. He felt as if someone had just entered his brain and began scattering all of his thoughts, starting and stopping all of his reflexes. In the inevitable pause, Jarlaxle brought his other arm forward, launching a dagger that smacked Entreri in the gut and bounced away.

The barrage of discordant, paralyzing emotions continued to blast away in Entreri's mind, and he stumbled back. He hardly felt the motion and was somewhat confused a moment later, as the fuzziness began to clear, to find that he was on the other side of the small room sitting against the wall and facing a smiling Jarlaxle.

Entreri closed his eyes and at last forced the confusing jumble of thoughts completely away. He assumed that Rai-guy, the drow wizard who had imbued both Entreri and Jarlaxle with stoneskin spells that they could spar with all of their hearts without fear of injuring each other, had intervened. When he glanced that way, he saw that the wizard was nowhere to be seen. He turned back to Jarlaxle, guessing then that the mercenary had used yet another in his seemingly endless bag of tricks. Perhaps he had used his newest magical acquisition, the powerful Crenshinibon, to overwhelm Entreri's concentration.

"Perhaps you *are* slowing down, my friend," Jarlaxle remarked.

"What a pity that would be. It is good that you defeated your avowed enemy when you did, for Drizzt Do'Urden has many centuries of youthful speed left in him."

Entreri scoffed at the words, though in truth, the thought gnawed at him. He had lived his entire life on the very edge of perfection and preparedness. Even now, in the middle years of his life, he was confident that he could defeat almost any foe—with pure skill or by out-thinking any enemy, by properly preparing any battlefield—but Entreri didn't want to slow down. He didn't want to lose that edge of fighting brilliance that had so marked his life.

He wanted to deny Jarlaxle's words, but he could not, for he knew in his heart that he had truly lost that fight with Drizzt, that if Kimmuriel Oblodra had not intervened with his psionic powers, then Drizzt would have been declared the victor.

"You did not outmatch me with speed," the assassin started to argue, shaking his head.

Jarlaxle came forward, his glowing eyes narrowing dangerously— a threatening expression, a look of rage, that the assassin rarely saw upon the handsome face of the always-in-control dark elf mercenary leader.

"I have *this!*" Jarlaxle announced, pulling wide his cloak and showing Entreri the tip of the artifact, Crenshinibon, the Crystal Shard, tucked neatly into one pocket. "Never forget that. Without it, I could likely still defeat you, though you are good, my friend— better than any human I have ever known. But with this in my possession . . . you are but a mere mortal. Joined in Crenshinibon, I can destroy you with but a thought. Never forget that."

Entreri lowered his gaze, digesting the words and the tone, sharpening that image of the uncharacteristic expression on Jarlaxle's always smiling face. *Joined in Crenshinibon? . . . but a mere mortal?* What in the Nine Hells did that mean? *Never forget that,* Jarlaxle had said, and indeed, this was a lesson that Artemis Entreri would not soon dismiss.

When he looked back up again, Entreri saw Jarlaxle wearing his typical expression, that sly, slightly amused look that conferred to all who saw it that this cunning drow knew more than he did, knew more than he possibly could.

Seeing Jarlaxle relaxed again also reminded Entreri of the novelty of these sparring events. The mercenary leader would not spar with any other. Rai-guy was stunned when Jarlaxle had told him that he meant to battle Entreri on a regular basis.

Entreri understood the logic behind that thinking. Jarlaxle survived, in part, by remaining mysterious, even to those around him. No one could ever really get a good look at the mercenary leader. He kept allies and opponents alike off-balance and wondering, always wondering, and yet, here he was, revealing so much to Artemis Entreri.

"Those daggers," Entreri said, coming back at ease and putting on his own sly expression. "They were merely illusions."

"In your mind, perhaps," the dark elf replied in his typically cryptic manner.

"They were," the assassin pressed. "You could not possibly carry so many, nor could any magic create them that quickly."

"As you say," Jarlaxle replied. "Though you heard the clang as your own weapons connected with them and felt the weight as they punctured your cloak."

"I *thought* I heard the clang," Entreri corrected, wondering if he had at last found a chink in the mercenary's never-ending guessing game.

"Is that not the same thing?" Jarlaxle replied with a laugh, but it seemed to Entreri as if there was a darker side to that chuckle.

Entreri lifted that cloak, to see several of the daggers—solid metal daggers—still sticking in its fabric folds, and to find several more holes in the cloth. "Some were illusions, then," he argued unconvincingly.

Jarlaxle merely shrugged, never willing to give anything away.

With an exasperated sigh, Entreri started out of the room.

"Do keep ever present in your thoughts, my friend, that an illusion can kill you if you believe in it," Jarlaxle called after him.

Entreri paused and glanced back, his expression grim. He wasn't used to being so openly warned or threatened, but he knew that with this one particular companion, the threats were never, ever idle.

"And the real thing can kill you whether you believe in it or not," Entreri replied, and he turned back for the door.

The assassin departed with a shake of his head, frustrated and yet intrigued. That was always the way with Jarlaxle, Entreri mused, and what surprised him even more was that he found that aspect of the clever drow mercenary particularly compelling.

⊷━┿━┿━━

That is the one, Kimmuriel Oblodra signaled to his two companions, Rai-guy and Berg'inyon Baenre, the most recent addition to the surface army of Bregan D'aerthe.

The favored son of the most powerful house in Menzoberranzan, Berg'inyon had grown up with all the drow world open before him—to the level that a drow male in Menzoberranzan could achieve, at least—but his mother, the powerful Matron Baenre, had led a disastrous assault on a dwarven kingdom, ending in her death and throwing all the great drow city into utter chaos. In that time of ultimate confusion and apprehension, Berg'inyon had thrown his hand in with Jarlaxle and the ever elusive mercenary band of Bregan D'aerthe. Among the finest of fighters in all the city, and with familial connections to still-mighty House Baenre, Berg'inyon was welcomed openly and quickly promoted, elevated to the status of high lieutenant. Thus, he was not here now serving Rai-guy and Kimmuriel, but as their peer, taken out on a sort of training mission.

He considered the human Kimmuriel had targeted, a shapely woman posing in the dress of a common street whore.

27

You have read her thoughts? Rai-guy signaled back, his fingers weaving an intricate pattern, perfectly complementing the various expressions and contortions of his handsome and angular drow features.

Raker spy, Kimmuriel silently assured his companion. *The coordinator of their group. All pass her by, reporting their finds.*

Berg'inyon shifted nervously from foot to foot, uncomfortable around the revelations of the strange and strangely powerful Kimmuriel. He hoped that Kimmuriel wasn't reading his thoughts at that moment, for he was wondering how Jarlaxle could ever feel safe with this one about. Kimmuriel could walk into someone's mind, it seemed, as easily as Berg'inyon could walk through an open doorway. He chuckled then but disguised it as a cough, when he considered that clever Jarlaxle likely had that doorway somehow trapped. Berg'inyon decided that he'd have to learn the technique, if there was one, to keep Kimmuriel at bay.

Do we know where the others might be? Berg'inyon's hands silently asked.

Would the show be complete if we did not? came Rai-guy's responding gestures. The wizard smiled widely, and soon all three of the dark elves wore sly, hungry expressions.

Kimmuriel closed his eyes and steadied himself with long, slow breaths.

Rai-guy took the cue, pulling an eyelash encased in a bit of gum arabic out of one of his several belt pouches. He turned to Berg'inyon and began waggling his fingers. The drow warrior flinched reflexively—as most sane people would do when a drow wizard began casting in their direction.

The first spell went off, and Berg'inyon, rendered invisible, faded from view. Rai-guy went right back to work, now aiming a spell designed mentally to grab at the target, to hold the spy fast.

The woman flinched and seemed to hold for a second, but shook out of it and glanced around nervously, now obviously on her guard.

Rai-guy growled and went at the spell again. Invisible Berg'inyon stared at him with an almost mocking smile—yes, there were advantages to being invisible! Rai-guy continually demeaned humans, called them every drow name for offal and carrion. On the one hand, he was obviously surprised that this one had resisted the hold spell—no easy mental task—but on the other, Berg'inyon noted, the blustery wizard had prepared more than one of the spells. One, without any resistance, should have been enough.

This time, the woman took one step, and held fast in her walking pose.

Go! Kimmuriel's fingers waved. Even as he gestured, the powers of his mind opened the doorway between the three drow and the woman. Suddenly she was there, though she was still on the street, but only a couple of strides away. Berg'inyon leaped out and grabbed the woman, tugging her hard into the extra-dimensional space, and Kimmuriel shut the door.

It had happened so fast that to any watching on the street, it would have seemed as if the woman had simply disappeared.

The psionicist raised his delicate black hand up to the victim's forehead, melding with her mentally. He could feel the horror in there, for though her physical body had been locked in Rai-guy's stasis, her mind was working and she knew indeed that she now stood before dark elves.

Kimmuriel took just a moment to bask in that terror, thoroughly enjoying the spectacle. Then he imparted psionic energies to her. He built around her an armor of absorbing kinetic energy, using a technique he had perfected in Entreri's battle with Drizzt Do'Urden.

When it was done, he nodded.

Berg'inyon became visible again almost immediately, as his fine drow sword slashed across the woman's throat, the offensive strike dispelling the defensive magic of Rai-guy's invisibility spell. The drow warrior went into a fast dance, slashing and thrusting with both of his fine swords, stabbing hard, even chopping once with both blades, a heavy drop down onto the woman's head.

But no blood spewed forth, no groans of pain came from the woman, for Kimmuriel's armor accepted each blow, catching and holding the tremendous energy offered by the drow warrior's brutal dance.

It went on and on for several minutes, until Rai-guy warned that the spell of holding was nearing its end. Berg'inyon backed away, and Kimmuriel closed his eyes again as Rai-guy began yet another casting.

Both onlookers, Kimmuriel and Berg'inyon, smiled wickedly as Rai-guy produced a tiny ball of bat guano that held a sulfuric aroma and shoved it, along with his finger into the woman's mouth, releasing his spell. A flash of fiery light appeared in the back of the woman's mouth, disappearing as it slid down her throat.

The sidewalk was there again, very close, as Kimmuriel opened a second dimension portal to the same spot on the street, and Rai-guy roughly shoved the woman back out.

Kimmuriel shut the door, and they watched, amused.

The hold spell released first, and the woman staggered. She tried to call out, but coughed roughly from the burn in her throat. A strange expression came over her, one of absolute horror.

She feels the energy contained in the kinetic barrier, Kimmuriel explained. *I hold it no longer—only her own will prevents its release.*

How long? a concerned Rai-guy asked, but Kimmuriel only smiled and motioned for them to watch and enjoy.

The woman broke into a run. The three drow noted other people moving about her, some closing cautiously—other spies, likely—and others seeming merely curious. Still others grew alarmed and tried to stay away from her.

All the while, she tried to scream out, but just kept hacking from the continuing burn in her throat. Her eyes were wide, so horrifyingly and satisfyingly wide! She could feel the tremendous energies within her, begging release, and she had no idea how she might accomplish that.

She couldn't hold the kinetic barrier, and her initial realization of the problem transformed from horror into confusion. All of Berg'inyon's terrible beating came out then, so suddenly. All of the slashes and the stabs, the great chop and the twisting heart thrust, burst over the helpless woman. To those watching, it seemed almost as if she simply fell apart, gallons of blood erupting about her face, head, and chest.

She went down almost immediately, but before anyone could even begin to react, could run away or charge to her aid, Rai-guy's last spell, a delayed fireball, went off, immolating the already dead woman and many of those around her.

Outside the blast, wide-eyed stares came at the charred corpse from comrade and ignorant onlooker alike, expressions of the sheerest terror that surely pleased the three merciless dark elves.

A fine display. Worthy indeed.

For Berg'inyon, the spectacle served a second purpose, a clear reminder to him to take care around these fellow lieutenants himself. Even taking into consideration the high drow standards for torture and murder, these two were particularly adept, true masters of the craft.

CHAPTER

3

He had his old room back. He even had his name back. The memories of the authorities in Luskan were not as long as they claimed.

The previous year, Morik the Rogue had been accused of attempting to murder the honorable Captain Deudermont of the good ship *Sea Sprite*, a famous pirate hunter. Since in Luskan accusation and conviction were pretty much the same thing, Morik had faced the prospect of a horrible death in the public spectacle of Prisoner's Carnival. He had actually been in the process of realizing that ultimate torture when Captain Deudermont, horrified by the gruesome scene, had offered a pardon.

Pardoned or not, Morik had been forever banned from Luskan on pain of death. He had returned anyway, of course, the following year. At first he'd taken on an assumed identity, but gradually he had regained his old trappings, his true mannerisms, his connections on the streets, his apartment, and, finally, his name and the reputation it carried. The authorities knew it too, but having plenty of other thugs to torture to death, they didn't seem to care.

Morik could look back on that awful day at Prisoner's Carnival with a sense of humor now. He thought it perfectly ironic that he had been tortured for a crime that he hadn't even committed when there were so many crimes of which he could be rightly convicted.

It was all a memory now, the memory of a whirlwind of intrigue and danger by the name of Wulfgar. He was Morik the Rogue once more, and all was as it had once been . . . almost.

For now there was another element, an intriguing and also terrifying element, that had come into Morik's life. He walked up to the door of his room cautiously, glancing all about the narrow hallway, studying the shadows. When he was confident that he was alone, he walked up tight to the door, shielding it from any magically prying eyes, and began the process of undoing nearly a dozen deadly traps, top to bottom along both sides of the jamb. That done, he took out a ring of keys and undid the locks—one, two, three—then he clicked open the door. He disarmed yet another trap—this one explosive—then entered, closing and securing the door and resetting all the traps. The complete process took him more than ten minutes, yet he performed this ritual every time he came home. The dark elves had come into Morik's life, unannounced and uninvited. While they had promised him the treasure of a king if he performed their tasks, they had also promised him and had shown him the flip side of that golden coin as well.

Morik checked the small pedestal at the side of the door next. He nodded, satisfied to see that the orb was still in place in the wide vase. The vessel was coated with contact poison and maintained a sensitive pressure release trap. He had paid dearly for that particular orb—an enormous amount of gold that would take him a year of hard thievery to retrieve—but in Morik's fearful eyes, the item was well worth the price. It was enchanted with a powerful anti-magic dweomer that would prevent dimensional doors from opening in his room, that would prevent wizards from strolling in on the other side of a teleportation spell.

Never again did Morik the Rogue wish to be awakened by a dark elf standing at the side of his bed, looming over him.

All of his locks were in place, his orb rested in its protected vessel, and yet some subtle signal, an intangible breeze, a tickling on the hairs at the back of his neck, told Morik that something was out of place. He glanced all around, from shadow to shadow, to the drapes that still hung over the window he had long ago bricked up. He looked to his bed, to the tightly tucked sheets, with no blankets hanging below the edge. Bending just a bit, Morik saw right through the bottom of the bed. There was no one hiding under there.

The drapes, then, he thought, and he moved in that general direction but took a circuitous route so that he wouldn't force any action from the intruder. A sudden shift and quick-step brought him there, dagger revealed, and he pulled the drapes aside and struck hard, catching only air.

Morik laughed in relief and at his own paranoia. How different his world had become since the arrival of the dark elves. Always now he was on the edge of his nerves. He had seen the drow a total of only five times, including their initial encounter way back when Wulfgar was new to the city and they, for some reason that Morik still did not completely understand, wanted him to keep an eye on the huge barbarian.

He was always on his edge, always wary, but he reminded himself of the potential gains his alliance with the drow would bring. Part of the reason that he was Morik the Rogue again, from what he had been able to deduce, had to do with a visit to a particular authority by one of Jarlaxle's henchmen.

He gave a sigh of relief and let the drapes swing back, then froze in surprise and fear as a hand clamped over his mouth and the fine edge of a dagger came tight against his throat.

"You have the jewels?" a voice whispered in his ear, a voice showing incredible strength and calm despite its quiet tone. The hand slipped off of his mouth and up to his forehead, forcing his head back just enough to remind him of how vulnerable and open his throat was.

Morik didn't answer, his mind racing through many possibilities—the least likely of which seeming to be his potential escape, for that

hand holding him revealed frightening strength
ing the dagger at his throat was too, too steady. Wh.
might be, Morik understood immediately that he was .

"I ask one more time; then I end my frustration, ...ne
whisper.

"You are not drow," Morik replied, as much to buy some time as to
ensure that this man—and he knew that it was a man and certainly
no dark elf—would not act rashly.

"Perhaps I am, though under the guise of a wizard's spell," the
assailant replied. "But that could not be—or could it?—since no
magic will work in this room." As he finished, he roughly pushed
Morik away, then grabbed his shoulder to spin the frightened rogue
around as he fell back.

Morik didn't recognize the man, though he still understood that he
was in imminent danger. He glanced down at his own dagger, and it
seemed a pitiful thing indeed against the magnificent, jewel-handled
blade his opponent carried—almost a reflection of the relative
strengths of their wielders, Morik recognized with a wince.

Morik the Rogue was as good a thief as roamed the streets of
Luskan, a city full of thieves. His reputation, though bloated by
bluff, had been well-earned across the bowels of the city. This man
before him, older than Morik by a decade, perhaps, and standing so
calm and so balanced . . .

This man had gotten into his apartment and had remained there
unobserved despite Morik's attempted scrutiny. Morik noted then
that the bed sheets were rumpled—but hadn't he just looked at them,
to see them perfectly smooth?

"You are not drow," Morik dared to say again.

"Not all of Jarlaxle's agents are dark elves, are they, Morik the
Rogue?" the man replied.

Morik nodded and slipped his dagger into its sheath at his belt,
a move designed to alleviate the tension, something that Morik
desperately wanted to do.

"The jewels?" the man asked.

Morik could not hide the panic from his face.

"You should have purchased them from Telsburgher," the man remarked. "The way was clear and the assignment was not difficult."

"The way would have been clear," Morik corrected, "but for a minor magistrate who holds old grudges."

The intruder continued to stare, showing neither intrigue nor anger, telling Morik nothing at all about whether or not he was even interested in any excuses.

"Telsburgher is ready to sell them to me," Morik quickly added, "at the agreed price. His hesitation is only a matter of his fear that there will be retribution from Magistrate Jharkheld. The evil man holds an old grudge. He knows that I am back in town and wishes to drag me back to his Prisoner's Carnival, but he cannot, by word of his superiors, I am told. Thank Jarlaxle for me."

"You thank Jarlaxle by performing as instructed," the man replied, and Morik nervously shifted from foot to foot. "He helps you to fill his purse, not to fill his heart with good feelings."

Morik nodded. "I fear to go after Jharkheld," he explained. "How high might I strike without incurring the wrath of the greater powers of Luskan, thus ultimately wounding Jarlaxle's purse?"

"Jharkheld is not a concern," the man answered with a tone so assured that Morik found that he believed every word. "Complete the transaction."

"But . . ." Morik started to reply.

"This night," came the answer, and the man turned away and started for the door.

His hands worked in amazing circles right before Morik's eyes as trap after trap after lock fell open. It had taken Morik several minutes to get through that door, and that with an intricate knowledge of every trap—which he had set—and with the keys for the three supposedly difficult locks, and yet, within the span of two minutes, the door now swung open wide.

hand holding him revealed frightening strength and the hand holding the dagger at his throat was too, too steady. Whoever his attacker might be, Morik understood immediately that he was overmatched.

The man glanced back and tossed something to the floor at Morik's feet.

A wire.

"The one on your bottom trap had stretched beyond usefulness," the man explained. "I repaired it for you."

He went out then and closed the door, and Morik heard the clicks and sliding panels as all the locks and traps were efficiently reset.

Morik went to his bed cautiously and pulled the bed sheets aside. A hole had been cut into his mattress, perfectly sized to hold the intruder. Morik gave a helpless laugh, his respect for Jarlaxle's band multiplying. He didn't even have to go over to his trapped vase to know that the orb now within it was a fake and that the real one had just walked out his door.

Entreri blinked as he walked out into the late afternoon Luskan sun. He dropped a hand into his pocket, to feel the enchanted device he had just taken from Morik. This small orb had frustrated Rai-guy. It defeated his magic when he'd tried to visit Morik himself, as it was likely doing now. That thought alone pleased Entreri greatly. It had taken Bregan D'aerthe nearly a tenday to discern the source of Morik's sudden distance, how the man had made his room inaccessible to the prying eyes of the wizards. Thus, Entreri had been sent. He held no illusions that his trip had to do with his thieving prowess, but rather, it was simply because the dark elves weren't certain of how resistant Morik might be and simply hadn't wished to risk any of their brethren in the exploration. Certainly Jarlaxle wouldn't have been pleased to learn that Rai-guy and Kimmuriel had forced Entreri to go, but the pair knew that Entreri wouldn't go to Jarlaxle with the information.

So Entreri had played message boy for the two formidable, hated dark elves.

His instructions upon taking the orb and finishing his business with Morik had been explicit and precise. He was to place the orb aside and use the magical signal whistle Rai-guy had given him to call to the dark elves in faraway Calimport, but he wasn't in any hurry.

He knew that he should have killed Morik, both for the man's impertinence in trying to shield himself and for failing to produce the required jewels. Rai-guy and Kimmuriel would demand such punishment, of course. Now he'd have to justify his actions, to protect Morik somewhat.

He knew Luskan fairly well, having been through the city several times, including an extended visit only a few days before, when he, along with several other drow agents, had learned the truth of Morik's magic-blocking device. Wandering the streets, he soon heard the shouts and cheers of the vicious Prisoner's Carnival. He entered the back of the open square just as some poor fool was having his intestines pulled out like a great length of rope. Entreri hardly noticed the spectacle, concentrating instead on the sharp-featured, diminutive, robed figure presiding over the torture.

The man screamed at the writhing victim, telling him to surrender his associates, there and then, before it was too late. "Secure a chance for a more pleasant afterlife!" the magistrate screeched, his voice as sharp as his angry, angular features. "Now! Before you die!"

The man only wailed. It seemed to Entreri as if he was far beyond any point of even comprehending the magistrate's words.

He died soon enough and the show was over. The people began filtering out of the square, most nodding their heads and smiling, speaking excitedly of Jharkheld's fine show this day.

That was all Entreri needed to hear.

He moved shadow to shadow, following the magistrate down the short walk from the back of the square to the tower that housed the quarters of the officials of Prisoner's Carnival as well as the dungeons holding those who would soon face the public tortures.

He mused at his own good fortune in carrying Morik's orb, for it gave him some measure of protection from any wizard hired to further secure the tower. That left only sentries and mechanical traps in his way.

Artemis Entreri feared neither.

He went into the tower as the sun disappeared in the west.

"They have too many allies," Rai-guy insisted.

"They would be gone without a trace," Jarlaxle replied with a wide smile. "Simply gone."

Rai-guy groaned and shook his head, and Kimmuriel, across the room and sitting comfortably in a plush chair, one leg thrown over the cushioning arm, looked up at the ceiling and rolled his eyes.

"You continue to doubt me?" Jarlaxle asked, his tone light and innocent, not threatening. "Consider all that we have already accomplished here in Calimport and across the surface. We have agents in several major cities, including Waterdeep."

"We are *exploring* agents in other cities," Rai-guy corrected. "We have but one currently working, the little rogue in Luskan." He paused and glanced over at his psionicist counterpart and smiled. "Perhaps."

Kimmuriel chuckled as he considered their second agent now working in Luskan, the one Jarlaxle did not know had left Calimport.

"The others are preliminary," Rai-guy went on. "Some are promising, others not so, but none are worthy of the title of agent at this time."

"Soon, then," said Jarlaxle, coming forward in his own comfortable chair. "Soon! They will become profitable partners or we will find others—not so difficult a thing to do among the greedy humans. The situation here in Calimport . . . look around you. Can you doubt our wisdom in coming here? The gems and jewels are flowing fast, a direct line to a drow population eager to expand their possessions beyond the limited wealth of Menzoberranzan."

"Fortunate are we if the houses of Ched Nasad determine that we are undercutting their economy," Rai-guy, who hailed from that other drow city, remarked sarcastically.

Jarlaxle scoffed at the notion.

"I cannot deny the profitability of Calimport," the wizard lieutenant went on, "yet when we first planned our journey to the surface, we all agreed that it would show immediate and strong returns. As we all agreed it would likely be a short tenure, and that, after the initial profits, we would do well to reconsider our position and perhaps retreat to our own land, leaving only the best of the trading connections and agents in place."

"So we should reconsider, and so I have," said Jarlaxle. "It seems obvious to me that we underestimated the potential of our surface operations. Expand! Expand, I say."

Again came the disheartened expressions. Kimmuriel was still staring at the ceiling, as if in abject denial of what Jarlaxle was proposing.

"The Rakers desire that we limit our trade to this one section," Jarlaxle reminded, "yet many of the craftsmen of the more exotic goods—merchandise that would likely prove most attractive in Menzoberranzan—are outside of that region."

"Then we cut a deal with the Rakers, let them in on the take for this new and profitable market to which they have no access," said Rai-guy, a perfectly reasonable suggestion in light of the history of Bregan D'aerthe, a mercenary and opportunistic band that always tried to use the words "mutually beneficial" as their business credo.

"They are pimples," Jarlaxle replied, extending his thumb and index finger in the air before him and pressing them together as if he was squeezing away an unwanted blemish. "They will simply disappear."

"Not as easy a task as you seem to believe," came a feminine voice from the doorway, and the three glanced over to see Sharlotta Vespers gliding into the room, dressed in a long gown slit high enough to reveal one very shapely leg. "The Rakers pride themselves on spreading their organizational lines far and wide. You could destroy all of their houses and all of their known agents, even all of the people dealing with all of their agents, and still leave many witnesses."

"Who would do what?" Jarlaxle asked, but he was still smiling, even patting his chair for Sharlotta to go over and sit with him, which she did, curling about him familiarly.

The sight of it made Rai-guy glance again at Kimmuriel. Both knew that Jarlaxle was bedding the human woman, the most powerful remnant—along with Entreri—of the old Basadoni Guild, and neither of them liked the idea. Sharlotta was a sly one, as humans go, almost sly enough to be accepted among the society of drow. She had even mastered the language of the drow and was now working on the intricate hand signals of the dark elven silent code. Rai-guy found her perfectly repulsive, and Kimmuriel, though seeing her as exotic, did not like the idea of having her whispering dangerous suggestions into Jarlaxle's ear.

In this particular matter, though, it seemed to both of them that Sharlotta was on their side, so they didn't try to interrupt her as they usually did.

"Witnesses who would tell every remaining guild," Sharlotta explained, "and who would inform the greater powers of Calimshan. The destruction of the Rakers Guild would imply that a truly great power had secretly come to Calimport."

"One has," Jarlaxle said with a grin.

"One whose greatest strength lies in remaining secret," Sharlotta replied.

Jarlaxle pushed her from his lap, right off the chair, so that she had to move quickly to get her shapely legs under her in time to prevent falling unceremoniously on her rump.

The mercenary leader then rose as well, pushing right past Sharlotta as if her opinion mattered not at all, and moving closer to his more important lieutenants. "I once envisioned Bregan D'aerthe's role on the surface as that of importer and exporter," he explained. "This we have easily achieved. Now I see the truth of the human dominated societies, and that is a truth of weakness. We can go further—we *must* go further."

"Conquest?" Rai-guy asked sourly, sarcastically.

"Not as Baenre attempted with Mithral Hall," Jarlaxle eagerly explained. "More a matter of absorption." Again came that wicked smile. "For those who will play."

"And those who will not simply disappear?" Rai-guy asked, but his sarcasm seemed lost on Jarlaxle, who only smiled all the wider.

"Did you not execute a Raker spy only the other day?" Jarlaxle asked.

"There is a profound difference in defending our privacy and trying to expand our borders," the wizard replied.

"Semantics," Jarlaxle said with a laugh. "Simply semantics."

Behind him, Sharlotta Vespers bit her lip and shook her head, fearing that her newfound benefactors might be about to make a tremendous and very dangerous blunder.

From an alley not so far away, Entreri listened to the shouts and confusion coming from the tower. When he had entered, he'd gone downstairs first, to find a particularly unpleasant prisoner to free. Once he had ushered the man to relative safety, to the open tunnels at the back of the dungeons, he had gone upstairs to the first floor, then up again, moving quietly and deliberately along the shadowy, torch-lit corridors.

Finding Jharkheld's room proved easy enough.

The door hadn't even been locked.

Had he not just witnessed the magistrate's work at Prisoner's Carnival, Artemis Entreri might have reasoned with him concerning Morik. Now the way was clear for Morik to complete his task and proffer the jewels.

Entreri wondered if the escaped prisoner, the obvious murderer of poor Jharkheld, had been found in the maze of tunnels yet. What misery the man would face. A wry grin found its way onto Entreri's face, for he hardly felt any guilt about using the wretch for his own gain. The idiot should have known better, after all. Why would someone come in unannounced and at obvious great personal risk to save him? Why hadn't he even questioned Entreri while the assassin was releasing him from the shackles? Why, if he was smart enough to deserve his life, hadn't he tried to capture Entreri in his place, to put this unasked-for and unknown savior up in the shackles in his stead, to face the executioner? So many prisoners came through these dungeons that the gaolers likely wouldn't even have been aware of the change.

So, his fate was the thug's own to accept, and in Entreri's thinking, of his own doing. Of course, the thug would claim that someone else had helped him to escape, had set it all up to make it look like it was his doing.

Prisoner's Carnival hardly cared for such excuses.

Nor did Artemis Entreri.

He dismissed all thoughts of those problems, glanced around to ensure that he was alone, and placed the magic dispelling orb along the side of the alley. He walked across the way and blew his whistle. He wondered then how this might work. Magic would be needed, after all, to get him back to Calimport, but how might that work if he had to take the orb along? Wouldn't the orb's dweomer simply dispel the attempted teleportation?

A blue screen of light appeared beside him. It was a magical doorway, he knew, and not one of Rai-guy's, but rather the doing of Kimmuriel Oblodra. So that was it, he mused. Perhaps the orb wouldn't work against psionics.

Or perhaps it would, and that thought unsettled the normally unshakable Entreri profoundly as he moved to collect the item. What would happen if the orb somehow did affect Kimmuriel's dimension warp? Might he wind up in the wrong place—even in another plane of existence, perhaps?

Entreri shook that thought away as well. Life was risky when dealing with drow, magical orbs or not. He took care to pocket the orb slyly, so that any prying eyes would have a difficult time making out the movement in the dark alley, then strode quickly up to the portal, and with a single deep breath, stepped through.

He came out dizzy, fighting hard to hold his balance, in the guild hall's private sorcery chambers back in Calimport, hundreds and hundreds of miles away.

There stood Kimmuriel and Rai-guy, staring at him hard.

"The jewels?" Rai-guy asked in the drow language, which Entreri understood, though not well.

"Soon," the assassin replied in his shaky command of Deep Drow. "There was a problem."

Both dark elves lifted their white eyebrows in surprise.

"*Was*," Entreri emphasized. "Morik will have the jewels presently."

"Then Morik lives," Kimmuriel remarked pointedly. "What of his attempts to hide from us?"

"More the attempts of local magistrates to seal him off from any outside influences," Entreri lied. "One local magistrate," he quickly corrected, seeing their faces sour. "The issue has been remedied."

Neither drow seemed pleased, but neither openly complained.

"And this local magistrate had magically sealed off Morik's room from outside, prying eyes?" Rai-guy asked.

"And all other magic," Entreri answered. "It has been corrected."

"With the orb?" Kimmuriel added.

"Morik proffered the orb," Rai-guy remarked, narrowing his eyes.

"He apparently did not know what he was buying," Entreri said calmly, not getting alarmed, for he recognized that his ploys had worked.

Rai-guy and Kimmuriel would hold their suspicions that it had been Morik's work, and not that of any minor official, of course. They would suspect that Entreri had bent the truth to suit his own needs, but the assassin knew that he hadn't given them anything overt enough for them to act upon—at least, not without raising the ire of Jarlaxle.

Again, the realization that his security was almost wholly based on the mercenary leader did not sit well with Entreri. He didn't like being dependent, equating the word with weakness.

He had to turn the situation around.

"You have the orb," Rai-guy remarked, holding out his slender, deceivingly delicate hand.

"Better for me than for you," the assassin dared to reply, and that declaration set the two dark elves back on their heels.

Even as he finished speaking, though, Entreri felt the tingling in his pocket. He dropped a hand to the orb, and his sensitive fingers felt a subtle vibration coming from deep within the enchanted item. Entreri's gaze focused on Kimmuriel. The drow was standing with his eyes closed, deep in concentration.

Then he understood. The orb's enchantment would do nothing against any of Kimmuriel's formidable mind powers, and Entreri had seen this psionic trick before. Kimmuriel was reaching into the latent energy within the orb and was exciting that energy to explosive levels.

Entreri toyed with the idea of waiting until the last moment then throwing the orb into Kimmuriel's face. How he would enjoy the sight of that wretched drow caught in one of his own tricks!

With a wave of his hand, Kimmuriel opened a dimensional portal, from the room to the nearly deserted dusty street outside. It was a portal large enough for the orb, but that would not allow Entreri to step through.

Entreri felt the energy building, building ... the vibrations were not so subtle any longer. Still he held back, staring at Kimmuriel—just staring and waiting, letting the drow know that he was not afraid.

In truth this was no contest of wills. Entreri had a mounting explosion in his pocket, and Kimmuriel was far enough away so that he would feel little effect from it other than the splattering of Entreri's blood. Again the assassin considered throwing the orb into Kimmuriel's face, but again he realized the futility of such a course.

Kimmuriel would simply stop exciting the latent energy within the orb, would shut off the explosion as completely as dipping a torch into water snuffed out its flame. Entreri would have given Rai-guy and Kimmuriel all the justification they needed to utterly destroy him. Jarlaxle might be angry, but he couldn't and wouldn't deny them their right to defend themselves.

Artemis Entreri wasn't ready for such a fight.

Not yet.

He tossed the orb out through the open door and watched, a split second later, as it exploded into dust.

The magical door went away.

"You play dangerous games," Rai-guy remarked.

"Your drow friend is the one who brought on the explosion," Entreri casually replied.

"I speak not of that," the wizard retorted. "There is a common saying among your people that it is foolhardy to send a child to do a man's work. We have a similar saying, that it is foolhardy to send a human to do a drow's work."

Entreri stared at him hard, having no response. This whole situation was starting to feel like those days when he had been trapped down in Menzoberranzan, when he had known that, in a city of twenty thousand dark elves, no matter how good he got, no matter how perfect his craft, he would never be considered any higher in society's rankings than twenty thousand and one.

Rai-guy and Kimmuriel tossed out a few phrases between themselves, insults mostly, some crude, some subtle, all aimed at Entreri.

He took them, every one, and said nothing, because he could say nothing. He kept thinking of Dallabad Oasis and a particular sword and gauntlet combination.

He accepted their demeaning words, because he had to.

For now.

CHAPTER

4

Antreri stood in the shadows of the doorway, listening with great curiosity to the soliloquy taking place in the room. He could only make out small pieces of the oration. The speaker, Jarlaxle, was talking quickly and excitedly in the drow tongue. Entreri, in addition to his limited Deep Drow vocabulary, couldn't hear every word from this distance.

"They will not stay ahead of us, because we move too quickly," the mercenary leader remarked. Entreri heard and was able to translate every word of that line, for it seemed as if Jarlaxle was cheering someone on. "Yes, street by street they will fall. Who can stand against us joined?"

"Us *joined?*" the assassin silently echoed, repeating the drow word over and over to make sure that he was translating it properly. *Us?* Jarlaxle could not be speaking of his alliance with Entreri, or even with the remnants of the Basadoni Guild. Compared to the strength of Bregan D'aerthe, these were minor additions. Had Jarlaxle made some new deal, then, without Entreri's knowledge? A deal with some pasha, perhaps, or an even greater power?

The assassin bent in closer, listening particularly for any names of demons or devils—or of illithids, perhaps. He shuddered at the thought of any of the three. Demons were too unpredictable and too savage to serve any alliance. They would do whatever served their specific needs at any particular moment, without regard for the greater benefit to the alliance. Devils were more predictable—were *too* predictable. In their hierarchical view of the world, they inevitably sat on top of the pile.

Still, compared to the third notion that had come to him, that of the illithids, Entreri was almost hoping to hear Jarlaxle utter the name of a mighty demon. Entreri had been forced to deal with illithids during his stay in Menzoberranzan—the mind flayers were an unavoidable side of life in the drow city—and he had no desire to ever, ever, see one of the squishy-headed, wretched creatures again.

He listened a bit longer, and Jarlaxle seemed to calm down and to settle more comfortably into his seat. The mercenary leader was still talking, just muttering to himself about the impending downfall of the Rakers, when Entreri strode into the room.

"Alone?" the assassin asked innocently. "I thought I heard voices."

He noted with some relief that Jarlaxle wasn't wearing his magical, protective eye patch this day, which made it unlikely that the drow had just encountered, or soon planned to encounter, any illithids. The eye patch protected against mind magic, and none in all the world were more proficient at such things as the dreaded mind flayers.

"Sorting things out," Jarlaxle explained, and his ease with the common tongue of the surface world seemed no less fluent than that of his native language. "There is so much afoot."

"Danger, mostly," Entreri replied.

"For some," said Jarlaxle with a chuckle.

Entreri looked at him doubtfully.

"Surely you do not believe that the Rakers can match our power?" the mercenary leader asked incredulously.

"Not in open battle," Entreri answered, "but that is how it has been with them for many years. They cannot match many, blade to blade, and yet they have ever found a way to survive."

"Because they are fortunate."

"Because they are intricately tied to greater powers," Entreri corrected. "A man need not be physically powerful if he is guarded by a giant."

"Unless the giant has more tightly befriended a rival," Jarlaxle interjected. "And giants are known to be unreliable."

"You have arranged this with the greater lords of Calimport?" Entreri asked, unconvinced. "With whom, and why was I not involved in such a negotiation?"

Jarlaxle shrugged, offering not a clue.

"Impossible," Entreri decided. "Even if you threatened one or more of them, the Rakers are too long-standing, too entrenched in the power web of all Calimshan, for such treachery against them to prosper. They have allies to protect them against other allies. There is no way that even Jarlaxle and Bregan D'aerthe could have cleared the opposition to such a sudden and destabilizing shift in the power structure of the region as the decimation of the Rakers."

"Perhaps I have allied with the most powerful being ever to come to Calimport," Jarlaxle said dramatically, and typically, cryptically.

Entreri narrowed his dark eyes and stared at the outrageous drow, looking for clues, any clues, as to what this uncharacteristic behavior might herald. Jarlaxle was often cryptic, always mysterious, and ever ready to grab at an opportunity that would bring him greater power or profits, and yet, something seemed out of place here. To Entreri's thinking, the impending assault on the Rakers was a blunder, which was something the legendary Jarlaxle never did. It seemed obvious, then, that the cunning drow had indeed made some powerful connection or ally, or was possessed of some deeper understanding of the situation. This Entreri doubted since he, not Jarlaxle, was the best connected person on Calimport's streets.

Even given one of those possibilities, though, something just didn't seem quite right to Entreri. Jarlaxle was cocky and arrogant—of course he was!—but never before had he seemed this self-assured, especially in a situation as potentially explosive as this.

The situation seemed only more explosive if Entreri looked beyond the inevitability of the downfall of the Rakers. He knew well the murderous power of the dark elves and held no doubt that Bregan D'aerthe would slaughter the competing guild, but there were so many implications to that victory—too many, certainly, for Jarlaxle to be so comfortable.

"Has your role in this been determined?" Jarlaxle asked.

"No role," Entreri answered, and his tone left no doubt that he was pleased by that fact. "Rai-guy and Kimmuriel have all but cast me aside."

Jarlaxle laughed aloud, for the truth behind that statement—that Entreri had been willingly cast aside—was all too obvious.

Entreri stared at him and didn't crack a smile. Jarlaxle had to know the dangers he had just walked into, a potentially catastrophic situation that could send him and Bregan D'aerthe fleeing back to the dark hole of Menzoberranzan. Perhaps that was it, the assassin mused. Perhaps Jarlaxle longed for home and was slyly facilitating the move. The mere thought of that made Entreri wince. Better that Jarlaxle kill him outright than drag him back there.

Perhaps Entreri would be set up as an agent, as was Morik in Luskan. No, the assassin decided, that would not suffice. Calimport was more dangerous than Luskan, and if the power of Bregan D'aerthe was forced away, he would not take such a risk. Too many powerful enemies would be left behind.

"It will begin soon, if it has not already," Jarlaxle remarked. "Thus, it will be over soon."

Sooner than you believe, Entreri thought, but he kept silent. He was a man who survived through careful calculation, by weighing scrupulously the consequences of every step and every word. He knew Jarlaxle to be a kindred spirit, but he could not reconcile that with the action that was being undertaken this very night, which, in searching it from any angle, seemed a tremendous and unnecessary gamble.

What did Jarlaxle know that he did not?

No one ever looked more out of place anywhere than did Sharlotta Vespers as she descended the rung ladder into one of Calimport's sewers. She was wearing her trademark long gown, her hair neatly coiffed as always, her exotic face painted delicately to emphasize her brown, almond-shaped eyes. Still, she was quite at home there, and anyone who knew her would not have been surprised to find her there.

Especially if they considered her warlord escorts.

"What word from above?" Rai-guy asked her, speaking quickly and in the drow tongue. The wizard, despite his misgivings about Sharlotta, was impressed by how quickly she had absorbed the language.

"There is tension," Sharlotta replied. "The doors of many guilds are locked fast this night. Even the Copper Ante is accepting no patrons—an unprecedented event. The streets know that something is afoot."

Rai-guy flashed a sour look at Kimmuriel. The two had just agreed that their plans depended mostly on stealth and surprise, that all of the elements of the Basadoni Guild and Bregan D'aerthe would have to reach their objectives nearly simultaneously to ensure that few witnesses remained.

How much this seemed like Menzoberranzan! In the drow city, one house going after another—a not-uncommon event—would measure success not only by the result of the actual fighting, but by the lack of credible witnesses left to produce evidence of the treachery. Even if every drow in the great city knew without doubt which house had precipitated the battle, no action would ever be taken unless the evidence demanding it was overwhelming.

But this was not Menzoberranzan, Rai-guy reminded himself. Up here, suspicion would invite investigation. In the drow city, suspicion without undeniable evidence only invited quiet praise.

"Our warriors are in place," Kimmuriel remarked. "The drow are beneath the guild houses, with force enough to batter through, and the Basadoni soldiers have surrounded the main three buildings. It will be swift, for they cannot anticipate the attack from below."

Rai-guy kept his gaze upon Sharlotta as his associate detailed the situation, and he did not miss a slight arch of one of her eyebrows. Had Bregan D'aerthe been betrayed? Were the Rakers setting up defenses against the assault from below?

"The agents have been isolated?" the drow wizard pressed to Sharlotta, referring to the first round of the invasion: the fight with—or rather, the assassinations of—Raker spies in the streets.

"The agents are not to be found," Sharlotta replied matter-of-factly, a surprising tone given the enormity of the implications.

Again Rai-guy glanced at Kimmuriel.

"All is in place," the psionicist reminded.

"Keego's swarm cramps the tunnels," Rai-guy replied, his words an archaic drow proverb referring to a long-ago battle in which an overwhelming swarm of goblins led by the crafty, rebellious slave, Keego, had been utterly destroyed by a small and sparsely populated city of dark elves. The drow had gone out from their homes to catch the larger force in the tight tunnels beyond the relatively open drow city. Simply translated, given the current situation, Rai-guy's words followed up Kimmuriel's remark. All was in place to fight the wrong battle.

Sharlotta looked at the wizard curiously, and he understood her confusion, for the soldiers of Bregan D'aerthe waiting in the tunnels beneath the Rakers' houses hardly constituted a "swarm."

Of course, Rai-guy hardly cared whether Sharlotta understood or not.

"Have we traced the course of the missing agents?" Rai-guy asked Sharlotta. "Do we know where they have fled?"

"Back to the houses, likely," the woman replied. "Few are on the streets this night."

Again, the less-than-subtle hint that too much had been revealed. Had Sharlotta herself betrayed them? Rai-guy fought the urge to interrogate her on the spot, using drow torture techniques that would quickly and efficiently break down any human. If he did so, he knew, he would have to answer to Jarlaxle, and Rai-guy was not ready for that fight . . . yet.

If he called it all off at that critical moment—if all the fighters, Basadoni and dark elf, returned to the guild house with their weapons unstained by Raker blood—Jarlaxle would not be pleased. The drow was determined to see this conquest through despite the protests of all of his lieutenants.

Rai-guy closed his eyes and logically sifted through the situation, trying to find some safer common ground. There was one Raker house far removed from the others, and likely only lightly manned. While destroying it would do little to weaken the structure and effectiveness of the opposition guild, perhaps such a conquest would quiet Jarlaxle's expected rampage.

"Recall the Basadoni soldiers," the wizard ordered. "Have their retreat be a visible one—instruct some to enter the Copper Ante or other establishments."

"The Copper Ante's doors are closed," Sharlotta reminded him.

"Then open them," Rai-guy instructed. "Tell Dwahvel Tiggerwillies that there is no need for her and her diminutive clan to cower this night. Let our soldiers be seen about the streets—not as a unified fighting force, but in smaller groups."

"What of Bregan D'aerthe?" Kimmuriel asked with some concern. Not as much concern, Rai-guy noted, as he would have expected, given that he had just countermanded Jarlaxle's explicit orders.

"Reposition Berg'inyon and all of our magic-users to the eighth position," Rai-guy replied, referring to the sewer hold beneath the exposed Raker house.

Kimmuriel arched his white eyebrows at that. They knew the

maximum resistance they could expect from that lone outpost, and it hardly seemed as if Berg'inyon and more magic-users would be needed to win out easily in that locale.

"It must be executed as completely and carefully as if we were attacking House Baenre itself," Rai-guy demanded, and Kimmuriel's eyebrows went even higher. "Redefine the plans and reposition all necessary drow forces to execute the attack."

"We could summon our kobold slaves alone to finish this task," Kimmuriel replied derisively.

"No kobolds and no humans," Rai-guy explained, emphasizing every word. "This is work for drow alone."

Kimmuriel seemed to catch on to Rai-guy's thinking then, for a wry smile showed on his face. He glanced at Sharlotta, nodded back at Rai-guy, and closed his eyes. He used his psionic energies to reach out to Berg'inyon and the other Bregan D'aerthe field commanders.

Rai-guy let his gaze settle fully on Sharlotta. To her credit, her expression and posture did not reveal her thoughts. Still, Rai-guy felt certain she was wondering if he had come to suspect her or some other Raker informant.

"You said that our power would prove overwhelming," Sharlotta remarked.

"For today's battle, perhaps," Rai-guy replied. "The wise thief does not steal the egg if his action will awaken the dragon."

Sharlotta continued to stare at him, continued to wonder, he knew. He enjoyed the realization that this too-clever human woman, guilty or not, was suddenly worried. She turned for the ladder again and took a step up.

"Where are you going?" Rai-guy asked.

"To recall the Basadoni soldiers," she replied, as if the explanation should have been obvious.

Rai-guy shook his head and motioned for her to step down. "Kimmuriel will relay the commands," he said.

Sharlotta hesitated—Rai-guy enjoyed the moment of confusion and concern—but she did step back down to the tunnel floor.

⊶══❙═══❙⊷

Berg'inyon could not believe the change in plans—what was the point of this entire offensive if the bulk of the Rakers' Guild escaped the onslaught? He had grown up in Menzoberranzan, and in that matriarchal society, males learned how to take orders without question. So it was now for Berg'inyon.

He had been trained in the finest battle tactics of the greatest house of Menzoberranzan and had at his disposal a seemingly overwhelming force for the task at hand, the destruction of a small, exposed Raker house—an outpost sitting on unfriendly streets. Despite his trepidation at the change in plans, his private questioning of the purpose of this mission, Berg'inyon Baenre wore an eager smile.

The scouts, the stealthiest of the stealthy drow, returned. Only minutes before, they had been inserted into the house above through wizard-made tunnels.

Drow fingers flashed, the silent hand gesture code.

While Berg'inyon's confidence mounted, so did his confusion over why this target alone had been selected. There were only a score of humans in the small house above, and none of them seemed to be magic-users. According to the drow scouts' assessment they were street thugs—men who survived by keeping to favorable shadows.

Under the keen eyes of a dark elf, there were no favorable shadows.

While Berg'inyon and his army had a strong idea of what they would encounter in the house above them, the humans could not understand the monumental doom that lay below them.

You have outlined to the group commanders all routes of retreat? Berg'inyon's fingers and facial gestures asked. He made it clear from the fact that he signaled retreat with his left hand that he was referring to any possible avenues their enemies might take to run away.

The wizards are positioned accordingly, one scout silently replied.

The lead hunters have been given their courses, another added.

Berg'inyon nodded, flashed the signal for commencing the operation, then moved to join his assault group. His would be the last group to enter the building, but they were the ones who would cut the fastest path to the very top.

There were two wizards in Berg'inyon's group. One stood with his eyes closed, ready to convey the signal. The other positioned himself accordingly, his eyes and hands pointed up at the ceiling, a pinch of seeds from the Underdark selussi fungus in one hand.

It is time, came a magical whisper, one that seeped through the walls and to the ears of all the drow.

The magic-user eyeing the ceiling began his spellcasting, weaving his hands as if tracing joining semicircles with each, thumbs touching, little fingers touching, back and forth, back and forth, chanting quietly all the while.

He finished with a chant that sounded more like a hiss, and reached his outstretched fingers to the ceiling.

That part of the stone ceiling began to ripple, as if the wizard had stabbed his fingers into clear water. The wizard held the pose for many seconds. The rippling increased until the stone became an indistinct blur.

The stone above the wizard disappeared—was just gone. In its place was an upward reaching corridor that cut through several feet of stone to end at the ground floor of the Raker house.

One unfortunate Raker had been caught by surprise, his heels right over the edge of the suddenly appearing hole. His arms worked great circles as he tried to maintain his balance. The drow warriors shifted into position under the hole and leaped. Enacting their innate drow levitation abilities, they floated up, up.

The first dark elf floating up beside the falling Raker grabbed him by the collar and yanked him backward, tumbling him into the hole. The human managed to land in a controlled manner, feet first, then buckling his legs and tumbling to the side to absorb the shock. He came up with equal grace, drawing a dagger.

His face blanched when he saw the truth about him: dark elves—drow!—were floating up into his guild house. Another drow, handsome and strong, holding the finest-edged blade the Raker could ever have imagined, faced him.

Maybe he tried to reason with the dark elf, offering his surrender, but while his mouth worked in a logical, hide-saving manner, his body, paralyzed by stark terror, did not. He still held his knife out before him as he spoke, and since Berg'inyon did not understand well the language of the surface dwellers, he had no way of understanding the Raker's intent.

Nor was the drow about to pause to figure it out. His fine sword stabbed forward and slashed down, taking the dagger and the hand that held it. A quick retraction re-gathered his balance and power, and out went the sword again. Straight and sure, it tore through flesh and sliced rib, biting hard at the foolish man's heart.

The man fell, quite dead, and still wearing that curious, stunned expression.

Berg'inyon didn't pause long enough to wipe his blade. He crouched, sprang straight up, and levitated fast into the house. His encounter had delayed him no more than a span of a few heartbeats, and yet, the floor of the room and the corridor beyond the open door was already littered with human corpses.

Berg'inyon's team exited the room soon after, before the wizard's initial passwall spell had even expired. Not a drow had been more than slightly injured and not a human remained alive. The Raker house held no treasure when they were done—not even the few coins several of the guildsmen had secretly tucked under loose floorboards—and even the furniture was gone. Magical fires had consumed every foot of flooring and all of the partitioning walls. From the outside, the house seemed quiet and secure. Inside, it was no more than a charred and empty husk.

Bregan D'aerthe had spoken.

"I accept no accolades," Berg'inyon Baenre remarked when he met up with Rai-guy, Kimmuriel, and Sharlotta. It was a common drow saying, with clear implications that the vanquished opponent was not worthy enough for the victor to take any pride in having defeated him.

Kimmuriel gave a wry smile. "The house was effectively purged," he said. "None escaped. You performed as was required. There is no glory in that, but there is acceptance."

As he had done all day, Rai-guy continued his scrutiny of Sharlotta Vespers. Was the human woman even comprehending the sincerity of Kimmuriel's words, and if so, did that allow her any insight into the true power that had come to Calimport? For any guild to so completely annihilate one of another's houses was no small feat—unless the attacking guild happened to be comprised of drow warriors who understood the complexities of inter-house warfare better than any race in all the world. Did Sharlotta recognize this? And if she did, would she be foolish enough to try to use it to her advantage?

Her expression now was mostly stone-faced, but with just a trace of intrigue, a hint to Rai-guy that the answer would be yes, to both questions. The drow wizard smiled at that, a confirmation that Sharlotta Vespers was walking onto very dangerous ground. *Quiensin ful biezz coppon quangolth cree, a drow,* went the old saying in Menzoberranzan, and elsewhere in the drow world. Doomed are those who believe they understand the designs of the drow.

"What did Jarlaxle learn to change his course so?" Berg'inyon asked.

"Jarlaxle has learned nothing of yet," Rai-guy replied. "He chose to remain behind. The operation was mine to wage."

Berg'inyon started to redirect his question to Rai-guy then, but he stopped in midsentence and merely offered a bow to the appointed leader.

"Perhaps later you will explain to me the source of your decision, that I will better understand our enemies," he said respectfully.

Rai-guy gave a slight nod.

"There is the matter of explaining to Jarlaxle," Sharlotta remarked, in her surprising command of the drow tongue. "He will not accept your course with a mere bow."

Rai-guy's gaze darted over at Berg'inyon as she finished, quickly enough to catch the moment of anger flash through his red-glowing eyes. Sharlotta's observations were correct, of course, but coming from a non-drow, an *iblith*—which was also the drow word for excrement—they intrinsically cast an insulting reflection upon Berg'inyon, who had so accepted the offered explanation. It was a minor mistake, but a few more quips like that against the young Baenre, Rai-guy knew, and there would remain too little of Sharlotta Vespers for anyone ever to make a proper identification of the pieces.

"We must tell Jarlaxle," the drow wizard put in, moving the conversation forward. "To us out here, the course change was obviously required, but he has secluded himself, too much so perhaps, to view things that way."

Kimmuriel and Berg'inyon both looked at him curiously—why would he speak so plainly in front of Sharlotta, after all?—but Rai-guy gave them a quick and quiet signal to follow along.

"We could implicate Domo and the wererats," Kimmuriel put in, obviously catching on. "Though I fear that we will then have to waste our time in slaughtering them." He looked to Sharlotta. "Much of this will fall to you."

"The Basadoni soldiers were the first to leave the fight," Rai-guy added. "And they will be the ones to return without blood on their blades." Now all three gazes fell upon Sharlotta.

The woman held her outward calm quite well. "Domo and the wererats, then," she agreed, thinking things through, obviously, as she went. "We will implicate them without faulting them. Yes, that is the way. Perhaps they did not know of our plans and coincidentally hired on with Pasha Da'Daclan to guard the sewers. As we did not wish to reveal ourselves fully to the coward Domo, we held to the unguarded regions, mostly around the eighth position."

The three drow exchanged looks, and nodded for her to continue.

"Yes," Sharlotta went on, gathering momentum and confidence. "I can turn this into an advantage with Pasha Da'Daclan as well. He felt the press of impending doom, no doubt, and that fear will only heighten when word of the utterly destroyed outer house reaches him. Perhaps he will come to believe that Domo is much more powerful than any of us believed, and that he was in league with the Basadonis, and that only House Basadoni's former dealings with the Rakers cut short the assault."

"But will that not implicate House Basadoni clearly in the one executed attack?" asked Kimmuriel, playing the role of Rai-guy's mouthpiece, drawing Sharlotta in even deeper.

"Not that we played a role, but only that we allowed it to happen," Sharlotta reasoned. "A turn of our heads in response to their increased spying efforts against our guild. Yes, and if this is conveyed properly, it will only serve to make Domo seem even more powerful. If we make the Rakers believe that they were on the edge of complete disaster, they will behave more reasonably, and Jarlaxle will find his victory." She smiled as she finished, and the three dark elves returned the look.

"Begin," Rai-guy offered, waving his hand toward the ladder leading out of their sewer quarters.

Sharlotta smiled again, the ignorant fool, and left them.

"Her deception against Pasha Da'Daclan will necessarily extend, to some level, to Jarlaxle," Kimmuriel remarked, clearly envisioning the web Sharlotta was foolishly weaving about herself.

"You have come to fear that something is not right with Jarlaxle," Berg'inyon bluntly remarked, for it was obvious that these two would not normally act so independently of their leader.

"His views have changed," Kimmuriel responded.

"You did not wish to come to the surface," Berg'inyon said with a wry smile that seemed to question the motives of his companions' reasoning.

"No, and glad will we be to see the heat of Narbondel again," Rai-guy agreed, speaking of the great glowing clock of Menzoberranzan, a pillar that revealed its measurements with heat to the dark elves, who viewed the Underdark world in the infrared spectrum of light. "You have not been up here long enough to appreciate the ridiculousness of this place. Your heart will call you home soon enough."

"Already," Berg'inyon replied. "I have no taste for this world, nor do I like the sight or smell of any I have seen up here, Sharlotta Vespers least of all."

"Her and the fool Entreri," said Rai-guy. "Yet Jarlaxle favors them both."

"His tenure in Bregan D'aerthe may be nearing its end," said Kimmuriel, and both Berg'inyon and Rai-guy opened their eyes wide at such a bold proclamation.

In truth, though, both were harboring the exact same sentiments. Jarlaxle had reached far in merely bringing them to the surface. Perhaps he'd reached too far for the rogue band to continue to hold much favor among their former associates, including most of the great houses back in Menzoberranzan. It was a gamble, and one that might indeed pay off, especially as the flow of exotic and desirable goods increased to the city.

The plan, however, had been for a short stay, only long enough to establish a few agents to properly facilitate the flow of trade. Jarlaxle had stepped in more deeply then, conquering House Basadoni and renewing his ties with the dangerous Entreri. Then, seemingly for his own amusement, Jarlaxle had gone after the most hated rogue, Drizzt Do'Urden. After completing his business with the outcast and stealing the mighty artifact Crenshinibon, he had let Drizzt walk away, had even forced Rai-guy to use a Lolth-bestowed spell of healing to save the miserable renegade's life.

And now this, a more overt grab for not profit but power, and in a place where none of Bregan D'aerthe other than Jarlaxle wished to remain.

Jarlaxle had taken small steps along this course, but he had put a long and winding road behind him. He brought all of Bregan D'aerthe further and further from their continuing mission, from the allure that had brought most of the members, Rai-guy, Kimmuriel, and Berg'inyon among them, into the organization in the first place.

"What of Sharlotta Vespers?" Kimmuriel asked.

"Jarlaxle will eliminate that problem for us," Rai-guy replied.

"Jarlaxle favors her," Berg'inyon reminded.

"She just entered into a deception against him," Rai-guy replied with all confidence. "We know this, and she knows that we know, though she has not yet considered the potentially devastating implications. She will follow our commands from this point forward."

The drow wizard smiled as he considered his own words. He always enjoyed seeing an *iblith* fall into the web of drow society, learning piece by piece that the sticky strands were layered many levels deep.

"I know of your hunger, for I share in it," Jarlaxle remarked. "This is not as I had envisioned, but perhaps it was not yet time."

Perhaps you place too much faith in your lieutenants, the voice in his head replied.

"No, they saw something that we, in our hunger, did not," Jarlaxle reasoned. "They are troublesome, often annoying, and not to be trusted when their personal gain is at odds with their given mission, but that was not the case here. I must examine this more carefully. Perhaps there are better avenues toward our desired goal."

The voice started to respond, but the drow mercenary cut short the dialogue, shutting it out.

The abruptness of that dismissal reminded Crenshinibon that its respect for the dark elf was well-placed. This Jarlaxle was as strong of will and as difficult to beguile as any wielder the ancient sentient artifact had ever known, even counting the great demon lords who had often joined with Crenshinibon through the centuries.

In truth, the only wielder the artifact had ever known who could so readily and completely shut out its call had been the immediate predecessor to Jarlaxle, another drow, Drizzt Do'Urden. That one's mental barrier had been constructed of morals. Crenshinibon would have been no better off in the hands of a goodly priest or a paladin, fools all and blind to the need to attain the greatest levels of power.

All that only made Jarlaxle's continued resistance even more impressive, for the artifact understood that this one held no such conscience-based mores. There was no intrinsic understanding within Jarlaxle that Crenshinibon was some evil creation and thus to be avoided out of hand. No, to Crenshinibon's reasoning, Jarlaxle viewed everyone and everything he encountered as tools, as vehicles to carry him along his desired road.

The artifact could build forks along that road, and perhaps even sharper turns as Jarlaxle wandered farther and farther from the path, but there would be no abrupt change in direction at this time.

Crenshinibon, the Crystal Shard, did not even consider seeking a new wielder, as it had often done when confronting obstacles in the past. While it sensed resistance in Jarlaxle, that resistance did not implicate danger or even inactivity. To the sentient artifact, Jarlaxle was powerful and intriguing, and full of the promise of the greatest levels of power Crenshinibon had ever known.

The fact that this drow was not a simple instrument of chaos and destruction, as were so many of the demon lords, or an easily duped human—perhaps the most redundant thought the artifact had ever considered—only made him more interesting.

They had a long way to go together, Crenshinibon believed.

The artifact would find its greatest level of power. The world would suffer greatly.

CHAPTER

5

Others have tried, and some have even come close," said Dwahvel Tiggerwillies, the halfling entrepreneur and leader of the only real halfling guild in all the city, a collection of pickpockets and informants who regularly congregated at Dwahvel's Copper Ante. "Some have even supposedly gotten their hands on the cursed thing."

"Cursed?" Entreri asked, resting back comfortably in his chair—a pose Artemis Entreri rarely assumed.

So unusual was the posture, that it jogged Entreri's own thoughts about this place. It was no accident that this was the only room in all the city in which Artemis Entreri had ever partaken of liquor—and even that only in moderate amounts. He had been coming here often of late—ever since he had killed his former associate, the pitiful Dondon Tiggerwillies, in the room next door. Dwahvel was Dondon's cousin, and she knew of the murder but knew, too, that Entreri had, in some respects, done the wretch a favor. Whatever ill will Dwahvel harbored over that incident couldn't hold anyway, not when her pragmatism surfaced.

Entreri knew that and knew that he was welcomed here by Dwahvel and all of her associates. Also, he knew that the Copper Ante was likely the most secure house in all of the city. No, its defenses were not formidable—Jarlaxle could flatten the place with a small fraction of the power he had brought to Calimport—but its safeguards against prying eyes were as fine as those of a wizards' guild. That was the area, as opposed to physical defenses, where Dwahvel utilized most of her resources. Also, the Copper Ante was known as a place to purchase information, so others had a reason to keep it secure. In many ways, Dwahvel and her comrades survived as Sha'lazzi Ozoule survived, by proving of use to all potential enemies.

Entreri didn't like the comparison. Sha'lazzi was a street profiteer, loyal to no one other than Sha'lazzi. He was no more than a middleman, collecting information with his purse and not his wits, and auctioning it away to the highest bidder. He did no work other than that of salesman, and in that regard, the man was very good. He was not a contributor, just a leech, and Entreri suspected that Sha'lazzi would one day be found murdered in an alley, and that no one would care.

Dwahvel Tiggerwillies might find a similar fate, Entreri realized, but if she did, her murderer would find many out to avenge her.

Perhaps Artemis Entreri would be among them.

"Cursed," Dwahvel decided after some consideration.

"To those who feel its bite."

"To those who feel it at all," Dwahvel insisted.

Entreri shifted to the side and tilted his head, studying his surprising little friend.

"Kohrin Soulez is trapped by his possession of it," Dwahvel explained. "He builds a fortress about himself because he knows the value of the sword."

"He has many treasures," Entreri reasoned, but he knew that Dwahvel was right on this matter, at least as far as Kohrin Soulez was concerned.

"That one treasure alone invites the ire of wizards," Dwahvel predictably responded, "and the ire of those who rely upon wizards for their security."

Entreri nodded, not disagreeing, but neither was he persuaded by Dwahvel's arguments. Charon's Claw might indeed be a curse for Kohrin Soulez, but if that was so it was because Soulez had entrenched himself in a place where such a weapon would be seen as a constant lure and a constant threat. Once he got his hands on the powerful sword, Artemis Entreri had no intention of staying anywhere near to Calimport. Soulez's chains would be his escape.

"The sword is an old artifact," Dwahvel remarked, drawing Entreri's attention more fully. "Everyone who has ever claimed it has died with it in his hands."

She thought her warning dramatic, no doubt, but the words had little effect on Entreri. "Everyone dies, Dwahvel," the assassin replied without hesitation, his response fueled by the living hell that had come to him in Calimport. "It is how one lives that matters."

Dwahvel looked at him curiously, and Entreri wondered if he had, perhaps, revealed too much, or tempted Dwahvel too much to go and learn even more about the reality of the power backing Entreri and the Basadoni Guild. If the cunning halfling ever learned too much of the truth, and Jarlaxle or his lieutenants learned of her knowledge, then none of her magical wards, none of her associates—even Artemis Entreri—and none of her perceived usefulness would save her from Jarlaxle's merciless soldiers. The Copper Ante would be gutted, and Entreri would find himself without a place in which to relax.

Dwahvel continued to stare at him, her expression a mixture of professional curiosity and personal—what was it?—compassion?

"What is it that so unhinges Artemis Entreri?" she started to ask, but even as the words came forth, so too came the assassin, his jeweled dagger flashing out of his belt as he leaped out of the chair and across the expanse, too quickly for Dwahvel's guards to even register the movement, too quickly for Dwahvel to even realize what was happening.

He was simply there, hovering over her, her hairy head pulled back, his dagger just nicking her throat.

But she felt it—how she felt the bite of that vicious, life-stealing dagger. Entreri had opened a tiny wound, yet through it Dwahvel could feel her very life-force being torn out of her body.

"If such a question as that ever echoes outside of these walls," the assassin promised, his breath hot on her face, "you will regret that I did not finish this strike."

He backed away then, and Dwahvel quickly threw up one hand, fingers flapping back and forth, the signal to her crossbowmen to hold their shots. With her other hand, she rubbed her neck, pinching at the tiny wound.

"You are certain that Kohrin Soulez still has it?" Entreri asked, more to change the subject and put things back on a professional level than to gather any real information.

"He had it, and he is still alive," the obviously shaken Dwahvel answered. "That seems proof enough."

Entreri nodded and assumed his previous posture, though the relaxed position did not fit the dangerous light that now shone in his eyes.

"You still wish to leave the city by secure routes?" Dwahvel asked.

Entreri gave a slight nod.

"We will need to utilize Domo and the were—" the halfling guildmaster started to say, but Entreri cut her short.

"No."

"He has the fastest—"

"No."

Dwahvel started to argue yet again. Fulfilling Entreri's request that she get him out of Calimport without anyone knowing it would prove no easy feat, even with Domo's help. Entreri was publicly and intricately tied to the Basadoni Guild, and that guild had drawn the watchful eyes of every power in Calimport. She stopped short, and this time Entreri hadn't interrupted her with a word but rather with a look, that all-too-dangerous look that Artemis Entreri had perfected decades before. It was the look that told his target that the time was fast approaching for final prayers.

"It will take some more time, then," Dwahvel remarked. "Not long, I assure you. An hour perhaps."

"No one is to know of this other than Dwahvel," Entreri instructed quietly, so that the crossbowmen in the shadows of the room's corners couldn't hear. "Not even your most trusted lieutenants."

The halfling blew a long, resigned sigh. "Two hours, then," she said.

Entreri watched her go. He knew that she couldn't possibly accede to his wishes to get him out of Calimport without anyone at all knowing of the journey—the streets were too well monitored—but it was a strong reminder to the halfling guildmaster that if anyone started talking about it too openly, Entreri would hold her personally responsible.

The assassin chuckled at the thought, for he couldn't imagine himself killing Dwahvel. He liked and respected the halfling, both for her courage and her skills.

He did need this departure to remain secret, though. If some of the others, particularly Rai-guy or Kimmuriel, found out that he had gone out, they would investigate and soon, no doubt, discern his destination. He didn't want the two dangerous drow studying Kohrin Soulez.

Dwahvel returned soon after, well within the two hours she had pessimistically predicted, and handed Entreri a rough map of this section of the city, with a route sketched on it.

"There will be someone waiting for you at the end of Crescent Avenue," she explained. "Right before the bakery."

"Detailing the second stretch your halflings have determined to be clear for travel," the assassin reasoned.

Dwahvel nodded. "My kin and other associates."

"And, of course, they will watch the movements as each map is collected," Entreri indicated.

Dwahvel shrugged. "You are a master of disguises, are you not?"

Entreri didn't answer. He set out immediately, exiting the Copper Ante and turning down a dark ally, emerging on the other side looking as though he had gained fifty pounds and walking with a pronounced limp.

He was out of Calimport within the hour, running along the northwestern road. By dawn, he was on a dune, looking down upon the Dallabad Oasis. He considered Kohrin Soulez long and hard, recalling everything he knew about the old man.

"Old," he said aloud with a sigh, for in truth, Soulez was in his early fifties, less than fifteen years older than Artemis Entreri.

The assassin turned his thoughts to the palace-fortress itself, trying to recall vivid details about the place. From this angle, all Entreri could make out were a few palm trees, a small pond, a single large boulder, a handful of tents including one larger pavilion, and behind them all, seeming to blend in with the desert sands, a brown, square-walled fortress. A handful of robed sentries walked around the fortress walls, seeming quite bored. The fortress of Dallabad did not appear very formidable—certainly nothing against the likes of Artemis Entreri—but the assassin knew better.

He had visited Soulez and Dallabad on several occasions when he had been working for Pasha Basadoni, and again more recently, when he had been in the service of Pasha Pook. He knew of the circular building within those square wall with its corridors winding in tighter and tighter circles toward the great treasury rooms of Kohrin Soulez, culminating in the private quarters of the oasis master himself.

Entreri considered Dwahvel's last description of the man and his place in the context of those memories and chuckled as he recognized the truth of her observations. Kohrin Soulez was indeed a prisoner.

Still, that prison worked well in both directions, and there was no way that Entreri could easily slip in and take that which he desired. The palace was a fortress, and a fortress full of soldiers specifically trained to thwart any attempts by the too-common thieves of the region.

The assassin thought that Dwahvel was wrong on one point, though. Kohrin himself, and not Charon's Claw, was the source of that prison. The man was so fearful of losing his prized weapon that he allowed it to dominate and consume him. His own fear of losing the sword had paralyzed him from taking any chances with it. When had Soulez last left Dallabad? the assassin wondered. When had he last visited the open market or chatted with his old associates on Calimport's streets?

No, people made their own prisons, Entreri knew, and knew well, for hadn't he, in fact, done the same thing in his obsession with Drizzt Do'Urden? Hadn't he been consumed by a foolish need to do battle with an insignificant dark elf who really had nothing to do with him?

Confident that he would never again make such an error, Artemis Entreri looked down upon Dallabad and smiled widely. Yes, Kohrin Soulez had done well to design his fortress against any would-be thieves skulking in from shadow to shadow or under cover of the darkness of night, but how would those many sentries fare when an army of dark elves descended upon them?

⊷━━⊶

"You were with him when he learned of the retreat," Sharlotta Vespers asked Entreri the next night, soon after the assassin had quietly returned to Calimport. "How did Jarlaxle accept the news?"

"With typical nonchalance," Entreri answered honestly. "Jarlaxle has led Bregan D'aerthe for centuries. He is not one to betray that which is in his heart."

"Even to Artemis Entreri, who can read a man's eyes and tell him what he had for dinner the night before?" Sharlotta asked, grinning.

That smirk couldn't hold against the deadly calm expression that came over Entreri's face. "You do not begin to understand these new allies who have come to join with us," he said in all seriousness.

"To conquer us, you mean," Sharlotta replied, the first time since the takeover that Entreri had heard her even hint ill will against the dark elves. He wasn't surprised—who wouldn't quickly come to hate the wretched drow? On the other hand, Entreri had always known Sharlotta as someone who accepted whatever allies she could find, as long as they brought to her the power she so desperately craved.

"If they so choose," Entreri replied without missing a beat and in a most serious tone. "Underestimate any facet of the dark elves, from their fighting abilities to whether or not they betray themselves with expressions, and you will wind up dead, Sharlotta."

The woman started to respond but did not, fighting hard to keep an uncharacteristic hopelessness off of her expression. He knew she was beginning to feel the same way he had during his journey to Menzoberranzan, the same way that he was beginning to feel once more, particularly whenever Rai-guy and Kimmuriel were around. There was something humbling about even being near these handsome, angular creatures. The drow always knew more than they should and always revealed less than they knew. Their mystery was only heightened by the undeniable power behind their often subtle threats. And always there was that damned condescension toward anyone who was not drow. In the current situation, where Bregan D'aerthe could obviously easily overwhelm the remnants of House Basadoni, Artemis Entreri included, that condescension took on even uglier tones. It was a poignant and incessant reminder of who was the master and who was the slave.

He recognized that same feeling in Sharlotta, growing with every passing moment, and he almost used that to enlist her aid in his secret scheme to take Dallabad and its greatest prize.

Almost—then Entreri considered the course and was shocked that his feelings toward Rai-guy and Kimmuriel had almost brought forth such a blunder as that. For all his life, with only very rare exceptions, Artemis Entreri had worked alone, had used his wits to ensnare unintentional and unwitting allies. Cohorts inevitably knew too much for Entreri ever to be comfortable with them. The one exception he now made, out of simple necessity, was Dwahvel Tiggerwillies, and she, he was quite sure, would never double-cross him, not even under the questioning of the dark elves. That had always been the beauty of Dwahvel and her halfling comrades.

Sharlotta, however, was a completely different sort, Entreri now pointedly reminded himself. If he tried to enlist Sharlotta in his plan to go after Kohrin Soulez, he'd have to watch her closely forever after. She'd likely take the information from him and run to Jarlaxle, or even to Rai-guy and Kimmuriel, using Entreri's soon-to-be-lifeless body as a ladder with which to elevate herself.

Besides, Entreri did not need to bring up Dallabad to Sharlotta, for he had already made arrangements toward that end. Dwahvel would entice Sharlotta toward Dallabad with a few well-placed lies, and Sharlotta, who was predictable indeed when one played upon her sense of personal gain, would take the information to Jarlaxle, only strengthening Entreri's personal suggestions that Dallabad would prove a meaningful and profitable conquest.

"I never thought I would miss Pasha Basadoni," Sharlotta remarked off-handedly, the most telling statement the woman had yet made.

"You hated Basadoni," Entreri reminded.

Sharlotta didn't deny that, but neither did she change her stance.

"You did not fear him as much as you fear the drow, and rightly so," Entreri remarked. "Basadoni was loyal, thus predictable. These dark elves are neither. They are too dangerous."

"Kimmuriel told me that you lived among them in Menzoberranzan," Sharlotta mentioned. "How did you survive?"

"I survived because they were too busy to bother with killing me," Entreri honestly replied. "I was *dobluth* to them, a non-drow outcast, and not worth the trouble. Also, it seems to me now that Jarlaxle might have been using me to further his understanding of the humans of Calimport."

That brought a chuckle to Sharlotta's thick lips. "I would hardly consider Artemis Entreri the typical human of Calimport," she said. "And if Jarlaxle had believed that all men were possessed of your abilities, I doubt he would have dared come to the city, even if all of Menzoberranzan marched behind him."

Entreri gave a slight bow, taking the compliment in polite stride, though he never had use for flattery. To Entreri's way of thinking, one was good enough or one wasn't, and no amount of self-serving chatter could change that.

"And that is our goal now, for both our sakes," Entreri went on. "We must keep the drow busy, which would seem not so difficult a task given Jarlaxle's sudden desire rapidly to expand his surface empire. We are safer if House Basadoni is at war."

"But not within the city," Sharlotta replied. "The authorities are starting to take note of our movements and will not stand idly by much longer. We are safer if the drow are engaged in battle, but not if that battle extends beyond house-to-house."

Entreri nodded, glad that Dwahvel's little suggestions to Sharlotta that other eyes might be pointing their way had brought the clever woman to these conclusions so quickly. Indeed, if House Basadoni reached too far and too fast, the true power of the house would likely be discovered. Once the realm of Calimshan came to that revelation, their response against Jarlaxle's band would be complete and overwhelming. Earlier on, Entreri had entertained just such a scenario, but he had come to dismiss it. He doubted that he, or any other *iblith* of House Basadoni, would survive a Bregan D'aerthe retreat.

That ultimate chaos, then, had been relegated to the status of a backup plan.

"But you are correct," Sharlotta went on. "We must keep them busy—their military arm, at least."

Entreri smiled and easily held back the temptation to enlist her then and there against Kohrin Soulez. Dwahvel would take care of that, and soon, and Sharlotta would never even figure out that she had been used for the gain of Artemis Entreri.

Or perhaps the clever woman would come to see the truth.

Perhaps, then, Entreri would have to kill her.

To Artemis Entreri, who had suffered the double-dealing of Sharlotta Vespers for many years, it was not an unpleasant thought.

CHAPTER

6

Artemis Entreri surely recognized the voice but hardly the tone. In all the months he had spent with Jarlaxle, both here and in the Underdark, he had never known the mercenary leader to raise his voice in anger.

Jarlaxle was shouting now, and to Entreri's pleasure as much as his curiosity, he was shouting at Rai-guy and Kimmuriel.

"It will symbolize our *ascension*," Jarlaxle roared.

"It will allow our enemies a focal point," Kimmuriel countered.

"They will not see it as anything more than a new guild house," Jarlaxle came back.

"Such structures are not uncommon," came Rai-guy's response, in calmer, more controlled tones.

Entreri entered the room then, to find the three standing and facing each other. A fourth drow, Berg'inyon Baenre, sat back comfortably against one wall.

"They will not know that drow were behind the construction of the tower," Rai-guy went on, after a quick and dismissive glance at the human, "but they will recognize that a new power has come to the Basadoni Guild."

"They know that already," Jarlaxle reasoned.

"They suspect it, as they suspect that old Basadoni is dead," Rai-guy retorted. "Let us not confirm their suspicions. Let us not do their reconnaissance for them."

Jarlaxle narrowed his one visible eye—the magical eye patch was over his left this day—and turned his gaze sharply at Entreri. "You know the city better than any of us," he said. "What say you? I plan to construct a tower, a crystalline image of Crenshinibon similar to the one in which you destroyed Drizzt Do'Urden. My associates here fear that such an act will prompt dangerous responses from other guilds and perhaps even the greater authorities of Calimshan."

"From the wizards' guild, at least," Entreri put in calmly. "A dangerous group."

Jarlaxle backed off a step in apparent surprise that Entreri had not readily gone along with him. "Guilds construct new houses all the time," the mercenary leader argued. "Some more lavish than anything I plan to create with Crenshinibon."

"But they do so by openly hiring out the proper craftsmen—and wizards, if magic is necessary," Entreri explained.

He was thinking fast on his feet here, totally surprised by Jarlaxle's dangerous designs. He didn't want to side with Rai-guy and Kimmuriel completely, though, because he knew that such an alliance would never serve him. Still, the notion of constructing an image of Crenshinibon right in the middle of Calimport seemed foolhardy at the very least.

"There you have it," Rai-guy cut in with a chortle. "Even your lackey does not believe it to be a wise or even feasible option."

"Speak your words from your own mouth, Rai-guy," Entreri promptly remarked. He almost expected the volatile wizard to make a move on him then and there, given the look of absolute hatred Rai-guy shot his way.

"A tower in Calimport would invite trouble," Entreri said to Jarlaxle, "though it is not impossible. We could, perhaps, hire a wizard of the prominent guild as a front for our real construction. Even that would be more easily accomplished if we set our sights on the outskirts of the city, out in the desert, perhaps, where the tower can better bask in the brilliant sunlight."

"The point is to erect a symbol of our strength," Jarlaxle put in. "I hardly wish to impress the little lizards and vipers that will view our tower in the empty desert."

"Bregan D'aerthe has always been better served by hiding its strength," Kimmuriel dared to interject. "Are we to change so successful a policy here in a world full of potential enemies? Time and again you seem to forget who we are, Jarlaxle, and *where* we are."

"We can mask the true nature of the tower's construction for a handsome price," Entreri reasoned. "And perhaps I can discern a location that will serve your purposes," he said to Jarlaxle, then turned to Kimmuriel and Rai-guy, "and alleviate your well-founded fears."

"You do that," Rai-guy remarked. "Show some worth and prove me wrong."

Entreri took the left-handed compliment with a quiet chuckle. He already had the perfect location in mind, yet another prompt to push Jarlaxle and Bregan D'aerthe against Kohrin Soulez and Dallabad Oasis.

"Have we heard any response from the Rakers?" Jarlaxle asked, walking to the side of the room and taking his seat.

"Sharlotta Vespers is meeting with Pasha Da'Daclan this very hour," Entreri replied.

"Will he not likely kill her in retribution?" Kimmuriel asked.

"No loss for us," Rai-guy quipped sarcastically.

"Pasha Da'Daclan is too intrigued to—" Entreri began.

"Impressed, you mean," corrected Rai-guy.

"He is too *intrigued*," Entreri said firmly, "to act so rashly as that. He harbors no anger at the loss of a minor outpost, no doubt, and is more interested in weighing our true strength and intentions. Perhaps he will kill her, mostly to learn if such an act might illicit a response."

"If he does, perhaps we will utterly destroy him and all of his guild," Jarlaxle said, and that raised a few eyebrows.

Entreri was less surprised. The assassin was beginning to suspect that there was some method behind Jarlaxle's seeming madness. Typically, Jarlaxle would have been the type to find a way for his relationship to be mutually beneficial with a man as entrenched in the power structures as Pasha Da'Daclan of the Rakers. The mercenary dark elf didn't often waste time, energy, and valuable soldiers in destruction—no more than was necessary for him to gain the needed foothold. At this time, the foothold in Calimport was fairly secure, and yet Jarlaxle's hunger seemed only to be growing.

Entreri didn't understand it, but he wasn't too worried, figuring that he could find some way to use it to his own advantage.

"Before we take any action against Da'Daclan, we must weaken his outer support," the assassin remarked.

"Outer support?" The question came from both Jarlaxle and Rai-guy.

"Pasha Da'Daclan's arms have a long reach," Entreri explained. "I suspect that he has created some outer ring of security, perhaps even beyond Calimport's borders."

From the look on the faces of the dark elves, Entreri realized that he had just successfully laid the groundwork, and that nothing more needed to be said at that time. In truth, he knew Pasha Da'Daclan better than to believe that the old man would harm Sharlotta Vespers. Such overt revenge simply wasn't Da'Daclan's way. No, he would invite the continued dialogue with Sharlotta, because for the Basadonis to have moved so brazenly against him as to destroy one of his outer houses, they would, by his reasoning, have to have some new and powerful weapons or allies. Pasha Da'Daclan wanted to know if the attack had been precipitated by the mere cocksureness of the new leaders of the guild—if Basadoni was indeed dead, as the common rumors implied—or by well-placed confidence. The fact that Sharlotta herself, who in the event of Basadoni's death would certainly have been elevated to the very highest levels within the organization, had come out to him hinted, at least, at the second explanation for the attack. In that instance, Pasha Da'Daclan wasn't about to invite complete disaster.

So Sharlotta would leave Da'Daclan's house very much alive, and she would hearken to Dwahvel Tiggerwillies's previous call. When she returned to Jarlaxle late that night, the mercenary would hear confirmation that Da'Daclan had an ally outside the city, an ally, Entreri would later explain, whose location would be the perfect setting for a new and impressive tower.

Yes, this was all going along quite well, in the assassin's estimation.

"Silence Kohrin Soulez, and Pasha Da'Daclan has no voice outside of Calimport," Sharlotta Vespers explained to Jarlaxle that same evening.

"He needs no voice outside the city," Jarlaxle returned. "Given the information that you and my other lieutenants have provided, there is too much backing for the human right here within Calimport for us wisely to consider any course of true conquest."

"But Pasha Da'Daclan does not understand that," Sharlotta replied without hesitation.

It was obvious to Jarlaxle that the woman had thought this through quite extensively. She had returned from her meeting with Da'Daclan, and later meetings with her street informants, quite excited and animated. She hadn't really accomplished anything conclusive with Da'Daclan, but she had sensed that the man was on the defensive. He was truly worried about the state of complete destruction that had befallen his outer, minor house. Da'Daclan didn't understand Basadoni's new level of power, nor the state of control within the Basadoni Guild, and that too made him nervous.

Jarlaxle rested his angular chin in his delicate black hand. "He believes Pasha Basadoni to be dead?" he asked for the third time, and for the third time, Sharlotta answered, "Yes."

"Should that not imply a new weakness, then, within the guild?" the mercenary leader reasoned.

"Perhaps in your world," Sharlotta replied, "where the drow houses are ruled by Matron Mothers who serve Lolth directly. Here the loss of a leader implies nothing more than instability, and that, more than anything else, frightens rivals. The guilds do not normally wage war because to do so would be detrimental to all sides. This is something the old pashas have learned through years, even decades, of experience. It's something they have passed down to their children, or other selected followers, for generations."

Of course it all made sense to Jarlaxle, but he held his somewhat perplexed look, prompting her to continue. In truth, Jarlaxle was learning more about Sharlotta than about anything to do with the social workings of Calimport's underground guilds.

"As a result of our attack, Pasha Da'Daclan believes the rumors that speak of old Basadoni's death," the woman continued. "To Da'Daclan's thinking, if Basadoni is dead—or has at least lost control of the guild—then we are more dangerous by far." Sharlotta flashed her wicked and ironic smile.

"So with every outer strand we cut—first the minor house and now this Dallabad Oasis—we lessen Da'Daclan's sense of security," Jarlaxle reasoned.

"And make it easier for me to force a stronger treaty with the Rakers," Sharlotta explained. "Perhaps Da'Daclan will even give over to us the entire block about the destroyed minor house to appease us. His base of operations is gone from that area anyway."

"Not so big a prize," Jarlaxle remarked.

"Ah yes, but how much more respect will the other guilds offer to Basadoni when they learn that Pasha Da'Daclan turned over some of his ground to us after we so wronged him?" Sharlotta purred. Her continuing roll of intrigue, her building of level upon level of gain, heightened Jarlaxle's respect for her.

"Dallabad Oasis?" he asked.

"A prize in and of itself," Sharlotta was quick to answer, "even without the gains it will afford us in our game with Pasha Da'Daclan."

Jarlaxle thought it over for a bit, nodded, and, with a sly look at Sharlotta, nodded toward the bed. Thoughts of great gain had ever been an aphrodisiac for Jarlaxle.

⊷══⊶

Jarlaxle paced his room later that night, having dismissed Sharlotta that he could consider in private the information she had brought to him. According to the woman—who had been so ill-briefed by Dwahvel—Dallabad Oasis was working as a relay point for Pasha Da'Daclan, the exit for information to Da'Daclan's more powerful allies far from Calimport. Run by some insignificant functionary named Soulez, Dallabad was an independent fortress. It was not an official part of the Rakers or any other guild from the city. Soulez apparently accepted payment to serve as information-relay, and also, Sharlotta had explained, sometimes collected tolls along the northwestern trails.

Jarlaxle continued to pace, digesting the information, playing it in conjunction with the earlier suggestions of Artemis Entreri. He felt the telepathic intrusion of his newest ally then, but he merely adjusted his magical eye patch to ward off the call.

There had to be some connection here, some truth within the truth, some planned relationship between Dallabad's tenuous position and the mere convenience of this all. Hadn't Entreri earlier suggested that Jarlaxle conquer some place outside of Calimport where he could more safely set up a crystalline tower?

And now this: a perfect location practically handed over to him for conquest, a place so conveniently positioned for Bregan D'aerthe to make a double gain.

The mental intrusions continued. It was a strong call, the strongest Jarlaxle had ever felt through his eye patch.

He wants something, Crenshinibon said in the mercenary leader's head.

Jarlaxle started to dismiss the shard, thinking that his own reasoning could bring him to a clearer picture of this whole situation, but Crenshinibon's next statement leaped past the conclusions he was slowly forming.

Artemis Entreri has deeper designs here, the shard insisted. *An old grudge, perhaps, or some treasure within the obvious prize.*

"Not a grudge," Jarlaxle said aloud, removing the protective eye patch so that he and the shard could better communicate. "If Entreri harbored such feelings as that, then he would see to this Soulez creature personally. Ever has he prided himself on working alone."

You believe the sudden imposition of Dallabad Oasis, a place never before mentioned, into both the equation of the Rakers and our need to construct a tower to be a mere fortunate coincidence? the shard asked, and before Jarlaxle could even respond, Crenshinibon made its assessment clear. *Artemis Entreri harbors some ulterior motive for an assault against Dallabad Oasis. There can be no doubt. Likely, he knew that our informants would bring to us the suggestion that conquering Dallabad would frighten Pasha Da'Daclan and considerably strengthen our bargaining power with him.*

"More likely, Artemis Entreri arranged for our informants to come to that very conclusion," Jarlaxle reasoned, ending with a chuckle.

Perhaps he views this as a way toward our destruction, the shard imparted. *That he can break free of us and rule on his own.*

Jarlaxle was shaking his head before the full reasoning even entered his mind. "If Artemis Entreri wished to be free of us, he would find some excuse to depart the city."

And run as faraway as Morik the Rogue, perhaps? came the ironic thought.

It was true enough, Jarlaxle had to admit. Bregan D'aerthe had already proven that its arms on the surface world were long indeed, long enough, perhaps, to catch a runaway deserter. Still, Jarlaxle highly doubted the shard's last reasoning. First of all, Artemis Entreri was wise enough to understand that Bregan D'aerthe would not go blindly against Dallabad or any other foe. Also, to Jarlaxle's thinking, such a ploy to bring about Bregan D'aerthe's downfall on the surface would be far too risky—and would it not be more easily accomplished merely by telling the greater authorities of Calimshan that a band of dark elves had come to Calimport?

He offered all of the reasoning to Crenshinibon, building common ground with the artifact that the most likely scenario here involved the shard's second line of reasoning, that of a secret treasure within the oasis.

The drow mercenary closed his eyes and absorbed the Crystal Shard's feelings on these plausible and growing suspicions and laughed again when he learned that he and the artifact had both come to accept the conclusion and were of like mind concerning it. Both were more amused and impressed than angry. Whatever Entreri's personal motives, and whether or not the information connecting Dallabad to Pasha Da'Daclan held any truth or not, the oasis would be a worthy and seemingly safe acquisition.

More so to the artifact than to the dark elf, for Crenshinibon had made it quite clear to Jarlaxle that it needed to construct an image of itself, a tower to collect the brilliant sunlight.

A step closer to its ever-present, final goal.

CHAPTER

7

Kohrin Soulez held his arm up before him, focusing his thoughts on the black, red-laced gauntlet that he wore on his right hand. Those laces seemed to pulse now, an all-too-familiar feeling for the secretive and secluded man.

Someone was trying to look in on him and his fortress at Dallabad Oasis.

Soulez forced his concentration deeper into the magical glove. He had recently been approached by a mediator from Calimport inquiring about a possible sale of his beloved sword, Charon's Claw. Soulez, of course, had balked at the absurd notion. He held this item more dear to his heart than he had any of his numerous wives, even above his many, many children. The offer had been serious, promising wealth beyond imagination for the single item.

Soulez had gained enough understanding of Calimport's guildsmen and had been in possession of Charon's Claw long enough to know what a serious offer, obviously refused and without room for bargaining, might bring, and so he was not surprised to find that prying eyes were seeking him out now. Since further investigation had whispered that the would-be purchaser might be Artemis Entreri and the Basadoni Guild, Soulez had been watching carefully for those eyes in particular.

They would look for weakness but would find none, and thus, he believed, they would merely go away.

As Soulez fell deeper into the energies of the gauntlet, he came to recognize a new element, dangerous only because it hinted that the would-be thief this time might not be so easily dissuaded. These were not the magical energies of a wizard he felt, nor the prayers of a divining priest. No, this energy was different than the expected, but certainly nothing beyond the understanding of Soulez and the gauntlet.

"Psionics," he said aloud, looking past the gauntlet to his lieutenants, who were standing at attention about his throne room.

Three of them were his own children. The fourth was a great military commander from Memnon, and the fifth was a renowned, and now retired, thief from Calimport. Conveniently, Soulez thought, a former member of the Basadoni Guild.

"Artemis Entreri and the Basadonis," Soulez told them, "if it is them, have apparently found access to a psionicist."

The five lieutenants muttered among themselves about the implications of that.

"Perhaps that has been Artemis Entreri's edge for all these years," the youngest of them, Kohrin Soulez's daughter, Ahdahnia, remarked.

"Entreri?" laughed Preelio, the old thief. "Strong of mind? Certainly. Psionics? Bah! He never needed them, so fine was he with the blade."

"But whoever seeks my treasure has access to the mind powers," said Soulez. "They believe that they have found an edge, a weakness of mine and of my treasure's, that they can exploit. That only makes them more dangerous, of course. We can expect an attack."

All five of the lieutenants stiffened at that proclamation, but none seemed overly concerned. There was no grand conspiracy against Dallabad among the guilds of Calimport. Kohrin Soulez had paid dearly to certify that information right away. The five knew that no one guild, or even two or three of the guilds banded together, could muster the power to overthrow Dallabad—not while Soulez carried the sword and the gauntlet and could render any wizards all but ineffective.

"No soldiers will break through our walls," Ahdahnia remarked with a confident smirk. "No thieves will slide through the shadows to the inner structures."

"Unless through some devilish mind power," Preelio put in, looking to the elder Soulez.

Kohrin Soulez only laughed. "They *believe* they have found a weakness," he reiterated. "I can stop them with this—" he held up the glove—"and of course, I have other means." He let the thought hang in the air, his smile bringing grins to the faces of all in attendance. There was a sixth lieutenant, after all, one little seen and little bothered, one used primarily as an instrument of interrogation and torture, one who preferred to spend as little time with the humans as possible.

"Secure the physical defenses," Soulez instructed them. "I will see to the powers of the mind."

He waved them away and sat back, focusing again on his mighty black gauntlet, on the red stitching that ran through it like veins of blood. Yes, he could feel the meager prying, and while he wished that the jealous folk would simply leave him to his business in peace, he believed that he would enjoy this little bit of excitement.

He knew that Yharaskrik certainly would.

⊷═╍═⊶

Far below Kohrin Soulez's throne room, in deep tunnels that few of Soulez's soldiers even knew existed, Yharaskrik was already well aware that someone or something using psionic energies had breached the oasis. Yharaskrik was a mind flayer, an illithid, a humanoid creature with a bulbous head that resembled a huge brain, with several tentacles protruding from the part of his face where a nose, mouth, and chin should have been. Illithids were horrible to behold, and could be quite formidable physically, but their real powers lay in the realm of the mind, in psionic energies that dwarfed the powers of human practitioners, even of drow practitioners. Illithids could simply overwhelm an opponent with stunning blasts of mental energies, and either enslave the unfortunate victim, his mind held in a fugue state, or move in for a feast, attaching their horrid tentacles to the helpless victim and burrowing in to suck out brain matter.

Yharaskrik had been working with Kohrin Soulez for many years. Soulez considered the creature as much an indentured servant as a minion. He believed he had cut a fair deal with the creature after Soulez had apparently rendered Yharaskrik helpless in a short battle, capturing the illithid's mind blast within the magical netting of his gauntlet and thus leaving Yharaskrik open to a devastating counterstrike with the deadly sword. In truth, had Soulez gone for that strike, Yharaskrik would have melted away into the stone, using energies not directed against Soulez and thus beyond the reach of the gauntlet.

Soulez had not pressed the attack, though, as Yharaskrik's communal brain had calculated. The opportunistic man had struck a deal instead, offering the illithid its life and a comfortable place to do its meditation—or whatever else it was that illithids did—in exchange for certain services whenever they were needed, primarily to aid in the defense of Dallabad Oasis.

In all these years, Kohrin Soulez had never once harbored any suspicions that coming to Dallabad in such a capacity had been Yharaskrik's duty all along, that the illithid had been chosen among its strange kin to seek out and study the black and red gauntlet, as mind flayers were often sent to learn of anything that could so block their devastating energies. In truth, Yharaskrik had learned little of use concerning the gauntlet over the years, but the creature was never anxious about that. Brilliant illithids were among the most patient of all the creatures in the multiverse, savoring the process more than the goal. Yharaskrik was quite content in its tunnel home.

Some psionic force had tickled the illithid's sensibility, and Yharaskrik felt enough of the stream of energy to know that it was no other illithid psionically prying about Dallabad Oasis.

The mind flayer, as confident in his superiority as all of his kind, was more intrigued than concerned. He was actually a bit perturbed that the fool Soulez had captured that psychic call with his gauntlet, but now the call had returned, redirected. Yharaskrik had called back, bringing his roving mind eye down, down, to the deep caverns.

The illithid did not try to hide its surprise when it discerned the source of that energy, nor did the creature on the other end, a drow, even begin to mask his own stunned reaction.

Haszakkin! the drow's thoughts instinctively screamed, their word for illithid—a word that conveyed a measure of respect the drow rarely gave to any creature that was not drow.

Dyon G'ennivalz? Yharaskrik asked, the name of a drow city the illithid had known well in its younger days.

Menzoberranzan, came the psionic reply.

House Oblodra, the brilliant creature imparted, for that atypical drow house was well known among all the mind flayer communities of Faerûn's Underdark.

No more, came Kimmuriel's response.

Yharaskrik sensed anger there, and understood it well as Kimmuriel relayed the memories of the downfall of his arrogant family. There had been, during the Time of Troubles, a period when magic, but not psionics, had ceased to function. In that too-brief time, the leaders of House Oblodra had challenged the greater houses of Menzoberranzan, including mighty Matron Baenre herself. The energies shifted with the shifting of the gods, and psionics had become temporarily impotent, while the powers of conventional magic had returned. Matron Baenre's response to the threats of

House Oblodra had wiped the structure and all of the family—except for Kimmuriel, who had wisely used his ties with Jarlaxle and Bregan D'aerthe to make a hasty retreat—from the city, dropping it into the chasm called the Clawrift.

You seek the conquest of Dallabad Oasis? Yharaskrik asked, fully expecting an answer, for creatures communicating through psionics often held their own loyalties to each other even above those of their kindred.

Dallabad will be ours before the night has passed, Kimmuriel honestly replied.

The connection abruptly ended, and Yharaskrik understood the hasty retreat as Kohrin Soulez sauntered into the dark chamber, his right hand clad in the cursed gauntlet that so interfered with psionic energy.

The illithid bowed before his supposed master.

"We have been scouted," Soulez said, getting right to the point, his tension obvious as he stood before the horrid mind flayer.

"Mind's eye," the illithid agreed in its physical, watery voice. "I sensed it."

"Powerful?" Soulez asked.

Yharaskrik gave a quiet gurgle, the illithid equivalent of a resigned shrug, showing his lack of respect for any psionicist that was not illithid. It was an honest appraisal, even though the psionicist in question was drow and not human, and tied to a drow house that was well known among Yharaskrik's people. Still, though the mind flayer was not overly concerned about any battle he might see against the drow psionicist, Yharaskrik knew the dark elves well enough to understand that the Oblodran psionicist would likely be the least of Kohrin Soulez's problems.

"Power is always a relative concept," the illithid answered cryptically.

Kohrin Soulez felt the tingling of magical energy as he ascended the long spiral staircase that took him back to the ground level of his palace in Dallabad. The guildmaster broke into a run, scrambling, muscles working to their limits and his old bones feeling no pain. He thought that the attack must already be underway.

He calmed somewhat, slowing and huffing and puffing to catch his breath. He came up into the guild house to find many of his soldiers milling about, talking excitedly, but seeming more curious than terrified.

"Is it yours, Father?" asked Ahdahnia, her dark eyes gleaming.

Kohrin Soulez stared at her curiously, and taking the cue, Ahdahnia led him to an outer room with an east-facing window.

There it stood, right in the middle of Dallabad Oasis, *within* the outer walls of Kohrin Soulez's fortress.

A crystalline tower, gleaming in the bright sunlight, an image of Crenshinibon, the calling card of doom.

Kohrin Soulez's right hand throbbed with tingling energy as he looked at the magical structure. His gauntlet could capture magical energy and even turn it back against the initiator. It had never failed him, but in just looking at this spectacular tower the guildmaster suddenly recognized that he and his toys were puny things indeed. He knew without even going out and trying that he could not hope to drag the magical energies from that tower, that if he tried, it would consume him and his gauntlet. He shuddered as he pictured a physical manifestation of that absorption, an image of Kohrin Soulez frozen as a gargoyle on the top rim of that magnificent tower.

"Is it yours, Father?" Ahdahnia asked again.

The eagerness left her voice and the sparkle left her eyes as Kohrin turned to her, his face bloodless.

Outside of Dallabad fortress's wall, under the shelter of a copse of palm trees and surrounded by globes of magical darkness, Jarlaxle called to the tower. Its outer wall elongated, and sent forth a tendril, a stairway tunnel that breached the darkness globes and reached to the mercenary's feet. Secure that his soldiers were all in place, Jarlaxle ascended the stairs into the tower proper. With a thought to the Crystal Shard, he retracted the tunnel, effectively sealing himself in.

From that high vantage point in the middle of the fortress courtyard, Jarlaxle watched the unfolding drama around him.

Could you dim the light? he telepathically asked the tower.

Light is strength, Crenshinibon answered.

For you, perhaps, the mercenary replied. *For me, it is uncomfortable.*

Jarlaxle felt a sensation akin to a chuckle from the Crystal Shard, but the artifact did comply and thicken its eastern wall, considerably dulling the light in the room. It also provided a floating chair for Jarlaxle, so that he could drift about the perimeter of the room, studying the battle that would soon unfold.

Notice that Artemis Entreri will partake of the attack, the Crystal Shard remarked, and it sent the chair floating to the northern side of the room. Jarlaxle took the cue and focused hard down below, outside the fortress wall, to the tents and trees and boulders. Finally, with helpful guidance from the artifact, the drow spotted the figure lurking about the shadows.

He did not do so when we planned the attack on Pasha Da'Daclan, Crenshinibon added. Of course, the Crystal Shard knew that Jarlaxle was considering the same thing. The implications continued to follow the line that Entreri had some secret agenda here, some private gain that was either outside of the domain of Bregan D'aerthe, or held some consequence within the second level of the band's hierarchy.

Either way, both Jarlaxle and Crenshinibon thought it more amusing than in any way threatening.

The floating chair drifted back across the small circular room, putting Jarlaxle in line with the first diversionary attack, a series of darkness globes at the top of the outer wall. The soldiers there went into a panic, running and crying out to reform a defensive line away from the magic, but even as they moved back—in fairly good order, Jarlaxle noted—the real attack began, bubbling up from the ground within the fortress courtyard.

Rai-guy had crossed the courtyard, ten difficult feet at a time, casting a series of passwall spells out of a wand. Now, from a natural tunnel that he had fortunately located below the fortress, the drow wizard enacted the last of those passwalls, vanishing a section of stone and dirt.

Immediately the soldiers of Bregan D'aerthe arose, floating with drow levitation into the courtyard, enacting darkness globes above them to confuse their enemies and to lessen the blinding impact of the hated sun.

"We should have attacked at night," Jarlaxle said aloud.

Daytime is when my power is at its peak, Crenshinibon responded immediately, and Jarlaxle felt the rest of the thought keenly. Crenshinibon was none-too-subtly reminding him that it was more powerful than all of Bregan D'aerthe combined.

That expression of confidence was more than a little disconcerting to the mercenary leader, for reasons that he hadn't yet begun to untangle.

Rai-guy stood in the hole, issuing orders to those dark elves running and leaping into levitation, floating up and eager for battle. The wizard was particularly animated this day. His blood was up, as always during a conquest, but he was not pleased at all that Jarlaxle had decided to launch the attack at dawn, a seemingly foolish trade-off of putting his soldiers, used to a world of blackness, at a disadvantage, for the simple gain of constructing a crystalline tower vantage point. The appearance of the tower was an amazing thing, without doubt, one that showed the power of the invaders clearly to those defending inside. Rai-guy did not diminish the value of striking such terror, but every time he saw one of his soldiers squint painfully as he rose up out of the hole into the daylight, the wizard considered his leader's continuing surprising behavior and gritted his teeth in frustration.

Also, the mere fact that they were using dark elves openly against the fortress seemed more than a bit of a gamble. Could they not have accomplished this conquest, as they had planned to do with Pasha Da'Daclan, by striking openly with human, perhaps even kobold soldiers, while the dark elves infiltrated more quietly? What would be left of Dallabad after the conquest now, after all? Almost all remaining alive within—and there would be many, since the dark elves led every assault with their trademark sleep-poisoned hand crossbow darts—would have to be executed anyway, lest they communicate the truth of their conquerors.

Rai-guy reminded himself of his place in the guild and knew it would take a monumental error on the part of Jarlaxle, one that cost the lives of many of Bregan D'aerthe, for him to rally enough support truly to overthrow Jarlaxle. Perhaps this would be that mistake.

The wizard heard a change in the timbre of the shouts from above. He glanced up, taking note that the sunlight seemed brighter, that the globes of magical darkness had gone away. The magically created shaft, too, suddenly disappeared, capturing a pair of levitating soldiers within it as the stone and dirt rematerialized. It lasted only a moment, as if something suddenly reached out and grabbed away the magic that was trying to dispel Rai-guy's vertical passwall dweomers. That moment was long enough to destroy utterly the two unfortunate drow soldiers.

The wizard cursed at Jarlaxle, but under his breath.

He reminded himself to keep safe and to see, in the end, if this attack, even if a complete failure, might not prove personally beneficial.

◁━━▷

Kohrin Soulez fell back. His sensibilities were stung, both by the realization that these were dark elves that had come to secluded Dallabad, and by the magical counterattack that had overwhelmed his gauntlet. He had come out from the main house to rally his soldiers, the blood-red blade of Charon's Claw bared and waving, leaving streaks of ashy blackness in the air. Soulez had run to the area of obvious invasion, where globes of darkness and screams of pain and terror heralded the fighting.

Dispelling those globes was no major task for the gauntlet, nor was closing the hole in the ground through which the enemy continued to arrive, but Soulez had nearly been overwhelmed by a wave of energy that countered the countering energy he was exerting himself. It was a blast of magical power so raw and pure that he could not hope to contain it. He knew it had come from the tower.

The tower!

The dark elves!

His doom was at hand!

He fell back into the main house, ordering his soldiers to fight to the last. As he ran along the more deserted corridors leading to his private chambers, his dear Ahdahnia right behind him, he called out to Yharaskrik to come and whisk him away.

There was no answer.

"He has heard me," Soulez assured his daughter anyway. "We need only escape long enough for Yharaskrik to come to us. Then we will run out to inform the lords of Calimport that the dark elves have come."

"The traps and locks along the hallways will keep our enemies at bay," Ahdahnia replied.

Despite the surprising nature of their enemies, the woman actually believed the claim. These long corridors weaving along the somewhat circular main house of Dallabad were lined with heavy, metal-banded doors of stone and wood layers that could defeat most intrusions, wizardly or physical. Also, the sheer number of traps in place between the outer walls and Kohrin Soulez's inner sanctuary would deter and daunt the most seasoned of thieves.

But not the most clever.

Artemis Entreri had worked his way unnoticed to the base of the fortress's northern wall. It was no small feat—an impossible one under normal circumstances, for there was an open field surrounding the fortress, running nearly a hundred feet to the trees and tents and boulders, and several of the small ponds that marked the place—but this was not a normal circumstance. With a tower materializing *inside* the fortress, most of the guards were scurrying about, trying to find some answers as to whether it was an invading enemy or some secret project of Kohrin Soulez's. Even those guards on the walls couldn't help but stare in awe at that amazing sight.

Entreri dug himself in. His borrowed black cloak—a camouflaging drow *piwafwi* that wouldn't last long in the sun—offered him some protection should any of the guards lean over the twenty foot wall and look down at him.

The assassin waited until the sounds of fighting erupted from within.

To untrained eyes, the wall of Kohrin Soulez's fortress would have seemed a sheer thing indeed, all of polished white marble joints forming an attractive contrast to the brownish sandstone and gray granite. To Entreri, though, it seemed more of a stairway than a wall, with many seam-steps and finger-holds.

He was up near the top in a matter of seconds. The assassin lifted himself up just enough to glance over at the two guards anxiously reloading their crossbows. They were looking in the direction of the courtyard where the battle raged.

Over the wall without a sound went the *piwafwi*-cloaked assassin. He came down from the wall only a few moments later, dressed as one of Kohrin Soulez's guards.

Entreri joined in with some others running frantically around to the front courtyard, but he broke away from them as he came in sight of the fighting. He melted back against the wall and toward the open, main door, where he spotted Kohrin Soulez. The guildmaster was battling drow magic and waving that wondrous sword. Entreri kept several steps ahead of the man as he was forced to fall back. The assassin entered the main building before Soulez and his daughter.

Entreri ran, silent and unseen, along those corridors, through the open doors, past the unset traps, ahead of the two fleeing nobles and those soldiers trailing their leader to secure the corridor behind him. The assassin reached the main door of Soulez's private chambers with enough time to spare to recognize that the alarms and traps on this portal were indeed in place and to do something about them.

Thus, when Ahdahnia Soulez pushed open that magnificent, gold-leafed door, leading her father into his seemingly secure chamber, Artemis Entreri was already there, standing quietly ready behind a floor-to-ceiling tapestry.

❦

The three Dallabad soldiers—well-trained, well-armed, and well-armored with shining chain and small bucklers—faced off against the three dark elves along the western wall of the fortress. The men, frightened as they were, kept the presence of mind to form a triangular defense, using the wall behind them to secure their backs.

The dark elves fanned out and came at them in unison. Their amazing drow swords—two for each warrior—worked circular attack routines so quickly that the paired weapons seemed to blur the line between where one sword stopped and the other began.

The humans, to their credit, held strong their position, offered parries and blocks wherever necessary, and suppressed any urge to scream out in terror and charge blindly—as some of their nearby comrades were doing to disastrous results. Gradually, talking quickly between them to analyze each of their enemy's movements, the trio began to decipher the deceptive and brilliant drow sword dance, enough so, at least, to offer one or two counters of their own.

Back and forth it went, the humans wisely holding their position, not following any of the individually retreating dark elves and thus weakening their own defenses. Blade rang against blade, and the magical swords Kohrin Soulez had provided his best-trained soldiers matched up well enough against the drow weapons.

The dark elves exchanged words the humans did not understand. Then the three drow attacked in unison, all six swords up high in a blurring dance. Human swords and shields came up to meet the challenge and the resulting clang of metal against metal rang out like a single note.

That note soon changed, diminished, and all three of the human soldiers came to recognize, but not completely to comprehend, that their attackers had each dropped one sword.

Shields and swords up high to meet the continuing challenge, they only understood their exposure below the level of the fight when they heard the clicks of three small crossbows and felt the sting as small darts burrowed into their bellies.

The dark elves backed off a step. Tonakin Ta'salz, the central soldier, called out to his companions that he was hit, but that he was all right. The soldier to Tonakin's left started to say the same, but his words were slurred and groggy. Tonakin glanced over just in time to see him tumble facedown in the dirt. To his right, there came no response at all.

Tonakin was alone. He took a deep breath and skittered back against the wall as the three dark elves retrieved their dropped swords. One of them said something to him that he did not understand, but while the words escaped him, the expression on the drow's face did not.

He should have fallen down asleep, the drow was telling him. Tonakin agreed wholeheartedly as the three came in suddenly, six swords slashing in brutal and perfectly coordinated attacks.

To his credit, Tonakin Ta'salz actually managed to block two of them.

And so it went throughout the courtyard and all along the wall of the fortress. Jarlaxle's mercenaries, using mostly physical weapons but with more than a little magic thrown in, overwhelmed the soldiers of Dallabad. The mercenary leader had instructed his killers to spare as many as possible, using sleep darts and accepting surrender. He noted, though, that more than a few were not waiting long enough to find out if any opponents who had resisted the sleep poison might offer a surrender.

The dark elf leader merely shrugged at that, hardly concerned. This was open battle, the kind that he and his mercenaries didn't see often enough. If too many of Kohrin Soulez's soldiers were killed for the oasis fortress to properly function, then Jarlaxle and Crenshinibon would simply find replacements. In any case, with Soulez chased back into his house by the sheer power of the Crystal Shard, the assault had already reached its second stage.

It was going along beautifully. The courtyard and wall were already secured, and the house had been breached at several points. Now Kimmuriel and Rai-guy at last came onto the scene.

Kimmuriel had several of the captives who were still awake dragged before him, forcing them to lead the way into the house. He would use his overpowering will to read their thoughts as they walked him and the drow through the trapped maze to the prize that was Soulez.

Jarlaxle rested back in the crystalline tower. A part of him wanted to go down and join in the fun, but he decided instead to remain and share the moment with his most powerful companion, the Crystal Shard. He even allowed the artifact to thin the eastern wall once more, allowing more sunlight into the room.

❈━━❈

"Where is he?" Kohrin Soulez fumed, stomping about the room. "Yharaskrik!"

"Perhaps he cannot get through," Ahdahnia reasoned. She moved nearer to the tapestry as she spoke.

Entreri knew he could step out and take her down, then go for his prize. He held the urge, intrigued and wary.

"Perhaps the same force from the tower—" Ahdahnia went on.

"No!" Kohrin Soulez interrupted. "Yharaskrik is beyond such things. His people see things—everything—differently."

Even as he finished, Ahdahnia gasped and skittered back across Entreri's field of view. Her eyes went wide as she looked back in the direction of her father, who had walked out of Entreri's very limited line of sight.

Confident that the woman was too entranced by whatever it was that she was watching, Entreri slipped down low to one knee and dared peek out around the tapestry.

He saw an illithid step out of the psionic dimensional doorway and into the room to stand before Kohrin.

A mind flayer!

The assassin fell back behind the tapestry, his thoughts whirling.

Very few things in all the world could rattle Artemis Entreri, who had survived life on the streets from a tender young age and had risen to the very top of his profession, who had survived Menzoberranzan and many, many encounters with dark elves. One of those few things was a mind flayer. Entreri had seen a few in the dark elf city, and he abhorred them more than any other creature he had ever met. It wasn't their appearance that so upset the assassin, though they were brutally ugly by any but illithid standards. No, it was their very demeanor, their different view of the world, as Kohrin had just alluded to.

Throughout his life, Artemis Entreri had gained the upper hand because he understood his enemies better than they understood him. He had found the dark elves a bit more of a challenge, based on the fact that the drow were too experienced—were simply too good at conspiring and plotting for him to gain any real comprehension . . . any that he could hold confidence in, at least.

With illithids, though he had only dealt with them briefly, the disadvantage was even more fundamental and impossible to overcome. There was no way Artemis Entreri could understand that particular enemy because there was no way he could bring himself to any point where he could view the world as an illithid might.

No way.

So Entreri tried to make himself very small. He listened to every word, every inflection, every intake of breath, very carefully.

"Why did you not come earlier to my call?" Kohrin Soulez demanded.

"They are dark elves," Yharaskrik responded in that bubbling, watery voice that sounded to Entreri like a very old man with too much phlegm in his throat. "They are within the building."

"You should have come earlier!" Ahdahnia cried. "We could have beaten—" Her voice left her with a gasp. She stumbled backward and seemed about to fall. Entreri knew the mind flayer had just hit her with some scrambling burst of mental energy.

"What do I do?" Kohrin Soulez wailed.

"There is nothing you can do," answered Yharaskrik. "You cannot hope to survive."

"P-par-parlay with them, F-father!" cried the recovering Ahdahnia. "Give them what they want—else you cannot hope to survive."

"They will take what they want," Yharaskrik assured her, and turned back to Kohrin Soulez. "You have nothing to offer. There is no hope."

"Father?" Ahdahnia asked, her voice suddenly weak, almost pitiful.

"You attack them!" Kohrin Soulez demanded, holding his deadly sword out toward the illithid. "Overwhelm them!"

Yharaskrik made a sound that Entreri, who had mustered enough willpower to peek back around the tapestry, recognized to be an expression of mirth. It wasn't a laugh, actually, but more like a clear, gasping cough.

Kohrin Soulez, too, apparently understood the meaning of the reply, for his face grew very red.

"They are drow. Do you now understand that?" the illithid asked. "There is no hope."

Kohrin Soulez started to respond, to demand again that Yharaskrik take the offensive, but as if he had suddenly come to figure it all out, he paused and stared at his octopus-headed companion. "You knew," he accused. "When the psionicist entered Dallabad, he conveyed . . ."

"The psionicist was drow," the illithid confirmed.

"*Traitor!*" Kohrin Soulez cried.

"There is no betrayal. There was never friendship, or even alliance," the illithid remarked logically.

"But you *knew!*"

Yharaskrik didn't bother to reply.

"Father?" Ahdahnia asked again, and she was trembling visibly.

Kohrin Soulez's breath came in labored gasps. He brought his left hand up to his face and wiped away sweat and tears. "What am I to do?" he asked, speaking to himself. "What will . . ."

Yharaskrik began that coughing laughter again, and this time, it sounded clearly to Entreri that the creature was mocking pitiful Soulez.

Kohrin Soulez composed himself suddenly and glared at the creature. "This amuses you?" he asked.

"I take pleasure in the ironies of the lesser species," Yharaskrik responded. "How much your whines sound as those of the many you have killed. How many have begged for their lives futilely before Kohrin Soulez, as he will now futilely beg for his at the feet of a greater adversary than he can possibly comprehend?"

"But an adversary that you know well!" Kohrin cried.

"I prefer the drow to your pitiful kind," Yharaskrik freely admitted. "They never beg for mercy that they know will not come. Unlike humans, they accept the failings of individual-minded creatures. There is no greater joining among them, as there is none among you, but they understand and accept that fallibility." The illithid gave a slight bow. "That is all the respect I now offer to you, in the hour of your death," Yharaskrik explained. "I would throw energy your way, that you might capture it and redirect it against the dark elves—and they are close now, I assure you—but I choose not to."

Artemis Entreri recognized clearly the change that came over Kohrin Soulez then, the shift from despair to nothing-to-lose anger that he had seen so many times during his decades on the tough streets.

"But I wear the gauntlet!" Kohrin Soulez said powerfully, and he moved the magnificent sword out toward Yharaskrik. "I will at least get the pleasure of first witnessing your end!"

But even as he made the declaration, Yharaskrik seemed to melt into the stone at his feet and was gone.

"Damn him!" Kohrin Soulez screamed. "Damn you—" His tirade cut short as a pounding came on the door.

"Your wand!" the guildmaster cried to his daughter, turning to face her, in the direction of the floor-to-ceiling tapestry that decorated his private chamber.

Ahdahnia just stood there, wide-eyed, making no move to reach for the wand at her belt. Her expression changing not at all, she crumpled to the floor.

There stood Artemis Entreri.

Kohrin Soulez's eyes widened as he watched her descent, but as if he hardly cared for the fall of Ahdahnia other than its implications for his own safety, his gaze focused clearly on Entreri.

"It would have been so much easier if you had merely sold the blade to me," the assassin remarked.

"I knew this was your doing, Entreri," Soulez growled back at him, advancing a step, the blood-red blade gleaming at the ready.

"I offer you one more chance to sell it," Entreri said, and Soulez stopped short, his expression one of pure incredulity. "For the price of her life," the assassin added, pointing down at Ahdahnia with his jeweled dagger. "Your own life is yours to bargain for, but you'll have to make that bargain with others."

Another bang sounded out in the corridor, followed by the sounds of some fighting.

"They are close, Kohrin Soulez," Entreri remarked, "close and overwhelming."

"You brought dark elves to Calimport," Soulez growled back at him.

"They came of their own accord," Entreri replied. "I was merely wise enough not to try to oppose them. So I make my offer, but only this one last time. I can save Ahdahnia—she is not dead but merely asleep." To accentuate his point, he held up a small crossbow quarrel of unusual design, a drow bolt that had been tipped with sleeping poison. "Give me the sword and gauntlet—now—and she lives. Then you can bargain for your own life. The sword will do you little good against the dark elves, for they need no magic to destroy you."

"But if I am to bargain for my life, then why not do so with the sword in hand?" Kohrin Soulez asked.

In response, Entreri glanced down at the sleeping form of Ahdahnia.

"I am to trust that you will keep your word?" Soulez answered.

Entreri didn't answer, other than to fix the man with a cold stare.

There came a sharp rap on the heavy door. As if incited by that sound of imminent danger, Kohrin Soulez leaped forward, slashing hard.

Entreri could have killed Ahdahnia and still dodged, but he did not. He slipped back behind the tapestry and went down low, scrambling along its length. He heard the tearing behind him as Soulez slashed and stabbed. Charon's Claw easily sliced the heavy material, even took chunks out of the wall behind it.

Entreri came out the other side to find Soulez already moving in his direction, the man wearing an expression that seemed half crazed, even jubilant.

"How valuable will the drow elves view me when they enter to find Artemis Entreri dead?" he squealed, and he launched a thrust, feint and slash for the assassin's shoulder.

Entreri had his own sword out then, in his right hand, his dagger still in his left, and he snapped it up, driving the slash aside. Soulez was good, very good, and he had the formidable weapon back in close defensively before the assassin could begin to advance with his dagger.

Respect kept Artemis Entreri back from the man, and more importantly, from that devastating weapon. He knew enough about Charon's Claw to understand that a simple nick from it, even one on his hand that he might suffer in a successful parry, would fester and grow and would likely kill him.

Confident that he'd find the right opening, the deadly assassin stalked the man slowly, slowly.

Soulez attacked again with a low thrust that Entreri hopped back from, and a thrust high that the assassin ducked. Entreri slapped at the red blade with his sword and thrust at his opponent's center mass. It was a brilliantly quick routine that would have left almost any opponent at least shallowly stabbed.

He never got near to hitting Entreri. Then he had to scramble and throw out a cut to the side to keep the assassin, who had somehow quick-stepped to his right while slapping hard at the third thrust, at bay.

Kohrin Soulez growled in frustration as they came up square again, facing each other from a distance of about ten feet, with Entreri continuing that composed stalk. Now Soulez also moved, angling to intercept.

He was dragging his back foot behind him, Entreri noted, keeping ready to change direction, trying to cut off the room and any possible escape routes.

"You so desperately desire Charon's Claw," Soulez said with a chuckle, "but do you even begin to understand the true beauty of the weapon? Can you even guess at its power and its tricks, assassin?"

Entreri continued to back and pace—back to the left, then back to the right—allowing Soulez to shrink down the battlefield. The assassin was growing impatient, and also, the sounds on the door indicated that the resistance in the hallway had come to an end. The door was magnificent and strong, but it would not hold out long, and Entreri wanted this finished before Rai-guy and the dark elves arrived.

"You think I am an old man," Soulez remarked, and he came forward in a short rush, thrusting.

Entreri picked it off and this time came forward with a counter of his own, rolling his sword under Soulez's blade and sliding it out. The assassin turned and stepped ahead, dagger rushing forward, but he had to disengage from the powerful sword too soon. The angle of the parry was forcing the enchanted blade dangerously close to

Entreri's exposed hand, and without the block, he had to skitter into a quick retreat as Soulez slashed across.

"I am an old man," Soulez continued, sounding undaunted, "but I draw strength from the sword. I am your fighting equal, Artemis Entreri, and with this sword you are surely doomed."

He came on again, but Entreri retreated easily, sliding back toward the wall opposite the door. He knew he was running out of room, but to him that only meant that Kohrin Soulez was running out of room, too, and out of time.

"Ah, yes, run back, little rabbit," Soulez taunted. "I know you, Artemis Entreri. I know you. Behold!" As he finished, he began waving the sword before him, and Entreri had to blink, for the blade began trailing blackness.

No, not trailing, the assassin realized to his surprise, but emitting blackness. It was thick ash that held in place in the air in great sweeping opaque fans, altering the battlefield to Kohrin Soulez's designs.

"I know you!" Soulez cried and came forward, sweeping, sweeping more ash screens into the air.

"Yes, you know me," Entreri answered calmly, and Soulez slowed. The timbre of Entreri's voice had reminded him of the power of this particular opponent. "You see me at night, Kohrin Soulez, in your dreams. When you look into the darkest shadows of those nightmares, do you see those eyes looking back at you?"

As he finished, he came forward a step, tossing his sword slightly into the air before him, and at just the right angle so that the approaching sword was the only thing Kohrin Soulez could see.

The room's door exploded into a thousand tiny little pieces.

Soulez hardly noticed, coming forward to meet the attack, slapping the apparently thrusting sword on top, then below and to the side. So beautifully angled was Entreri's toss that the man's own quick parry strikes, one countering the spin of the other, gave Soulez the illusion that Entreri was still holding the other end of the blade.

He leaped ahead, through the opaque fans of the sword's conjured ash, and struck hard for where he knew the assassin had to be.

Soulez stiffened, feeling the sting in his back. Entreri's dagger cut into his flesh.

"Do you see those eyes looking back at you from the shadows of your nightmares, Kohrin Soulez?" Entreri asked again. "Those are my eyes."

Soulez felt the dagger pulling at his life-force. Entreri hadn't driven it home yet, but he didn't have to. The man was beaten, and he knew it. Soulez dropped Charon's Claw to the floor and let his arm slip down to his side.

"You are a devil," he growled at the assassin.

"I?" Entreri answered innocently. "Was it not Kohrin Soulez who would have sacrificed his daughter for the sake of a mere weapon?"

As he finished, he was fast to reach down with his free hand and yank the black gauntlet from Soulez's right hand. To Soulez's surprise, the glove fell to the floor right beside the sword.

From the open doorway across the room came the sound of a voice, melodic yet sharp, and speaking in a language that rolled but was oft-broken with harsh and sharp consonant sounds.

Entreri backed away from the man. Soulez turned around to see the ash lines drifting down to the floor, showing him several dark elves standing in the room.

⊲⊨══⊨⊳

Kohrin Soulez took a deep, steadying breath. He had dealt with worse than drow, he silently reminded himself. He had parlayed with an illithid and had survived meetings with the most notorious guildmasters of Calimport. Soulez focused on Entreri then, seeing the man engaged in conversation with the apparent leader of the dark elves, seeing the man drifting farther and farther from him.

There, right beside him, lay his precious sword, his greatest possession—an artifact he would indeed protect even at the cost of his own daughter's life.

Entreri moved a bit farther from him. None of the drow were advancing or seemed to pay Soulez any heed at all.

Charon's Claw, so conveniently close, seemed to be calling to him.

Gathering all his energy, tensing his muscles and calculating the most fluid course open to him, Kohrin Soulez dived down low, scooped the black, red-stitched gauntlet onto his right hand, and before he could even register that it didn't seem to fit him the same way, scooped up the powerful, enchanted sword.

He turned toward Entreri with a growl. "Tell them that I will speak with their leader . . ." he started to say, but his words quickly became a jumble, his tone going low and his pace slowing, as if something was pulling at his vocal chords.

Kohrin Soulez's face contorted weirdly, his features seeming to elongate in the direction of the sword.

All conversation in the room stopped. All eyes turned to stare incredulously at Soulez.

"T-to the Nine . . . Nine Hells with y-you, Entreri!" the man stammered, each word punctuated by a croaking groan.

"What is he doing?" Rai-guy demanded of Entreri.

The assassin didn't answer, just watched in amusement as Kohrin Soulez continued to struggle against the power of Charon's Claw. His face elongated again and wisps of smoke began wafting up from his body. He tried to cry out, but only an indecipherable gurgle came forth. The smoke increased, and Soulez began to tremble violently, all the while trying to scream out.

Nothing more than smoke poured from his mouth.

It all seemed to stop then, and Soulez stood staring at Entreri and gasping.

The man lived just long enough to put on the most horrified and stunned expression Artemis Entreri had ever seen. It was an expression that pleased Entreri greatly. There was something too familiar in the way in which Soulez had abandoned his daughter.

Kohrin Soulez erupted in a sudden, sizzling burst. The skin burned off his head, leaving no more than a whitened skull and wide, horrified eyes.

Charon's Claw hit the hard floor again, making more of a dull thump than any metallic ring. The skull-headed corpse of Kohrin Soulez crumpled in place.

"Explain," Rai-guy demanded.

Entreri walked over and, wearing a gauntlet that appeared identical to the one Kohrin Soulez had but not a match for the other since it was shaped for the same hand, reached down and calmly gathered up his newest prize.

"Pray I do not go to the Nine Hells, as you surely will, Kohrin Soulez," the deadly assassin said to the corpse. "For if I see you there, I will continue to torment you throughout eternity."

"Explain!" Rai-guy demanded more forcefully.

"Explain?" Entreri echoed, turning to face the angry drow wizard. He gave a shrug, as if the answer seemed obvious. "I was prepared, and he was a fool."

Rai-guy glared at him ominously, and Entreri only smiled back, hoping his amused expression would tempt the wizard to action.

He held Charon's Claw now, and he wore the gauntlet that could catch and redirect magic.

The world had just changed in ways that the wretched Rai-guy couldn't begin to understand.

CHAPTER

8

The tower will remain. Jarlaxle has declared it," said Kimmuriel. "The fortress weathered our attack well enough to keep Dallabad operating smoothly, and without anyone outside of the oasis even knowing that an assault had taken place."

"Operating," Rai-guy echoed, spitting the distasteful word out. He stared at Entreri, who walked beside him into the crystal tower. Rai-guy's look made it quite clear that he considered the events of this day the assassin's doing and planned on holding Entreri personally responsible if anything went wrong. "Is Bregan D'aerthe to become the overseers of a great toll booth, then?"

"Dallabad will prove more valuable to Bregan D'aerthe than you assume," Entreri replied in his stilted use of the drow language. "We can keep the place separate from House Basadoni as far as all others are concerned. The allies we place out here will watch the road and gather news long before those in Calimport are aware. We can run many of our ventures from out here, farther from the prying eyes of Pasha Da'Daclan and his henchmen."

"And who are these trusted allies who will operate Dallabad as a front for Bregan D'aerthe?" Rai-guy demanded. "I had thought of sending Domo."

"Domo and his filthy kind will not leave the offal of the sewers," Sharlotta Vespers put in.

"Too good a hole for them," Entreri muttered.

"Jarlaxle has hinted that perhaps the survivors of Dallabad will suffice," Kimmuriel explained. "Few were killed."

"Allied with a conquered guild," Rai-guy remarked with a sigh, shaking his head. "A guild whose fall we brought about."

"A very different situation from allying with a fallen house of Menzoberranzan," Entreri declared, seeing the error in the dark elf's apparent internal analogy. Rai-guy was viewing things through the dark glass of Menzoberranzan, was considering the generational feuds and grudges that members of the various houses, the various families, held for each other.

"We shall see," the drow wizard replied, and he motioned for Entreri to hang back with him as Kimmuriel, Berg'inyon, and Sharlotta started up the staircase to the second level of the magical crystalline tower.

"I know that you desired Dallabad for personal reasons," Rai-guy said when the two were alone. "Perhaps it was an act of vengeance, or that you might wear that very gauntlet upon your hand and carry that same sword you now have sheathed on your hip. Either way, do not believe you've done anything here I don't understand, human."

"Dallabad is a valuable asset," Entreri replied, not backing away an inch. "Jarlaxle has a place where he can safely construct and maintain the crystalline tower. There was gain here to be had by all."

"Even to Artemis Entreri," Rai-guy remarked.

In answer, the assassin drew forth Charon's Claw, presenting it horizontally to Rai-guy for inspection, letting the drow wizard see the beauty of the item. The sword had a slender, razor-edged, gleaming red blade, its length inscribed with designs of cloaked figures and tall scythes, accentuated by a black blood trough running along its center. Entreri opened his hand enough for the wizard to see the skull-bobbed pommel, with a hilt that appeared like whitened vertebrae. Running from it toward the crosspiece, the hilt was carved to resemble a backbone and rib-cage, and the crosspiece itself resembled a pelvic skeleton, with legs spread out wide and bent back toward the head, so that the wielder's hand fit neatly within the "bony" boundaries. All of the pommel, hilt and crosspiece was white, like bleached bones—perfectly white, except for the eye sockets of the skull pommel, which seemed like black pits at one moment and flared with red fires the next.

"I am pleased with the prize I earned," Entreri admitted.

Rai-guy stared hard at the sword, but his gaze inevitably kept drifting toward the other, less-obvious treasure: the black, red-stitched gauntlet on Entreri's hand.

"Such weapons can be more of a curse than a blessing, human," the wizard remarked. "They are possessed of arrogance, and too often does that foolish pride spill over into the mind of the wielder, to disastrous result."

The two locked stares, with Entreri's expression melting into a wry grin. "Which end would you most like to feel?" he asked, presenting the deadly sword closer to Rai-guy, matching the wizard's obvious threat with one of his own.

Rai-guy narrowed his dark eyes, and walked away.

Entreri held his grin as he watched the wizard move up the stairs, but in truth, Rai-guy's warning had struck a true chord to him. Indeed, Charon's Claw was strong of will—Entreri could feel that clearly—and if he was not careful with the blade always, it could surely lead him to disaster or destroy him as it had utterly slaughtered Kohrin Soulez.

Entreri glanced down at his own posture, reminding himself—a humble self-warning—not to touch any part of the sword with his unprotected hand.

Even Artemis Entreri could not deny a bit of caution against the horrific death he had witnessed when Charon's Claw had burned the skin from the head of Kohrin Soulez.

"Crenshinibon easily dominates the majority of the survivors," Jarlaxle announced to his principal advisors a short while later in an audience chamber he had crafted of the second level the magical tower. "To those outside of Dallabad Oasis, the events of this day will seem like nothing more than a coup within the Soulez family, followed by a strong alliance to the Basadoni Guild."

"Ahdahnia Soulez agreed to remain?" Rai-guy asked.

"She was willing to assume the mantle of Dallabad even before Crenshinibon invaded her thoughts," Jarlaxle explained.

"Loyalty," Entreri remarked under his breath.

Even as the assassin was offering the sarcastic jibe, Rai-guy admitted, "I am beginning to like the young woman more already."

"But can we trust her?" Kimmuriel asked.

"Do you trust me?" Sharlotta Vespers interjected. "It would seem a similar situation."

"Except that her guildmaster was also her father," Kimmuriel reminded.

"There is nothing to fear from Ahdahnia Soulez or any of the others who will remain at Dallabad," Jarlaxle put in, forcefully, thus ending the philosophical debate. "Those who survived and will continue to do so belong to Crenshinibon now, and Crenshinibon belongs to me."

Entreri didn't miss the doubting look that flashed briefly across Rai-guy's face at the moment of Jarlaxle's final proclamation, and in truth, he, too, wondered if the mercenary leader wasn't a bit confused as to who owned whom.

"Kohrin Soulez's soldiers will not betray us," Jarlaxle went on with all confidence. "Nor will they even remember the events of this day, but rather, they will accept the story we tell them to put forth as truth, if that is what we choose. Dallabad Oasis belongs to Bregan D'aerthe now as surely as if we had installed an army of dark elves here to facilitate the operations."

"And you trust the woman Ahdahnia to lead, though we just

murdered her father?" Kimmuriel said more than asked.

"Her father was killed by his obsession with that sword; so she told me herself," Jarlaxle replied, and as he spoke, all gazes turned to regard the weapon hanging easily at Entreri's belt. Rai-guy, in particular, kept his dangerous glare upon Entreri, as if silently reiterating the warnings of their last conversation.

The wizard meant those warnings to be a threat to Entreri, a reminder to the assassin that he, Rai-guy, would be watching Entreri's every move much more closely now, a reminder that he believed that the assassin had, in effect, used Bregan D'aerthe for the sake of his personal gain—a very dangerous practice.

"You do not like this," Kimmuriel remarked to Rai-guy when the two were back in Calimport.

Jarlaxle had remained behind at Dallabad Oasis, securing the remnants of Kohrin Soulez's forces and explaining the slight shift in direction that Ahdahnia Soulez should now undertake.

"How could I?" Rai-guy responded. "Every day, it seems that our purpose in coming to the surface has expanded. I had thought that we would be back in Menzoberranzan by this time, yet our footpads have tightened on the stone."

"On the sand," Kimmuriel corrected, in a tone that showed he, too, was not overly pleased by the continuing expansion of Bregan D'aerthe's surface ventures.

Originally, Jarlaxle had shared plans to come to the surface and establish a base of contacts, humans mostly, who would serve as profiteering front men for the trading transactions of the mercenary drow band. Though he had never specified the details, Jarlaxle's original explanation had made the two believe that their time on the surface would be quite limited.

But now they had expanded, had even constructed a physical

structure, with more apparently planned, and had added a second base to the Basadoni conquest. Worse than that, both dark elves were thinking, though not openly saying, perhaps there was something even more behind Jarlaxle's continuing shift of attitude. Perhaps the mercenary leader had erred in taking a certain relic from the renegade Do'Urden.

"Jarlaxle seems to have taken a liking to the surface," Kimmuriel went on. "We all knew that he had tired somewhat of the continuing struggles within our homeland, but perhaps we underestimated the extent of that weariness."

"Perhaps," Rai-guy replied. "Or perhaps our friend merely needs to be reminded that this is not our place."

Kimmuriel stared at him hard, his expression clearly asking how one might "remind" the great Jarlaxle of anything.

"Start at the edges," Rai-guy answered, echoing one of Jarlaxle's favorite sayings, and favorite tactics for Bregan D'aerthe. Whenever the mercenary band went into infiltration or conquest mode, they started gnawing at the edges of their opponent—circling the perimeter and chewing, chewing—as they continued their ever-tightening ring. "Has Morik yet delivered the jewels?"

<hr />

There it lay before him, in all its wicked splendor.

Artemis Entreri stared long and hard at Charon's Claw, the fingers on both of his unprotected hands rubbing in against his moist palms. Part of him wanted to reach out and grasp the sword, to effect now the battle that he knew would soon enough be fought between his own willpower and that of the sentient weapon. If he won that battle, the sword would truly be his, but if he lost. . . .

He recalled, and vividly, the last horrible moments of Kohrin Soulez's miserable life.

It was exactly that life, though, that so propelled Entreri in this seemingly suicidal direction. He would not be as Soulez had been. He would not allow himself to be a prisoner to the sword, a man trapped in a box of his own making. No, he would be the master, or he would be dead.

But still, that horrific death. . . .

Entreri started to reach for the sword, steeling his willpower against the expected onslaught.

He heard movement in the hallway outside his room.

He had the glove on in a moment and scooped up the sword in his right hand, moving it to its sheath on his hip in one fluid movement even as the door to his private chambers—if any chambers for a human among Bregan D'aerthe could be considered private—swung open.

"Come," instructed Kimmuriel Oblodra, and he turned and started away.

Entreri didn't move, and as soon as the drow realized it, he turned back. Kimmuriel had a quizzical look upon his handsome, angular face. That look of curiosity soon turned to one of menace, though, as he considered the standing, but hardly moving assassin.

"You have a most excellent weapon now," Kimmuriel remarked. "One to greatly complement your nasty dagger. Fear not. Neither Rai-guy nor I have underestimated the value of that gauntlet you seem to keep forever upon your right hand. We know its powers, Artemis Entreri, and we know how to defeat it."

Entreri continued to stare, unblinking, at the drow psionicist. A bluff? Or had resourceful Kimmuriel and Rai-guy indeed found some way around the magic-negating gauntlet? A wry smile found its way onto Entreri's face, a look bolstered by the assassin's complete confidence that whatever secret Kimmuriel might now be hinting of would do the drow little good in their immediate situation. Entreri knew, and his look made Kimmuriel aware as well, that he could cross the room then and there, easily defeat any of Kimmuriel's psionically created defenses with the gauntlet, and run him through with the mighty sword.

If the drow, so cool and so powerful, was bothered or worried at all, he did a fine job of masking it.

But so did Entreri.

"There is work to be done in Luskan," Kimmuriel remarked at length. "Our friend Morik still has not delivered the required jewels."

"I am to go and serve as messenger again?" Entreri asked sarcastically.

"No message for Morik this time," Kimmuriel said coldly. "He has failed us."

The finality of that statement struck Entreri profoundly, but he managed to hide his surprise until Kimmuriel had turned around and started away once more. The assassin understood clearly, of course, that Kimmuriel had, in effect, just told him to got to Luskan and murder Morik. The request did not seem so odd, given that Morik apparently was not living up to Bregan D'aerthe's expectations. Still, it seemed out of place to Entreri that Jarlaxle would so willingly and easily cut his only thread to a market as promising as Luskan without even asking for some explanation from the tricky little rogue. Jarlaxle had been acting strange, to be sure, but was he as confused as that?

It occurred to Entreri even as he started after Kimmuriel that perhaps this assassination had nothing to do with Jarlaxle.

His feelings, and fears, were only strengthened when he entered the small room. He came in not far behind Kimmuriel but found Rai-guy, and Rai-guy alone, waiting for him.

"Morik has failed us yet again," the wizard stated immediately. "There can be no further chances for him. He knows too much of us, and with such an obvious lack of loyalty, well, what are we to do? Go to Luskan and eliminate him. A simple task. We care not for the jewels. If he has them, spend them as you will. Just bring me Morik's heart." As he finished, he stepped aside, clearing the way to a magical portal he had woven, the blurry image inside showing Entreri the alleyway beside Morik's building.

"You will need to remove the gauntlet before you stride through," Kimmuriel remarked, slyly enough for Entreri to wonder if perhaps this whole set-up was but a ruse to force him into an unguarded position. Of course, the resourceful assassin had considered that very thing on the walk over, so he only chuckled at Kimmuriel, walked up to the portal, and stepped right through.

He was in Luskan now, and he looked back to see the magical portal closing behind him. Kimmuriel and Rai-guy were looking at him with expressions that showed everything from confusion to anger to intrigue.

Entreri held up his gloved hand in a mocking wave as the pair faded out of sight. He knew they were wondering how he could exercise such control over the magic-dispelling gauntlet. They were trying to get a feel for its power and its limitations, something that even Entreri had not yet figured out. He certainly didn't mean to offer any clues to his quiet adversaries, thus he had changed from the real magical gauntlet to the decoy that had so fooled Soulez.

When the portal closed he started out of the alleyway, changing once again to the real gauntlet and dropping the fake one into a small sack concealed under the folds of his cloak at the back of his belt.

He went to Morik's room first and found that the little thief had not added any further security traps or tricks. That surprised Entreri, for if Morik was again disappointing his merciless leaders he should have been expecting company. Furthermore, the thief obviously had not fled the small apartment.

Not content to sit and wait, Entreri went back out onto Luskan's streets, making his way from tavern to tavern, from corner to corner. A few beggars approached him, but he sent them away with a glare. One pickpocket actually went for the purse he had secured to his belt on the right side. Entreri left him sitting in the gutter, his wrist shattered by a simple twist of the assassin's hand.

Sometime later, and thinking that it was about time for him to return to Morik's abode, the assassin came into an establishment on Half-Moon Street known as the Cutlass. The place was nearly empty, with a portly barkeep rubbing away at the dirty bar and a skinny little man sitting across from him, chattering away. Another figure among the few patrons remaining in the place caught Entreri's attention.

The man was sitting comfortably and quietly at the far left end of the bar with his back against the wall and the hood of his weathered cloak pulled over his head. He appeared to be sleeping, judging from his rhythmic breathing, the hunch of his shoulders, and the loll of his head, but Entreri caught a few tell-tale signs—like the fact that the rolling head kept angling to give the supposedly sleeping man a fine view of all around him—that told him otherwise.

The assassin didn't miss the slight tensing of the shoulders when that angle revealed his presence to the supposedly sleeping man.

Entreri strode up to the bar, right beside the nervous, skinny little man, who said, "Arumn's done serving for the night."

Entreri glanced over, his dark eyes taking a full measure of this one. "My gold is not good enough for you?" he asked the barkeep, turning back slowly to consider the portly man behind the bar.

Entreri noted that the barkeep took a long, good measure of him. He saw respect coming into Arumn's eyes. He wasn't surprised. This barkeep, like so many others, survived primarily by understanding his clientele. Entreri was doing little to hide the truth of his skills in his graceful, solid movements. The man pretending to sleep at the bar said nothing, and neither did the nervous one.

"Ho, Josi's just puffing out his chest, is all," the barkeep, Arumn, remarked, "though I had planned on closing her up early. Not many looking for drink this night."

Satisfied with that, Entreri glanced to the left, to the compact form of the man pretending to be asleep. "Two honey meads," he said, dropping a couple of shining gold coins on the bar, ten times the cost of the drinks.

The assassin continued to watch the "sleeper," hardly paying any heed at all to Arumn or nervous little Josi, who was constantly shifting at his other side. Josi even asked Entreri his name, but the assassin ignored him. He just continued to stare, taking a measure, studying every movement and playing them against what he already knew of Morik.

He turned back when he heard the clink of glass on the bar. He scooped up one drink in his gloved right hand, bringing the dark liquid to his lips, while he grasped the second glass in his left hand, and instead of lifting it, just sent it sliding fast down the bar, angled slightly for the outer lip, perfectly set to dump onto the supposedly-sleeping man's lap.

The barkeep cried out in surprise. Josi Puddles jumped to his feet, and even started toward Entreri, who simply ignored him.

The assassin's smile widened when Morik, and it was indeed Morik, reached up at the last moment and caught the mead-filled missile, bringing his hand back and wide to absorb the shock of the catch and to make sure that any liquid that did splash over did not spill on him.

Entreri slid off the barstool, took up his glass of mead and motioned for Morik to go with him outside. He had barely taken a step, though, when he sensed a movement toward his arm. He turned back to see Josi Puddles reaching for him.

"No, ye don't!" the skinny man remarked. "Ye ain't leavin' with Arumn's glasses."

Entreri watched the hand coming toward him and lifted his gaze to look Josi Puddles straight in the eye, to let the man know, with just a look and just that awful, calm and deadly demeanor, that if he so much as brushed Entreri's arm with his hand, he would surely pay for it with his life.

"No, ye . . ." Josi started to say again, but his voice failed him and his hand stopped moving. He knew. Defeated, the skinny man sank back against the bar.

"The gold should more than pay for the glasses," Entreri remarked to the barkeep, and Arumn, too, seemed quite unnerved.

The assassin headed for the door, taking some pleasure in hearing the barkeep quietly scolding Josi for being so stupid.

The street was quiet outside, and dark, and Entreri could sense the uneasiness in Morik. He could see it in the man's cautious stance and in the way his eyes darted about.

"I have the jewels," Morik was quick to announce. He started in the direction of his apartment, and Entreri followed.

The assassin thought it interesting that Morik presented him with the jewels—and the size of the pouch made Entreri believe that the thief had certainly met his master's expectations—as soon as they entered the darkened room. If Morik had them, why hadn't he simply given them over on time? Certainly Morik, no fool, understood the volatile and extremely dangerous nature of his partners.

"I wondered when I would be called upon," Morik said, obviously trying to appear completely calm. "I have had them since the day after you left but have gotten no word from Rai-guy or Kimmuriel."

Entreri nodded, but showed no surprise—and in truth, when he thought about it, the assassin wasn't really surprised at all. These were drow, after all. They killed when convenient, killed when they felt like it. Perhaps they had sent Entreri here to slay Morik in the hopes that Morik would prove the stronger. Perhaps it didn't matter to them either way. They would merely enjoy the spectacle of it.

Or perhaps Rai-guy and Kimmuriel were anxious to clip away at the entrenchment that Jarlaxle was obviously setting up for Bregan D'aerthe. Kill Morik and any others like him, sever all ties, and go home. He lifted his black gauntlet into the air, seeking any magical emanations. He detected some upon Morik and some other minor dweomers in and around the room, but nothing that seemed to him to be any kind of scrying spell. It wasn't that he could have done anything about any spells or psionics divining the area, anyway. Entreri had come to understand already that the gauntlet could only grab at spells directed at him specifically. In truth, the thing was really quite limited. He might catch one of Rai-guy's lightning bolts and hurl it back at the wizard, but if Rai-guy filled the room with a fireball. . . .

"What are you doing?" Morik asked the distracted assassin.

"Get out of here," Entreri instructed. "Out of this building and out of the city altogether, for a short while at least."

The obviously puzzled Morik just stared at him.

"Did you not hear me?"

"That order comes from Jarlaxle?" Morik asked, seeming quite confused. "Does he fear that I have been discovered, that he, by association, has been somehow implicated?"

"I tell you to begone, Morik," Entreri answered. "I, and not Jarlaxle, nor, certainly, Rai-guy or Kimmuriel."

"Do I threaten you?" asked Morik. "Am I somehow impeding your ascension within the guild?"

"Are you that much a fool?" Entreri replied.

"I have been promised a king's treasure!" Morik protested. "The only reason I agreed—"

"Was because you had no choice," Entreri interrupted. "I know that to be true, Morik. Perhaps that lack of choice is the only thing that saves you now."

Morik was shaking his head, obviously upset and unconvinced. "Luskan is my home," he started to say.

Charon's Claw came out in a red and black flash. Entreri swiped down beside Morik, left and right, then slashed across right above the man's head. The sword left a trail of black ash with all three swipes so that Entreri had Morik practically boxed in by the opaque walls. So quickly had he struck, the dazed and dazzled rogue hadn't even had a chance to draw his weapon.

"I was not sent to collect the jewels or even to scold and warn you, fool," Entreri said coldly—so very, very coldly. "I was sent to kill you."

"But . . ."

"You have no idea the level of evil with which you have allied yourself," the assassin went on. "Flee this place—this building *and* this city. Run for all your life, fool Morik. They will not look for you if they cannot find you easily—you are not worth their trouble. So run away, beyond their vision and take hope that you are free of them."

Morik stood there, encapsulated by the walls of black ash that still magically hung in the air, his jaw hanging open in complete astonishment. He looked left and right, just a bit, and swallowed hard, making it clear to Entreri that he had just then come to realize how overmatched he truly was. Despite the assassin's previous visit, easily getting through all of Morik's traps, it had taken this display of brutal swordsmanship to show Morik the deadly truth of Artemis Entreri.

"Why would they . . . ?" Morik dared to ask. "I am an ally, eyes for Bregan D'aerthe in the northland. Jarlaxle himself instructed me to . . ." He stopped at the sound of Entreri's laughter.

"You are *iblith*," Entreri explained. "Offal. Not of the drow. That alone makes you no more than a plaything to them. They *will* kill you—I am to kill you here and now by their very words."

"Yet you defy them," Morik said, and it wasn't clear from his tone if he had come around yet truly to believe Entreri or not.

"You are thinking that this is some test of your loyalty," Entreri correctly guessed, shaking his head with every word. "The drow do not test loyalty, Morik, because they expect none. With them, there is only the predictability of actions based in simple fear."

"Yet you are showing yourself disloyal by letting me go," Morik remarked. "We are not friends, with no debt and little contact between us. Why do you tell me this?"

Entreri leaned back and considered that question more deeply than Morik could have expected, allowing the thief's recognition of illogic to resonate in his thoughts. For surely Entreri's actions here made little logical sense. He could have been done with his business and back on his way to Calimport, without any real threat to him. By contrast, and by all logical reasoning, there would be little gain for Entreri in letting Morik walk away.

Why this time? the assassin asked himself. He had killed so many, and often in situations similar to this, often at the behest of a guildmaster seeking to punish an impudent or threatening underling. He had followed orders to kill people whose offense had never been made known to him, people, perhaps, similar to Morik, who had truly committed no offense at all.

No, Artemis Entreri couldn't quite bring himself to accept that last thought. His killings, every one, had been committed against people associated with the underworld, or against mis-informed do-gooders who had somehow become entangled in the wrong mess, impeding the assassin's progress. Even Drizzt Do'Urden, that paladin in drow skin, had named himself as Entreri's enemy by preventing the assassin from retrieving Regis the halfling and the magical ruby pendant the little fool had stolen from Pasha Pook. It had taken years, but to Entreri, kill-ing Drizzt Do'Urden had been the justified culmination of the drow's unwanted and immoral interference. In Entreri's mind and in his heart, those who had died at his hands had played the great game, had tossed aside their innocence in pursuit of power or material gain.

In Entreri's mind, everyone he had killed had indeed deserved it, because he was a killer among killers, a survivor in a brutal game that would not allow it to be any other way.

"Why?" Morik asked again, drawing Entreri from his contemplation.

The assassin stared at the rogue for a moment, and offered a quick and simple answer to a question too complex for him to sort out properly, an answer that rang of more truth than Artemis Entreri even realized.

"Because I hate drow more than I hate humans."

PART 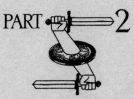 2

WHICH THE TOOL?
WHICH THE MASTER?

Entreri again teamed with Jarlaxle?

What an odd pairing that seems, and to some (and initially to me, as well) a vision of the most unsettling nightmare imaginable. There is no one in all the world, I believe, more crafty and ingenious than Jarlaxle of Bregan D'aerthe, the consummate opportunist, a wily leader who can craft a kingdom out of the dung of rothé. Jarlaxle, who thrived in the matriarchal society of Menzoberranzan as completely as any Matron Mother.

Jarlaxle of mystery, who knew my father, who claims a past friendship with Zaknafein.

How could a drow who befriended Zaknafein ally with Artemis Entreri? At quick glance, the notion seems incongruous, even preposterous. And yet, I do believe Jarlaxle's claims of the former and know the latter to be true—for the second time.

Professionally, I see no mystery in the union. Entreri has ever preferred a position of the shadows, serving as the weapon of a high-paying master—no, not master. I doubt that Artemis Entreri has ever known a master. Rather, even in the service of the guilds, he worked as a sword for hire. Certainly such a skilled mercenary could find a place within Bregan D'aerthe, especially since they've come to the surface and likely need humans to front and cover their true identity. For Jarlaxle, therefore, the alliance with Entreri is certainly a convenient thing.

But there is something else, something more, between them. I know this from the way Jarlaxle spoke of the man, and from the simple fact that the mercenary leader went so far out of his way to arrange the last fight between me and Entreri. It was for the sake of Entreri's state of mind, no less, and certainly as no favor to me, and as no mere source of entertainment for Jarlaxle. He cares for Entreri as a friend might, even as he values the assassin's multitude of skills.

There lies the incongruity.

For though Entreri and Jarlaxle have complementary professional skills, they do not seem well matched in temperament or in moral standards—two essentials, it would seem, for any successful friendship.

Or perhaps not.

Jarlaxle's heart is far more generous than that of Artemis Entreri. The mercenary can be brutal, of course, but not randomly so. Practicality guides his moves, for his eye is ever on the potential gain, but even in that light of efficient pragmatism, Jarlaxle's heart often overrules his lust for profit. Many times has he allowed my escape, for example, when bringing my head to Matron Malice or Matron Baenre would have brought him great gain. Is Artemis Entreri similarly possessed of such generosity?

Not at all.

In fact, I suspect that if Entreri knew that Jarlaxle had saved me from my apparent death in the tower, he would have first tried to kill me and turned his anger upon Jarlaxle. Such a battle might well yet occur, and if it does, I believe that Artemis Entreri will learn that he is badly overmatched. Not by Jarlaxle individually, though the mercenary leader is crafty and reputedly a fine warrior in his own right, but by the pragmatic Jarlaxle's many, many deadly allies.

Therein lies the essence of the mercenary leader's interest in, and control of, Artemis Entreri. Jarlaxle sees the man's value and does not fear him, because what Jarlaxle has perfected, and what Entreri is sorely lacking in, is the ability to build an interdependent organization. Entreri won't attempt to kill Jarlaxle because Entreri will need Jarlaxle.

Jarlaxle will make certain of that. He weaves his web all around him. It is a network that is always mutually beneficial, a network in which all security—against Bregan D'aerthe's many dangerous rivals—inevitably depends upon the controlling and calming influence that is Jarlaxle. He is the ultimate consensus builder, the purest of diplomats, while Entreri is a loner, a man who must dominate all around him.

Jarlaxle coerces. Entreri controls.

But with Jarlaxle, Entreri will never find any level of control. The mercenary leader is too entrenched and too intelligent for that.

And yet, I believe that their alliance will hold, and their friendship will grow. Certainly there will be conflicts and perhaps very dangerous ones for both parties. Perhaps Entreri has already learned the truth of my departure and has killed Jarlaxle or died trying. But the longer the alliance holds, the stronger it will become, the more entrenched in friendship.

I say this because I believe that, in the end, Jarlaxle's philosophy will win out. Artemis Entreri is the one of this duo who is limited by fault. His desire for absolute control is fueled by his inability to trust. While that desire has led him to become as fine a fighter as I have ever known, it has also led him to an existence that even he is beginning to recognize as empty.

Professionally, Jarlaxle offers Artemis Entreri security, a base for his efforts, while Entreri gives Jarlaxle and all of Bregan D'aerthe a clear connection to the surface world.

But personally, Jarlaxle offers even more to Entreri, offers him a chance to finally break out of the role that he has assumed as a solitary creature. I remember Entreri upon our departure from Menzoberranzan, where we were both imprisoned, each in his own way. He was with Bregan D'aerthe then as well, but down in that city, Artemis Entreri looked into a dark and empty mirror that he did not like. Why, then, is he now returned to Jarlaxle's side?

It is a testament to the charm that is Jarlaxle, the intuitive understanding that that most clever of dark elves holds for creating desire and

*alliance. The mere fact that Entreri is apparently with Jarlaxle once
again tells me that the mercenary leader is already winning the inevitable clash between their basic philosophies, their temperament and
moral standards. Though Entreri does not yet understand it, I am sure,
Jarlaxle will strengthen him more by example than by alliance.*

*Perhaps with Jarlaxle's help, Artemis Entreri will find his way out
of his current empty existence.*

Or perhaps Jarlaxle will eventually kill him.

Either way, the world will be a better place, I think.

—Drizzt Do'Urden

CHAPTER

9

The Copper Ante was fairly busy this evening, with halflings mostly crowding around tables, rolling bones or playing other games of chance and all whispering about the recent events in and around the city. Every one of them spoke quietly, though, for among the few humans in the tavern that night were two rather striking figures, operatives central to the recent tumultuous events.

Sharlotta Vespers was very aware of the many stares directed her way, and she knew that many of these halflings were secret allies of her companion this night. She had almost refused Entreri's invitation for her to come and meet with him privately here, in the house of Dwahvel Tiggerwillies, but she recognized the value of the place. The Copper Ante was beyond the prying eyes of Rai-guy and Kimmuriel, a condition necessary, so Entreri had said, for any meeting.

"I can't believe you openly walk Calimport's streets with that sword," Sharlotta remarked quietly.

"It is rather distinctive," Entreri admitted, but there wasn't the slightest hint of alarm in his voice.

"It's a well-known blade," Sharlotta answered. "Anyone who knew of Kohrin Soulez and Dallabad knows he would never willingly part with it, yet here you are, showing it to all who would glance your way. One might think that a clear connection between the downfall of Dallabad and House Basadoni."

"How so?" Entreri asked, and he took pleasure indeed at the look of sheer exasperation that washed over Sharlotta.

"Kohrin is dead and Artemis Entreri is wearing his sword," Sharlotta remarked dryly.

"He is dead, and thus the sword is no longer of any use to him," Entreri flippantly remarked. "On the streets, it is understood that he was killed in a coup by his very own daughter, who, by all rumors, had no desire to be captured by Charon's Claw as was Kohrin."

"Thus it falls to the hands of Artemis Entreri?" Sharlotta asked incredulously.

"It has been hinted that Kohrin's refusal to sell at the offered price—an absurd amount of gold—was the very catalyst for the coup," Entreri went on, leaning back comfortably in his chair. "When Ahdahnia learned that he refused the transaction. . . ."

"Impossible," Sharlotta breathed, shaking her head. "Do you really expect that tale to be believed?"

Entreri smiled wryly. "The words of Sha'lazzi Ozoule are often believed," he remarked. "Inquiries to purchase the sword were made through Sha'lazzi only days before the coup at Dallabad."

That set Sharlotta back in her chair as she tried hard to digest and sort through all of the information. On the streets, it was indeed being said that Kohrin had been killed in a coup—Jarlaxle's domination of the remaining Dallabad forces through use of the Crystal Shard had provided consistency in all of the reports coming out of the oasis. As long as Crenshinibon's dominance held out, there was no evidence at all to reveal the truth of the assault on Dallabad. If Entreri had spoken truly—and Sharlotta had no reason to think that he had not—the refusal by Kohrin to sell Charon's Claw would be linked not to any theft or any attack by House Basadoni, but rather as one of the catalysts for the coup.

Sharlotta stared hard at Entreri, her expression a mixture of anger and admiration. He had covered every possible aspect of his procurement of the coveted sword beforehand. Sharlotta, given her understanding of Entreri's relationship with the dangerous Rai-guy and Kimmuriel, held no doubts that Entreri had helped guide the dark elves to Dallabad specifically with the intent of collecting that very sword.

"You weave a web with many layers," the woman remarked.

"I have been around dark elves for far too long," Entreri casually replied.

"But you walk the very edge of disaster," said Sharlotta. "Many of the guilds had already linked the downfall of Dallabad with House Basadoni, and now you openly parade about with Charon's Claw. The other rumors are plausible, of course, but your actions do little to distance us from the assassination of Kohrin Soulez."

"Where stands Pasha Da'Daclan or Pasha Wroning?" Entreri asked, feigning concern.

"Da'Daclan is cautious and making no overt moves," Sharlotta replied. Entreri held his grin private at her earnest tones, for she had obviously taken his bait. "He is far from pleased with the situation, though, and the strong inferences concerning Dallabad."

"As they all will be," Entreri reasoned. "Unless Jarlaxle grows too bold with his construction of crystalline towers."

Again he spoke with dramatically serious tones, more to measure Sharlotta's reaction than to convey any information the woman didn't already know. He did note a slight tremor in her lip. Frustration? Fear? Disgust? Entreri knew that Rai-guy and Kimmuriel were not happy with Jarlaxle, and that the two independent-minded lieutenants, perhaps, were thinking that the influences of the sentient and dominating Crystal Shard might be causing some serious problems. They had sent him after Morik to weaken the guild's presence on the surface, obviously, but why, then, was Sharlotta still alive? Had she thrown in with the two potential usurpers to Bregan D'aerthe's dark throne?

"The deed is completed now and cannot be undone," Entreri remarked. "Indeed I did desire Charon's Claw—what warrior would not?—but with Sha'lazzi Ozoule spreading his tales of a generous offer to buy being refused by Kohrin, and with Ahdahnia Soulez speaking openly of her disdain for her father's choices, particularly concerning the sword, it all plays to the advantage of Bregan D'aerthe and our work here. Jarlaxle needed a haven to construct the tower, and we gave him one. Bregan D'aerthe now has eyes beyond the city, where we might watch all mounting threats that are outside of our immediate jurisdiction. Everyone wins."

"And Entreri gets the sword," Sharlotta remarked.

"Everyone wins," the assassin said again.

"Until we step too far, and too boldly, and all the world unites against us," said Sharlotta.

"Jarlaxle has lived on such a precipice for centuries," Entreri replied. "He has not stumbled over yet."

Sharlotta started to respond but held her words at the last moment. Entreri knew them anyway, words taken from her by the quick give and take of the conversation, the mounting excitement and momentum bringing a rare unguarded moment. She was about to remark that never in all those centuries had Jarlaxle possessed Crenshinibon, the clear inference being that never in those centuries had Crenshinibon possessed Jarlaxle.

"Say nothing of our concerns to Rai-guy and Kimmuriel," Entreri bade her. "They are fearful enough, and frightened creatures, even drow, can make serious errors. You and I will watch from afar—perhaps there is a way out of this if it comes to an internal war."

Sharlotta nodded, and rightly took Entreri's tone as a dismissal. She rose, nodded again, and moved out of the room.

Entreri didn't believe that nod for a moment. He knew the woman would likely go running right to Rai-guy and Kimmuriel, attempting to bend this conversation her way. But that was the point of it all, was it not? Entreri had just forced Sharlotta's hand, forced her to show her true alliances in this ever-widening web of intrigue. Certainly his last claim, that there might be a way out for the two of them, would ring hollow to Sharlotta, who knew him well, and knew well that he would never bother to take her along with him on any escape from Bregan D'aerthe. He'd put a dagger in her back as surely as he had killed any previous supposed partners, from Tallan Belmer to Rassiter the wererat. Sharlotta knew that, and Entreri knew she knew it.

It did occur to the assassin that perhaps Sharlotta, Rai-guy, and Kimmuriel were correct in their apparent assessment that Crenshinibon was having unfavorable influences on Jarlaxle, that the artifact was leading the cunning mercenary in a direction that could spell doom for Bregan D'aerthe's surface ambitions. That hardly mattered to Entreri, of course, who wasn't sure the retreat of the dark elves back to Menzoberranzan would be such a bad thing. What was more important, to Entreri's thinking, were the dynamics of his relationship with the principles of the mercenary band. Rai-guy and Kimmuriel were notorious racists and hated him as they hated anyone who was not drow—more, even, because Entreri's skill and survival instincts threatened them profoundly. Without Jarlaxle's protection, it wasn't hard for Artemis Entreri to envision his fate. While he felt somewhat bolstered by his acquisition of Charon's Claw, the bane of wizards, he hardly thought it evened the odds in any battle he might find with the duo of the drow wizard-cleric and psionicist. If those two wound up in command of Bregan D'aerthe, with over a hundred drow warriors at their immediate disposal . . .

Entreri didn't like the odds at all.

He knew, without doubt, that Jarlaxle's fall would almost immediately precede his own.

Kimmuriel walked along the tunnels beneath Dallabad with some measure of trepidation. This was a *haszakkin*, after all, an illithid—unpredictable and deadly. Still, the drow had come alone, had deceived Rai-guy that he might do so.

There were some things that psionicists alone could understand and appreciate.

Around a sudden bend in the tunnel, Kimmuriel came upon the bulbous-headed creature, sitting calmly on a rock against the back end of an alcove. Yharaskrik's eyes were closed, but he was awake, Kimmuriel knew, for he could feel the mental energy beaming out from the creature.

I chose well in siding with Bregan D'aerthe, it would seem, the illithid telepathically remarked. *There was never any doubt.*

The drow are stronger than the humans, Kimmuriel agreed, using the illithid's telepathic link to impart his exact thoughts.

Stronger than these *humans*, Yharaskrik corrected.

Kimmuriel bowed, figuring to let the matter drop there, but Yharaskrik had more to discuss.

Stronger than Kohrin Soulez, the illithid went on. *Crippled, he was, by his obsession with a particular magical item.*

That brought some understanding to Kimmuriel, some logical connection between the mind flayer and the pitiful gang of Dallabad Oasis. Why would a creature as great as Yharaskrik waste its time with such inferior beings, after all?

You were sent to observe the powerful sword and the gauntlet, he reasoned.

We wish to understand that which can sometimes defeat our attacks, Yharaskrik freely admitted. *Yet neither item is without limitations. Neither is as powerful as Kohrin Soulez believed, or your attack would never have succeeded.*

We have discerned as much, Kimmuriel agreed.

My time with Kohrin Soulez was nearing its end, said Yharaskrik, a clear inference that the illithid—creatures known as among the most meticulous of all in the multiverse—believed that it had learned every secret of the sword and gauntlet.

The human, Artemis Entreri, confiscated both the gauntlet and Charon's Claw, the drow psionicist explained.

That was his intent, of course, the illithid replied. *He fears you and wisely so. You are strong in will, Kimmuriel of House Oblodra.*

The drow bowed again.

Respect the sword named Charon's Claw, and even more so the gauntlet the human now wears on his hand. With these, he can turn your powers back against you if you are not careful.

Kimmuriel imparted his assurances that Artemis Entreri and his dangerous new weapon would be closely watched. *Are your days of watching the paired items now ended?* he asked as he finished.

Perhaps, Yharaskrik answered.

Or perhaps Bregan D'aerthe could find a place suited to your special talents, Kimmuriel offered. He didn't think it would be hard to persuade Jarlaxle of such an arrangement. Dark elves often allied with illithids in the Underdark.

Yharaskrik's pause was telling to the perceptive and intelligent drow. "You have a better offer?" Kimmuriel asked aloud, and with a chuckle.

Better it would be if I remained to the side of events, unknown to Bregan D'aerthe other than to Kimmuriel Oblodra, Yharaskrik answered in all seriousness.

The response at first confused Kimmuriel and made him think that the illithid feared that Bregan D'aerthe would side with Entreri and Charon's Claw if any such conflict arose between Yharaskrik and Entreri, but before he could begin to offer his assurances against that, the illithid imparted a clear image to him, one of a crystalline tower shining in the sun above the palm trees of Dallabad Oasis.

"The towers?" Kimmuriel asked aloud. "They are just manifestations of Crenshinibon."

Crenshinibon. The word came to Kimmuriel with a sense of urgency and great importance.

It is an artifact, the drow telepathically explained. *A new toy for Jarlaxle's collection.*

Not so, came Yharaskrik's response. *Much more than that, I fear, as should you.*

Kimmuriel narrowed his red-glowing eyes, focusing carefully on Yharaskrik's thoughts, which he expected might confirm the fears he and Rai-guy had long been discussing.

Weave into the thoughts of Jarlaxle, I cannot, the illithid went on. *He wears a protective item.*

The eye patch, Kimmuriel silently replied. *It denies entrance to his mind by wizard, priest, or psionicist.*

But such a simple tool cannot defeat the encroachment of Crenshinibon, Yharaskrik explained.

How do you know of the artifact?

Crenshinibon is no mystery to my people, for it is an ancient item indeed, and one that has crossed the trails of the illithids on many occasions, Yharaskrik admitted. *Indeed, Crenshinibon, the Crystal Shard, despises us, for we alone are quite beyond its tempting reach. We alone as a great race are possessed of the mental discipline necessary to prevent the Crystal Shard from its greatest desires of absolute control. You, too, Kimmuriel, can step beyond the orb of Crenshinibon's influence and easily.*

The drow took a long moment to contemplate the implications of that claim, but naturally, he quickly came to the conclusion that Yharaskrik was relating that psionics alone might fend the intrusions of the Crystal Shard, since Jarlaxle's potent eye patch was based in wizardly magic and not the potent powers of the mind.

Crenshinibon's primary attack is upon the ego, the illithid explained. *It collects slaves with promises of greatness and riches.*

Not unlike the drow, Kimmuriel related, thinking of the tactics Bregan D'aerthe had used on Morik.

Yharaskrik laughed a gurgling, bubbly sound. *The more ambitious the wielder, the easier he will be controlled.*

But what if the wielder is ambitious yet ultimately cautious? Kimmuriel asked, for never had he known Jarlaxle to allow his ambition to overrule good judgment—never before, at least, for only recently had he, Rai-guy, and others come to question the wisdom of the mercenary leader's decisions.

Some lessers can deny the call, the illithid admitted, and it was obvious to Kimmuriel that Yharaskrik considered anyone who was not illithid or who was not at least a psionicist a lesser. *Crenshinibon has little sway over paladins and goodly priests, over righteous kings and noble peasants, but one who desires more—and who of the lesser races, drow included, does not?—and who is not above deception and destruction to further his ends, will inevitably sink into Crenshinibon's grasp.*

It made perfect sense to Kimmuriel, of course, and explained why Drizzt Do'Urden and his "heroic" friends had seemingly put the artifact away. It also explained Jarlaxle's recent behavior, confirming Kimmuriel's suspicions that Bregan D'aerthe was indeed being led astray.

I would not normally refuse an offer of Bregan D'aerthe, Yharaskrik imparted a moment later, after Kimmuriel had digested the information. *You and your reputable kin would be amusing at the least—and likely enlightening and profitable as well—but I fear that all of Bregan D'aerthe will soon fall under the domination of Crenshinibon.*

And why would Yharaskrik fear such a thing, if Crenshinibon becomes leader in order to take us in the same ambitious direction that we have always pursued? Kimmuriel asked, and he feared that he already knew the answer.

I trust not the drow, Yharaskrik admitted, *but I understand enough of your desires and methods to recognize that we need not be enemies among the cattle humans. I trust you not, but I fear you not, because you would find no gain in facilitating my demise. Indeed, you understand that I am connected to the one community that is my people, and that if you killed me you would be making many powerful enemies.*

Kimmuriel bowed, acknowledging the truth of the illithid's observations.

Crenshinibon, however, Yharaskrik went on, *acts not with such rationality. It is all-devouring, a scourge upon the world, controlling all that it can and consuming that which it cannot. It is the bane of devils, yet the love of demons, a denier of laws for the sake of the destruction wrought by chaos. Your Lady Lolth would idolize such an artifact and truly enjoy the chaos of its workings—except of course that Crenshinibon, unlike her drow agents, works not for any ends, but merely to devour. Crenshinibon will bring great power to Bregan D'aerthe—witness the new willing slaves it has made for you, among them the very daughter of the man you overthrew. In the end, Crenshinibon will abandon you, will bring upon you foes too great to fend. This is the history of the Crystal Shard, repeated time and again through the centuries. It is unbridled hunger without discipline, doomed to bloat and die.*

Kimmuriel unintentionally winced at the thoughts, for he could see that very path being woven right before the still-secretive doorstep of Bregan D'aerthe.

All-devouring, Yharaskrik said again. *Controlling all that it can and consuming that which it cannot.*

And you are among that which it cannot, Kimmuriel reasoned.

"As are you," Yharaskrik said in its watery voice. "Tower of Iron Will and Mind Blank," the illithid recited, two typical and readily available mental defense modes that psionicists often used in their battles with each other.

Kimmuriel growled, understanding well the trap that the illithid had just laid for him, the alliance of necessity that Yharaskrik, obviously fearing that Kimmuriel might betray him to Jarlaxle and the Crystal Shard, had just forced upon him. He knew those defensive mental postures, of course, and if the Crystal Shard came after him, seeking control, now that he knew the two defenses would prevent the intrusions, he would inevitably and automatically summon them up. For, like any psionicist, like any reasoning being, Kimmuriel's ego and id would never allow such controlling possession.

He stared long and hard at the illithid, hating the creature, and yet sympathizing with Yharaskrik's fears of Crenshinibon. Or, perhaps, it occurred to him that Yharaskrik had just saved him. Crenshinibon would have come after him, to dominate if not to destroy, and if Kimmuriel had discovered the correct ways to block the intrusion in time, then he would have suddenly become an enemy in an unfavorable position, as opposed to now, when he, and not Crenshinibon, properly understood the situation at hand.

"You will shadow us?" he asked the illithid, hoping the answer would be yes.

He felt a wave of thoughts roll through him, ambiguous and lacking any specifics, but indicating clearly that Yharaskrik meant to keep a watchful eye on the dangerous Crystal Shard.

They were allies, then, out of necessity.

"I do not like her," came the high-pitched, excited voice of Dwahvel Tiggerwillies. The halfling shuffled over to take Sharlotta's vacated seat at Entreri's table.

"Is it her height and beauty that so offend you?" Entreri sarcastically replied.

Dwahvel shot him a perfectly incredulous look. "Her dishonesty," the halfling explained.

That answer raised Entreri's eyebrow. Wasn't everyone on the streets of Calimport, Entreri and Dwahvel included, basically a manipulator? If a claim of dishonesty was a reason not to like someone in Calimport, then the judgmental person would find herself quite alone.

"There is a difference," Dwahvel explained, intercepting a nearby waiter with a wave of her hand and taking a drink from his laden tray.

"So it comes back to that height and beauty problem, then," Entreri chided with a smile.

His own words did indeed amuse him, but what caught his fancy even more was the realization that he could, and often did, talk to Dwahvel in such a manner. In all of his life, Artemis Entreri had known very few people with whom he could have a casual conversation, but he found himself so at ease with Dwahvel that he had even considered hiring a wizard to determine if she was using some charming magic on him. In fact, then and there, Entreri clenched his gloved fist, concentrating briefly on the item to see if he could determine any magical emanations coming from Dwahvel, aimed at him.

There was nothing, only honest friendship, which to Artemis Entreri was a magic more foreign indeed.

"I have often been jealous of human women," Dwahvel answered sarcastically, doing well to keep a perfectly straight face. "They are often tall enough to attract even ogres, after all."

Entreri chuckled, an expression from him so rare that he actually surprised himself in hearing it.

"There is a difference between Sharlotta and many others, yourself included," Dwahvel went on. "We all play the game—that is how we survive, after all—and we all deceive and plot, twisting truths and lies alike to reach our own desired ends. The confusion for some, Sharlotta included, lies in those ends. I understand you. I know your desires, your goals, and know that I impede those goals at my peril. But I trust as well that, as long as I do not impede those goals, I'll not find the wrong end of either of your fine blades."

"So thought Dondon," Entreri put in, referring to Dondon Tiggerwillies, Dwahvel's cousin and once Entreri's closest friend in the city. Entreri had murdered the pitiful Dondon soon after his return from his final battle with Drizzt Do'Urden.

"Your actions against Dondon did not surprise him, I assure you," Dwahvel remarked. "He was a good enough friend to you to have killed you if he had ever found you in the same situation as you found him. You did him a favor."

Entreri shrugged, hardly sure of that, not even sure of his own motivations in killing Dondon. Had he done so to free Dondon from his own gluttonous ends, from the chains that kept him locked in a room and in a state of constant incapacity? Or had he killed Dondon simply because he was angry at the failed creature, simply because he could not stand to look at the miserable thing he had become any longer?

"Sharlotta is not trustworthy because you cannot understand her true goals and motivations," Dwahvel continued. "She desires power, yes, as do many, but with her, one can never understand where she might be thinking that she can find that power. There is no loyalty there, even to those who maintain consistency of character and action. No, that one will take the better deal at the expense of any and all."

Entreri nodded, not disagreeing in the least. He had never liked Sharlotta, and like Dwahvel, he had never even begun to trust her. There were no scruples or codes within Sharlotta Vespers, only blatant manipulation.

"She crosses the line every time," Dwahvel remarked. "I have never been fond of women who use their bodies to get that which they desire. I've got my own charms, you know, and yet I have never had to stoop to such a level."

The lighthearted ending brought another smile to Entreri's face, and he knew that Dwahvel was only half joking. She did indeed have her charms: a pleasant appearance and fine, flattering dress, as sharp a wit as was to be found, and a keen sense of her surroundings.

"How are you getting on with your new companion?" Dwahvel asked.

Entreri looked at her curiously—she did have a way of bouncing about a conversation.

"The sword," Dwahvel clarified, feigning exasperation. "You have it now, or it has you."

"*I* have *it*," Entreri assured her, dropping his hand to the bony hilt.

Dwahvel eyed him suspiciously.

"I have not yet fought my battle with Charon's Claw," Entreri admitted to her, hardly believing that he was doing so, "but I do not think it so powerful a weapon that I need fear it."

"As Jarlaxle believes with Crenshinibon?" Dwahvel asked, and again, Entreri's eyebrow lifted high.

"He constructed a crystalline tower," the ever-observant halfling argued. "That is one of the most basic desires of the Crystal Shard, if the old sages are to be believed."

Entreri started to ask her how she could possibly know of any of that, of the shard and the tower at Dallabad and of any connection, but he didn't bother. Of course Dwahvel knew. She always knew—that was one of her charms. Entreri had dropped enough hints in their many discussions for her to figure it all out, and she did have an incredible number of other sources as well. If Dwahvel Tiggerwillies learned that Jarlaxle carried an artifact known as Crenshinibon, then there would be little doubt that she would go to the sages and pay good coin to learn every little-known detail about the powerful item.

"He thinks he controls it," Dwahvel said.

"Do not underestimate Jarlaxle," Entreri replied. "Many have. They all are dead."

"Do not underestimate the Crystal Shard," Dwahvel returned without hesitation. "Many have. They all are dead."

"A wonderful combination then," Entreri said matter-of-factly. He dropped his chin in his hand, stroking his smooth cheek and bringing his finger to a pinch at the small tuft of hair that remained on his chin, considering the conversation and the implications. "Jarlaxle can handle the artifact," he decided.

Dwahvel shrugged noncommitally.

"Even more than that," Entreri went on, "Jarlaxle will welcome the union if Crenshinibon proves his equal. That is the difference between him and me," he explained, and though he was speaking to Dwahvel, he was, in fact, really talking to himself, sorting out his many feelings on this complicated issue. "He will allow Crenshinibon to be his partner, if that is necessary, and will find ways to make their goals one and the same."

"But Artemis Entreri has no partners," Dwahvel reasoned.

Entreri considered the words carefully, and even glanced down at the powerful sword he now wore, a sword possessed of sentience and influence, a sword whose spirit he surely meant to break and dominate. "No," he agreed. "I have no partners, and I want none. The sword is mine and will serve me. Nothing less."

"Or?"

"Or it will find its way into the acid mouth of a black dragon," Entreri strongly assured the halfling, growling with every word, and Dwahvel wasn't about to argue with those words spoken in that tone.

"Who is the stronger then," Dwahvel dared to ask, "Jarlaxle the partner or Entreri the loner?"

"I am," Entreri assured her without the slightest hesitation. "Jarlaxle might seem so for now, but inevitably he will find a traitor among his partners who will bring him down."

"You never could stand the thought of taking orders," Dwahvel said with a laugh. "That is why the shape of the world so bothers you!"

"To take an order implies that you must trust the giver of such," Entreri retorted, and the tone of his banter showed that he was taking no offense. In fact, there was an eagerness in his voice rarely heard, a true testament to those many charms of Dwahvel Tiggerwillies. "That, my dear little Dwahvel, is why the shape of the world so bothers me. I learned at a very young age that I cannot trust in or count on anyone but myself. To do so invites deceit and despair and opens a vulnerability that can be exploited. To do so is a weakness."

Now it was Dwahvel's turn to sit back a bit and digest the words. "But you have come to trust in me, it would seem," she said, "merely by speaking with me such. Have I brought out a weakness in you, my friend?"

Entreri smiled again, a crooked smile that didn't really tell Dwahvel whether he was amused or merely warning her not to push this observation too far.

"Perhaps it is merely that I know you and your band well enough to hold no fear of you," the cocky assassin remarked, rising from his seat and stretching. "Or maybe it is merely that you have not yet been foolish enough to try to give me an order."

Still that grin remained, but Dwahvel, too, was smiling, and sincerely. She saw it in Entreri's eyes now, that little hint of appreciation. Perhaps their talks were a bit of weakness to Entreri's jaded way of thinking. The truth of it, whether he wanted to admit it or not, was that he did indeed trust her, perhaps more deeply than he had ever trusted anyone in all of his life. At least, more deeply than he had since that first person—and Dwahvel figured that it had to have been a parent or a close family friend—had so deeply betrayed and wounded him.

Entreri headed for the door, that casual, easy walk of his, perfect in balance and as graceful as any court dancer. Many heads turned to watch him go—so many were always concerned with the whereabouts of deadly Artemis Entreri.

Not so for Dwahvel, though. She had come to understand this relationship, this friendship of theirs, not long after Dondon's death. She knew that if she ever crossed Artemis Entreri, he would surely kill her, but she knew, too, where those lines of danger lay.

Dwahvel's smile was indeed genuine and comfortable and confident as she watched her dangerous friend leave the Copper Ante that night.

CHAPTER

10

"My master, he says that I am to pay you, yes?" the slobbering little brown-skinned man said to one of the fortress guards. "Kohrin Soulez is Dallabad, yes? My master, he says I pay Kohrin Soulez for water and shade, yes?"

The Dallabad soldier looked to his amused companion, and both of them regarded the little man, who continued bobbing his head stupidly.

"You see that tower?" the first asked, drawing the little man's gaze with his own toward the crystalline structure gleaming brilliantly over Dallabad. "That is Ahdahnia's tower. Ahdahnia Soulez, who now rules Dallabad."

The little man looked up at the tower with obvious awe. "Ah-dahn-ee-a," he said carefully, slowly, as if committing it to memory. "Soulez, yes? Like Kohrin."

"The daughter of Kohrin Soulez," the guard explained. "Go and tell your master that Ahdahnia Soulez now rules Dallabad. You pay her, through me."

The little man's head bobbed frantically. "Yes, yes," he agreed, handing over the modest purse, "and my master will meet with her, yes?"

The guard shrugged. "If I get around to asking her, perhaps," he said, and he held his hand out, and the little man looked at it curiously.

"If I find the time to bother to tell her," the guard said pointedly.

"I pay you to tell her?" the little man asked, and the other guard snorted loudly, shaking his head at the little man's continuing stupidity.

"You pay me, I tell her," the guard said plainly. "You do not pay me, and your master does not meet with her."

"But if I pay you, we . . . he, meets with her?"

"If she so chooses," the guard explained. "I will tell her. I can promise no more than that."

The little man's head continued to bob, but his stare drifted off to the side, as if he was considering the options laid out before him. "I pay," he agreed, and handed over another, smaller, purse.

The guard snatched it away and bounced it in his hand, checking the weight, and shook his head and scowled, indicating clearly that it was not enough.

"All I have!" the little man protested.

"Then get more," ordered the guard.

The little man hopped all about, seeming unsure and very concerned. He reached for the second purse, but the guard pulled it back and scowled at him. A bit more shuffling and hopping, and the little man gave a shriek and ran off.

"You think they will attack?" the other guard asked, and it was obvious from his tone that he wasn't feeling very concerned about the possibility.

The group of six wagons had pulled into Dallabad that morning, seeking reprieve from the blistering sun. The drivers were twenty strong, and not one of them seemed overly threatening, and not one of them even looked remotely like any wizard. Any attack that group made against Dallabad's fortress would likely bring only a few moments of enjoyment to the soldiers now serving Ahdahnia Soulez.

"I think that our little friend has already forgotten his purse," the first soldier replied. "Or at least, he has forgotten the truth of how he lost it."

The second merely laughed. Not much had changed at the oasis since the downfall of Kohrin Soulez. They were still the same pirating band of toll collectors. Of course the guard would tell Ahdahnia of the wagon leader's desire to meet with her—that was how Ahdahnia collected her information, after all. As for his extortion of some of the stupid little wretch's funds, that would fade away into meaninglessness very quickly.

Yes, little had really changed.

⚔

"So it is true that Kohrin is dead," remarked Lipke, the coordinator of the scouting party, the leader of the "trading caravan."

He glanced out the slit in his tent door to see the gleaming tower, the source of great unease throughout Calimshan. While it was no great event that Kohrin Soulez had at last been killed, nor that his daughter had apparently taken over Dallabad Oasis, rumors tying this event to another not-so-minor power shift among a prominent guild in Calimport had put the many warlords of the region on guard.

"It is also true that his daughter has apparently taken his place," Trulbul replied, pulling the padding from the back collar of his shirt, the "hump" that gave him the slobbering, stooped-over appearance. "Curse her name for turning on her father."

"Unless she had no choice in the matter," offered Rolmanet, the third of the inner circle. "Artemis Entreri has been seen in Calimport with Charon's Claw. Perhaps Ahdahnia sold it to him, as some rumors say. Perhaps she bartered it for the magic that would construct that tower, as say others. Or perhaps the foul assassin took it from the body of Kohrin Soulez."

"It has to be Basadoni," Lipke reasoned. "I know Ahdahnia, and she would not have so viciously turned against her father, not over the sale of a sword. There is no shortage of gold in Dallabad."

"But why would the Basadoni Guild leave her in command of Dallabad?" asked Trulbul. "Or more particularly, how would they leave her in command, if she holds any loyalty to her father? Those guards were not Basadoni soldiers," he added. "I am sure of it. Their skin shows the weathering of the open desert, as with all the Dallabad militia, and not the grime of Calimport's streets. Kohrin Soulez treated his guild well—even the least of his soldiers and attendants always had gold for the gambling tents when we passed through here. Would so many so quickly abandon their loyalties to the man?"

The three looked at each other for a moment and burst into laughter. Loyalty had never been the strong suit of any of Calimshan's guilds and gangs.

"Your point is well taken," Trulbul admitted, "yet it still does not seem right to me. Somehow there is more to this than a simple coup."

"I do not believe that either of us disagrees with you," Lipke replied. "Artemis Entreri carries Kohrin's mighty sword, yet if it is a simple matter that Ahdahnia Soulez decided that the time had come to secure Dallabad Oasis for herself, would she so quickly part with such a powerful defensive item? Is this not the time when she will likely be most open to reprisals?"

"Unless she hired Entreri to kill her father, with payment to be Charon's Claw," Rolmanet reasoned. He was nodding as he improvised the words, thinking that he had stumbled onto something very plausible, something that would explain much.

"If that is so, then this is the most expensive assassination Calimshan has known in centuries," Lipke remarked.

"But if not that, then what?" a frustrated Rolmanet asked.

"Basadoni," Trulbul said definitively. "It has to be Basadoni. They extended their grasp within the city, and now they have struck out again, hoping it to be away from prying eyes. We must confirm this."

The others were nodding, reluctantly it seemed.

◆━━━◆

Jarlaxle, Kimmuriel, and Rai-guy sat in comfortable chairs in the second level of the crystalline tower. An enchanted mirror, a collaboration between the magic of Rai-guy and Crenshinibon, conveyed the entire conversation between the three scouts, as it had followed the supposedly stupid little hunched man from the moment he had handed his purses over to the guard outside the fortress.

"This is not acceptable," Rai-guy dared to remark, turning to face Jarlaxle. "We are grasping too far and too fast, inviting prying eyes."

Kimmuriel sent his thoughts to his wizardly friend. *Not here. Not within the tower replica of Crenshinibon.* Even as he sent the message, he felt the energies of the shard tugging at him, prying around the outside of his mental defenses. With Yharaskrik's warnings echoing in his mind, and surely not wanting to alert Crenshinibon to the truth of his nature at that time, Kimmuriel abruptly ceased all psionic activity.

"What do you plan to do with them?" Rai-guy asked more calmly. He glanced at Kimmuriel, relaying to his friend that he had gotten the message and would heed the wise thoughts well.

"Destroy them," Kimmuriel reasoned.

"Incorporate them," Jarlaxle corrected. "There are a score in their party, and they are obviously connected to other guilds. What fine spies they will become."

"Too dangerous," Rai-guy remarked.

"Those who submit to the will of Crenshinibon will serve us," Jarlaxle replied with utmost calm. "Those who do not will be executed."

Rai-guy didn't seem convinced. He started to reply, but Kimmuriel put his hand on his friend's forearm and motioned for him to let it go.

"You will deal with them?" Kimmuriel asked Jarlaxle. "Or would you prefer that we send in soldiers to capture them and drag them before the Crystal Shard for judgment?"

"The artifact can reach their minds from the tower," Jarlaxle replied. "Those who submit will willingly slay those who do not."

"And if those who do not are the greater?" Rai-guy had to ask, but again, Kimmuriel motioned for him to be quiet, and this time, the psionicist rose and bade the wizard to follow him away.

"With the changes in Dallabad's hierarchy and the tower so evident, we will have to remain fully on our guard for some time to come," Kimmuriel did say to Jarlaxle.

The mercenary leader nodded. "Crenshinibon is ever wary," he explained.

Kimmuriel smiled in reply, but in truth, Jarlaxle's assurances were only making him more nervous, were only confirming to him that Yharaskrik's information concerning the devastating Crystal Shard was, apparently, quite accurate.

The two left their leader alone then with his newest partner, the sentient artifact.

Rolmanet and Trulbul blinked repeatedly as they exited their tent into the stinging daylight. All about them, the other members of their band worked methodically, if less than enthusiastically, brushing the horses and camels and filling the waterskins for the remaining journey to Calimport.

Others should have been out scouting the perimeter of the oasis and doing guard counts on Dallabad fortress, but Rolmanet soon realized that all seventeen of the remaining force was about. He also noticed that many kept glancing his way, wearing curious expressions.

One man in particular caught Rolmanet's eye. "Did he not already fill those skins?" Rolmanet quietly asked his companion.

"And should he not be at the east wall, counting sentries?" As he finished, he turned to Trulbul, and his last words faded away as he considered his companion, the man standing quietly, staring up at the crystalline tower with a wistful look in his dark eyes.

"Trulbul?" Rolmanet asked, starting toward the man but, sensing that something was amiss, changing his mind and stepping away instead.

An expression of complete serenity came over Trulbul's face. "Can you not hear it?" he asked, glancing over to regard Rolmanet. "The music . . ."

"Music?" Rolmanet glanced at the man curiously, and snapped his gaze back to regard the tower and listened carefully.

"Beautiful music," Trulbul said rather loudly, and several others nearby nodded their agreement.

Rolmanet fought hard to steady his breathing and at least appear calm. He did hear the music then, a subtle note conveying a message of peace and prosperity, promising gain and power and . . . demanding. Demanding fealty.

"I am staying at Dallabad," Lipke announced suddenly, coming out of the tent. "There is more opportunity here than with Pasha Broucalle."

Rolmanet's eyes widened in spite of himself, and he had to fight very hard to keep from glancing all around in alarm or from simply running away. He was gasping now as it all came clear to him: a wizard's spell, he believed, charming enemies into friends.

"Beautiful music," another man off to the side agreed.

"Do you hear it?" Trulbul asked Rolmanet.

Rolmanet fought very hard to steady himself, to paint a serene expression upon his face, before turning back to stare at his friend.

"No, he does not," Lipke said from afar before Rolmanet had even completed the turn. "He does not see the opportunity before us. He will betray us!"

"It is a spell!" Rolmanet cried loudly, drawing his curved sword.

"A wizard's enchantment to ensnare us in his grip. Fight back! Deny it, my friends!"

Lipke was at him, slashing hard with his sword, a blow that skilled Rolmanet deftly parried. Before he could counter, Trulbul was there beside Lipke, following the first man's slash with a deadly thrust at Rolmanet's heart.

"Can you not understand?" Rolmanet cried frantically, and only luck allowed him to deflect that second attack.

He glanced about as he retreated steadily, seeking allies and taking care for more enemies. He noted another fight over by the water, where several men had fallen over another, knocking him to the ground and kicking and beating him mercilessly. All the while, they screamed at the man that he could not hear the music, that he would betray them in this, their hour of greatest glory.

Another man, obviously resisting the tempting call, rushed away to the side, and the group took up the chase, leaving the beaten man facedown in the water.

A third fight erupted on the other side.

Rolmanet turned to his two opponents, the two men who had been his best friends for several years now. "It is a lie, a trick!" he insisted. "Can you not understand?"

Lipke came at him hard with a cunning low thrust, followed by an upward slash, a twisting hand-over maneuver, and yet another upward slash that forced Rolmanet to lean backward, barely keeping his balance. On came Lipke, another straight-ahead charge and thrust, with Rolmanet quite vulnerable.

Trulbul's blade slashed across, intercepting Lipke's killing blow.

"Wait!" Trulbul cried to the astonished man. "Rolmanet speaks the truth! Look more deeply at the promise, I beg!"

Lipke was fully into the coercion of the Crystal Shard. He did pause, only long enough to allow Trulbul to believe that he was indeed reflecting on the seeming inconsistency here. As Trulbul nodded, grinned, and lowered his blade, Lipke hit him with a slashing cut that opened wide his throat.

He turned back to see Rolmanet in full flight, running to the horses tethered beside the water.

"Stop him! Stop him!" Lipke cried, giving chase. Several others came in as well, trying to cut off any escape routes as Rolmanet scrambled onto his horse and turned the beast around, hooves churning the sand. The man was a fine rider, and he picked his path carefully, and they could not hope to stop him.

He thundered out of Dallabad, not even pausing to try to help the other resister, who had been cut off, forced to turn, and would soon be caught and overwhelmed. No, Rolmanet's path was straight and fast, a dead gallop down the sandy road toward distant Calimport.

Jarlaxle's thoughts, and those of Crenshinibon, angled the magical mirror to follow the retreat of the lone escapee.

The mercenary leader could feel the power building within the crystalline tower. It was a quiet humming noise as the structure gathered in the sunlight, focusing it more directly through a series of prisms and mirrors to the very tip of the pointed tower. He understood what Crenshinibon meant to do, of course. Given the implications of allowing someone to escape, it seemed a logical course.

Do not kill him, Jarlaxle instructed anyway, and he wasn't sure why he issued the command. *There is little he can tell his superiors that they do not already know. The spies have no idea of the truth behind Dallabad's overthrow, and will only assume that a wizard . . .* He felt the energy continuing to build, with no conversation, argument or otherwise, coming back at him from the artifact.

Jarlaxle looked into the mirror at the fleeing, terrified man. The more he thought about it, the more he realized that he was right, that there was no real reason to kill this one. In fact, allowing him to return to his masters with news of such a complete failure might actually serve Bregan D'aerthe. Likely these were no minor spies sent on such an important mission as this, and the manner in which the band was purely overwhelmed would impress—perhaps enough so that the other pashas would come to Dallabad openly to seek truce and parlay.

Jarlaxle filtered all of that through his thoughts to the Crystal Shard, reiterating his command to halt, for the good of the band, and secretly, because he simply didn't want to kill a man if he did not have to,

He felt the energy building, building, now straining release.

"Enough!" he said aloud. "Do not!"

"What is it, my leader?" came Rai-guy's voice, the wizard and his sidekick psionicist rushing back into the room.

They entered to see Jarlaxle standing, obviously angry, staring at the mirror.

Then how that mirror brightened! There was a flash as striking, and as painful to sensitive drow eyes, as the sun itself. A searing beam of pure heat energy shot out of the tower's tip, shooting down across the sands to catch the rider and his horse, enveloping them in a white-yellow shroud.

It was over in an instant, leaving the charred bones of Rolmanet and his horse lying on the empty desert sands.

Jarlaxle closed his eyes and clenched his teeth, suppressing his urge to scream out.

"Impressive display," Kimmuriel said.

"Fifteen have come over to us, and it would seem the other five are dead," Rai-guy remarked. "The victory is complete."

Jarlaxle wasn't so sure of that, but he composed himself and turned a calm look upon his lieutenants. "Crenshinibon will discern those who are most easily and completely dominated," he informed the wary pair. "They will be sent back to their guild—or guilds, if this was a collaboration—with a proper explanation for the defeat.

The others will be interrogated—and they will willingly submit to all of our questions—so that we might learn everything about this enemy that came prying into our affairs."

Rai-guy and Kimmuriel exchanged a glance that Jarlaxle did not miss, a clear indication that they had seen him distressed when they had entered. What they might discern from that, the mercenary leader did not know, but he wasn't overly pleased at that moment.

"Entreri is back in Calimport?" he asked.

"At House Basadoni," Kimmuriel answered.

"As we should all be," Jarlaxle decided. "We will ask our questions of our newest arrivals and give them over to Ahdahnia. Leave Berg'inyon and a small contingent behind to watch over the operation here."

The two glanced at each other again but offered no other response. They bowed and left the room.

Jarlaxle stared into the mirror at the blackened bones of the man and horse.

It had to be done, came the whisper of Crenshinibon into his mind. *His escape would have brought more curious eyes, better prepared. We are not yet ready for that.*

Jarlaxle recognized the lie for what it was. Crenshinibon feared no prying, curious eyes, feared no army at all. The Crystal Shard, in its purest of arrogance, believed that it would simply convert the majority of any attacking force, turning them back on any who did not submit to its will. How many could it control? Jarlaxle wondered. Hundreds? Thousands? Millions?

Images of domination, not merely of the streets of Calimport, not merely of the city itself, but of the entire realm, flittered through his thoughts as Crenshinibon "heard" the silent questions and tried to answer.

Jarlaxle shifted his eye patch and focused on it, lessening the connection with the artifact, and tightened his willpower to try to keep his thoughts as much to himself as possible. No, he knew,

Crenshinibon had not killed the fleeing man for fear of any retribution. Nor had it struck out with such overwhelming fury against that lone rider because it did not agree with the merits of Jarlaxle's arguments against doing so.

No, the Crystal Shard had killed the man precisely because Jarlaxle had ordered it not to do so, because the mercenary leader had crossed over the line of the concept of partner and had tried to assume control.

That Crenshinibon would not allow.

If the artifact could so easily disallow such a thing, could it also step back over the line the other way?

The rather disturbing notion did not bring much solace to Jarlaxle, who had spent the majority of his life serving as no man's, nor Matron Mother's, slave.

"We have new allies under our domination, and thus we are stronger," Rai-guy remarked sarcastically when he was alone with Kimmuriel and Berg'inyon.

"Our numbers grow," Berg'inyon agreed, "but so too mounts the danger of discovery."

"And of treachery," Kimmuriel added. "Witness that one of the spies, under the influence of Jarlaxle's artifact, turned against us when the fighting started. The domination is not complete, nor is it unbreakable. With every unwitting soldier we add in such a manner, we run the risk of an uprising from within. While it is unlikely that any would so escape the domination and subsequently cause any real damage to us—they are merely humans, after all—we cannot dismiss the likelihood that one will break free and escape us, delivering the truth of the new Basadoni Guild and of Dallabad to some of the guilds."

"We already have agreed upon the consequences of Bregan

D'aerthe being discovered for what it truly is," Rai-guy added ominously. "This group came to Dallabad looking specifically for the answers behind the facade, and the longer we stretch that facade, the more likely that we will be discovered. We are forfeiting our anonymity in this foolish quest for expansion."

The other two remained very silent for a long while. Then Kimmuriel quietly asked, "Are you going to explain this to Jarlaxle?"

"Should we be addressing this problem to Jarlaxle," Rai-guy countered, his voice dripping with sarcasm, "or to the true leader of Bregan D'aerthe?"

That bold proclamation gave the other two even more pause. There it was, set out very clearly, the notion that Jarlaxle had lost control of the band to a sentient artifact.

"Perhaps it is time for us to reconsider our course," Kimmuriel said somberly.

Both he and Rai-guy had served under Jarlaxle for a long, long time, and both understood the tremendous weight of the implications of Kimmuriel's remark. Wresting Bregan D'aerthe from Jarlaxle would be something akin to stealing House Baenre away from Matron Baenre during the centuries of her iron-fisted rule. In many ways, Jarlaxle, so cunning, so layered in defenses and so full of understanding of everything around him, might prove an even more formidable foe.

Now the course seemed obvious to the three, a coup that had been building since the first expansive steps of House Basadoni.

"I have a source who can offer us more information on the Crystal Shard," Kimmuriel remarked. "Perhaps there is a way to destroy it or at least temporarily to cripple its formidable powers so that we can get to Jarlaxle."

Rai-guy looked to Berg'inyon and both nodded grimly.

Artemis Entreri was beginning to understand just how much trouble was brewing for Jarlaxle and therefore for him. He heard about the incident at Dallabad soon after the majority of the dark elves returned to House Basadoni, and knew from the looks and the tone of their voices that several of Jarlaxle's prominent underlings weren't exactly thrilled by the recent events.

Neither was Entreri. He knew that Rai-guy's and Kimmuriel's complaints were quite valid, knew that Jarlaxle's expansionist policies were leading Bregan D'aerthe down a very dangerous road indeed. When the truth about House Basadoni's change and the takeover of Dallabad eventually leaked out—and Entreri was now harboring few doubts that it would—all the guilds and all the lords and every power in the region would unite against Bregan D'aerthe. Jarlaxle was cunning, and the band of mercenaries was indeed powerful—even more so with the Crystal Shard in their possession—but Entreri held no doubts that they would be summarily destroyed, every one.

No, the assassin realized, it wouldn't likely come to that. The groundwork had been clearly laid before them all, and Entreri held little doubt that Kimmuriel and Rai-guy would move against Jarlaxle and soon. Their scowls were growing deeper by the day, their words a bit bolder.

That understanding raised a perplexing question to Entreri. Was the Crystal Shard actually spurring the coup, as Lady Lolth often did among the houses in Menzoberranzan? Was the artifact reasoning that perhaps either of the more volatile magic-using lieutenants might be a more suitable wielder? Or was the coup being inspired by the actions of Jarlaxle under the prodding, if not the outright influence, of Crenshinibon?

Either way, Entreri knew that he was becoming quite vulnerable, even with his new magical acquisitions. However he played through the scenario, Jarlaxle alone remained the keystone to his survival.

The assassin turned down a familiar avenue, moving inconspicuously among the many street rabble out this evening, keeping to the shadows and keeping to himself. He had to find some way to get Jarlaxle back in command and on strong footing. He needed for Jarlaxle to be in control of Bregan D'aerthe—not only of their actions but of their hearts as well. Only then could he fend a coup—a coup that could only mean disaster for Entreri.

Yes, he had to secure Jarlaxle's position. Then he had to find a way to get himself far, far away from the dark elves and their dangerous intrigue.

The sentries at the Copper Ante were hardly surprised to see him and even informed him that Dwahvel was expecting him and waiting for him in the back room.

She had already heard of the most recent events at Dallabad, he realized, and he shook his head, reminding himself that he should not be surprised, and also reminding himself that it was just her amazing ability for the acquisition of knowledge that had brought him to Dwahvel this evening.

"It was House Broucalle of Memnon," Dwahvel informed him as soon as he entered and sat on the plush pillows set upon the floor opposite the halfling.

"They were quick to move," Entreri replied.

"The crystalline tower is akin to a huge beacon set out on the wasteland of the desert," Dwahvel replied. "Why do your compatriots, with their obvious need for secrecy, so call attention to themselves?"

Entreri didn't answer verbally, but the expression on his face told Dwahvel much of his fears.

"They err," Dwahvel concurred with those fears. "They have House Basadoni, a superb front for their exotic trading business. Why reach further and invite a war that they cannot hope to win?"

Still Entreri did not answer.

"Or was that the whole purpose for the band of drow to come to the surface?" Dwahvel asked with sincere concern. "Were you, too, perhaps, misinformed about the nature of this band, led to believe that they were here for profit—mutual profit, potentially—when in fact they are but an advanced war party, setting the stage for complete disaster for Calimport and all Calimshan?"

Entreri shook his head. "I know Jarlaxle well," he replied. "He came here for profit—mutual profit for those who work along with him. That is his way. I do not think he would ever serve in anything as potentially disastrous as a war party. Jarlaxle is not a warlord, in any capacity. He is an opportunist and nothing more. He cares little for glory and much for comfort."

"And yet he invites disaster by erecting such an obvious, and obviously inviting, monument as that remarkable tower," Dwahvel answered. She tilted her plump head, studying Entreri's concerned expression carefully. "What is it?" she asked.

"How great is your knowledge of Crenshinibon?" the assassin asked. "The Crystal Shard?"

Dwahvel scrunched up her face, deep in thought for just a moment, and shook her head. "Cursory," she admitted. "I know of its tower images but little more."

"It is an artifact of exceeding power," Entreri explained. "I am not so certain that the sentient item's goals and Jarlaxle's are one and the same."

"Many artifacts have a will of their own," Dwahvel stated dryly. "That is rarely a good thing."

"Learn all that you can about it," Entreri bade her, "and quickly, before that which you fear inadvertently befalls Calimport." He paused and considered the best course for Dwahvel to take in light of fairly recent events. "Try to find out how Drizzt came to possess it, and where—"

"What in the Nine Hells is a Drizzt?" Dwahvel asked.

Entreri started to explain but just stopped and laughed,

remembering how very wide the world truly was. "Another dark elf," he answered, "a dead one."

"Ah, yes," said Dwahvel. "Your rival. The one you call 'Do'Urden.'"

"Forget him, as have I," Entreri instructed. "He is only relevant here because it was from him that Jarlaxle's minions acquired the Crystal Shard. They impersonated a priest of some renown and power, a cleric named Cadderly, I believe, who resides somewhere in or around the Snowflake Mountains."

"A long journey," the halfling remarked.

"A worthwhile one," Entreri replied. "And we both know that distance is irrelevant to a wizard possessing the proper spells."

"This will cost you greatly."

With just a twitch of his honed leg muscles, a movement that would have been difficult for a skilled fighter half his age, Entreri rose up tall and fearsome before Dwahvel, then leaned over and patted her on the shoulder—with his gloved right hand.

She got the message.

CHAPTER

11

It is what you desired all along, Kimmuriel said to Yharaskrik.

The illithid feigned surprise at the drow psionicist's blunt proposition. Yharaskrik had explaining to Kimmuriel how he might fend the intrusions of the Crystal Shard. The illithid desired that the situation be brought to this very point all along.

Who will possess it? Yharaskrik silently asked. *Kimmuriel or Rai-guy?*

Rai-guy, the drow answered. *He and Crenshinibon will perfectly complement one another—by Crenshinibon's own impartations to him from afar.*

So you both believe, the illithid responded. *Perhaps, though, Crenshinibon sees you as a threat—a likely and logical assumption— and is merely goading you into this so that you and your comrades might be thoroughly destroyed.*

I have not dismissed that possibility, Kimmuriel returned, seeming quite at ease. *That is why I have come to Yharaskrik.*

The illithid paused for a long while, digesting the information. *The Crystal Shard is no minor item,* the creature explained. *To ask of me—*

A temporary reprieve, Kimmuriel interrupted. *I do not wish to pit Yharaskrik against Crenshinibon, for I understand that the artifact would overwhelm you.* He imparted those thoughts without fear of insulting the mind flayer. Kimmuriel understood that the perfectly logical illithids were not possessed of ego beyond reason. Certainly they believed their race to be superior to most others, to humans, of course, and even to drow, but within that healthy confidence there lay an element of reason that prevented them from taking insult to statements made of perfect logic. Yharaskrik knew that the artifact could overwhelm any creature short of a god.

There is, perhaps, a way, the illithid replied, and Kimmuriel's smile widened. *A Tower of Iron Will's sphere of influence could encompass Crenshinibon and defeat its mental intrusions, and its commands to any towers it has constructed near the battlefield. Temporarily,* the creature added emphatically. *I hold no illusions that any psionic force short of that conducted by a legion of my fellow illithids could begin to permanently weaken the powers of the great Crystal Shard.*

"Long enough for the downfall of Jarlaxle," Kimmuriel agreed aloud. "That is all that I require." He bowed and took his leave then, and his last words echoed in his mind as he stepped through the dimensional doorway that would bring him back to Calimport and the private quarters he shared with Rai-guy.

The downfall of Jarlaxle! Kimmuriel could hardly believe that he was a party to this conspiracy. Hadn't it been Jarlaxle, after all, who had offered him refuge from his own Matron Mother and vicious female siblings of House Oblodra, and who had then taken him in and sheltered him from the rest of the city when Matron Baenre had declared that House Oblodra must be completely eradicated? Aside from any loyalty he held for the mercenary leader, there remained the practical matter of the problem of decapitating Bregan D'aerthe. Jarlaxle above all others had facilitated the rise of the mercenary band, had brought them to prominence more than a century before, and no one in all the band, not even self-confident Rai-guy, doubted for a moment how important Jarlaxle was politically for the survival of Bregan D'aerthe.

All those thoughts stayed with Kimmuriel as he made his way

back to Rai-guy's side, to find the drow thick into the plotting of the attacks they would use to bring Jarlaxle down.

"Your new friend can give us that which we require?" the eager wizard-cleric asked as soon as Kimmuriel arrived.

"Likely," Kimmuriel replied.

"Neutralize the Crystal Shard, and the attack will be complete," Rai-guy said.

"Do not underestimate Jarlaxle," Kimmuriel warned. "He has the Crystal Shard now and so we must first eliminate that powerful item, but even without it, Jarlaxle has spent many years solidifying his hold on Bregan D'aerthe. I would not have gone against him before the acquisition of the artifact."

"But it is just that acquisition that has weakened him," Rai-guy explained. "Even the common soldiers fear this course we have taken."

"I have heard some remark that they cannot believe our rise in power," Kimmuriel argued. "Some have proclaimed that we will dominate the surface world, that Jarlaxle will take Bregan D'aerthe to prominence among the weakling humans, and return in glory to conquer Menzoberranzan."

Rai-guy laughed aloud at the proclamation. "The artifact is powerful, I do not doubt, but it is limited. Did not the mind flayer tell you that Crenshinibon sought to reach its limit of control?"

"Whether or not the fantasy conquest can occur is irrelevant to our present situation," Kimmuriel replied. "What matters is whether or not the soldiers of Bregan D'aerthe believe in it."

Rai-guy didn't have an argument for that line of reasoning, but still, he wasn't overly concerned. "Though Berg'inyon is with us, the drow will be limited in their role in the battle," he explained. "We have humans at our disposal now and thousands of kobolds."

"Many of the humans were brought into our fold by Crenshinibon," Kimmuriel reminded. "The Crystal Shard will have little difficulty in dominating the kobolds, if Yharaskrik cannot completely neutralize it."

"And we have the wererats," Rai-guy went on, unfazed. "Shape-changers are better suited to resisting mental intrusions. Their internal strife denies any outside influences."

"You have enlisted Domo?"

Rai-guy shook his head. "Domo is difficult," he admitted, "but I have enlisted several of his wererat lieutenants. They will fall to our cause if Domo is eliminated. To that end, I have had Sharlotta Vespers inform Jarlaxle that the wererat leader has been speaking out of turn, revealing too much about Bregan D'aerthe, to Pasha Da'Daclan, and we believe to the leader of the guild that came to investigate Dallabad."

Kimmuriel nodded, but his expression remained concerned. Jarlaxle was a tough opponent in games of the mind—he might see the ruse for what it was, and use Domo to turn the wererats back to his side.

"His actions now will be telling," Rai-guy admitted. "Crenshini-bon, no doubt, will want to believe Sharlotta's tale, but Jarlaxle will desire to proceed more cautiously before acting against Domo."

"You believe that the wererat leader will be dead this very day," Kimmuriel reasoned after a moment.

Rai-guy smiled. "The Crystal Shard has become Jarlaxle's strength and thus his weakness," he said with a wicked grin.

◆━━◆

"First the gauntlet and now this," Dwahvel Tiggerwillies said with a profound sigh. "Ah, Entreri, what shall I ever do for extra coin when you are no more?"

Entreri didn't appreciate the humor. "Be quick about it," he instructed.

"Sharlotta's actions have made you very nervous," Dwahvel

171

remarked, for she had observed the woman busily working the streets during the last few hours, with many of her meetings with known operatives of the wererat guild.

Entreri just nodded, not wanting to share the latest news with Dwahvel—just in case. Things were moving fast now, he knew, too fast. Rai-guy and Kimmuriel were laying the groundwork for their assault, but at least Jarlaxle had apparently caught on to some of the budding problems. The mercenary leader had summoned Entreri just a few moments before, telling the man that he had to go and meet with a particularly wretched wererat by the name of Domo. If Domo was in on the conspiracy, Entreri suspected that Rai-guy and Kimmuriel would soon have a hole to fill in their ranks.

"I will return within two hours," Entreri explained. "Have it ready."

"We have no proper material to make such an item as you requested," Dwahvel complained.

"Color and consistency alone," Entreri replied. "The material does not need to be exact."

Dwahvel shrugged.

Entreri went out into Calimport's night, moving swiftly, his cloak pulled tight around his shoulders. Not far from the Copper Ante, he turned down an alley. Then after a quick check to ensure that he was not being followed, he slipped down an open sewer hole into the tunnels below the city.

A few moments later, he stood before Jarlaxle in the appointed chamber.

"Sharlotta has informed me that Domo has been whispering secrets about us," Jarlaxle remarked.

"The wererat is on the way?"

Jarlaxle nodded. "And likely with many allies. You are prepared for the fight?"

Entreri wore the first honest grin he had known in several days. Prepared for a fight with wererats? How could he not be? Still he could not dismiss the source of Jarlaxle's information. He realized that Sharlotta was working both ends of the table here, that she was in tight with Rai-guy and Kimmuriel but was in no overt way severing her ties to Jarlaxle. He doubted that Sharlotta and her drow allies had set this up as the ultimate battle for control of Bregan D'aerthe. Such intricate planning would take longer, and the sewers of Calimport would not be a good location for a fight that would grow so very obvious.

Still . . .

"Perhaps you should have stayed at Dallabad for a while," Entreri remarked, "within the crystalline tower, overseeing the new operation."

"Domo hardly frightens me," Jarlaxle replied.

Entreri stared at him hard. Could he really be so oblivious to the apparent underpinnings of a coup within Bregan D'aerthe? If so, did that enhance the possibility that the Crystal Shard was indeed prompting the disloyal actions of Rai-guy and Kimmuriel? Or did it mean, perhaps, that Entreri was being too cautious here, was seeing demons and uprisings where there were none?

The assassin took a deep breath and shook his head, clearing his thoughts.

"Sharlotta could be mistaken," the assassin did say. "She would have reasons of her own to wish to be rid of troublesome Domo."

"We will know soon enough," Jarlaxle replied, nodding in the direction of a tunnel, where the wererat leader, in the form of a huge humanoid rat, was approaching, along with three other ratmen.

"My dear Domo," Jarlaxle greeted, and the wererat leader bowed.

"It is good that you came to us," Domo replied. "I do not enjoy any journeys to the surface at this time, not even to the cellars of House Basadoni. There is too much excitement, I fear."

Entreri narrowed his eyes and considered the wretched lycanthrope, thinking that answer curious, at least, but trying hard not to interpret it one way or the other.

"Do the agents of the other guilds similarly come down to meet with you?" Jarlaxle asked, a question that surely set Domo back on his heels.

Entreri stared hard at the drow now, catching on that Crenshinibon was instructing Jarlaxle to put Domo on his guard, to get him thinking of any potentially treasonous actions that they might be more easily read. Still, it seemed to him that Jarlaxle was moving too quickly here, that a little small talk and diplomacy might have garnered the necessary indicators without resorting to any crude mental intrusions by the sentient artifact.

"On those rare occasions when I must meet with agents of other guilds, they often do come to me," Domo answered, trying to remain calm, though he betrayed his sudden edge to Entreri when he shifted his weight from one foot to the other. The assassin calmly dropped his hands to his belt, hooking his wrists over the pommels of his two formidable weapons, a posture that seemed more relaxed and comfortable, but also one that had him in touch with his weapons, ready to draw and strike.

"And have you met with any recently?" Jarlaxle asked.

Domo winced, and winced again, and Entreri caught on to the truth of it. The artifact was trying to scour his thoughts then and there.

The three wererats behind the leader glanced at each other and shifted nervously.

Domo's face contorted, began to form into his human guise, and went back almost immediately to the trapping of the wererat. A low, feral growl escaped his throat.

"What is it?" one of the wererats behind him asked.

Entreri could see the frustration mounting on Jarlaxle's face. He glanced back to Domo curiously, wondering if he had perhaps underestimated the ugly creature.

Jarlaxle and Crenshinibon simply could not get a fix on the wererat's thoughts, for the Crystal Shard's intrusion had brought about the lycanthropic internal strife, and that wall of red pain and rage had now denied any access.

Jarlaxle, growing increasingly frustrated, stared at the wererat hard.

He betrayed us, Crenshinibon decided suddenly.

Jarlaxle's thoughts filled with doubt and confusion, for he had not seen any such revelation.

A moment of weakness, came Crenshinibon's call. *A flash of the truth within that wall of angry torment. He betrayed us . . . twice.*

Jarlaxle turned to Entreri, a subtle signal, but one that the eager assassin, who hated wererats profoundly, was quick to catch and amplify.

Domo and his associates caught it, too, and their swords came flashing out of their scabbards. By the time they'd drawn their weapons, Entreri was on the charge. Charon's Claw waved in the air before him, painting a wall of black ash that Entreri could use to segment the battleground and prevent his enemies from coordinating their movements.

He spun to the left, around the ash wall, ducking as he turned so that he came around under the swing of Domo's long and slender blade. Up went the assassin's sword, taking Domo's far and wide. Entreri, still in a crouch, scrambled forward, his dagger leading.

Domo's closest companion came on hard, though, forcing Entreri to skitter back and slash down with his sword to deflect the attack. He went into a roll, over backward, and planted his right hand, pushing hard to launch him back to his feet, working those feet quickly as he landed to put him in nearly the same position as when he had started. The foolish wererat followed, leaving Domo and its two companions on the other side of the ash wall.

Behind Entreri, Jarlaxle's hand pumped once, twice, thrice, and daggers sailed past Entreri, barely missing his head, plunging through the ash wall, blasting holes in the drifting curtain.

On the other side came a groan, and Entreri realized that Domo's companions were down to two.

A moment later, down to one, for the assassin met the wererat's charge full on, his sword coming up in a rotating fashion, taking the thrusting blade aside. Entreri continued forward, and so did the wererat, thinking to bite at the man.

How quickly it regretted that choice when Entreri's dagger blade filled its mouth.

A sudden second thrust yanked the creature's head back, and the assassin disengaged and quickly turned. He saw yet another of the beasts coming fast through the ash wall and heard the footsteps of a retreating Domo.

Down he went into a shoulder roll, under the ash wall, catching the ankles of the charging wererat and sending it flying over him to fall facedown right before Jarlaxle.

Entreri didn't even slow, rolling forward and back to his feet and running off full speed in pursuit of the fleeing wererat. Entreri was no stranger to the darkness, even the complete blackness of the tunnels. Indeed, he had done some of his best work down there, but recognizing the disadvantage he faced against infravision-using wererats, he held his powerful sword before him and commanded it to bring forth light—hoping that it, like many magical swords, could produce some sort of glow.

That magical glow surprised him, for it was a light of blackish hue and nothing like Entreri had ever seen before, giving all the corridor a surrealistic appearance. He glanced down at the sword, trying to see how blatant a light source it appeared, but he saw no definitive glow and hoped that meant that he might use a bit of stealth, at least, despite the fact that he was the source of the light.

He came to a fork and skidded to a stop, turning his head and focusing his senses.

The slight echo of a footfall came from the left, so on he ran.

<hr />

Jarlaxle finished the prone wererat in short order, pumping his arm repeatedly and hitting the squirming creature with dagger after dagger. He put a hand in his pocket, on the Crystal Shard, as he ran through the gap in the ash wall, trying to catch up with his companion.

Guide me, he instructed the artifact.

Up, came the unexpected reply. *They have returned to the streets.*

Jarlaxle skidded to a stop, puzzled.

Up! came the more emphatic silent cry. *To the streets.*

The mercenary leader rushed back the other way, down the corridor to the ladder that would take him back up through the sewer grate and into the alley outside the neighborhood of the Copper Ante.

Guide me, he instructed the shard again.

We are too exposed, the artifact returned. *Keep to the shadows and move back to House Basadoni—Artemis Entreri and Domo lie in that direction.*

<hr />

Entreri rounded a bend in the corridor, slowing cautiously. There, standing before him, was Domo and two more wererats, all holding swords. Entreri started forward, thinking himself seen, and figuring to attack before the three could organize their defenses. He stopped abruptly, though, when the ratman to Domo's left whispered.

"I smell him. He is near."

"Too near," agreed the other lesser creature, squinting, the tell-tale red glow of infravision evident in its eyes.

Why did they even need that infravision? Entreri wondered. He could see them clearly in the black light of Charon's Claw, as clearly as if they were all standing in a dimly lit room. He knew that he should go straight in and attack, but his curiosity was piqued now and so he stepped out from the wall, in clear view, in plain sight.

"His smell is thick," Domo agreed. All three were glancing about nervously, their swords waving. "Where are the others?"

"They have not come but should have been here," the one to his left answered. "I fear we are betrayed."

"Damn the drow to the Nine Hells, then," Domo said.

Entreri could hardly believe they could not see him—yet another wondrous effect of the marvelous sword. He wondered if perhaps they could see him had they been focusing their eyes in the normal spectrum of light, but that, he realized, had to be a question for another day. Concentrating now on moving perfectly silently, he slid one foot, and then the other, ahead of him, moving to Domo's right.

"Perhaps we should have listened more carefully to the dark elf wizard," the one to the left went on, his voice a whisper.

"To go against Jarlaxle?" Domo asked incredulously. "That is doom. Nothing more."

"But . . ." the other started to argue, but Domo began whispering harshly, sticking his finger in the other's face.

Entreri used their distraction to get right up behind the third of the group, his dagger tip coming against the wererat's spine. The creature stiffened as Entreri whispered into its ear. "Run," he said.

The ratman sped off down the corridor, and Domo stopped his arguing long enough to chase his fleeing soldier a few steps, calling threats out after him.

"Run," said Entreri, who had shifted across the way to the side of the remaining lesser wererat.

This one, though, didn't run, but let out a shriek and spun, its sword slashing across at chest level.

Entreri ducked below the blade easily and came up with a stab that brought his deadly jeweled dagger under the wererat's ribs and up into its diaphragm. The creature howled again, but then spasmed and convulsed violently.

"What is it?" Domo asked, spinning about. "What?"

The wererat fell to the floor, twitching still as it died. Entreri stood there, in the open, dagger in hand. He called up a glow from his smaller blade.

Domo jumped back, bringing his sword out in front of him. "Dancing blade?" he asked quietly. "Is this you, wizard drow?"

"Dancing blade?" Entreri repeated quietly, looking down at his glowing dagger. It made no sense to him. He looked back to Domo, to see the glow leave the wererat's eyes as he shifted from ratman, to nearly human form. Likewise his vision shifted from the infrared to the normal viewing spectrum.

He nearly jumped out of his boots again, as the specter of Artemis Entreri came clear to him. "What trick is that?" the wererat gasped.

Entreri wasn't even sure how to answer. He had no idea what Charon's Claw was doing with its black light. Did it block infravision completely but apparently hold a strange illuminating effect that was clearly visible in the normal spectrum? Did it act like a black campfire then, even though Entreri felt no heat coming from the blade? Infravision could be severely limited by strong heat sources.

It was indeed intriguing—one of so many riddles that seemed to be presenting themselves before Artemis Entreri—but again, it was a riddle to be solved another day.

"So you are without allies," he said to Domo. "It is you and I alone."

"Why does Jarlaxle fear me?" Domo asked as Entreri advanced a step.

The assassin stopped. "Fear you? Or loathe you? They are not the same thing, you know."

"I am his ally!" Domo protested. "I stood beside him, even against the advances of his lessers."

"So you said to him," Entreri remarked, glancing down at the still-twitching, still-groaning form. "What do you know? Speak it clearly and quickly, and perhaps you will walk out of here."

Domo's rodent eyes narrowed angrily. "As Rassiter walked away from your last meeting?" he asked, referring to one of his greatest predecessors in the wererat guild, a powerful leader who had served Pasha Pook along with Entreri, and whom Entreri had subsequently murdered—a deed never forgotten by the wererats of Calimport.

"I ask you one last time," Entreri said calmly.

He caught a slight movement to the side and knew that the first wererat had returned, waiting in the shadows to leap out at him. He was hardly surprised and hardly afraid.

Domo gave a wide, toothy smile. "Jarlaxle and his companions are not as unified a force as you believe," he teased.

Entreri advanced another step. "You must do better than that," he said, but before the words even left his mouth, Domo howled and leaped at him, stabbing with his slender sword.

Entreri barely moved Charon's Claw, just angled the blade to intercept Domo's and slide it off to the side.

The wererat retracted the strike at once, thrust again, and again. Each time Entreri, with barely any motion at all, positioned his parry perfectly and to a razor-thin angle, with Domo's sword stabbing past him, missing by barely an inch.

Again the wererat retracted and this time came across with a great slash.

But he had stepped too far back, and Entreri had to lean only slightly backward for the blade to swish harmlessly past before him.

The expected charge came from Domo's companion in the shadows to the side, and Domo played his part in the routine perfectly, rushing ahead with a powerful thrust.

Domo didn't understand the beauty, the efficiency, of Artemis Entreri. Again Charon's Claw caught and turned the attack, but this time, Entreri rolled his hand right over, and under the outside of Domo's blade. He pulled in his gut as he threw Domo's blade up high, and brought forth another wall of ash, blackening the air between him and the wererat. Following his own momentum, Entreri went into a complete spin, around to the right. As he came back square with Domo he brought his right arm swishing down, the sword trailing ash, while his left crossed his body over the down-swing, launching his jeweled dagger right into the gut of the charging wererat.

Charon's Claw did a complete circuit in the air between the combatants, forming a wide, circular wall. Domo came ahead right through it with yet another stubborn thrust, but Entreri wasn't there. He dived to the side into a roll and came up and around with a powerful slash at the legs of the wererat still struggling with the dagger in its belly. To the assassin's surprise and delight, the mighty sword sheared through not only the wererat's closest knee, but through the other as well. The creature tumbled to the stone, howling in agony, its life-blood pouring out freely.

Entreri hardly slowed, spinning about and coming up powerfully, slapping Domo's sword out wide yet again, and snapping Charon's Claw down and across to pick off a dagger neatly thrown by the wererat leader.

Domo's expression changed quickly then, his last trick obviously played. Now it was Entreri's turn to take the offensive, and he did so with a powerful thrust high, thrust center, thrust low routine that had Domo inevitably skittering backward, fighting hard merely to keep his balance.

Entreri, leaping ahead, didn't make it any easier on the over-matched creature. His sword worked furiously, sometimes throwing ash, sometimes not, and all with a precision designed to limit Domo's vision and options. Soon he had the wererat nearly to the back wall, and a glance from Domo told Entreri that he wasn't thrilled about the prospect of getting cornered.

Entreri took the cue to slash and slash again, bringing up a wall of ash perpendicular to the floor then perpendicular to the first, an L-shaped design that blocked Domo's vision of Entreri and his vision of the area to his immediate right.

With a growl, the wererat went right with a desperate thrust, thinking that Entreri would use the ash wall to try to work around him. He hit only air. Then he felt the assassin's presence at his back, for the man, anticipating the anticipation, had simply gone around the other way.

Domo threw his sword to the ground. "I will tell you everything," he cried. "I will—"

"You already did," Entreri assured him and the wererat stiffened as Charon's Claw sliced through his backbone and drove on to the hilt, coming out the front just below Domo's ribs.

"It . . . hurts," Domo gasped.

"It is supposed to," Entreri replied, and he gave the sword a sudden jerk, and Domo gasped, and he died.

Entreri tore his blade free and rushed to retrieve his dagger. His thoughts were whirling now, as Domo's confirmation of some kind of an uprising within Bregan D'aerthe incited a plethora of questions. Domo had not been Jarlaxle's deceiver, nor was he in on the plotting against the mercenary leader—of that much, at least, Entreri was pretty sure. Yet it was Jarlaxle who had prompted this attack on Domo.

Or was it?

Wondering just how much the Crystal Shard was playing Jarlaxle's best interests against Jarlaxle, Artemis Entreri scrambled out of Calimport's sewers.

◄┼══┼►

"Beautiful," Rai-guy remarked to Kimmuriel, the two of them using a mirror of scrying to witness Artemis Entreri's return to House Basadoni. The wizard broke the connection almost immediately after, though, for the look upon the cunning assassin's face told him that Entreri might be sensing the scrying. "He unwittingly does our bidding. The wererats will stand against Jarlaxle now."

"Alas for Domo," Kimmuriel said, laughing. He stopped abruptly, though, and assumed a more serious demeanor. "But what of Entreri? He is formidable—even more so with that gauntlet and sword—and is too wise to believe that he would be better served in joining our cause. Perhaps we should eliminate him before turning our eyes toward Jarlaxle."

Rai-guy thought it over for just a moment, and nodded his agreement. "It must come from a lesser," he said. "From Sharlotta and her minions, perhaps, as they will be little involved in the greater coup."

"Jarlaxle would not be pleased if he came to understand that we were going against Entreri," Kimmuriel agreed. "Sharlotta, then, and not as a straightforward command. I will plant the thought in her that Entreri is trying to eliminate her."

"If she came to believe that, she would likely simply run away," Rai-guy remarked.

"She is too full of pride for that," Kimmuriel came back. "I will also make it clear to her, subtly and through other sources, that Entreri is not in the favor of many of Bregan D'aerthe, that even Jarlaxle has grown tired of his independence. If she believes that Entreri stands alone in some vendetta or rivalry against her, and that she can utilize the veritable army at her disposal to destroy him, then she will not run but will strike and strike hard." He gave another laugh. "Though unlike you, Rai-guy, I am not so certain that Sharlotta and all of House Basadoni will be able to get the job done."

"They will keep him occupied and out of our way, at least," Rai-guy replied. "Once we have finished with Jarlaxle . . ."

"Entreri will likely be far gone," Kimmuriel observed, "running as Morik has run. Perhaps we should see to Morik, if for no other reason than to hold him up as an example to Artemis Entreri."

Rai-guy shook his head, apparently recognizing that he and Kimmuriel had far more pressing problems than the disposition of a minor deserter in a faraway and insignificant city. "Artemis Entreri cannot run far enough away," he said determinedly. "He is far too great a nuisance for me ever to forget him or forgive him."

Kimmuriel thought that statement might be a bit extravagant, but in essence, he agreed with the sentiment. Perhaps Entreri's greatest crime was his own ability, the drow psionicist mused. Perhaps his rise above the standards of humans alone was the insult that so sparked hatred in Rai-guy and in Kimmuriel. The psionicist, and the wizard as well, were wise enough to appreciate that truth.

But that didn't make things any easier for Artemis Entreri.

CHAPTER

12

Layer after layer!" Entreri raged. He pounded his fist on the small table in the back room of the Copper Ante. It was still the one place in Calimport where he could feel reasonably secure from the ever-prying eyes of Rai-guy and Kimmuriel—and how often he had felt those eyes watching him of late! "So many layers that they roll back onto each other in a never-ending loop!"

Dwahvel Tiggerwillies leaned back in her chair and studied the man curiously. In all the years she had known Artemis Entreri, she had never seen him so animated or so angry—and when Artemis Entreri was angry, those anywhere in the vicinity of the assassin did well to take extreme care. Even more surprising to the halfling was the fact that Entreri was so angry so soon after killing the hated Domo. Usually killing a wererat put him in a better mood for a day at least. Dwahvel could understand his frustration, though. The man was dealing with dark elves, and though Dwahvel had little real knowledge of the intricacies of drow culture, she had witnessed enough to understand that the dark elves were the masters of intrigue and deception.

"Too many layers," Entreri said more calmly, his rage played out. He turned to Dwahvel and shook his head. "I am lost within the web within the web. I hardly know what is real anymore."

"You are still alive," Dwahvel offered. "I would guess, then, that you are doing something right."

"I fear that I erred greatly in killing Domo," Entreri admitted, shaking his head. "I have never been fond of wererats, but this time, perhaps, I should have let him live, if only to provide some opposition to the growing conspiracy against Jarlaxle."

"You do not even know if Domo and his wretched, lying companions were speaking truthfully when they uttered words about the drow conspiracy," Dwahvel reminded. "They may have been doing that as misinformation that you would take back to Jarlaxle, thus bringing about a rift in Bregan D'aerthe. Or Domo might have been sputtering for the sake of saving his own head. He knows your relationship with Jarlaxle and understands that you are better off as long as Jarlaxle is in command."

Entreri just stared at her. Domo knew all of that? Of course he did, the assassin told himself. As much as he hated the wererat, he could not dismiss the creature's cunning in controlling that most difficult of guilds.

"It is irrelevant anyway," Dwahvel went on. "We both know that the ratmen will be minor players at best in any internal struggles of Bregan D'aerthe. If Rai-guy and Kimmuriel start a coup, Domo and his kin would do little to dissuade them."

Entreri shook his head again, thoroughly frustrated by it all. Alone he believed that he could outfight or out-think any drow, but they were not alone, were never alone. Because of that harmony of movement within the band's cliques, Entreri could not be certain of the truth of anything. The addition of the Crystal Shard was merely compounding matters, blurring the truth about the source of the coup—if there was a coup—and making the assassin honestly wonder if Jarlaxle was in charge or was merely a slave to the sentient artifact. As much as Entreri knew that Jarlaxle would protect him, he understood that the Crystal Shard would want him dead.

"You dismiss all that you once learned," Dwahvel remarked, her voice soothing and calm. "The drow play no games beyond those that Pasha Pook once played—or Pasha Basadoni, or any of the others, or all of the others together. Their dance is the same as has been going on in Calimport for centuries."

"But the drow are better dancers."

Dwahvel smiled and nodded, conceding the point. "But is not the solution the same?" she asked. "When all is a facade. . . ." She let the words hang out in the air, one of the basic truths of the streets, and one that Artemis Entreri surely knew as well as anyone. "When all is a facade . . . ?" she said again, prompting him.

Entreri forced himself to calm down, forced himself to dismiss the overblown respect, even fear, he had been developing toward the dark elves, particularly toward Rai-guy and Kimmuriel. "In such situations, when layer is put upon layer," he recited, a basic lesson for all bright prospects within the guild structures, "when all is a facade, wound within webs of deception, the truth is what you make of it."

Dwahvel nodded. "You will know which path is real, because that is the path you will make real," she agreed. "Nothing pains a liar more than when an opponent turns one of his lies into truth."

Entreri nodded his agreement, and indeed he felt better. He knew that he would, which was why he had slipped out of House Basadoni after sensing that he was being watched and had gone straight to the Copper Ante.

"Do you believe Domo?" the halfling asked.

Entreri considered it for a moment, and nodded. "The hourglass has been turned, and the sand is flowing," he stated. "Have you the information I requested?"

Dwahvel reached under the low dust ruffle of the chair in which she was sitting and pulled out a portfolio full of parchments. "Cadderly," she said, handing them over.

"What of the other item?"

Again the halfling's hand went down low, this time producing a small sack identical to the one Jarlaxle now carried on his belt, and,

Entreri knew without even looking, containing a block of crystal similar in appearance to Crenshinibon.

Entreri took it with some trepidation, for it was, to him, the final and irreversible acknowledgment that he was indeed about to embark upon a very dangerous course, perhaps the most dangerous road he had ever walked in all his life.

"There is no magic about it," Dwahvel assured him, noting his concerned expression. "Just a mystical aura I ordered included so that it would replicate the artifact to any cursory magical inspection."

Entreri nodded and hooked the pouch on his belt, behind his hip so that it would be completely concealed by his cloak.

"We could just get you out of the city," Dwahvel offered. "It would have been far cheaper to hire a wizard to teleport you far, far away."

Entreri chuckled at the thought. It was one that had crossed his mind a thousand times since Bregan D'aerthe had come to Calimport, but one that he had always dismissed. How far could he run? Not farther than Rai-guy and Kimmuriel could follow, he understood.

"Stay close to him," Dwahvel warned. "When it happens, you will have to be the quicker."

Entreri nodded and started to rise, but paused and stared hard at Dwahvel. She honestly cared how he managed in this conflict, he realized, and the truth of that—that Dwahvel's concern for him had little to do with her own personal gain—struck him profoundly. It showed him something he'd not known often in his miserable existence—a friend.

He didn't leave the Copper Ante right away but went into an adjoining room and began ruffling through the reams of information that Dwahvel had collected on the priest, Cadderly. Would this man be the answer to Jarlaxle's dilemma and thus Entreri's own?

Frustration more than anything else guided Jarlaxle's movements as he made his swift way back to Dallabad, using a variety of magical items to facilitate his silent and unseen passage, but not—pointedly not—calling upon the Crystal Shard for any assistance.

This was it, the drow leader realized, the true test of his newest partnership. It had struck Jarlaxle that perhaps the Crystal Shard had been gaining too much the upper hand in their relationship, and so he had decided to set the matter straight.

He meant to take down the crystalline tower.

Crenshinibon knew it, too. Jarlaxle could feel the artifact's unhappy pulsing in his pouch, and he wondered if the powerful item might force a desperate showdown of willpower, one in which there could emerge only one victor.

Jarlaxle was ready for that. He was always willing to share in responsibility and decision-making, as long as it eventually led to the achievement of his own goals. Lately, though, he'd come to sense, the Crystal Shard seemed to be altering those very goals. It seemed to be bending him more and more in directions not of his choosing.

Soon after the sun had set, a very dark Calimshan evening, Jarlaxle stood before the crystalline tower, staring hard at it. He strengthened his resolve and mentally bolstered himself for the struggle that he knew would inevitably ensue. With a final glance around to make certain that no one was nearby, he reached into his pouch and took out the sentient artifact.

No! Crenshinibon screamed in his thoughts, the shard obviously knowing exactly what it was the dark elf meant to do. *I forbid this. The towers are a manifestation of my—of our strength and indeed heighten that strength. To destroy one is forbidden!*

Forbidden? Jarlaxle echoed skeptically.

It is not in the best interests of—

I decide what is in my best interests, Jarlaxle strongly interrupted. *And now it is in my interest to tear down this tower.* He focused all his mental energies into a singular and powerful command to the Crystal Shard.

And so it began, a titanic, if silent, struggle of willpower. Jarlaxle, with his centuries of accumulated knowledge and perfected cunning, was pitted squarely against the ages-old dweomer that was the Crystal Shard. Within seconds of the battle, Jarlaxle felt his will bend backward, as if the artifact meant to break his mind completely. It seemed to him as if every fear he had ever harbored in every dark corner of his imagination had become real, stalking inexorably toward his thoughts, his memories, his very identity.

How naked he felt! How open to the darts and slings of the mighty Crystal Shard!

Jarlaxle composed himself and worked very hard to separate the images, to single out each horrid manifestation and isolate it from the others. Then, focusing as much as he possibly could on that one vividly imagined horror, he counterattacked, using feelings of empowerment and strength, calling upon all of those many, many experiences he had weathered to become this leader of Bregan D'aerthe, this male dark elf who had for so long thrived in the matriarchal hell that was Menzoberranzan.

One after another the nightmares fell before him. As his internal struggles began to subside, Jarlaxle sent his willpower out of his inner mind, out to the artifact, issuing that singular, powerful command:

Tear down the crystalline tower!

Now came the coercion, the images of glory, of armies falling before fields of crystalline towers, of kings coming to him on their knees, bearing the treasures of their kingdoms, of the Matron Mothers of Menzoberranzan anointing him as permanent ruler of their council, speaking of him in terms previously reserved for Lady Lolth herself.

This second manipulation was, in many ways, even more difficult for Jarlaxle to control and defeat. He could not deny the allure of the images. More importantly, he could not deny the possibilities for Bregan D'aerthe and for him, given the added might that was the Crystal Shard.

He felt his resolve slipping away, a compromise reached that would allow Crenshinibon and Jarlaxle both to find all they desired.

He was ready to release the artifact from his command, to admit the ridiculousness of tearing down the tower, to give in and reform their undeniably profitable alliance.

But he remembered.

This was no partnership, for the Crystal Shard was no partner, no real, controllable, replaceable and predictable partner. No, Jarlaxle reminded himself. It was an artifact, an enchanted item, and though sentient it was a created intelligence, a method of reasoning based upon a set and predetermined goal. In this case, apparently, its goal was the acquisition of as many followers and as much power as its magic would allow.

While Jarlaxle could sympathize, even agree with that goal, he reminded himself pointedly and determinedly that he would have to be the one in command. He fought back against the temptations, denied the Crystal Shard its manipulations as he had beaten back its brute force attack in the beginning of the struggle.

He felt it, as tangible as a snapping rope, a click in his mind that gave him his answer.

Jarlaxle was the master. His were the decisions that would guide Bregan D'aerthe and command the Crystal Shard.

He knew then, without the slightest bit of doubt, that the tower was his to destroy, and so he led the shard again to that command. This time, Jarlaxle felt no anger, no denial, no recriminations, only sadness.

The beaten artifact began to hum with the energies needed to deconstruct its large magical replica.

Jarlaxle opened his eyes and smiled with satisfaction. The fight had been everything he had feared it would be, but in the end, he knew without doubt he had triumphed. He felt the tingling as the essence of the crystalline tower began to weaken. Its binding energy would be stolen away. Then the material bound together by Crenshinibon's magic would dissipate to the winds. The way he commanded it—and he knew that Crenshinibon could comply— there would be no explosions, no crashing walls, just fading away.

Jarlaxle nodded, as satisfied as with any victory he had ever known in his long life of struggles.

He pictured Dallabad without the tower and wondered what new spies would then show up to determine where the tower had gone, why it had been there in the first place, and if Ahdahnia was, therefore, still in charge.

"Stop!" he commanded the artifact. "The tower remains, by *my* word."

The humming stopped immediately and the Crystal Shard, seeming very humbled, went quiet in Jarlaxle's thoughts.

Jarlaxle smiled even wider. Yes, he would keep the tower, and he decided in the morning he would construct a second one beside the first. The twin towers of Dallabad. Jarlaxle's twin towers.

At least two.

For now the mercenary leader did not fear those towers, nor the source that had inspired him to erect the first one. No, he had won the day and could use the mighty Crystal Shard to bring him to new heights of power.

And Jarlaxle knew it would never threaten him again.

Artemis Entreri paced the small room he had rented in a non-descript inn far from House Basadoni and any of the other street guilds. On a small table to the side of the bed was his black, red-stitched gauntlet, with Charon's Claw lying right beside it, the red blade gleaming in the candlelight.

Entreri was not certain of this at all. He wondered what the innkeeper might think if he came in later to find Entreri's skull-headed corpse smoldering on the floor.

It was a very real possibility, the assassin reminded himself. Every time he used Charon's Claw, it showed him a new twist, a new trick, and he understood sentient magic well enough to understand that the more powers such a sword possessed, the greater its willpower. Entreri had already seen the result of a defeat in a willpower battle with this particularly nasty sword. He could picture the horrible end of Kohrin Soulez as vividly as if it had happened that very morning, the man's facial skin rolling up from his bones as it melted away.

But he had to do this and now. He would soon be going against the Crystal Shard, and woe to him if, at that time, he was still waging any kind of mental battle against his own sword. With just that fear in mind, he had even contemplated selling the sword or hiding it away somewhere, but as he considered his other likely enemies, Rai-guy and Kimmuriel, he realized that he had to keep it.

He had to keep it, and he had to dominate it completely. There could be no other way.

Entreri walked toward the table, rubbing his hands together, then bringing them up to his lips, and blowing into them.

He turned around before he reached the sword, thinking, thinking, seeking some alternative. He wondered again if he could sell the vicious blade or hand it over to Dwahvel to lock in a deep hole until after the dark elves had left Calimport and he could, perhaps, return.

That last thought, of being chased from the city by Jarlaxle's wretched lieutenants, fired a sudden anger in the assassin, and he strode determinedly over to the table. Before he could again consider the potential implications, he growled and reached over, snapping up Charon's Claw in his bare hand.

He felt the immediate tug—not a physical tug, but something

deeper, something going to the essence of Artemis Entreri, the spirit of the man. The sword was hungry—how he could feel that hunger! It wanted to consume him, to obliterate his very essence simply because he was bold enough, or foolish enough, to grasp it without that protective gauntlet.

Oh, how it wanted him!

He felt a twitching in his cheek, an excitement upon his skin, and wondered if he would combust. Entreri forced that notion away and concentrated again on winning the mental battle.

The sentient sword pulled and pulled, relentlessly, and Entreri could hear something akin to laughter in his head, a supreme confidence that reminded him that Charon's Claw would not tire, but he surely would. Another thought came, the realization that he could not even let go of the weapon if he chose to, that he had locked in this combat and there could be no turning back, no surrender.

That was the ploy of the devilish sword, to impart a sense of complete hopelessness on the part of anyone challenging it, to tell the challenger, in no uncertain terms, that the fight would be to the bitter and disastrous end. For so many before Entreri, such a message had resulted in a breaking of the spirit that the sword had used as a springboard to complete its victory.

But with Entreri, the ploy only brought forth greater feelings of rage, a red wall of determined and focused anger and denial.

"You are mine!" the assassin growled through gritted teeth. "You are a possession, a thing, a piece of beaten metal!" He lifted the gleaming red blade before him and commanded it to bring forth its black light.

It did not comply. The sword kept attacking Entreri as it had attacked Kohrin Soulez, trying to defeat him mentally that it might burn away his skin, trying to consume him as it had so many before him.

"You are mine," he said again, his voice calm now, for while the sword had not relented its attack, Entreri's confidence that he could fend that attack began to rise.

He felt a sudden sting within him, a burning sensation as Charon's Claw threw all of its energy into him. Rather than deny it he welcomed that energy and took it from the sword. It mounted to a vibrating crescendo and broke apart.

The black light appeared in the small room, and Entreri's smile gleamed widely within it. The light was confirmation that Entreri had overwhelmed Charon's Claw, that the sword was indeed his now. He lowered the blade, taking several deep breaths to steady himself, trying not to consider the fact that he had just come back from the very precipice of obliteration.

That did not matter anymore. He had beaten the sword, had broken the sword's spirit, and it belonged to him now as surely as did the jeweled dagger he wore on his other hip. Certainly he would ever after have to take some measure of care that Charon's Claw would try to break free of him, but that was, at most, a cursory inconvenience.

"You are mine," he said again, calmly, and he commanded the sword to dismiss the black light.

The room was again bathed in only candlelight. Charon's Claw, the sword of Artemis Entreri, offered no arguments.

Jarlaxle *thought* he knew. Jarlaxle *thought* that he had won the day.

Because Crenshinibon made him think that. Because Crenshinibon wanted the battle between the mercenary leader and his upstart lieutenants to be an honest one, so that it could then determine which would be the better wielder.

The Crystal Shard still favored Rai-guy, because it knew that drow to be more ambitious and more willing, even eager, to kill.

But the possibilities here with Jarlaxle did not escape the artifact. Turning him within the layers of deception had been no easy thing, but indeed, Crenshinibon had taken Jarlaxle exactly to that spot where it had desired he go.

At dawn the very next morning, a second crystalline tower was erected at Dallabad Oasis.

CHAPTER

13

Y̶ou understand your role in every contingency?" Entreri asked Dwahvel at their next meeting, an impromptu affair conducted in the alley beside the Copper Ante, an area equally protected from divining wizards by Dwahvel's potent anti-spying resources.

"In every contingency that you have outlined," the halfling replied with a warning smirk.

"Then you understand every contingency," Entreri answered without hesitation. He returned her grin with one of complete confidence.

"You have thought *every* possibility through?" the halfling asked doubtfully. "These are dark elves, the masters of manipulation and intrigue, the makers of the layers of their own reality and of the rules within that layered reality."

"And they are not in their homeland and do not understand the nuances of Calimport," Entreri assured her. "They view the whole world as an extension of Menzoberranzan, an extension in temperament, and more importantly, in how they measure the reactions of those around them. I am *iblith*, thus inferior, and thus, they will not expect the turn their version of reality is about to take."

"The time has come?" Dwahvel asked, still doubtfully. "Or are you bringing the critical moment upon us?"

"I have never been a patient man," Entreri admitted, and his wicked grin did not dissipate with the admission but intensified.

"Every contingency," Dwahvel remarked, "thus every layer of the reality you intend to create. Beware, my competent friend, that you do not get lost somewhere in the mixture of your realities."

Entreri started to scowl but held back the negative thoughts, recognizing that Dwahvel was offering him sensible advice here, that he was playing a most dangerous game with the most dangerous foes he had ever known. Even in the best of circumstances, Artemis Entreri realized that his success, and therefore his very life, would hang on the movements of a split second and would be forfeited by the slightest turn of bad luck. This culminating scenario was not the precision strike of the trained assassin but the desperate move of a cornered man.

Still, when he looked at his halfling friend, Entreri's confidence and resolve were bolstered. He knew that Dwahvel would not disappoint him in this, that she would hold up her end of the reality-making process.

"If you succeed, I'll not see you again," the halfling remarked. "And if you fail, I'll likely not be able to find your blasted and torn corpse."

Entreri took the blunt words for the offering of affection that he knew they truly were. His smile was wide and genuine—so rare a thing for the assassin.

"You will see me again," he told Dwahvel. "The drow will grow weary of Calimport and will recede back to their sunless holes where they truly belong. Perhaps it will happen in months, perhaps in years, but they will eventually go. That is their nature. Rai-guy and Kimmuriel understand that there is no long-term benefit for them or for Bregan D'aerthe in expanding any trading business on the surface. Discovery would mean all-out war. That is the main focus of their ire with Jarlaxle, after all. So they will go, but you will remain, and I will return."

"Even if the drow do not kill you now, am I to believe that your road will be any less dangerous once you're gone?" the halfling asked with a snort that ended in a grin. "Is there any such road for Artemis Entreri? Not likely, I say. Indeed, with your new weapon and that defensive gauntlet, you will likely take on the assassinations of prominent wizards as your chosen profession. And, of course, eventually one of those wizards will understand the truth of your new toys and their limitations, and he will leave you a charred and smoking husk." She chuckled and shook her head. "Yes, go after Khelben, Vangerdahast, or Elminster himself. At least your death will be painlessly quick."

"I did say I was not a patient man," Entreri agreed.

To his surprise, and to the halfling's as well, Dwahvel then rushed up to him and leaped upon him, wrapping him in a hug. She broke free quickly and backed away, composing herself.

"For luck and nothing more," she said. "Of course I prefer your victory to that of the dark elves."

"If only the dark elves," Entreri said, needing to keep this conversation lighthearted.

He knew what awaited him. It would be a brutal test of his skills—of all of his skills—and of his nerve. He walked the very edge of disaster. Again, he reminded himself that he could indeed count on the reliability of one Dwahvel Tiggerwillies, that most competent of halflings. He looked at her hard then and understood that she was going to play along with his last remark, was not going to give him the satisfaction of disagreeing, of admitting that she considered him a friend.

Artemis Entreri would have been disappointed in her if she had.

"Beware that you do not catch yourself within the very layers of lies that you have perpetrated," Dwahvel said after the assassin as he started away, already beginning to blend seamlessly into the shadows.

Entreri took those words to heart. The potential combinations of the possible events was indeed staggering. Improvisation alone might

keep him alive in this critical time, and Entreri had survived the
entirety of his life on the very edge of disaster. He had been forced to
rely on his wits, on complete improvisation, dozens of times, scores
of times, and had somehow managed to survive. In his mind, he
held contingency plans to counter every foreseeable event. While he
kept confidence in himself and in those he had placed strategically
around him, he did not for one moment dismiss the fact that if one
eventuality materialized that he had not counted on, if one wrong
turn appeared before him and he could not find a way around that
bend, he would die.

And, given the demeanor of Rai-guy, he would die horribly.

The street was busy, as were most of the avenues in Calimport, but
the most remarkable person on it seemed the most unremarkable.
Artemis Entreri, wearing the guise of a beggar, kept to the shadows,
not moving suspiciously from one to another, but blending invisibly
against the backdrop of the bustling street.

His movements were not without purpose. He kept his prey in
sight at every moment.

Sharlotta Vespers attempted no such anonymity as she moved
along the thoroughfare. She was the recognized figurehead of House
Basadoni, walking bidden into the domain of dangerous Pasha
Da'Daclan. Many suspicious, even hateful eyes cast more than the
occasional glance her way, but none would move against her. She had
requested the meeting with Da'Daclan, on orders from Rai-guy, and
had been accepted under his protection. Thus, she walked now with
the guise of complete confidence, bordering on bravado.

She didn't seem to realize that one of those watching her, shadow-
ing her, was not under any orders from Pasha Da'Daclan.

Entreri knew this area well, for he had worked for the Rakers on
several occasions in the past. Sharlotta's demeanor told him without

doubt that she was coming for a formal parlay. Soon enough, as she passed one potential meeting area after another, he was able to deduce exactly where that meeting would take place. What he did not know, however, was how important this meeting might be to Rai-guy and Kimmuriel.

"Are you watching her every step with your strange mind powers, Kimmuriel?" he asked quietly

His mind worked through the contingency plans he had to keep available should that be the case. He didn't believe that the two drow, busy with planning of their own, no doubt, would be monitoring Sharlotta's every move, but it was certainly possible. If that came to pass, Entreri realized that he would know it, in no uncertain terms, very soon. He could only hope that he'd be ready and able to properly adjust his course.

He moved more quickly then, outpacing the woman by taking the side alleys, even climbing to one roof, and scrambling across to another and to another.

Soon after, he reached the house bordering the alley he believed Sharlotta would turn down, a suspicion only heightened by the fact that a sentry was in position on that very roof, overlooking the alley on the far side.

As silent as death, Entreri moved into position behind the sentry, with the man's attention obviously focused on the alleyway and completely oblivious to him. Working carefully, for he knew that others would be about, Entreri spent some amount of time casing the entire area, locating the two sentries on the rooftops across the way and one other on this side of the alley, on the adjoining roof of a building immediately behind the one Entreri now stood upon.

He watched those three more than the man directly in front of him, measured their every movement, their every turn of the head. Most of all, he gauged their focus. Finally, when he was certain that they were not attentive, the assassin struck, yanking his victim back behind a dormer.

A moment later, all four of Pasha Da'Daclan's sentries seemed in place once more, all of them honestly intent on the alleyway below as Sharlotta Vespers, a pair of Da'Daclan's guards at her back, turned into the alleyway.

Entreri's thoughts whirled. Five enemy soldiers, and a supposed comrade who seemed more of an enemy than the others. He didn't delude himself into thinking that these five were alone. Da'Daclan's stooges probably included a significant portion of the scores of people milling about on the main avenue.

Entreri went anyway, rolling over the edge of the roof of the two-story building, catching hold with his hand, stretching to his limit, and dropping agilely to the surprised Sharlotta's side.

"A trap," he whispered harshly, and he turned to face the two soldiers following her and held up his hand for them to halt. "Kimmuriel has a dimensional portal in place for our escape on the roof."

Sharlotta's facial expression went from surprise to anger to calm so quickly, each one buried in her practiced manner, that only Entreri caught the range of expressions. He knew that he had her befuddled, that his mention of Kimmuriel had given credence to his outlandish claim that this was a trap.

"I will take her from here," Entreri said to the guards. He heard movement farther along and across the alley, as two of the other three sentries, including the one on the same side of the alley as Entreri, came down to see what was going on.

"Who are you?" one of the soldiers following Sharlotta asked skeptically, his hand going inside his common traveling cloak to the hilt of a finely crafted sword.

"Go," Entreri whispered to Sharlotta.

The woman hesitated, so Entreri prompted her retreat in no uncertain terms. Out came the jeweled dagger and Charon's Claw, the assassin throwing back his cloak, revealing himself in all his splendor. He leaped forward, slashing with his sword and thrusting with his dagger at the second soldier.

Out came the swords in response. One picked off the swipe of Charon's Claw, but with the man inevitably retreating as he parried. That had been Entreri's primary goal. The second soldier, though, had less fortune. As his sword came forth to parry, Entreri gave a subtle twist of his wrist and looped his dagger over the blade, then thrust it home into the man's belly.

With others closing fast, the assassin couldn't follow through with the kill, but he did hold the strike long enough to bring forth the dagger's life-stealing energies to let the man know the purest horror he could ever imagine. The soldier wasn't really badly wounded, but he fell away to the ground, clutching his belly and howling in terror.

The assassin broke back, turning away from the wall where Sharlotta Vespers was scrambling to gain the roof.

The one who had fallen back from the sword slash came at Entreri from the left. Another came from the right, and two rushed across the alleyway, coming straight in. Entreri started right, sword leading, then turned back fast to the left. Even as the four began to compensate for the change—a change that was not completely unexpected—the assassin turned back fast to the right, charging in hard just as that soldier had begun to accelerate in pursuit.

The soldier found himself in a flurry of slashing and stabbing. He worked his own blades, a sword and dirk, quite well. The soldier was no novice to battle, but this was Artemis Entreri. Whenever the man moved to parry, Entreri altered the angle. His fury kept the ring of metal in the air for a long few seconds, but the dagger slipped through, gashing the soldier's right arm. As that limb drooped, Entreri went into a spin, Charon's Claw coming around fast to pick off a thrust from the man coming in at his back, then continuing through, over the wounded man's lowered defense, slashing him hard across the chest.

Also on that maneuver, Entreri's devilish sword trailed out the black ash wall. The line was horizontal, not vertical, so that ash did not impede the vision of his adversaries, but still the mere sight of it hanging there in midair gave them enough pause for Entreri to dispatch the man who had come in on his right. Then the assassin went into a wild flurry, sword waving and bringing up an opaque wall.

The remaining three soldiers settled back behind it, confused and trying to put some coordination into their movements. When at last they mustered the nerve to charge through the ash wall, they discovered that the assassin was nowhere to be found.

Entreri watched them from the rooftop, shaking his head at their ineptness, and also at the little values offered by this wondrous sword—a weapon to which he was growing more fond with each battle.

"Where is it?" Sharlotta called to him from across the way.

Entreri looked at her quizzically.

"The doorway?" Sharlotta asked. "Where is it?"

"Perhaps Da'Daclan has interfered," Entreri replied, trying to hide his satisfaction that apparently Rai-guy and Kimmuriel were not closely monitoring Sharlotta's movements. "Or perhaps they decided to leave us," he added, figuring that if he could throw a bit of doubt into Sharlotta Vespers' view of the world and her dark elven compatriots, then so be it.

Sharlotta merely scowled at that disturbing thought.

Noise from behind told them that the soldiers in the alleyway weren't giving up and reminded them that they were on hostile territory here. Entreri ran past Sharlotta, motioning for her to follow, then made the leap across the next alleyway to another building, then to a third, then down and out the back end of an alley, and finally, down into the sewers—a place that Entreri wasn't thrilled about entering at that time, given his recent assassination of Domo. He didn't remain underground for long, coming up in the more familiar territory beyond Da'Daclan's territory and closer to the Basadoni guild house.

Still leading, Entreri made his way along at a swift pace until he reached the alleyway beside the Copper Ante, where he abruptly stopped.

Seeming more angry than grateful, obviously doubting the sincerity of the escape and the very need for it, Sharlotta continued past, hardly glancing his way.

Until the assassin's sword came out and settled in front of her neck. "I think not," he remarked.

Sharlotta glanced sidelong at him, and he motioned for her to head down the alley beside Dwahvel's establishment.

"What is this?" the woman asked.

"Your only chance at continuing to draw breath," Entreri replied. When she still didn't move, he grabbed her by the arm, and with frightening strength yanked her in front of him heading down the alley. He pointedly reminded her to keep going, prodding her with his sword.

They came to a tiny room, having entered through a secret alley entrance. The room held a single chair, into which Entreri none-too-gently shoved Sharlotta.

"Have you lost what little sense you once possessed?" the woman asked.

"Am I the one bargaining secret deals with dark elves?" Entreri replied, and the look Sharlotta gave him in the instant before she found her control told him volumes about the truth of his suspicions.

"We have both been dealing as need be," the woman indignantly answered.

"Dealing? Or double-dealing? There is a difference, even with dark elves."

"You speak the part of a fool," snapped Sharlotta.

"Yet you are the one closer to death," Entreri reminded, and he came in very close, now with his jeweled dagger in hand, and a look on his face that told Sharlotta that he was certainly not bluffing here. Sharlotta knew well the life-stealing powers of that horrible dagger. "Why were you going to meet with Pasha Da'Daclan?" Entreri asked bluntly.

"The change at Dallabad has raised suspicions," the woman answered, an honest and obvious—if obviously incomplete—response.

"No suspicions that trouble Jarlaxle, apparently," Entreri reasoned.

"But some that could turn to serious trouble," Sharlotta went on, and Entreri knew that she was improvising here. "I was to meet with Pasha Da'Daclan to assure him the situation on the streets, and elsewhere, will calm to normal."

"That any expansion by House Basadoni is at its end?" Entreri asked doubtfully. "Would you not be lying, though, and would that not invite even greater wrath when the next conquest falls before Jarlaxle?"

"The next?"

"Have you come to believe that our suddenly ambitious leader means to stop?" Entreri asked.

Sharlotta spent a long while mulling that one over. "I have been told that House Basadoni will begin pulling back, to all appearances, at least," she said. "As long as we encounter no further outside influences."

"Like the spies at Dallabad," Entreri agreed.

Sharlotta nodded—a bit too eagerly, Entreri thought.

"Then Jarlaxle's hunger is at last sated, and we can get back to a quieter and safer routine," the assassin remarked.

Sharlotta did not respond.

Entreri's lips curled up into a smile. He knew the truth of it, of course, that Sharlotta had just blatantly lied to him. He would never have put it past Jarlaxle to have played such opposing games with his underlings in days past, leading Entreri in one direction and Sharlotta in another, but he knew that the mercenary leader was in the throes of Crenshinibon's hunger now, and given the information supplied by Dwahvel, he understood the truth of that. It was a truth very different from the lie Sharlotta had just outlined.

Sharlotta, by going to Da'Daclan and claiming that Jarlaxle had been behind the meeting, which meant that Rai-guy and Kimmuriel certainly had been, confirmed to Entreri that time was indeed running short.

He stepped back and paused, digesting all of the information, trying to reason when and where the actual in-fighting might occur. He noted, too, that Sharlotta was watching him very carefully.

Sharlotta moved with the grace and speed of a hunting cat, rolling off the chair to one knee, drawing and throwing a dagger at Entreri's heart, and bolting for the room's other, less remarkable doorway.

Entreri caught the dagger in midflight, turned it over in his hand and hurled it into that door with a thump, to stick, quivering, before Sharlotta's widening eyes.

He grabbed her and turned her roughly around, hitting her with a heavy punch across the face.

She drew out another dagger—or tried to. Entreri caught her wrist even as it came out of its concealed sheath, turning a quick spin under the arm and tugging so violently that all of Sharlotta's strength left her hand and the dagger fell harmlessly to the floor. Entreri tugged again, and let go. He leaped around in front of the woman, slapping her twice across the face, and grabbed her hard by the shoulders. He ran her backward, to crash back into the chair.

"Do you not even understand those with whom you play these foolish games?" he growled in her face. "They will use you to their advantage, and discard you. In their eyes you are *iblith*, a word that means "not drow," a word that also means offal. Those two, Rai-guy and Kimmuriel, are the greatest racists among Jarlaxle's lieutenants. You will find no gain beside them, Sharlotta the Fool, only horrible death."

"And what of Jarlaxle?" she cried out in response.

It was just the sort of instinctive, emotional explosion the assassin had been counting on. There it was, as clear as it could be, an admission that Sharlotta had fallen into league with two would-be kings of Bregan D'aerthe. He moved back from her, just a bit, leaving her ruffled in the chair.

"I offer you one chance," he said to her. "Not out of any favorable feelings I might hold toward you, because there are none, but because you have something I need."

Sharlotta straightened her shirt and tunic and tried to regain some of her dignity.

"Tell me everything," Entreri said bluntly. "All of this coup—when, where, and how. I know more than you believe, so try none of your foolish games with me."

Sharlotta smirked at him doubtfully. "You know nothing," she replied. "If you did, you'd know you've come to play the role of the idiot."

Even as the last word left her mouth, Entreri was there, back against her, one hand roughly grabbing her hair and yanking her head back, the other, holding his awful dagger point in at her exposed throat. "Last chance," he said, so very calmly. "And do remember that I do not like you, dearest Sharlotta."

The woman swallowed hard, her eyes locked onto Entreri's deadly gaze.

Entreri's reputation heightened the threat reflected in his eyes to the point where Sharlotta, with nothing to lose and no reason for loyalty to the dark elves, spilled all she knew of the entire plan, even the method Rai-guy and Kimmuriel planned to use to incapacitate the Crystal Shard—some kind of mind magic transformed into a lantern.

None of it came as any surprise to Entreri, of course. Still, hearing the words spoken openly did bring a shock to him, a reminder of how precarious his position truly had become. He quietly muttered his litany of creating his own reality within the strands of the layered web and reminded himself repeatedly that he was every bit the player as were his two opponents.

He moved away from Sharlotta to the inner door. He pulled free the stuck dagger and banged hard three times on the door. It opened a few moments later and a very surprised looking Dwahvel Tiggerwillies bounded into the room.

"Why have you come?" she started to ask of Entreri, but she stopped, her gaze caught by the ruffled Sharlotta. Again she turned to Entreri, this time her expression one of surprise and anger. "What have you done?" the halfling demanded of the assassin. "I'll play no part in any of the rivalries within House Basadoni!"

"You will do as you are instructed," the assassin replied coldly. "You will keep Sharlotta here as your comfortable but solitary guest until I return to permit her release."

"Permit?" Dwahvel asked doubtfully, turning from Entreri to Sharlotta. "What insanity have you brought upon me, fool?"

"The next insult will cost you your tongue," Entreri said coldly, perfectly playing the role. "You will do as I've instructed. Nothing more, nothing less. When this is finished, even Sharlotta will thank you for keeping her safe in times when none of us truly are."

Dwahvel stared hard at Sharlotta as Entreri spoke, making silent contact. The human woman gave the slightest nod of her head.

Dwahvel turned back to the assassin. "Out," she ordered.

Entreri looked to the alleyway door, so perfectly fitted that it was barely an outline on the wall.

"Not that way . . . it opens only in," Dwahvel said sourly, and she pointed to the conventional door. "That way." She moved up to him and pushed him along, out of the room, turning to close and lock the door behind them.

"It has come this far already?" Dwahvel asked when the two were safely down the corridor.

Entreri nodded grimly.

"But you are still on course for your plan?" Dwahvel asked. "Despite this unexpected turn?"

Entreri's smile reminded the halfling that nothing would be, or could be, unexpected.

Dwahvel nodded. "Logical improvisation," she remarked.

"You know your role," Entreri replied.

"And I thought I played it quite well," Dwahvel said with a smile.

"Too well," Entreri said to her as they reached another doorway farther along the wall up the alleyway. "I was not joking when I said I would take your tongue."

With that, he went out into the alley, leaving a shaken Dwahvel behind. After a moment, though, the halfling merely chuckled, doubting that Entreri would ever take her tongue, whatever insults she might throw his way.

Doubting, but not sure—never sure. That was the way of Artemis Entreri.

Entreri was out of the city before dawn, riding hard for Dallabad Oasis on a horse he'd borrowed without the owner's permission. He knew the road well. It was often congested with beggars and highwaymen. That knowledge didn't stop the assassin, though, didn't slow his swift ride one bit. When the sun rose over his left shoulder he only increased his pace, knowing that he had to get to Dallabad on time.

He'd told Dwahvel that Jarlaxle was back at the crystalline tower, where the assassin now had to go with all haste. Entreri knew the halfling would be prompt about her end of the plan. Once she released Sharlotta. . . .

Entreri put his head down and drove on in the growing morning sunlight. He was still miles away, but he could see the sharp focus at the top of the tower . . . no, towers, he realized, for he saw not one, but two pillars rising in the distance to meet the morning light.

He didn't know what that meant, of course, but he didn't worry about it. Jarlaxle was there, according to his many sources—informants independent of, and beyond the reach of Rai-guy and Kimmuriel and their many lackeys.

He sensed the scrying soon after and knew he was being watched. That only made the desperate assassin put his head down and drive the stolen horse on at greater speeds, determined to beat the brutal, self-imposed timetable.

"He goes to Jarlaxle with great haste, and we know not where Sharlotta Vespers has gone," Kimmuriel remarked to Rai-guy.

The two of them, along with Berg'inyon Baenre, watched the assassin's hard ride out from Calimport.

"Sharlotta may remain with Pasha Da'Daclan," Rai-guy replied. "We cannot know for certain."

"Then we should learn," said an obviously frustrated and nervous Kimmuriel.

Rai-guy looked at him. "Easy, my friend," he said. "Artemis Entreri is no threat to us but merely a nuisance. Better that all of the vermin gather together."

"A more complete and swift victory," Berg'inyon agreed.

Kimmuriel thought about it and held up a small square lantern, three sides shielded, the fourth open. Yharaskrik had given it to him with the assurance that, when Kimmuriel lit the candle and allowed its glow to fall over Crenshinibon, the powers of the Crystal Shard would be stunted. The effects would be temporary, the illithid had warned. Even confident Yharaskrik held no illusions that anything would hold the powerful artifact at bay for long.

But it wouldn't take long, Kimmuriel and the others knew, even if Artemis Entreri was at Jarlaxle's side. With the artifact shut down,

Jarlaxle's fall would be swift and complete, as would the fall of all of those, Entreri included, who stood beside him.

This day would be sweet indeed—or rather, this night. Rai-guy and Kimmuriel had planned to strike at night, when the powers of the Crystal Shard were at their weakest.

⊷═╪═⊶

"He is a fool, but one, I believe, acting on honest fears," Dwahvel Tiggerwillies said to Sharlotta when she joined the woman in the small room. "Find a bit of sympathy for him, I beg."

Sharlotta, the prisoner, looked at the halfling incredulously.

"Oh, he's gone now," said Dwahvel, "and so should you be."

"I thought I was your prisoner," the woman asked.

Dwahvel chuckled. "Forever and ever?" she asked with obvious sarcasm. "Artemis Entreri is afraid, and so you should be too. I know little about dark elves, I admit, but—"

"Dark elves?" Sharlotta echoed, feigning surprise and ignorance. "What has any of this to do with dark elves?"

Dwahvel laughed again. "The word is out," she said, "about Dallabad and House Basadoni. The power behind the throne is well-known around the streets."

Sharlotta started to mumble something about Entreri, but Dwahvel cut her short. "Entreri told me nothing," she explained. "Do you think I would need to deal with one as powerful as Entreri for such common information? I am many things, but I do not number fool among them."

The woman settled back in her chair, staring hard at the halfling. "You believe you know more than you really know," she said. "That is a dangerous mistake."

"I know only that I want no part of any of this," Dwahvel returned. "No part of House Basadoni or of Dallabad Oasis. No part of the feud between Sharlotta Vespers and Artemis Entreri."

"It would seem that you are already a part of that feud," the woman replied, her sparkling dark eyes narrowing.

Dwahvel shook her head. "I did and do as I had to do, nothing more," she said.

"Then I am free to leave?"

Dwahvel nodded and stood aside, leaving the path to the door open. "I came back here as soon as I was certain Entreri was long gone. Forgive me, Sharlotta, but I would not make of you an ally if doing so made Entreri an enemy."

Sharlotta continued to stare hard at the surprising halfling, but she couldn't argue with the logic of that statement. "Where has he gone?" she asked.

"Out of Calimport, my sources relay," Dwahvel answered. "To Dallabad, perhaps? Or long past the oasis—all the way along the road and out of Calimshan. I believe I might take that very route, were I Artemis Entreri."

Sharlotta didn't reply, but silently she agreed wholeheartedly. She was still confused by the recent events, but she recognized clearly that Entreri's supposed "rescue" of her was no more than a kidnapping of his own, so he could squeeze information out of her. And she had offered much, she understood to her apprehension. She had told him more than she should have, more than Rai-guy and Kimmuriel would likely find acceptable.

She left the Copper Ante trying to sort it all out. What she did know was that the dark elves would find her and likely soon. The woman nodded, recognizing the only real course left open before her, and started off with all speed for House Basadoni. She would tell Rai-guy and Kimmuriel of Entreri's treachery.

<hr>

Entreri looked at the sun hanging low in the eastern sky and took a deep, steadying breath. The time had passed. Dwahvel had released

Sharlotta, as arranged. The woman, no doubt, had run right to Rai-guy and Kimmuriel, thus setting into motion momentous events.

If the two dark elves were even still in Calimport.

If Sharlotta had not figured out the ruse within the kidnapping, and had gone off the other way, running for cover.

If the dark elves hadn't long ago found Sharlotta in the Copper Ante and leveled the place, in which case, Dallabad and the Crystal Shard might already be in Rai-guy's dangerous hands.

If, in learning of the discovery, Rai-guy and Kimmuriel hadn't just turned around and run back to Menzoberranzan.

If Jarlaxle still remained at Dallabad.

That last notion worried Entreri profoundly. The unpredictable Jarlaxle was, perhaps, the most volatile on a long list of unknowns. If Jarlaxle had left Dallabad, what trouble might he bring to every aspect of this plan? Would Kimmuriel and Rai-guy catch up to him unawares and slay him easily?

The assassin shook all of the doubts away. He wasn't used to feelings of self-doubt, even inadequacy. Perhaps that was why he so hated the dark elves. In Menzoberranzan, the ultimately capable Artemis Entreri had felt tiny indeed.

Reality is what you make of it, he reminded himself. He was the one weaving the layers of intrigue and deception here, so he—not Rai-guy and Kimmuriel, not Sharlotta, not even Jarlaxle and the Crystal Shard—was the one in command.

He looked at the sun again, and glanced to the side, to the imposing structures of the twin crystalline towers set among the palms of Dallabad, reminding himself that this time he, and no one else, had turned over that hourglass.

Reminding himself pointedly that the sand was running, that time was growing short, he kicked his horse's flanks and leaped away, galloping hard to the oasis.

CHAPTER

WHEN THE SAND RAN OUT

14

Entreri kept the notion that he had come to steal the Crystal Shard foremost in his mind. All he thought of was that he'd come to take it as his own, whatever the cost to Jarlaxle, though he made certain that he kept a bit of compassion evident whenever he thought of the mercenary leader. Entreri replayed that singular thought and purpose over and over again, suspecting that the artifact, in this place of its greatest power, would scan those thoughts.

Jarlaxle was waiting for him on the second floor of the tower in a round room sparsely adorned with two chairs and a small desk. The mercenary leader stood across the way, directly opposite the doorway through which Entreri entered. Jarlaxle put himself as far, Entreri noted, as he could be from the approaching assassin.

"Greetings," Entreri said.

Jarlaxle, curiously wearing no eye patch this day, tipped his broad-brimmed hat and asked, "Why have you come?"

Entreri looked at him as if surprised by the question, but turned the not-so-secret notion in his head to one appearing as an ironic twist: Why have I come indeed!

Jarlaxle's uncharacteristic scowl told the assassin that the Crystal Shard had heard those thoughts and had communicated them instantly to its wielder. No doubt, the artifact was now telling

Jarlaxle to dispose of Entreri, a suggestion the mercenary leader was obviously resisting.

"Your course is that of the fool," Jarlaxle remarked, struggling with the words as his internal battle heightened. "There is nothing here for you."

Entreri settled back on his heels, assuming a pensive posture. "Then perhaps I should leave," he said.

Jarlaxle didn't blink.

Hardly expecting one as cunning as Jarlaxle to be caught off guard, Entreri exploded into motion anyway, a forward dive and roll that brought him up in a run straight at his opponent.

Jarlaxle grabbed his belt pouch—he didn't even have to take the artifact out—and extended his other hand toward the assassin. Out shot a line of pure white energy.

Entreri caught it with his red-stitched gauntlet, took the energy in, and held it there. He held some of it, anyway, for it was too great a power to be completely held at bay. The assassin felt the pain, the intense agony, though he understood that only a small fraction of the shard's attack had gotten through.

How powerful was that item? he wondered, awestruck and thinking that he might be in serious trouble.

Afraid that the energy would melt the gauntlet or otherwise consume it, Entreri turned the magic right back out. He didn't throw it at Jarlaxle, for he hardly wanted to kill the drow. Entreri loosed it on the wall to the dark elf's side. It exploded in a blistering, blinding, thunderous blow that left both man and dark elf staggering to the side.

Entreri kept his course straight, dodging and parrying with his blade as Jarlaxle's arm pumped, sending forth a stream of daggers. The assassin blocked one, got nicked by a second, and squirmed about two more. He then came on fast, thinking to tackle the lighter dark elf.

He missed cleanly, slamming the wall behind Jarlaxle.

The drow was wearing a displacement cloak, or perhaps it was that ornamental hat, Entreri mused, but only briefly, for he understood that he was vulnerable and came right around, bringing Charon's Claw in a broad, ash-making sweep that cut the view between the opponents.

Hardly slowing, Entreri crashed straight through that visual barrier, his straightforwardness confusing Jarlaxle long enough for him to get by—and properly gauge his attack angle this time—close enough to work his own form of magic.

With skills beyond those of nearly any man alive, Entreri sheathed Charon's Claw, drew forth his dagger in his gloved hand, and pulled out his replica pouch with his other. He spun past Jarlaxle, deftly cutting the scrambling drow's belt pouch and catching it in the same gloved hand, while dropping the false pouch at the mercenary's feet.

Jarlaxle hit him with a series of sharp blows then, with what felt like an iron maul. Entreri went rolling away, glancing back just in time to pick off another dagger, then to catch the next in his side. Groaning and doubled over in pain, Entreri scrambled away from his adversary, who held, he now saw, a small warhammer.

"Do you think I need the Crystal Shard to destroy you?" Jarlaxle confidently asked, stooping over to retrieve the pouch. He held up the warhammer then and whispered something. It shrank into a tiny replica that Jarlaxle tucked up under the band of his great hat.

Entreri hardly heard him and hardly saw the move. The pain, though the dagger hadn't gone in dangerously far, was searing. Even worse, a new song was beginning to play in his head, a demand that he surrender himself to the power of the artifact he now possessed.

"I have a hundred ways to kill you, my former friend," Jarlaxle remarked. "Perhaps Crenshinibon will prove the most efficient in this, and in truth, I have little desire to torture you."

Jarlaxle clasped the pouch then, and a curious expression crossed his face.

Still, Entreri could hardly register any of Jarlaxle's words or movements. The artifact assailed him powerfully, reaching into his mind and showing such overwhelming images of complete despair that the mighty assassin nearly fell to his knees sobbing.

Jarlaxle shrugged and rubbed the moisture from his hand on his cloak, and produced yet another of his endless stream of daggers from his enchanted bracer. He brought it back, lining up the killing throw on the seemingly defenseless man.

"Please tell me why I must do this," the drow asked. "Was it the Crystal Shard calling out to you? Your own overblown ambitions, perhaps?"

The images of despair assailed him, a sense of hopelessness more profound than anything Entreri had ever known.

One thought managed to sort itself out in the battered mind of Artemis Entreri: Why didn't the Crystal Shard summon forth its energy and consume him then and there?

Because it cannot! Entreri's willpower answered. Because I am now the wielder, something that the Crystal Shard does not enjoy at all!

"Tell me!" Jarlaxle demanded.

Entreri summoned up all his mental strength, every ounce of discipline he had spent decades grooming, and told the artifact to cease, simply commanded it to shut down all connection to him. The sentient artifact resisted, but only for a moment. Entreri's wall was built of pure discipline and pure anger, and the Crystal Shard was closed off as completely as it had been during those days when Drizzt Do'Urden had carried it. The denial that Drizzt, a goodly ranger, had brought upon the artifact had been wrought of simple morality, while Entreri's was wrought of simple strength of will, but to the same effect. The shard was shut down.

And not an instant too soon, Entreri realized as he blinked open his eyes and saw a stream of daggers coming at him. He dodged and parried with his own dagger, hardly picking anything off cleanly, but deflecting the missiles so that they did not, at least, catch him squarely. One hit him in the face, high on his cheekbone and just under his eye, but he had altered the spin enough so that it slammed in pommel first and not point first. Another grazed his upper arm, cutting a long slash.

"I could have killed you with the return bolt!" Entreri managed to cry out.

Jarlaxle's arm pumped again, this dagger going low and clipping the dancing assassin's foot. The words did register, though, and the mercenary leader paused, his arm cocked, another dagger in hand, ready to throw. He stared at Entreri curiously.

"I could have struck you dead with your own attack," Entreri growled out through teeth gritted in pain.

"You feared you would destroy the shard," Jarlaxle reasoned.

"The shard's energy cannot destroy the shard!" Entreri snapped back.

"You came in here to kill me," Jarlaxle declared.

"No!"

"To take the Crystal Shard, whatever the cost!" Jarlaxle countered.

Entreri, leaning heavily back against the wall now, his legs growing weak from pain, mustered all his determination and looked the drow in the eye—though he did so with only one eye, for his other had already swollen tightly closed. "I came in here," he said slowly, accentuating every word, "making you believe, through the artifact, that such was my intent."

Jarlaxle's face screwed up in one of his very rare expressions of confusion, and his dagger arm began to slip lower. "What are you about?" he asked, his anger seemingly displaced now by honest curiosity.

"They are coming for you," Entreri vaguely explained. "You have to be prepared."

"They?"

"Rai-guy and Kimmuriel," the assassin explained. "They have

decided that your reign over Bregan D'aerthe is at its end. You have exposed the band to too many mighty enemies."

Jarlaxle's expression shifted several times, through a spectrum of emotions, confusion to anger. He looked down at the pouch he held in his hand.

"The artifact has deceived you," Entreri said, managing to straighten a bit as the pain at last began to wane. He reached down and, with trembling fingers, pulled the dagger out of his side and dropped it to the floor. "It pushes you past the point of reason," he went on. "And at the same time, it resents your ability to . . ."

He paused as Jarlaxle opened the pouch and reached in to touch the shard—the imitation item. Before he could begin again, Entreri noted a shimmering in the air, a bluish glow across the room. Then, suddenly, he was looking out as if through a window, at the grounds of Dallabad Oasis.

Through that portal stepped Rai-guy and Kimmuriel, along with Berg'inyon Baenre and another pair of Bregan D'aerthe soldiers.

Entreri forced himself to straighten, growled away the pain, knowing that he had to be at his best here or he would be lost indeed. He noted, then, even as Rai-guy brought forth a curious-looking lantern, that Kimmuriel had not dismissed his dimensional portal.

They were expecting the tower to fall, perhaps, or Kimmuriel was keeping open his escape route.

"You come unbidden," Jarlaxle remarked to them, and he pulled forth the shard from his pouch. "I will summon you when you are needed." The mercenary leader stood tall and imposing, his gaze locked onto Rai-guy. His expression was one of absolute competence, Entreri thought, one of command.

Rai-guy held forth the lantern, its glow bathing Jarlaxle and the shard in quiet light.

That was it, Entreri realized. That was the item to neutralize the Crystal Shard, the tip in the balance of the fight. The intruders had made one tactical error, the assassin knew, one Entreri had counted on. Their focus was the Crystal Shard, as well as it should have been, along with the assumption that Jarlaxle's toy would be the dominant artifact.

You see how they would deny you, Entreri telepathically imparted to the artifact, tucked securely into his belt. *Yet these are the ones you call to lead you to deserved glory?*

He felt the artifact's moment of confusion, felt its reply that Rai-guy would disable it only thereby to possess it, and that . . .

In that instant of confusion, Artemis Entreri exploded into motion, sending a telepathic roar into Crenshinibon, demanding that the tower be brought crumbling down. At the same time he leaped at Jarlaxle and drew forth Charon's Claw.

Indeed, caught so off its guard, the shard nearly obeyed. A violent shudder ran through the tower. It caused no real damage, but was enough of a shake to put Berg'inyon and the other two warriors, who were moving to intercept Entreri, off their balance and to interrupt Rai-guy's attempt to cast a spell.

Entreri altered direction, rushing at the closest drow warrior, batting the sword of the off-balance dark elf aside and stabbing him hard. The dark elf fell away, and the assassin brought his sword through a series of vertical sweeps, filling the air with black ash, filling the room with confusion.

He dived toward Jarlaxle into a sidelong roll. Jarlaxle stood transfixed, staring at the shard he held in his hand as if he had been betrayed.

"Forget it," the assassin cried, yanking Jarlaxle aside just as a hand crossbow dart—poisoned, of course—whistled past. "To the door," he whispered to Jarlaxle, shoving him forward. "Fight for your life!"

With a growl, Jarlaxle put the shard in his pouch and went into action beside the slashing, fighting assassin. His arm flashed repeatedly, sending a stream of daggers at Rai-guy, where they were defeated, predictably, by a stoneskin enchantment. Another barrage was sent at Kimmuriel, who merely absorbed their power into his kinetic barrier.

"Just give it to them!" Entreri cried unexpectedly. He crashed against Jarlaxle's side, taking the pouch back and tossing it to Rai-guy and Kimmuriel, or rather past the two, to the far edge of the room beyond Kimmuriel's magic door. Rai-guy turned immediately, trying to keep the mighty artifact in the glow of his lantern, and Kimmuriel scrambled for it. Entreri saw his one desperate chance.

He grabbed the surprised Jarlaxle roughly and pulled him along, charging for Kimmuriel's magical portal.

Berg'inyon met the charge head on, his two swords working furiously to find a hole in Entreri's defenses. The assassin, a rival of Drizzt Do'Urden, was no stranger to the two-handed style. He neatly parried while working around the skilled drow warrior.

Jarlaxle ducked fast under a swing by the other soldier, pulled the great feather from his magnificent hat, put it to his lips, and blew hard. The air before him filled with feathers.

The soldier cried out, slapping the things away. He hit one that did not so easily move and realized to his horror that he was now facing a ten-foot-tall, monstrous birdlike creature—a diatryma.

Entreri, too, added to the confusion by waving his sword wildly, filling the air with ash. He always kept his focus, though, kept moving around the slashing blades and toward the dimensional portal. He could easily get through it alone, he knew, and he had the real Crystal Shard, but for some reason he didn't quite understand, and didn't bother even to think about, he turned back and grabbed Jarlaxle again, pulling him behind.

The delay brought him some more pain. Rai-guy managed to fire off a volley of magic missiles that stung the assassin profoundly. Those the wizard had launched Jarlaxle's way, Entreri noted sourly, were absorbed by the broach on the band in his hat. Did this one ever run out of tricks?

"Kill them!" Entreri heard Kimmuriel yell, and he felt Berg'inyon's deadly sword coming in fast at his back.

Entreri found himself rolling, disoriented, out onto the sand of Dallabad, out the other side of Kimmuriel's magical portal. He kept his wits about him enough to keep scrambling, grabbing the similarly disoriented Jarlaxle and pulling him along.

"They have the shard!" the mercenary protested.

"Let them keep it!" Entreri cried back.

Behind him, on the other side of the portal, he heard Rai-guy's howling laughter. Yes, the drow wizard thought he now possessed the Crystal Shard, the assassin realized. He'd soon try to put it to use, no doubt calling forth a beam of energy as Jarlaxle had done to the fleeing spy. Perhaps that was why no pursuit came out of the portal.

As he ran, Entreri dropped his hand once more to the real Crystal Shard. He sensed that the artifact was enraged, shaken, and understood that it had not been pleased when Entreri had gone near to Jarlaxle, thus bringing it within the glow of Rai-guy's nullifying light.

"Dispel the magical doorway," he commanded the item. "Trap them and crush them."

Glancing back he saw that Kimmuriel's doorway, half of it within the province of Crenshinibon's absolute domain, was gone.

"The tower," Entreri instructed. "Bring it tumbling down and together we will construct a line of them across Faerûn!"

The promise, spoken so full of energy and enthusiasm, offering the artifact the very same thing it always offered its wielders, was seized upon immediately.

Entreri and Jarlaxle heard the ground rumbling beneath their feet.

They ran on, across the way to a campground beside the small pond of Dallabad. They heard cries from behind them, from soldiers of the fortress, and the cries of astonishment before them from traders who had come to the oasis.

Those cries only multiplied when the traders saw the truth of the two approaching, saw a dark elf coming at them!

Entreri and Jarlaxle had no time to engage the frightened, confused group. They ran straight for the horses that were tethered to a nearby wagon and pulled them free. In a few seconds, with a chorus of angry shouts and curses behind them, the duo charged out of Dallabad, riding hard, though Jarlaxle looked more than a little uncomfortable atop a horse in bright daylight.

Entreri was a fine rider, and he easily paced the dark elf, despite his posture, which was bent over and to the side in an attempt to keep his blood from flowing freely.

"They have the Crystal Shard!" Jarlaxle cried angrily. "How far can we run?"

"Their own magic defeated the artifact," Entreri lied. "It cannot help them now in their pursuit."

Behind them the first tower crashed down, and the second toppled atop the first in a thunderous explosion, all the binding energies gone, and all the magic fast dissipating to the wind.

Entreri held no illusions that Rai-guy and Kimmuriel, or their henchmen, had been caught in that catastrophe. They were too quick and too cunning. He could only hope that the wreckage had diverted them long enough for he and Jarlaxle to get far enough away. He didn't know the extent of his wounds, but he knew that they hurt badly, and that he felt very weak. The last thing he needed then was another fight with the wizard and psionicist or with a swordsman as skilled as Berg'inyon Baenre.

Fortunately, no pursuit became evident as the minutes turned to an hour, and both horses and riders had to slow to a stop, fully exhausted. In his head, Entreri heard the chanting promises of Crenshinibon, whispering to him to construct another tower then and there for shelter and rest.

He almost did it and wondered for a moment why he was even thinking of disagreeing with the Crystal Shard, whose methods seemed to lead to the very same goals that he now held himself.

With a smile of comprehension that seemed more a grimace to the pained assassin, Entreri dismissed the notion. Crenshinibon was clever indeed, sneaking always around the edges of opposition.

Besides, Artemis Entreri had not run away from Dallabad Oasis into the open desert unprepared. He slipped down from his horse, to find that he could hardly stand. Still, he managed to slip his backpack off his shoulders and drop it to the ground before him, then drop to one knee and pull at the strings.

Jarlaxle was soon beside him, helping him to open the pack.

"A potion," Entreri explained, swallowing hard, his breath becoming labored.

Jarlaxle fiddled around in the pack, producing a small vial with a bluish-white liquid within. "Healing?" he asked.

Entreri nodded and motioned for it.

Jarlaxle pulled it back. "You have much to explain," he said. "You attacked me, and you gave them the Crystal Shard."

Entreri, his brow thick with sweat, motioned again for the potion. He put his hand to his side and brought it back up, wet with blood. "A fine throw," he said to the dark elf.

"I do not pretend to understand you, Artemis Entreri," said Jarlaxle, handing over the potion. "Perhaps that is why I do so enjoy your company."

Entreri swallowed the liquid in one gulp, and fell back to a sitting position, closing his eyes and letting the soothing concoction go to work mending some of his wounds. He wished he had about five more of the things, but this one would have to suffice—and would, he believed, keep him alive and start him on the mend.

Jarlaxle watched him for a few moments, and turned his attention to a more immediate problem, glancing up at the stinging, blistering sun. "This sunlight will make for our deaths," he remarked.

In answer, Entreri shifted over and stuck his hand into his backpack, soon producing a small scale model of a brown tent. He brought it in close, whispered a few words, and tossed it off to the side. A few seconds later, the model expanded, growing to full-size and beyond.

"Enough!" Entreri said when it was big enough to comfortably hold him, the dark elf, and both of their horses.

"Not so hard to find on the open desert," Jarlaxle remarked.

"Harder than you believe," Entreri, still gasping with every word, assured him. "Once we're inside, it will recede into a pocket dimension of its own making."

Jarlaxle smiled. "You never told me you possessed such a useful desert tool," he said.

"Because I did not, until last night."

"Thus, you knew that it would come to this, with us out running in the open desert," the mercenary leader reasoned, thinking himself sly.

Far from arguing the point, Entreri merely shrugged as Jarlaxle helped him to his feet. "I hoped it would come to this," the assassin said.

Jarlaxle looked at him curiously, but didn't press the issue. Not then. He looked back in the direction of distant Dallabad, obviously wondering what had become of his former lieutenants, wondering how all of this had so suddenly come about. It was not often that the cunning Jarlaxle was confused.

"We have that which we desired," Kimmuriel reminded his outraged companion. "Bregan D'aerthe is ours to lead—back to the Underdark and Menzoberranzan where we belong."

"It is not the Crystal Shard!" Rai-guy protested, throwing the imitation piece to the floor.

Kimmuriel looked at him curiously. "Was our purpose to procure the item?"

"Jarlaxle still has it," Rai-guy growled back at him. "How long do you believe he will allow us our position of leadership? He should be dead, and the artifact should be mine."

Kimmuriel's sly expression did not change at the wizard's curious choice of words—words, he understood, inspired by Crenshinibon itself and the desire to hold Rai-guy as its slave. Yes, Yharaskrik had done well in teaching the drow psionicist the nuances of the powerful and dangerous artifact. Kimmuriel did agree, though, that their position was tenuous, given that mighty Jarlaxle was still alive.

Kimmuriel had never really wanted Jarlaxle as an enemy—not out of friendship to the older drow but out of simple fear. Perhaps Jarlaxle was already on his way back to Menzoberranzan, where he would rally the remaining members of Bregan D'aerthe, far more than half the band, against Rai-guy and Kimmuriel and those who might follow them back to the drow city. Perhaps Jarlaxle would call upon Gromph Baenre, the archmage of Menzoberranzan himself, to test his wizardly skills against those of Rai-guy.

It was not a pleasant thought, but Kimmuriel understood clearly that Rai-guy's frustration was far more involved with the wizard's other complaint, that the Crystal Shard and not Jarlaxle had gotten away.

"We have to find them," Rai-guy said a moment later. "I want Jarlaxle dead. How else might I ever know a reprieve?"

"You are now the leader of a mercenary band of males housed in Menzoberranzan," Kimmuriel replied. "You will find no reprieve, no break from the constant dangers and matron games. This is the trapping of power, my companion."

Rai-guy's returning expression was not one of friendship. He was angry, perhaps more so than Kimmuriel had ever seen him. He wanted the artifact desperately. So did Yharaskrik, Kimmuriel knew. Should they find a way to catch up to Jarlaxle and Crenshinibon, he had every intention of making certain that the illithid got it. Let Yharaskrik and his mighty mind flayer kin take control of

Crenshinibon, study it, and destroy it. Better that than having it in Rai-guy's hands back in Menzoberranzan—if it would even agree to go to Menzoberranzan, for Yharaskrik had told Kimmuriel that the artifact drew much of its power from the sunlight. How much more on his guard might Kimmuriel have to remain with Crenshinibon as an ally? The artifact would never accept him, would never accept the fact that he, with his mental disciplines, could deny it entrance and control of his mind.

He was tempted to work against Rai-guy now, to foil the search for Jarlaxle however he might, but he understood clearly that Jarlaxle, with or without the Crystal Shard, was far too powerful an adversary to be allowed to run free.

A knock on the door drew him from his contemplation. It opened, and Berg'inyon Baenre entered, followed by several drow soldiers dragging a chained and beaten Sharlotta Vespers behind them. More drow soldiers followed, escorting a bulky and imposing ratman.

Kimmuriel motioned for Sharlotta's group to move aside, that he could face the ratman directly.

"Gord Abrix at your service, good Kimmuriel Oblodra," the ratman said, bowing low.

Kimmuriel stared at him hard. "You lead the wererats of Calimport now?" he asked in his halting command of the common tongue.

Gord nodded. "The wererats in the service of House Basadoni," he said. "In the service of—"

"That is all you need to know, and all that you would ever be wise to speak," Rai-guy growled at him and the wererat, as imposing as he was, inevitably shrank back from the dark elves.

"Get him out of here," Kimmuriel commanded the drow escorts, in his own language. "Tell him we will call when we have decided the new course for the wererats."

Gord Abrix managed one last bow before being herded out of the room.

"And what of you?" Kimmuriel asked Sharlotta, and the mere fact that he could speak to her in his own language reminded him of this woman's resourcefulness and thus her potential usefulness.

"What have I done to deserve such treatment?" Sharlotta, stubborn to the end, replied.

"Why do you believe you had to do anything?" Kimmuriel calmly replied.

Sharlotta started to respond, but quickly realized that there was really nothing she could say against the simple logic of that question.

"We sent you to meet with Pasha Da'Daclan, a necessary engagement, yet you did not," Rai-guy reminded her.

"I was tricked by Entreri and captured," the woman protested.

"Failure is failure," Rai-guy said. "Failure brings punishment—or worse."

"But I escaped and warned you of Entreri's run to Jarlaxle's side," Sharlotta argued.

"Escaped?" Rai-guy asked incredulously. "By your own words, the halfling was too afraid to keep you and so she let you go."

Those words rang uncomfortably in Kimmuriel's thoughts. Had that, too, been a part of Entreri's plan? Because had not Kimmuriel and Rai-guy arrived at the crystalline tower in Dallabad at precisely the wrong moment for the coup? With the Crystal Shard hidden away somewhere and an imitation playing decoy to their greatest efforts? A curious thought, and one the drow psionicist figured he might just take up with that halfling, Dwahvel Tiggerwillies, at a later time.

"I came straight to you," Sharlotta said plainly and forcefully, speaking then like someone who had at last come to understand that she had absolutely nothing left to lose.

"Failure is failure," Rai-guy reiterated, just as forcefully.

"But we are not unmerciful," Kimmuriel added immediately. "I even believe in the possibility of redemption. Artemis Entreri put you in this unfortunate position, so you say, so find him and kill him. Bring me his head, or I shall take your own."

Sharlotta held up her hands helplessly. "Where to begin?" she asked. "What resources—"

"All the resources and every soldier of House Basadoni and of Dallabad, and the complete cooperation of that rat creature and its minions," Kimmuriel replied.

Sharlotta's expression remained skeptical, but there flashed a twinkle in her eyes that Kimmuriel did not miss. She was outraged at Artemis Entreri for all of this, at least as much as were Rai-guy and Kimmuriel. Yes, she was cunning and a worthy adversary. Her efforts to find and destroy Entreri would certainly aid Kimmuriel and Rai-guy's efforts to neutralize Jarlaxle and the dangerous Crystal Shard.

"When do I begin?" Sharlotta asked.

"Why are you still here?" Kimmuriel asked.

The woman took the cue and began scrambling to her feet. The drow guards took the cue, too, and rushed to help her up, quickly unlocking her chains.

CHAPTER

DEAR DWAHVEL

15

"Ah, my friend, how you have deceived me," Jarlaxle whispered to Entreri, whose wounds had far from healed, leaving him in a weakened, almost helpless state. As Entreri had floated into semiconsciousness, Jarlaxle, possessed of the magic to heal him fully, had instead taken the time to consider all that had happened.

He was in the process of trying to figure out if Entreri had saved him or damned him when he heard an all-too familiar call.

Jarlaxle's gaze fell over Entreri and a great smile widened on his black-skinned face. Crenshinibon! The man had Crenshinibon! Jarlaxle replayed the events in his mind and quickly figured that Entreri had done more than simply cut the pouch loose from Jarlaxle's belt in that first, unexpected attack. No, the clever—so clever!—human had switched Jarlaxle's pouch for an imitation pouch, complete with an imitation Crystal Shard.

"My sneaky companion," the mercenary remarked, though he wasn't sure if Entreri could hear him or not. "It is good to know that once again, I have not underestimated you!" As he finished, the mercenary leader went for Entreri's belt pouch, smiling all the while.

The assassin's hand snapped up and grabbed Jarlaxle by the arm.

Jarlaxle had a dagger in his free hand in the blink of an eye, prepared to stab it through the nearly helpless man's heart, but he noted that Entreri wasn't pressing the attack any further. The assassin wasn't reaching for his dagger or any other weapon, but rather, was staring at Jarlaxle plaintively. In his head, Jarlaxle could hear the Crystal Shard calling to him, beckoning him to finish this man off and take back the artifact that was rightfully his.

He almost did it, despite the fact that Crenshinibon's call wasn't nearly as powerful and melodious as it had been when he had been in possession of the artifact.

"Do not," Entreri whispered to him. "You cannot control it."

Jarlaxle pulled back, staring hard at the man. "But you can?"

"That is why it is calling to you," Entreri replied, his breath even more labored than it had been earlier, and blood flowing again from the wound in his side. "The Crystal Shard has no hold over me."

"And why is that?" Jarlaxle asked doubtfully. "Has Artemis Entreri taken up the moral code of Drizzt Do'Urden?"

Entreri started to chuckle, but grimaced instead, the pain nearly unbearable. "Drizzt and I are not so different in many ways," he explained. "In discipline, at least."

"And discipline alone will keep the Crystal Shard from controlling you?" Jarlaxle asked, his tone still one of abject disbelief. "So, you are saying that I am not as disciplined as either of—"

"No!" Entreri growled, and he nearly came up to a sitting position as he tightened his side against a wave of pain.

"No," he said more calmly a moment later, easing back and breathing hard. "Drizzt's code denied the artifact, as does my own—not a code of morality, but one of independence."

Jarlaxle fell back a bit, his expression going from doubtful to curious. "Why did you take it?"

Entreri looked at him and started to respond but wound up just grimacing. Jarlaxle reached under the folds of his cloak and produced a small orb, which he held out to Entreri as he began to chant.

The assassin felt better almost immediately, felt his wound closing and his breathing easier to control. Jarlaxle chanted for a few seconds, each one making Entreri feel that much better, but long before the healing had been completely facilitated, the mercenary stopped.

"Answer my question," he demanded.

"They were coming to kill you," Entreri replied.

"Obviously," said Jarlaxle. "Could you not have merely warned me?"

"It would not have been enough," Entreri insisted. "There were too many against you, and they knew that your primary weapon would be the artifact. Thus, they neutralized it, temporarily."

Jarlaxle's first instinct was to demand the Crystal Shard again, that he could go back and repay Rai-guy and Kimmuriel for their treachery. He held the thought, though, and let Entreri go on.

"They were right in wanting to take it from you," the assassin finished boldly.

Jarlaxle glared at him but just for a moment.

"Step back from it," Entreri advised. "Shut out its call and consider the actions of Jarlaxle over the last few tendays. You could not remain on the surface unless your true identity remained secret, yet you brought forth crystalline towers! Bregan D'aerthe, for all of its power, and with all of the power of Crenshinibon behind it, could not rule the world—not even the city of Calimport—yet look at what you tried to do."

Jarlaxle started to respond several times, but each of his arguments died in his throat before he could begin to offer them. The assassin was right, he knew. He had erred, and badly.

"We cannot go back and try to explain this to the usurpers," the mercenary remarked.

Entreri shook his head. "It was the Crystal Shard that inspired the coup against you," he explained, and Jarlaxle fell back as if slapped. "You were too cunning, but Crenshinibon figured that ambitious Rai-guy would easily fall to its chaotic plans."

"You say that to placate me," Jarlaxle accused.

"I say that because it is the truth, nothing more," Entreri replied.

Then he had to pause and grimace as a spasm of pain came over him. "And, if you take the time to consider it, you know that it is. Crenshinibon kept you moving in its preferred direction but not without interference."

"The Crystal Shard did not control me, or it did. You cannot have it both ways."

"It did manipulate you. How can you doubt that?" Entreri replied. "But not to the level that it knew it could manipulate Rai-guy."

"I went to Dallabad to destroy the crystal tower, something the artifact surely did not desire," Jarlaxle argued, "and yet, I could have done it! All interference from the shard was denied."

He continued, or tried to, but Entreri easily cut him short. "You *could* have done it?" the assassin asked incredulously.

Jarlaxle stammered to reply. "Of course."

"But you did not?"

"I saw no reason to drop the tower as soon as I knew that I could . . ." Jarlaxle started to explain, but when he actually heard the words coming out of his mouth, it hit him, and hard. He had been duped. He, the master of intrigue, had been fooled into believing that he was in control.

"Leave it with me," Entreri said to him. "The Crystal Shard tries to manipulate me, constantly, but it has nothing to offer me that I truly desire, and thus, it has no power over me."

"It will wear at you," Jarlaxle told him. "It will find every weakness and exploit them."

Entreri nodded. "Its time is running short," he remarked.

Jarlaxle looked at him curiously.

"I would not have spent the energy and the time pulling you away from those wretches if I did not have a plan," the assassin remarked.

"Tell me."

"In time," the assassin promised. "Now I beg of you not to take the Crystal Shard, and I beg of you, too, to allow me to rest."

He settled back and closed his eyes, knowing full well that the only defense he would have if Jarlaxle came at him was the Crystal Shard. He knew that if he used the artifact, it would likely find many, many ways to weaken his defenses and the effect might be that he would abandon his mission and simply let the artifact become his guide.

His guide to destruction, he knew, and perhaps to a fate worse than death.

When Entreri looked at Jarlaxle, he was somewhat comforted, for he saw again that clever and opportunistic demeanor, that visage of one who thought things through carefully before taking any definitive and potentially rash actions. Given all that Entreri had just explained to the mercenary drow, the retrieval of Crenshinibon would have to fall into that very category. No, he trusted that Jarlaxle would not move against him. The mercenary drow would let things play out a bit longer before making any move to alter a situation he obviously didn't fully comprehend.

With that thought in mind, Entreri fell fast asleep.

Even as he was drifting off, he felt the healing magic of Jarlaxle's orb falling over him again.

⌖

The halfling was surprised to see her fingers trembling as she carefully unrolled the note.

"Why Artemis, I did not even know you could write," Dwahvel said with a snicker, for the lines on the parchment were beautifully constructed, if a bit spare and efficient for Dwahvel's flamboyant flair. "My dear Dwahvel," she read aloud, and she paused and considered the words, not certain how she should take that greeting. Was it a formal and proper heading, or a sign of true friendship?

It occurred to the halfling then how little she really understood what went on inside of the heart of Artemis Entreri. The assassin had

235

always claimed that his only desire was to be the very best, but if that was true why didn't he put the Crystal Shard to devastating use soon after acquiring it? And Dwahvel knew that he had it. Her contacts at Dallabad had described in detail the tumbling of the crystalline towers, and the flight of a human, Entreri, and a dark elf, whom Dwahvel had to believe must be Jarlaxle.

All indications were that Entreri's plan had succeeded. Even without her eyewitness accounts and despite the well-earned reputations of his adversaries, Dwahvel had never doubted the man.

The halfling moved to her doorway and made certain it was locked. Then she took a seat at her small night table and placed the parchment flat upon it, holding down the ends with paperweights fashioned of huge jewels, and read on, deciding to hold her analysis for the second read through.

My dear Dwahvel,

And so the time has come for us to part ways, and I do so with more than a small measure of regret. I will miss our talks, my little friend. Rarely have I known one I could trust enough to so speak what was truly on my mind. I will do so now, one final time, not in any hopes that you will advise me of my way, but only so that I might more clearly come to understand my own feelings on these matters . . . but that was always the beauty of our talks, was it not?

Now that I consider those discussions, I recognize that you rarely offered any advice. In fact, you rarely spoke at all but simply listened. As I listened to my own words, and in hearing them, in explaining my thoughts and feelings to another, I came to sort them through. Was it your expressions, a simple nod, an arched eyebrow, that led me purposefully down different roads of reasoning?

I know not.

I know not—that has apparently become the litany of my

existence, Dwahvel. I feel as if the foundation upon which I have built my beliefs and actions is not a solid thing, but one as shifting as the sands of the desert. When I was younger, I knew all the answers to all the questions. I existed in a world of surety and certainty. Now that I am older, now that I have seen four decades of life, the only thing I know for certain is that I know nothing for certain.

It was so much easier to be a young man of twenty, so much easier to walk the world with a purpose grounded in—

Grounded in hatred, I suppose, and in the need to be the very best at my dark craft. That was my purpose, to be the greatest warrior in all of the world, to etch my name into the histories of Faerûn. So many people believed that I wished to achieve that out of simple pride, that I wanted people to tremble at the mere mention of my name for the sake of my vanity.

They were partially right, I suppose. We are all vain, whatever arguments we might make against the definition. For me, though, the desire to further my reputation was not as important as the desire—no, not the desire, but the need—truly to be the very best at my craft. I welcomed the increase in reputation, not for the sake of my pride, but because I knew that having such fear weaving through the emotional armor of my opponents gave me even more of an advantage.

A trembling hand does not thrust the blade true.

I still aspire to the pinnacle, fear not, but only because it offers me some purpose in a life that increasingly brings me no joy.

It seems a strange twist to me that I learned of the barren nature of my world only when I defeated the one person who tried in so many ways to show that very thing to me. Drizzt Do'Urden—how I still hate him!—perceived my life as an empty thing, a hollow trapping with no true benefit and no true happiness. I never really disagreed with his assessment, I merely believed that it did not matter. His reason for living was ever based upon his friends and community, while mine was more a life of the self. Either way, it seems to me as if it is just a play, and a pointless one, an act for the pleasure of the viewing gods, a walk that takes us up hills we perceive as huge, but that are really just little mounds, and through valleys that appear so very deep, but are really nothing at all that truly matters. All the pettiness of life itself is my complaint, I fear.

Or perhaps it was not Drizzt who showed me the shifting sands beneath my feet. Perhaps it was Dwahvel, who gave to me something I've rarely known and never known well.

A friend? I am still not certain that I understand the concept, but if I ever bother to attempt to sort through it, I will use our time together as a model.

Thus, this is perhaps a letter of apology. I should not have forced Sharlotta Vespers upon you, though I trust that you tortured her to death as I instructed and buried her far, far away.

How many times you asked me my plans, and always I merely laughed, but you should know, dear Dwahvel, that my intent is to steal a great and powerful artifact before other interested parties get their hands upon it. It is a desperate attempt, I know, but I cannot help myself, for the artifact calls to me, demands of me that I take it from its current, less-than-able wielder.

So I will have it, because I am indeed the best at my craft, and I will be gone, far, far from this place, perhaps never to return.

Farewell, Dwahvel Tiggerwillies, in whatever venture you attempt. You owe me nothing, I assure you, and yet I feel as if I am in your debt. The road before me is long and fraught with peril, but I have my goal in sight. If I attain it, nothing will truly bring me any harm.

Farewell!

—AE

Dwahvel Tiggerwillies pushed aside the parchment and wiped a tear from her eye, and laughed at the absurdity of it all. If anyone had told her months before that she would regret the day Artemis Entreri walked out of her life, she would have laughed at him and called him a fool.

But here it was, a letter as intimate as any of the discussions Dwahvel had shared with Entreri. She found that she missed those discussions already, or perhaps she lamented that there would be no such future talks with the man. None in the near future, at least.

Entreri would also miss those talks by his own words. That struck Dwahvel profoundly. To think that she had so engaged this man—this killer who had secretly ruled Calimport's streets off and on for more than twenty years. Had anyone ever become so close to Artemis Entreri?

None who were still alive, Dwahvel knew.

She reread the ending of the letter, the obvious lies concerning Entreri's intentions. He had taken care not to mention anything that would tell the remaining dark elves that Dwahvel knew anything about them or the stolen artifact, or anything about his proffering of the Crystal Shard. His lie about his instructions concerning Sharlotta certainly added even more security to Dwahvel, buying her, should the need arise, some compassion from the woman and her secret backers.

That thought sent a shudder along Dwahvel's spine. She really didn't want to depend on the compassion of dark elves!

It would not come to that, she realized. Even if the trail led to her and her establishment, she could willingly and eagerly show Sharlotta the letter and Sharlotta would then see her as a valuable asset.

Yes, Artemis Entreri had taken great pains to cover Dwahvel's efforts in the conspiracy, and that, more than any of the kind words he had written to her, revealed to her the depth of their friendship.

"Run far, my friend, and hide in deep holes," she whispered.

She gently rerolled the parchment and placed it in one of the drawers of her crafted bureau. The sound of that closing drawer resonated hard against Dwahvel's heart.

She would indeed miss Artemis Entreri.

PART 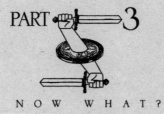 3

N O W   W H A T ?

There is a simple beauty in the absolute ugliness of demons. There is no ambiguity there, no hesitation, no misconception, about how one must deal with such creatures.

You do not parlay with demons. You do not hear their lies. You cast them out, destroy them, rid the world of them—even if the temptation is present to utilize their powers to save what you perceive to be a little corner of goodness.

This is a difficult concept for many to grasp and has been the downfall of many wizards and priests who have errantly summoned demons and allowed the creatures to move beyond their initial purpose—the answering of a question, perhaps—because they were tempted by the power offered by the creature. Many of these doomed spellcasters thought they would be doing good by forcing the demons to their side, by bolstering their cause, their army, with demonic soldiers. What ill, they supposed, if the end result proved to the greater good? Would not a goodly king be well advised to add "controlled" demons to his cause if goblins threatened his lands?

I think not, because if the preservation of goodness relies upon the use of such obvious and irredeemable evil to defeat evil, then there is nothing, truly, worth saving.

The sole use of demons, then, is to bring them forth only in times when they must betray the cause of evil, and only in a setting so controlled that there is no hope of their escape. Cadderly has done this within the secure summoning chamber of the Spirit Soaring, as have, I am sure, countless priests and wizards. Such a summoning is not without peril, though, even if the circle of protection is perfectly formed, for there is always a temptation that goes with the manipulation of powers such as a balor or a nalfeshnie.

Within that temptation must always lie the realization of irredeemable evil. Irredeemable. Without hope. That concept, redemption, must be the crucial determinant in any such dealings. Temper your blade when redemption is possible, hold it when redemption is at hand, and strike hard and without remorse when your opponent is beyond any hope of redemption.

Where on that scale does Artemis Entreri lie, I wonder? Is the man truly beyond help and hope?

Yes, to the former, I believe, and no to the latter. There is no help for Artemis Entreri because the man would never accept any. His greatest flaw is his pride—not the boasting pride of so many lesser warriors, but the pride of absolute independence and unbending self-reliance. I could tell him his errors, as could anyone who has come to know him in any way, but he would not hear my words.

Yet perhaps there may be hope of some redemption for the man. I know not the source of his anger, though it must have been great. And yet I will not allow that the source, however difficult and terrible it might have been, in any way excuses the man from his actions. The blood on Entreri's sword and trademark dagger is his own to wear.

He does not wear it well, I believe. It burns at his skin as might the breath of a black dragon and gnaws at all that is within him. I saw that during our last encounter, a quiet and dull ache at the side of his dark eyes. I had him beaten, could have killed him, and I believe that in many ways he hoped I would finish the task and be done with it, and end his mostly self-imposed suffering.

That ache is what held my blade, that hope within me that somewhere deep inside Artemis Entreri there is the understanding that *his path needs to change, that the road he currently walks is one of emptiness and ultimate despair. Many thoughts coursed my mind as I stood there, weapons in hand, with him defenseless before me. How could I strike when I saw that pain in his eyes and knew that such pain might well be the precursor to redemption? And yet how could I not, when I was well aware that letting Artemis Entreri walk out of that crystalline tower might spell the doom of others?*

Truly it was a dilemma, a crisis of conscience and of balance. I found my answer in that critical moment in the memory of my father, Zaknafein. To Entreri's thinking, I know, he and Zaknafein are not so different, and there are indeed similarities. Both existed in an environment hostile and to their respective perceptions evil. Neither, to their perceptions, did either go out of his way to kill anyone who did not deserve it. Are the warriors and assassins who fight for the wretched pashas of Calimport any better than the soldiers of the drow houses? Thus, in many ways, the actions of Zaknafein and those of Artemis Entreri are quite similar. Both existed in a world of intrigue, danger, and evil. Both survived their imprisonment through ruthless means. If Entreri views his world, his prison, as full of wretchedness as Zaknafein viewed Menzoberranzan, then is not Entreri as entitled to his manner as was Zaknafein, the weapons master who killed many, many dark elves in his tenure as patron of House Do'Urden?

It is a comparison I realized when first I went to Calimport, in pursuit of Entreri, who had taken Regis as prisoner (and even that act had justification, I must admit), and a comparison that truly troubled me. How close are they, given their abilities with the blade and their apparent willingness to kill? Was it, then, some inner feelings for Zaknafein that stayed my blade when I could have cut Entreri down?

No, I say, and I must believe, for Zaknafein was far more discerning in whom he would kill or would not kill. I know the truth of Zaknafein's heart. I know that Zaknafein was possessed of the ability to love, and the reality of Artemis Entreri simply cannot hold up against that.

Not in his present incarnation, at least, but is there hope that the man will find a light beneath the murderous form of the assassin?

Perhaps, and I would be glad indeed to hear that the man so embraced that light. In truth, though, I doubt that anyone or anything will ever be able to pull that lost flame of compassion through the thick and seemingly impenetrable armor of dispassion that Artemis Entreri now wears.

—Drizzt Do'Urden

CHAPTER

16

Danica sat on a ledge of an imposing mountain beside the field that housed the magnificent Spirit Soaring, a cathedral of towering spires and flying buttresses, of great and ornate windows of multicolored glass. Acres of grounds were striped by well-maintained hedgerows, many of them shaped into the likeness of animals, and one wrapping around and around itself in a huge maze.

The cathedral was the work of Danica's husband, Cadderly, a mighty priest of Deneir, the god of knowledge. This structure had been Cadderly's most obvious legacy, but his greatest one, to Danica's reasoning, were the twin children romping around the entrance to the maze and their younger sibling, sleeping within the cathedral. The twins had gone running into the hedgerow maze, much to the dismay of the dwarf Pikel Bouldershoulder. Pikel, a practitioner of the druidic ways—magic that his surly brother Ivan still denied—had created the maze and the other amazing gardens.

Pikel had gone running into the maze behind the children screaming, *"Eeek!"* and other such Pikelisms, and pulling at his green-dyed hair and beard. His maze wasn't quite ready for visitors yet, and the roots hadn't properly set.

Of course, as soon as Pikel had gone running in, the twins had sneaked right back out and were now playing quietly in front of the maze entrance. Danica didn't know how far along the confusing corridors the green-bearded dwarf had gone, but she had heard his voice fast receding and figured that he'd be lost in the maze, for the third time that day, soon enough.

A wind gust came whipping across the mountain wall, blowing Danica's thick mop of strawberry blond hair into her face. She blew some strands out of her mouth and tossed her head to the side, just in time to see Cadderly walking toward her.

What a fine figure he cut in his tan-white tunic and trousers, his light blue silken cape and his trademark blue, wide-brimmed, and plumed hat. Cadderly had aged greatly while constructing the Spirit Soaring, to the point where he and Danica honestly believed he would expire. Much to Danica's dismay Cadderly had expected to die and had accepted that as the sacrifice necessary for the construction of the monumental library. Soon after he had completed the construction of the main building—the details, like the ornate designs of the many doors and the golden leaf work around the beautiful archways, might never be completed—the aging process had reversed, and the man had grown younger almost as fast as he'd aged. Now he seemed a man in his late twenties with a spring in his step, and a twinkle in his eye every time he glanced Danica's way. Danica had even worried that this process would continue, and that soon she'd find herself raising four children instead of three.

He eventually grew no younger, though, stopping at the point where Cadderly seemed every bit the vivacious and healthy young man he had been before all the trouble had started within the Edificant Library, the structure that had stood on this ground before the advent of the chaos curse and the destruction of the old order of Deneir. The willingness to sacrifice everything for the new cathedral and the new order had sufficed in the eyes of Deneir, and thus, Cadderly Bonaduce had been given back his life, a life so enriched by the addition of his wife and their children.

"I had a visitor this morning," Cadderly said to her when he moved beside her. He cast a glance at the twins and smiled all the wider when he heard another frantic call from the lost Pikel.

Danica marveled at how her husband's gray eyes seemed to smile as well. "A man from Carradoon," she replied, nodding. "I saw him enter."

"Bearing word from Drizzt Do'Urden," Cadderly explained, and Danica turned to face him directly, suddenly very interested. She and Cadderly had met the unusual dark elf the previous year and had taken him back to the northland using one of Cadderly's wind-walking spells.

Danica spent a moment studying Cadderly, considering the intense expression upon his normally calm face. "He has retrieved the Crystal Shard," she reasoned, for when last she and Cadderly had been with Drizzt and his human companion, Catti-brie, they had spoken of just that. Drizzt promised that he would retrieve the ancient, evil artifact and bring it to Cadderly to be destroyed.

"He did," Cadderly said.

He handed a roll of parchment sheets to Danica. She took them and unrolled them. A smile crossed her face when she learned of the fate of Drizzt's lost friend, Wulfgar, freed from his prison at the clutches of the demon Errtu. By the time she got to the second page, though, Danica's mouth drooped open, for the note went on to describe the subsequent theft of the Crystal Shard by a rogue dark elf named Jarlaxle, who had sent one of his drow soldiers to Drizzt in the guise of Cadderly.

Danica paused and looked up, and Cadderly took back the parchments. "Drizzt believes the artifact has likely gone underground, back to the dark elf city of Menzoberranzan, where Jarlaxle makes his home," he explained.

"Well, good enough for Menzoberranzan, then," Danica said in all seriousness.

She and Cadderly had discussed the powers of the sentient shard at length, and she understood it to be a tool of destruction—

destruction of the wielder's enemies, of the wielder's allies, and ultimately of the wielder himself. There had never been, and to Cadderly's reasoning, could never be, a different outcome where Crenshinibon was concerned. To possess the Crystal Shard was, ultimately, a terminal disease, and woe to all those nearby.

Cadderly was shaking his head before Danica ever finished the sentiment. "The Crystal Shard is an artifact of sunlight, which is perhaps, in the measure of symbolism, its greatest perversion."

"But the drow are creatures of their dark holes," Danica reasoned. "Let them take it and be gone. Perhaps in the Underdark, the Crystal Shard's power will be lessened, even destroyed."

Again Cadderly was shaking his head. "Who is the stronger?" he asked. "The artifact or the wielder?"

"It sounds as if this particular dark elf was quite cunning," Danica replied. "To have fooled Drizzt Do'Urden is no easy feat, I would guess."

Cadderly shrugged and grinned. "I doubt that Crenshinibon, once it finds its way into the new wielder's heart—which it surely will unless this Jarlaxle is akin in heart to Drizzt Do'Urden—will allow him to retreat to the depths," he explained. "It is not necessarily a question of who is the stronger. The subtlety of the artifact is its ability to manipulate its wielder into agreement, not dominate him."

"And the heart of a dark elf would be easily manipulated," Danica reasoned.

"A typical dark elf, yes," Cadderly agreed.

A few moments of quiet passed as each considered the words and the new information.

"What are we to do, then?" Danica asked at length. "If you believe that the Crystal Shard will not allow a retreat to the sunless Underdark, then are we to allow it to wreak havoc on the surface world? Do we even know where it might be?"

Still deep in thought, Cadderly did not answer right away. The question of what to do, of what their responsibilities might be in this situation, went to the very core of the philosophical trappings of power. Was it Cadderly's place, because of his clerical power, to hunt down the new wielder of the Crystal Shard, this dark elf thief, and take the item by force, bringing it to its destruction? If that was the case, then what of every other injustice in the world? What of the pirates on the Sea of Fallen Stars? Was Cadderly to charter a boat and go out hunting them? What of the Red Wizards of Thay, that notorious band? Was it Cadderly's duty to seek them out and do battle with each and every one? Then there were the Zhentarim, the Iron Throne, the Shadow Thieves. . . .

"Do you remember when we met here with Drizzt Do'Urden and Catti-brie?" Danica asked, and it seemed to Cadderly that the woman was reading his mind. "Drizzt was distressed when we realized that our summoning of the demon Errtu had released the great beast from its banishment—a banishment handed out to it by Drizzt years before. What did you tell Drizzt about that to calm him?"

"The releasing of Errtu was no major problem," Cadderly admitted again. "There would always be a demon available to a sorcerer with evil designs. If not Errtu, then another."

"Errtu was just one of a number of agents of chaos," Danica reasoned, "as the Crystal Shard is just another element of chaos. Any havoc it brings would merely replace the myriad other tools of chaos in wreaking exactly that, correct?"

Cadderly smiled at her, staring intently into the seemingly limitless depths of her almond-shaped brown eyes. How he loved this woman. She was so much his partner in every aspect of his life. Intelligent and possessed of the greatest discipline Cadderly had ever known, Danica always helped him through any difficult questions and choices, just by listening and offering suggestions.

"It is the heart that begets evil, not the instruments of destruction," he completed the thought for her.

"Is the Crystal Shard the tool or the heart?" Danica asked.

"That is the question, is it not?" Cadderly replied. "Is the artifact akin to a summoned monster, an instrument of destruction for one whose heart was already tainted? Or is it a manipulator, a creator of evil where there would otherwise be none?" He held out his arms, having no real answer for that. "In either case, I believe I will contact some extra-planar sources and see if I can locate the artifact and this dark elf, Jarlaxle. I wish to know the use to which he has put the Crystal Shard, or perhaps even more troubling, the use to which the Crystal Shard plans to put him."

Danica started to ask what he might be talking about, but she figured it out before she could utter the words, and her lips grew very thin. Might the Crystal Shard, rather than let this Jarlaxle creature take it to the lightless Underdark, use him to spearhead an invasion by an army of drow? Might the Crystal Shard use the position and race of its new wielder to create havoc beyond anything it had ever known before? Even worse for them personally, if Jarlaxle had stolen the artifact by using an imitation of Cadderly, then Jarlaxle certainly knew of Cadderly. If Jarlaxle knew, the Crystal Shard knew—and knew, too, that Cadderly might have information about how to destroy it. A flash of worry crossed Danica's face, one that Cadderly could not miss, and she instinctively turned to regard her children.

"I will try to discover where he might be with the artifact, and what trouble they together might already be causing," Cadderly explained, not reading Danica's expression very well and wondering, perhaps, if she was doubting him.

"You do that," the more-than-convinced woman said in all seriousness. "Right away."

A squeal from inside the maze turned them both in that direction.

"Pikel," the woman explained.

Cadderly smiled. "Lost again?"

"Again?" Danica asked. "Or still?"

They heard some rumbling off to the side and saw Pikel's more traditional brother, Ivan Bouldershoulder, rolling toward the maze grumbling with every step. "Doo-dad," the yellow-bearded dwarf said sarcastically, referring to Pikel's pronunciation of his calling. "Yeah, Doo-dad," Ivan grumbled. "Can't even find his way out of a hedgerow."

"And you will help him?" Cadderly called to the dwarf.

Ivan turned curiously, noting the pair, it seemed, for the first time. "Been helpin' him all me life," he snorted.

Both Cadderly and Danica nodded and allowed Ivan his fantasy. They knew well enough, if Ivan did not, that his helping Pikel more often caused problems for both of the dwarves. Sure enough, within the span of a few minutes, Ivan's calls about being lost echoed no less than Pikel's. Cadderly and Danica, and the twins sitting outside the devious maze, thoroughly enjoyed the entertainment.

A few hours later, after preparing the proper sequence of spells and after checking on the magical circle of protection the young-again priest always used when dealing with even the most minor of the creatures of the lower planes, Cadderly sat in a cross-legged position on the floor of his summoning chamber, chanting the incantation that would bring a minor demon, an imp, to him.

A short while later, the tiny, bat-winged, horned creature materialized in the protection circle. It hopped all about, confused and angry, finally focusing on Cadderly. It spent some time studying the man, no doubt trying to get some clues to his demeanor. Imps were often summoned to the material plane, sometimes for information, other times to serve as familiars for wizards of evil weal.

"Deneir?" the imp asked in a coughing, raspy voice that Cadderly thought seemed both typical and fitting to its smoky natural environment. "You wear the clothing of a priest of Deneir."

The creature was staring at the red band on his hat, Cadderly knew, on which was set a porcelain-and-gold pendant depicting a candle burning above an eye, the symbol of Deneir.

Cadderly nodded.

"*Ahck!*" the imp said and spat upon the ground.

"Hoping for a wizard in search of a familiar?" Cadderly asked slyly.

"Hoping for anything other than you, priest of Deneir," the imp replied.

"Accept that which has been given to you," Cadderly said. "A glimpse of the material plane is better than none, after all, and a reprieve from your hellish existence."

"What do you want, priest of Deneir?"

"Information," Cadderly replied, but even as he said it, he realized that his questions would be difficult indeed, perhaps too much so for so minor a demon. "All that I require of you is that you give to me the name of a greater demonic source, that I might bring it forth."

The imp looked at him curiously, tilting its head as a dog might, and licking its thin lips with a pointed tongue.

"Nothing greater than a nalfeshnie," Cadderly quickly clarified, seeing the impish smile growing and wanting to limit the power of whatever being he next summoned. A nalfeshnie was no minor demon, but was certainly within Cadderly's power to control, at least long enough for him to get what he needed.

"Oh, I has a name for you, priest of Deneir . . ." the imp started to say, but it jerked spasmodically as Cadderly began to chant a spell of torment. The imp fell to the floor, writhing and spitting curses.

"The name?" Cadderly asked. "And I warn you, if you deceive me and try to trick me into summoning a greater creature, I will dismiss it promptly and find you again. This torment is nothing compared to that which I will exact upon you!"

He said the words with conviction and with strength, though in truth, it pained the gentle man to be doing even this level of torture, even upon a wretched imp. He reminded himself of the importance of his quest and bolstered his resolve.

"Mizferac!" the imp screamed out. "A glabrezu, and a stupid one!"

Cadderly released the imp from his spell of torment, and the creature gave a beat of its wings and righted itself, staring at him coldly. "I did your bidding, evil priest of Deneir. Let me go!"

"Be gone, then," said Cadderly, and even as the little beast began fading from view, offering a few obscene gestures, Cadderly had to toss in, "I will tell Mizferac what you said concerning its intelligence."

He did indeed enjoy that last expression of panic on the face of the little imp.

Cadderly brought Mizferac in later that same day and found the towering pincer-armed glabrezu to be the embodiment of all that he hated about demons. It was a nasty, vicious, conniving, and wretchedly self-serving creature that tried to get as much gain as it could out of every word. Cadderly kept their meeting short and to the point. The demon was to inquire of other extra-planar creatures about the whereabouts of a dark elf named Jarlaxle, who was likely on the surface of Faerûn. Furthermore, Cadderly put a powerful geas on the demon, preventing it from actually walking the material world, but retreating only back to the Abyss and using sources to discern the information.

"That will take longer," Mizferac said.

"I will call on you daily," Cadderly replied, putting as much anger without adding any passion whatsoever as he could into his timbre. "Each passing day I will grow more impatient, and your torment will increase."

"You make a terrible enemy in Mizferac, Cadderly Bonaduce, Priest of Deneir," the glabrezu replied, obviously trying to shake him with its knowledge of his name.

Cadderly, who heard the mighty song of Deneir as clearly as if it was a chord within his own heart, merely smiled at the threat. "If ever you find yourself free of your bonds and able to walk the surface of Toril, do come and find me, Mizferac the fool. It will please me greatly to reduce your physical form to ash and banish your spirit from this world for a hundred years."

The demon growled, and Cadderly dismissed it, simply and with just a wave of his hand and an utterance of a single word. He had heard every threat a demon could give and many times. After the trials the young priest had known in his life, from facing a red dragon to doing battle with his own father, to warring against the chaos curse, to, most of all, offering his very life up as sacrifice to his god, there was little any creature, demonic or not, could say to him that would frighten him.

He recalled the glabrezu every day for the next tenday, until finally the fiend brought him some news of the Crystal Shard and the drow, Jarlaxle, along with the surprising information that Jarlaxle no longer possessed the artifact, but traveled in the company of a human, Artemis Entreri, who did.

Cadderly knew that name well from the stories that Drizzt and Catti-brie had told him in their short stay at the Spirit Soaring. The man was an assassin, a brutal killer. According to the demon, Entreri, along with the Crystal Shard and the dark elf Jarlaxle, was on his way to the Snowflake Mountains.

Cadderly rubbed his chin as the glabrezu passed along the information—information that he knew to be true, for he had enacted a spell to make certain the demon had not lied to him.

"I have done as you demanded," the glabrezu growled, clicking its pincer-ended appendages anxiously. "I am released from your bonds, Cadderly Bonaduce."

"Then begone, that I do not have to look upon your ugly face any longer," the young priest replied.

The demon narrowed its huge eyes threateningly and clicked its pincers. "I will not forget this," it promised.

"I would be disappointed if you did," Cadderly replied casually.

"I was told that you have young children, fool," Mizferac remarked, fading from view.

"Mizferac, *ehugu-winance!*" Cadderly cried, catching the departing demon before it had dissipated back to the swirling smoke of the Abyss. Holding it in place by the sheer strength of his enchantment, Cadderly twisted the demon's physical form painfully by the might of his spell.

"Do I smell fear, human?" Mizferac asked defiantly.

Cadderly smiled wryly. "I doubt that, since a hundred years will pass before you are able to walk the material plane again." The threat, spoken openly, freed Mizferac of the summoning binding—and yet, the beast was not freed, for Cadderly had enacted another spell, one of exaction.

Mizferac created magical darkness to fill the room. Cadderly fell into his own chanting, his voice trembling with feigned terror.

"I can smell you, foolish mortal," Mizferac remarked, and Cadderly heard the voice from the side, though he guessed correctly that Mizferac was using ventriloquism to throw him off guard. The young priest was fully into the flow of Deneir's song now, hearing every beautiful note and accessing the magic quickly and completely. First he detected evil, easily locating the great negative force of the glabrezu—then another mighty negative force as the demon gated in a companion.

Cadderly held his nerve and continued casting.

"I will kill the children first, fool," Mizferac promised, and it began speaking to its new companion in the guttural tongue of the Abyss—one that Cadderly, through the use of another spell that he had enacted before he had ever brought Mizferac to him this day, understood perfectly. The glabrezu told its fellow demon to keep the foolish priest occupied while it went to hunt the children.

"I will bring them before you for sacrifice," Mizferac started to promise, but the end of the sentence came out as garbled screams as Cadderly's spell went off, creating a series of spinning, slicing blades all around the two demons. The priest then brought forth a globe of light to counter Mizferac's darkness. The spectacle of Mizferac and its companion, a lesser demon that looked like a giant gnat, getting sliced and chopped was revealed.

Mizferac roared and uttered a guttural word—one designed to teleport him away, Cadderly assumed. It failed. The young priest, so strong in the flow of Deneir's song, was the quicker. He brought forth a prayer that dispelled the demon's magic before Mizferac could get away.

A spell of binding followed immediately, locking Mizferac firmly in place, while the magical blades continued their spinning devastation.

"I will never forget this!" Mizferac roared, words edged with outrage and agony.

"Good, then you will know better than ever to return," Cadderly growled back.

He brought forth a second blade barrier. The two demons were torn apart, their material forms ripped into dozens of bloody pieces, thus banishing them from the material plane for a hundred years. Satisfied with that, Cadderly left his summoning chamber covered in demon blood. He'd have to find a suitable spell from Deneir to clean up his clothes.

As for the Crystal Shard, he had his answers—and it seemed to him a good thing that he had bothered to check, since a dangerous assassin, an equally dangerous dark elf, and the even more dangerous Crystal Shard were apparently on their way to see him.

He had to talk to Danica, to prepare all the Spirit Soaring and the order of Deneir, for the potential battle.

CHAPTER

A CALL FOR HELP

17

"There is something enjoyable about these beasts, I must admit," Jarlaxle noted when he and Entreri pulled up beside a mountain pass.

The assassin quickly dismounted and ran to the ledge to view the trail below—and to view the band of orcs he suspected were still stubbornly in pursuit. The pair had left the desert behind, at long last, entering a region of broken hills and rocky trails.

"Though if I had one of my lizards from Menzoberranzan, I could simply run away to the top of the hill and over the other side," the drow went on. He took off his great plumed hat and rubbed a hand over his bald head. The sun was strong this day, but the dark elf seemed to be handling it quite well—certainly better than Entreri would have expected of any drow under this blistering sun. Again the assassin had to wonder if Jarlaxle might have a bit of magic about him to protect his sensitive eyes. "Useful beasts, the lizards of Menzoberranzan," Jarlaxle remarked. "I should have brought some to the surface with me."

Entreri gave him a smirk and a shake of his head. "It will be hard enough getting into half the towns with a drow beside me," he remarked. "How much more welcoming might they be if I rode in on a lizard?"

He looked back down the mountainside, and sure enough, the

orc band was still pacing them, though the wretched creatures were obviously exhausted. Still, they followed as if compelled beyond their control.

It wasn't hard for Artemis Entreri to figure out exactly what might be so compelling them.

"Why can you not just take out your magical tent, that we can melt away from them?" Jarlaxle asked for the third time.

"The magic is limited," Entreri answered yet again.

He glanced back at Jarlaxle as he replied, surprised that the cunning drow would keep asking the same question. Was Jarlaxle, perhaps, trying to garner some information about the tent? Or even worse, was the Crystal Shard reaching out to the drow, subtly asking him to goad Entreri in that direction? If they did take out the tent and disappear, after all, they would have to reappear in the same place. That being true, had the Crystal Shard figured out how to send its telepathic call across the planes of existence? Perhaps the next time Entreri and Jarlaxle used the plane-shifting tent, they would return to the material plane to find an orc army, inspired by Crenshinibon, waiting for them.

"The horses grow weary," Jarlaxle noted.

"They can outrun orcs," Entreri replied.

"If we let them run free, perhaps."

"They're just orcs," Entreri muttered, though he could hardly believe how persistent this group remained.

He turned back to Jarlaxle, no longer doubting the drow's claim. The horses were indeed tired—they had been riding a long day before even realizing the orcs were following their trail. They had ridden the beasts practically into the desert sands in an effort to get out of that barren, wide-open region as quickly as possible.

Perhaps it was time to stop running.

"There are only about a score of them," Entreri remarked, watching their movements as they crawled over the lower slopes.

"Twenty against two," Jarlaxle reminded. "Let us go and hide in your tent, that the horses can rest, and come out and begin the chase anew."

"We can defeat them and drive them away," Entreri insisted, "if we choose and prepare the battlefield."

It surprised the assassin that Jarlaxle didn't look very eager about that possibility. "They're only orcs," Entreri said again.

"Are they?" Jarlaxle asked.

Entreri started to respond but paused long enough to consider the meaning behind the dark elf's words. Was this pursuit a chance encounter? Or was there something more to this seemingly nondescript band of monsters?

"You believe that Kimmuriel and Rai-guy are secretly guiding this band," Entreri stated more than asked.

Jarlaxle shrugged. "Those two have always favored using monsters as fodder," he explained. "They let the orcs—or kobolds, or whatever other creature is available—rush in to weary their opponents while they prepare the killing blow. It is nothing new in their tactics. They used such a ruse to take House Basadoni, forcing the kobolds to lead the charge and take the bulk of the casualties."

"It could be," Entreri agreed with a nod. "Or it could be a conspiracy of another sort, one with its roots in our midst."

It took Jarlaxle a few moments to sort that out. "Do you believe that I have urged the orcs on?" he asked.

In response, Entreri patted the pouch that held the Crystal Shard. "Perhaps Crenshinibon has come to believe that it needs to be rescued from our clutches," he said.

"The shard would prefer an orcish wielder to either you or me?" Jarlaxle asked doubtfully.

"I am not its wielder, nor will I ever be," Entreri answered sharply. "Nor will you, else you would have taken it from me our first night on the road from Dallabad, when I was too weak with my wounds to resist. I know this truth, so do you, and so does Crenshinibon. It understands that we are beyond its reach now, and it fears us, or fears me, at least, because it recognizes what is in my heart."

He spoke the words with perfect calm and perfect coldness, and it wasn't hard for Jarlaxle to figure out what he might be talking about. "You mean to destroy it," the drow remarked, and his tone made the sentence seem like an accusation.

"And I know how to do it," Entreri bluntly admitted. "Or at least, I know someone who knows how to do it."

The expressions that crossed Jarlaxle's handsome face ranged from incredulity to sheer anger to something less obvious, something buried deep. The assassin knew that he had taken a chance in proclaiming his intent so openly with the drow who had been fully duped by the Crystal Shard and who was still not completely convinced, despite Entreri's many reminders, that giving up the artifact had been a good thing to do. Was Jarlaxle's unreadable expression a signal to him that the Crystal Shard had indeed gotten to the drow leader once again and was even then working through, and with, Jarlaxle to find a way to get rid of Entreri's bothersome interference?

"You will never find the strength of heart to destroy it," Jarlaxle remarked.

Now it was Entreri's turn to wear a confused expression.

"Even if you discover a method, and I doubt that there is one, when the moment comes, Artemis Entreri will never find the heart to be rid of so powerful and potentially gainful an item as Crenshinibon," Jarlaxle proclaimed slyly. A grin widened across the dark elf's face. "I know you, Artemis Entreri," he said, grinning still, "and I know that you'll not throw away such power and promise, such beauty as Crenshinibon!"

Entreri looked at him hard. "Without the slightest hesitation," he said coldly. "And so would you, had you not fallen under its spell. I see that enchantment for what it is, a trap of temporary gain through reckless action that can only lead to complete and utter ruin. You disappoint me, Jarlaxle. I had thought you smarter than this."

Jarlaxle's expression, too, turned cold. A flash of anger lit his dark eyes. For just a moment, Entreri thought his first fight of the day was upon him, thought the dark elf would attack him. Jarlaxle closed his eyes, his body swaying as he focused his thoughts and his concentration.

"Fight the urge," the assassin found himself whispering under his breath. Entreri the consummate loner, the man who, for all his life, had counted on no one but himself, was surely surprised to hear himself now.

"Do we continue to run, or do we fight them?" Jarlaxle asked a moment later. "If these creatures are being guided by Rai-guy and Kimmuriel, we will learn of it soon enough—likely when we are fully engaged in battle. The odds of ten-to-one, of even twenty-to-one, against orcs on a mountain battlefield of our choosing does not frighten me in the least, but in truth, I do not wish to face my former lieutenants, even two-against-two. With his combination of wizardly and clerical powers, Rai-guy has variables enough to strike fear into the heart of Gromph Baenre, and there is nothing predictable, or even understandable, about many of Kimmuriel Oblodra's tactics. In all the years he has served me, I have not begun to sort the riddle that is Kimmuriel. I know only that he is extremely effective."

"Keep talking," Entreri muttered, looking back down at the orcs, who were much closer now, and at all the potential battlefield areas. "You are making me wish that I had left you and the Crystal Shard behind."

He caught a slight shift in Jarlaxle's expression as he said that, a subtle hint that perhaps the mercenary leader had been wondering all along why Entreri had bothered with both the theft and the rescue. If Entreri meant to destroy the Crystal Shard anyway, after all, why not just run away and leave it and the feud between Jarlaxle and his dangerous lieutenants behind?

"We will discuss that," Jarlaxle replied.

"Another time," Entreri said, trotting along the ledge to the right. "We have much to do, and our orc friends are in a hurry."

"Headlong into doom," Jarlaxle remarked quietly. He slid off of his horse and moved to follow Entreri.

Soon after, the pair had set up in a location on the northeastern side of the range, the steepest ascent. Jarlaxle worried that perhaps some of the orcs would come up from the other paths, the same ones they had taken, stealing from them the advantage of the higher ground, but Entreri was convinced that the artifact was calling out to the creatures insistently, and that they would alter their course to follow the most direct line to Crenshinibon. That line would take them up several high bluffs on this side of the hills, and along narrow and easily defensible trails.

Sure enough, within a few minutes of attaining their new perch, Entreri and Jarlaxle spotted the obedient and eager orc band, scrambling over stony outcroppings below them.

Jarlaxle began his customary chatting, but Entreri wasn't listening. He turned his thoughts inward, listening for the Crystal Shard, knowing that it was calling out to the orcs. He paid close heed to its subtle emanations, knowing them all too well from his time in possession of the item, for though he had denied the Crystal Shard, had made it as clear as possible that the artifact could offer him nothing, it had not relented its tempting call.

He heard that call now, drifting out over the mountain passes, reaching out to the orcs and begging them to come and find the treasure.

Halt the call, Entreri silently commanded the artifact. *These creatures are not worthy to serve either you or me as slaves.*

He sensed it then, a moment of confusion from the artifact, a moment of fleeting hope—there, Entreri knew without the slightest of doubts, Crenshinibon did desire him as a wielder!—followed by . . . questions. Entreri seized the moment to interject his own thoughts into the stream of the telepathic call. He offered no words, for he didn't even speak Orcish, and doubted that the creatures would understand any of the human tongues he did speak, but merely imparted images of orc slaves, serving the master dark elf. He figured Jarlaxle would be a more imposing figure to orcs than he. Entreri showed them one orc being eaten by drow, another being beaten and torn apart with savage glee.

"What are you doing, my friend?" he heard Jarlaxle's insistent call, in a loud voice that told him his drow companion had likely asked that same question several times already.

"Putting a little doubt into the minds of our ugly little camp-followers," Entreri replied. "Joining Crenshinibon's call to them in the hopes that they will hardly sort out one lie from the other."

Jarlaxle wore a perplexed expression indeed, and Entreri understood all the questions that were likely behind it, for he was harboring many of the same doubts. One lie from another indeed. Or were the promises of Crenshinibon truly lies? the assassin had to ask himself. Even beyond that fundamental confusion, the assassin understood that Jarlaxle would, and had to, fear Entreri's motivations. Was Entreri, perhaps, shading his words to Jarlaxle in a way that would make the mercenary drow come to agree with Entreri's assessment that he, and not the dark elf, should carry the Crystal Shard?

"Ignore whatever doubts Crenshinibon is now giving to you," Entreri said matter-of-factly, reading the dark elf's expression perfectly.

"Even if you speak the truth, I fear that you play a dangerous game with an artifact that is far beyond your understanding," Jarlaxle retorted after another introspective pause.

"I know what it is," Entreri assured him, "and I know that it understands the truth of our relationship. That is why the Crystal Shard so desperately wants to be free of me—and is thus calling to you once more."

Jarlaxle looked at him hard, and for just a moment, Entreri thought the drow might move against him.

"Do not disappoint me," the assassin said simply.

Jarlaxle blinked, took off his hat, and rubbed the sweat from his bald head again.

"There!" Entreri said, pointing down to the lower slopes, to where a fight had broken out between different factions among the orcs. Few of the ugly brutes seemed to be trying to make peace, as was the way with chaotic orcs. The slightest spark could ignite warfare within a tribe of the beasts that would continue at the cost of many lives until one side was simply wiped out. Entreri, with his imparted images of torture and slavery and images of a drow master, had done more than flick a little spark. "It would seem that some of them heeded my call over that of the artifact."

"And I had thought this day would bring some excitement," Jarlaxle remarked. "Shall we join them before they kill each other? To aid whichever side is losing, of course."

"And with our aid, that side will soon be winning," Entreri reasoned, and Jarlaxle's quick response came as no surprise.

"Of course," said the drow, "we are then honor-bound to join in with the side that is losing. It could be a complicated afternoon."

Entreri smiled as he worked his way around the ledge of the current perch, looking for a quick way down to the orcs.

By the time the pair got close to the fighting, they realized that their estimates of a score of orcs had been badly mistaken. There were at least fifty of the beasts, all running around in a frenzy now, whacking at each other with abandon, using clubs, branches, sharpened sticks, and a few crafted weapons.

Jarlaxle tipped his hat to the assassin, motioned for Entreri to go left, and went right, blending into the shadows so perfectly that Entreri had to blink to make sure they were not deceiving him. He knew that Jarlaxle, like all dark elves, was stealthy. Likewise he knew that while Jarlaxle's cloak was not the standard drow *piwafwi*, it did have many magical qualities. It surprised him that anyone, short of using a wizard's invisibility spell, could find a way so to completely hide that great plumed hat.

Entreri shook it off and ran to the left, finding an easy path of shadows through the sparse trees, boulders, and rocky ridges. He approached the first group of orcs—four of the beasts squared up in battle, three against one. Moving silently, the assassin worked his way around the back of the trio, thinking to even up the odds with a sudden strike. He knew he was making no noise, knew he was hiding perfectly from tree to tree to rock to ridge. He had performed attacks like this for nearly three decades, had perfected the stealthy strike to an unprecedented level—and these were only orcs, simple, stupid brutes.

How surprised Entreri was, then, when two of the fighting trio howled and leaped around, charging right for him. The orc they had been fighting, with complete disregard to the battle at hand, similarly charged at the assassin. The remaining orc opponent promptly cut it down as it ran past.

Hard-pressed, Entreri worked his sword left and right, parrying the thrusts of the two makeshift spears and shearing the tip off one in the process. He was back on his heels, in a position of terrible balance. Had he been fighting an opponent of true skill he surely would have been killed, but these were only orcs. Their weapons were poorly crafted and their tactics were utterly predictable. He had defeated their first thrusts, their only chance, and yet, still they came on, headlong, with abandon.

Charon's Claw waved before them, filling the air with an opaque wall of ash. They plunged right through—of course they did!—but Entreri had already skittered to the left, and he spun back behind the charge of the closest orc, plunging his dagger deep into the creature's side. He didn't retract the blade immediately, though he had broken free. He could have made an easy kill of the second stumbling orc. No, he used the dagger to draw out the life-force from the already dying creature, taking that life-force into his own body to speed the healing of his own previous wounds.

By the time he let the limp creature drop to the ground, the second orc was at him, stabbing wildly. Entreri caught the spear with the crosspiece of his dagger and easily turned it up high, over his shoulder, and ducked and stepped ahead, shearing across with a great sweep of Charon's Claw. The orc instinctively tried to block with its arm, but the sword cut right through the limb, and drove hard into the orc's side, splintering ribs and tearing a great hole in its lung, all the way to its heart.

Entreri could hardly believe that the third of the group was still charging at him after seeing how easily and completely he had destroyed its two companions. He casually planted his left foot against the chest of the drooping, dead creature impaled on his sword, and waited for the exact moment. When that moment came, he turned the dead orc and kicked it free, dropping it in the path of its charging, howling companion.

The orc tripped, diving headlong past Entreri. The assassin stabbed up hard with the dagger, catching the orc under the chin and driving the blade up into its head. He bent as the heavy orc continued its facedown dive, ending with him holding the creature's head from the ground and the orc twitching spasmodically as it died.

A twist and yank tore the dagger free, and Entreri paused only long enough to wipe both his blades on the dead beast's back before running off in pursuit of other prey.

His stride was more tempered this time, though, for his failure in approaching the trio from behind bothered him greatly. He believed he understood what had happened—the Crystal Shard had called out a warning to the group—but the thought that carrying the cursed item left him without his favored mode of attack and his greatest ability to defend himself was more than a little unsettling.

He charged across the side of the rock facing, picking shadows where he could find them but worrying little about cover. He understood that with the Crystal Shard on his belt, he was likely as obvious as he would be sitting beside a blazing campfire on a dark night. He came past one small area of brush onto the lower edge of sloping, bare stone. Cursing the open ground but hardly slowing, Entreri started across.

He saw the charge of another orc out of the corner of his eye, the creature rushing headlong at him, one arm back and ready to launch a spear his way.

The orc was barely five strides away when it threw, but Entreri didn't even have to parry the errant missile, just letting it fly harmlessly past. He did react to it, though, with dramatic movement, and that only spurred on the eager orc attacker.

It leaped at the seemingly vulnerable man, a flying tackle aimed for Entreri's waist. Two quick steps took the assassin out of harm's way, and he swished his sword down onto the orc's back as it flew past, cracking the powerful weapon right through the creature's backbone. The orc skidded down hard on its face, its upper torso and arms squirming wildly, but its legs making no movement of their own.

Entreri didn't even bother finishing the wretched creature. He just ran on. He had a direction sorted for his run, for he heard the unmistakable laughter of a drow who seemed to be having too much fun.

He found Jarlaxle standing atop a boulder amidst the largest tumult of battling orcs, spurring one side on with excited words that Entreri could not understand, while systematically cutting down their opponents with dagger after thrown dagger.

Entreri stopped in the shadow of a tree and watched the spectacle.

Sure enough, Jarlaxle soon changed sides, calling out to the other orcs, and launching that endless stream of daggers at members of the side he had just been urging on.

The numbers dwindled, obviously so, and eventually, even the stupid orcs caught on to the deadly ruse. As one, they turned on Jarlaxle.

The drow only laughed at them all the harder as a dozen spears came his way—every one of them missing the mark badly due to the displacement magic in the drow's cloak and the bad aim of the orcs. The drow countered, throwing one dagger after another. Jarlaxle spun around on his high perch, always seeking the closest orc, and always hitting home with a nearly perfect throw.

Out of the shadows came Entreri, a whirlwind of fury, dagger working efficiently, but sword waving wildly, building walls of floating ash as the assassin sliced up the battlefield to suit his designs. Inevitably, Entreri worked his way into a situation that put him one-on-one against an orc. Just as inevitably, that creature was down and dying within the span of a few thrusts and stabs.

Entreri and Jarlaxle walked slowly back up the mountain slope soon after, with the drow complaining at the meager take of silver pieces they had found on the orcs. Entreri was hardly listening, was more concerned with the call that had brought the creatures to them in the first place—the plea, the scream, for help from Crenshinibon. These were just a rag-tag band of orcs, but what more powerful creatures might the Crystal Shard find to come to its call next?

"The call of the shard is strong," he admitted to Jarlaxle.

"It has existed for centuries," the drow answered. "It knows well how to preserve itself."

"That existence is soon to end," Entreri said grimly.

"Why?" Jarlaxle asked with perfect innocence.

The tone more than the word stopped Entreri cold in his tracks and made him turn around to regard his surprising companion.

"Do we have to go through this all over again?" the assassin asked.

"My friend, I know why you believe the Crystal Shard to be unacceptable for either of us to wield, but why does that translate into the need to destroy it?" Jarlaxle asked. He paused and glanced around, and motioned for Entreri to follow and led the assassin to the edge of a fairly deep ravine, a remote valley. "Why not just throw it away then?" he asked. "Toss it from this cliff and let it land where it may?"

Entreri stared out at the remote vale and almost considered taking Jarlaxle's advice. Almost, but a very real truth rang clear in his mind. "Because it would find its way back to the hands of our adversaries soon enough," he replied. "The Crystal Shard saw great potential in Rai-guy,"

Jarlaxle nodded. "Sensible," he said. "Ever was that one too ambitious for his own good. Why do you care, though? Let Rai-guy have it and have all of Calimport, if the artifact can deliver the city to him. What does it matter to Artemis Entreri, who is gone from that place, and who will not return anytime soon in any event? Likely, my former lieutenant will be too preoccupied with the potential gains he might find with the artifact in his hands even to worry about our whereabouts. Perhaps freeing ourselves of the burden of the artifact will indeed save us from the pursuit we now fear at our backs."

Entreri spent a long moment musing over that reasoning, but one fact kept nagging at him. "The Crystal Shard knows I wish to see it destroyed," he replied. "It knows that in my heart I hate it and will find some way to be rid of the thing. Rai-guy knows the threat that is Jarlaxle. As long as you live, he can never be certain of his position within Bregan D'aerthe. What would happen if Jarlaxle reappeared in Menzoberranzan, reaching out to old comrades against the fools who tried to steal the throne of Bregan D'aerthe?"

Jarlaxle offered no response, but the twinkle in his dark eyes told Entreri that his drow companion would like nothing more than to play out that very scenario.

"He wants you dead," Entreri said bluntly. "He needs you dead, and with the Crystal Shard at his disposal, that might not prove to be an overly difficult task."

The twinkle in Jarlaxle's dark eyes remained, but after a moment's thought, he just shrugged and said, "Lead on."

Entreri did just that, back to their horses and back to the trails that would take them to the northeast, to the Snowflake Mountains and the Spirit Soaring. Entreri was quite pleased with the way he had handled Jarlaxle, quite pleased in the strength of his argument for destroying the Crystal Shard.

But it was all just so much dung, he knew, all a justification for that which was in his heart. Yes, he was determined to destroy the Crystal Shard, and would see the artifact obliterated, but it was not for any fear of retribution or of pursuit. Entreri wanted Crenshinibon destroyed simply because the mere existence of the dominating artifact revolted him. The Crystal Shard, in trying to coerce him, had insulted him profoundly. He didn't hold any notion that the wretched world would be a better place without the artifact, and hardly cared whether it would be or not, but he did believe that he would more greatly enjoy his existence in the world knowing that one less wretched and perverted item such as the Crystal Shard remained in existence.

Of course, as Entreri harbored these thoughts, Crenshinibon realized them as well. The Crystal Shard could only seethe, could only hope that it might find someone weaker of heart and stronger of arm to slay Artemis Entreri and free it from his grasp.

CHAPTER

18

It was Entreri," Sharlotta Vespers said with a sly grin as she examined the orc corpse on the side of the mountain a couple days later. "The precision of the cuts . . . and see, a dagger thrust here, a sword slash there."

"Many fight with sword and dirk," the wererat, Gord Abrix, replied. The wretch, wearing his human form at that time, moved his hands out wide as he spoke, revealing his own sword and dagger hanging on his belt.

"But few strike so well," Sharlotta argued.

"And these others," Berg'inyon Baenre agreed in his stilted command of the common tongue. He swung his arm about to encompass the many orcs lying dead around the base of a large boulder. "Wounds consistent with a dagger throw—and so many of them. Only one warrior that I know of carries such a supply as that."

"You are counting wounds, not daggers!" Gord Abrix argued.

"They are one and the same in a fight this frantic," Berg'inyon reasoned. "These are throws, not stabs, for there is no tearing about the sides of the cuts, just a single fast puncture. And I think it unlikely that anyone would throw a few daggers at one opponent, somehow run down and pull them free, then throw them at another."

"Where are these daggers, then, drow?" the wererat leader asked doubtfully.

"Jarlaxle's missiles are magical in nature and disappear," Berg'inyon answered coldly. "His supply is nearly endless. This is the work of Jarlaxle, I know—and not his best work, I warn both of you."

Sharlotta and Gord Abrix exchanged nervous glances, though the wererat leader still held that doubting expression.

"Have you not yet learned the proper respect for the drow?" Berg'inyon asked him pointedly and threateningly.

Gord Abrix went back on his heels and held his empty hands up before him.

Sharlotta eyed him closely. Gord Abrix wanted a fight, she knew, even with this dark elf standing before him. Sharlotta hadn't really seen Berg'inyon Baenre in action, but she had seen his lessers, dark elves who had spoken of this young Baenre with the utmost respect. Even those lessers would have had little trouble in slaughtering the prideful Gord Abrix. Yes, Sharlotta realized then and there, her own self-preservation would depend upon her getting as far away from Gord Abrix and his sewer dwellers as possible, for there was no respect here, only abject hatred for Artemis Entreri and a genuine dislike for the dark elves. No doubt, Gord Abrix would lead his companions, wererat and otherwise, into absolute devastation.

Sharlotta Vespers, the survivor, wanted no part of that.

"The bodies are cold, the blood dried, but they have not been cleanly picked," Berg'inyon observed.

"A couple of days, no more," Sharlotta added, and she looked to Gord Abrix, as did Berg'inyon.

The wererat nodded and smiled wickedly. "I will have them," he declared. He walked off to confer with his wererat companions, who had been standing off to the side of the battleground.

"He will have a straight passageway to the realm of death," Berg'inyon quietly remarked to Sharlotta when the two were alone.

Sharlotta looked at the drow curiously. She agreed, of course, but she had to wonder why, if the dark elves knew this, they were allowing Gord Abrix to hold so critical a role in this all-important pursuit.

"Gord Abrix thinks he will get them," she replied, "both of them, yet you do not seem so confident."

Berg'inyon chuckled at the remark—one he obviously believed absurd. "No doubt, Entreri is a deadly opponent," he said.

"More so than you understand," Sharlotta, who knew the assassin's exploits well, was quick to add.

"And yet he is still, by any measure, the easier of the prey," Berg'inyon assured her. "Jarlaxle has survived for centuries with his intelligence and skill. He thrives in a land more violent than Calimport could ever know. He ascends to the highest levels of power in a warring city that prevents the ascent of males. Our wretched companion Gord Abrix cannot understand the truth of Jarlaxle, nor can you, so I tell you this now—out of the respect I have gained for you in these short tendays—beware that one."

Sharlotta paused and stared long and hard at the surprising drow warrior. Offering her respect? The notion pleased her and made her fearful all at once, for Sharlotta had already learned to try to look beneath every word uttered by her dark elf comrades. Perhaps Berg'inyon had just paid her a high and generous compliment. Perhaps he was setting her up for disaster.

Sharlotta glanced down at the ground, biting her lower lip as she fell into her thoughts, sorting it all out. Perhaps Berg'inyon was setting her up, she reasoned again, as Rai-guy and Kimmuriel had set up Gord Abrix. As she thought of the mighty Jarlaxle and the item he possessed, she came to realize, of course, that there was no way Rai-guy could believe Gord Abrix and his ragged wererat band could possibly bring down the great Entreri and the great Jarlaxle. If that came to pass, then Gord Abrix would have the Crystal Shard in his possession, and what trouble might he bring about before Rai-guy and Kimmuriel could take it away from him? No, Rai-guy and Kimmuriel did not believe that the wererat leader would get anywhere near the Crystal Shard, and furthermore, they didn't want him anywhere near it.

Sharlotta looked back up at Berg'inyon to see him smiling slyly, as if he had just followed her reasoning as clearly as if she had spoken it aloud. "The drow always use a lesser race to lead the way into battle," the dark elf warrior said. "We never truly know, of course, what surprises our enemies might have in store."

"Fodder," Sharlotta remarked.

Berg'inyon's expression was perfectly blank, was absent of any sense of compassion at all, giving Sharlotta all the confirmation she needed.

A shudder coursed up Sharlotta's spine as she considered the sheer coldness of that look, dispassionate and inhuman, a less-than-subtle reminder to her that these dark elves were indeed very different, and much, much more dangerous. Artemis Entreri was, perhaps, the closest creature she had ever met in temperament to the drow, but it seemed to her that, in terms of sheer evil, even he paled in comparison. These long-lived dark elves had perfected the craft of efficient heartlessness to a level beyond human comprehension, let alone human mimicry. She turned to regard Gord Abrix and his eager wererats, and made a silent vow then to stay as far away from the doomed creatures as possible.

<hr />

The demon writhed on the floor in agony, its skin smoking, its blood boiling.

Cadderly did not pity the creature, though it pained him to have to lower himself to this level. He did not enjoy torture—even the torture of a demon, as deserving a creature as ever existed. He did not enjoy dealing with the denizens of the lower planes at all, but he had to for the sake of the Spirit Soaring, for the sake of his wife and children.

The Crystal Shard was coming to him, was coming for him, he knew, and his impending battle with the vile artifact might prove to be as important as his war had been against *Tuanta Quiro Miancay,* the dreaded Chaos Curse. It was as important as his construction of the Spirit Soaring, for what lasting effect might the remarkable cathedral hold if Crenshinibon reduced it to rubble?

"You know the answer," Cadderly said as calmly as he could. "Tell me, and I will release you."

"You are a fool, priest of Deneir!" the demon growled, its guttural words broken apart as spasm after spasm wracked its physical form. "Do you know the enemy you make in Mizferac?"

Cadderly sighed. "And so it continues," he said, as if he were speaking to himself, though well aware that Mizferac would hear his words and understand the painful implications of them with crystalline clarity.

"Release me!" the glabrezu demanded.

"Yokk tu Mizferac be-enck do-tu," Cadderly recited, and the demon howled and jerked wildly about the floor within the perfectly designed protective circle.

"This will take as long as you wish," Cadderly said coldly to the demon. "I have no mercy for your kind, I assure you."

"We . . . want . . . no . . . mercy," Mizferac growled. Then a great spasm wracked the beast, and it jerked wildly, rolling about and shrieking curses in its profane, demonic language.

Cadderly just quietly recited more of the exaction spell, bolstering his resolve with the continual reminder that his children might soon be in mortal danger.

"Ye wasn't lost! Ye was playing!" Ivan Bouldershoulder roared at his green-bearded brother.

"Doo-dad maze!" Pikel argued vehemently.

The normally docile dwarf's tone took his brother somewhat by surprise. "Ye getting talkative since ye becomed a doo-dad, ain't ye?" he asked.

"Oo oi!" Pikel shrieked, punching his fist in the air.

"Well, ye shouldn't be playin' in yer maze when Cadderly's at such dark business," Ivan scolded.

"Doo-dad maze," Pikel whispered under his breath, and he lowered his gaze.

"Yeah, whatever ye might be callin' it," grumbled Ivan, who had never been overly fond of his brother's woodland calling and considered it quite an unnatural thing for a dwarf. "He might be needin' us, ye fool." Ivan held up his great axe as he spoke, flexing the bulging muscles on his short but powerful arm.

Pikel responded with one of his patented grins and held up a wooden cudgel.

"Great weapon for fighting demons," Ivan muttered.

"Sha-la—" Pikel started.

"Yeah, I'm knowin' the name," Ivan cut in. "Sha-la-la. I'm think-ing that a demon might be callin' it kind-lind-ling."

Pikel's grin drooped into a severe frown.

The door to the summoning chamber pulled open and a very weary Cadderly emerged—or tried to. He tripped over something and sprawled facedown to the floor.

"Oops," said Pikel.

"Me brother put one o' his magic trips on the doorway," Ivan explained, helping the priest back to his feet. "We was worryin' that a demon might be walkin' out."

"So of course, Pikel would trip the thing to the floor and bash it with his club," Cadderly said dryly, pulling himself back to his feet.

"Sha-la-la!" Pikel squealed gleefully, completely missing the sarcasm in the young cleric's tone.

"Ain't one coming, is there?" Ivan asked, looking past Cadderly.

"The glabrezu, Mizferac, has been dismissed to its own foul

plane," Cadderly assured the dwarves. "I brought it forth again, thus rescinding the hundred year banishment I had just exacted upon it, to answer a specific question, and with that done, I had—and have, I hope—no further need of it."

"Ye should've kept him about just so me and me brother could bash him a few times," said Ivan.

"Sha-la-la!'" Pikel agreed.

"Save your strength, for I fear we will need it," Cadderly explained. "I have learned the secret to destroying the Crystal Shard, or at least, I have learned of the creature that might complete the task."

"Demon?" Ivan asked.

"Doo-dad?" Pikel added hopefully.

Cadderly, shaking his head, started to reply to Ivan, but paused to put a perfectly puzzled expression over the green-bearded dwarf. Embarrassed, Pikel merely shrugged and said, "Ooo."

"No demon," he said to the other dwarf at length. "A creature of this world."

"Giant?"

"Think bigger."

Ivan started to speak again, but paused, taking in Cadderly's sour expression and studying it in light of all that they had been through together.

"Let me guess one more time," the dwarf said.

Cadderly didn't answer.

"Dragon," Ivan said.

"Ooo," said Pikel.

Cadderly didn't answer.

"Red dragon," Ivan clarified.

"Ooo," said Pikel.

Cadderly didn't answer.

"Big red dragon," said the dwarf. "*Huge* red dragon! Old as the mountains."

"Ooo," said Pikel, three more times.

Cadderly merely sighed.

"Old Fyren's dead," Ivan said, and there was indeed a slight tremor in the tough dwarf's voice, for that fight with the great red dragon had nearly been the end of them all.

"Fyrentennimar was not the last of its kind, nor the greatest, I assure you," Cadderly replied evenly.

"Ye're thinking that we got to take the thing to another of the beasts?" Ivan asked incredulously. "To one bigger than old Fyren?"

"So I am told," explained Cadderly. "A red dragon, ancient and huge."

Ivan shook his head, and snapped a glare over Pikel, who said, "Ooo," once again.

Ivan couldn't help but chuckle. They had met up with mighty Fyrentennimar on their way to find the mountain fortress that housed the minions of Cadderly's own wicked father. Through Cadderly's powerful magic, the dragon had been "tamed" into flying Cadderly and the others across the Snowflake Mountains. A battle deeper in those mountains had broken the spell though, and old Fyren had turned on its temporary masters with a vengeance. Somehow, Cadderly had managed to hold onto enough magical strength to weaken the beast enough for Vander, a giant friend, to lop off its head, but Ivan knew, and so did the others, that the win had been as much a feat of luck as of skill.

"Drizzt Do'Urden told ye about another of the reds, didn't he?" Ivan remarked.

"I know where we can find one," Cadderly replied grimly.

Danica walked in, then, her smile wide—until she noted the expressions on the faces of the other three.

"Poof!" said Pikel and he walked out of the room, muttering squeaky little sounds.

A puzzled Danica watched him go. Then she turned to his brother.

"He's a doo-dad," Ivan explained, "and fearin' no natural creature.

There ain't nothin' less natural than a red dragon, I'm guessing, so he's not too happy right now." Ivan snorted and walked out behind his brother.

"Red dragon?" Danica asked Cadderly.

"Poof," the priest replied.

CHAPTER

19

Entreri frowned when he glanced from the not-too-distant village to his ridiculously plumed drow companion. The hat alone, with its wide brim and huge diatryma feather that always grew back after Jarlaxle used it to summon a real giant bird, would invite suspicion and likely open disdain, from the farmers of the village. Then there was the fact that the wearer was a dark elf. . . .

"You really should consider a disguise," Entreri said dryly, and shook his head, wishing he still had a particular magic item, a mask that could transform the wearer's appearance. Drizzt Do'Urden had once used the thing to get from the northlands around Waterdeep all the way to Calimport disguised as a surface elf.

"I have considered a disguise," the drow replied, and to Entreri's—temporary—relief, he pulled the hat from his head. A good start, it seemed.

Jarlaxle merely brushed the thing off and plopped it right back in place. "You wear one, as well," the drow protested to Entreri's scowl, pointing to the small-brimmed black hat Entreri now wore. The hat was called a bolero, named after the drow wizard who had given it its tidy shape and had imbued it, and several others of the same make, with certain magical properties.

"Not the hat!" the frustrated Entreri replied, and he rubbed a hand across his face. "These are simple farmers, likely with very

282

definite feelings about dark elves—and likely, those feelings are not favorable."

"For most dark elves, I would agree with them," said Jarlaxle, and he ended there, and merely kept riding on his way toward the village, as if Entreri had said nothing to him at all.

"Hence, the disguise," the assassin called after him.

"Indeed," said Jarlaxle, and he kept on riding.

Entreri kicked his heels into his horse's flanks, spurring the mount into a quick canter to bring him up beside the elusive drow. "I mean that you should consider wearing one," Entreri said plainly.

"But I am," the drow replied. "And you, Artemis Entreri, above all others, should recognize me! I am Drizzt Do'Urden, your most hated rival."

"What?" the assassin asked incredulously.

"Drizzt Do'Urden, the perfect disguise for me," Jarlaxle casually replied. "Does not Drizzt walk openly from town to town, neither hiding nor denying his heritage, even in those places where he is not well-known?"

"*Does* he?" Entreri asked slyly.

"*Did* he not?" Jarlaxle quickly replied, correcting the tense, for of course, as far as Artemis Entreri knew, Drizzt Do'Urden was dead.

Entreri stared hard at the drow.

"Well, did he not?" Jarlaxle asked plainly. "And it was Drizzt's nerve, I say, in parading about so openly, that prevented townsfolk from organizing against him and slaying him. Because he remained so obvious, it became obvious that he had nothing to hide. Thus, I use the same technique and even the same name. I am Drizzt Do'Urden, hero of Icewind Dale, friend of King Bruenor Battlehammer of Mithral Hall, and no enemy of these simple farmers. Rather, I might be of use to them, should danger threaten."

"Of course," Entreri replied. "Unless one of them crosses you, in which case you will destroy the entire town."

"There is always that," Jarlaxle admitted, but he didn't slow his mount, and he and Entreri were getting close to the village now, close enough to be seen for what they were—or at least, for what they were pretending to be.

There were no guards about, and the pair rode in undisturbed, their horses' hooves clattering on cobblestone roads. They pulled up before one two-story building, on which hung a shingle painted with a foamy mug of mead and naming the place as

Gent eman Briar's Good y
P ace of Si ing

in lettering old and weathered.

"Si ing," Jarlaxle read, scratching his head, and he gave a great and dramatic sigh. "This is a gathering hall for those of melancholy?"

"Not sighing," Entreri replied. He looked at Jarlaxle, snorted, and rolled off the side of his horse. "Sitting, or perhaps sipping. Not sighing."

"Sitting, then, or sipping," Jarlaxle announced, looping his right leg over his horse, and rolling over backward off the mount into a somersault to land gracefully on his feet. "Or perhaps a bit of both! Ha!" He ended with a great gleaming smile.

Entreri stared at him hard yet again, and just shook his head, thinking that perhaps he would have been better off leaving this one with Rai-guy and Kimmuriel.

A dozen patrons were inside the place, ten men and a pair of women, along with a grizzled old barkeep whose snarl seemed to be eternally etched upon his stubbly face, a locked expression amidst the leathery wrinkles and acne scars. One by one, the thirteen took note of the pair entering, and inevitably, each nodded or merely glanced away, and shot a stunned expression back at the duo, particularly at the dark elf, and sent a hand to the hilt of the nearest weapon. One man even leaped up from his chair, sending it skidding out behind him.

Entreri and Jarlaxle merely tipped their hats and moved to the bar, making no threatening movements and keeping their expressions perfectly friendly.

"What're ye about?" the barkeep barked at them. "Who're ye, and what's yer business?"

"Travelers," Entreri answered, "weary of the road and seeking a bit of respite."

"Well, ye'll not be finding it here, ye won't!" the barkeep growled. "Get yer hats back on yer ugly heads and get yer arses out me door!"

Entreri looked to Jarlaxle, who seemed perfectly unperturbed. "I do believe we will stay a bit," the drow stated. "I do understand your hesitance, good sir . . . good Eman Briar," he added, remembering the sign.

"Eman?" the barkeep echoed in obvious confusion.

"Eman Briar, so says your placard," Jarlaxle answered innocently.

"Eh?" the puzzled man asked, then his old yellow eyes lit up as he caught on. "*Gentle*man Briar," he insisted. "The L's all rotted away. *Gentleman* Briar."

"Your pardon, good sir," the charming and disarming Jarlaxle said with a bow. He gave a great sigh and threw a wink at Entreri's predictable scowl. "We have come in to sigh, sit, and sip, a bit of all three. We want no trouble and bring none, I assure you. Have you not heard of me? Drizzt Do'Urden of Icewind Dale, who reclaimed Mithral Hall for dwarven King Bruenor Battlehammer?"

"Never heard o' no Drizzit Dudden," Briar replied. "Now get ye outta me place afore me friends and me haul ye out!" His voice rose as he spoke, and several of the gathered men did, as well, moving together and readying their weapons.

Jarlaxle glanced around at the lot of them, smiling, seeming perfectly amused. Entreri, too, was quite entertained by it all, but he didn't bother looking around, just leaned back on his barstool, watching his friend and trying to see how Jarlaxle might wriggle out of this one. Of course, the ragged band of farmers hardly bothered the skilled assassin, especially since he was sitting next to the dangerous Jarlaxle. If they had to leave the town in ruin, so be it.

Thus, Entreri did not even search the ever-present silent call of the imprisoned Crystal Shard. If the artifact wanted these simple fools to take it from Entreri, then let them try!

"Did I not just tell you that I reclaimed a dwarven kingdom?" Jarlaxle asked. "And mostly without help. Hear me well, Gent Eman Briar. If you and your friends here try to expel me, your kin will be planting more than crops this season."

It wasn't so much what he said as it was the manner in which he said it, so casual, so confident, so perfectly assured that this group could not begin to frighten him. The men approaching slowed to a halt, all of them glancing to the others for some sign of leadership.

"Truly, I desire no trouble," Jarlaxle said calmly. "I have dedicated my life to erasing the prejudices—rightful conceptions, in many instances—that so many hold for my people. I am not merely a weary traveler, but a warrior for the causes of common men. If goblins attacked your fair town, I would fight beside you until they were driven away, or until my heart beat its last!" His voice continued a dramatic climb: "If a great dragon swooped down upon your village, I would brave its fiery breath, draw forth my weapons and leap to the parapets. . . ."

"I think they understand your point," Entreri said to him, grabbing him by the arm and easing him back to his seat.

Gentleman Briar snorted. "Ye're not even carryin' no weapon, drow," he observed.

"A thousand dead men have said the same thing," Entreri replied in all seriousness. Jarlaxle tipped his hat to the assassin. "But enough banter," Entreri added, hopping from his seat and pulling back his cloak to reveal his two fabulous weapons, the jeweled dagger and the magnificent Charon's Claw with its distinctive bony hilt. "If you mean to fight us, then do so now, that I can finish this business and still find a good meal, a better drink, and a warm bed before the fall of night. If not, then go back to your tables, I beg, and leave us in peace, else I'll forget my delusional paladin friend's desire to become the hero of the land."

Again, the patrons glanced nervously at each other, and some grumbled under their breaths.

"Gentleman Briar, they await your signal," Entreri remarked. "Choose well which signal that will be, or else find a way to mix blood with your drink, for you shall have gallons of it pooling about your tavern."

Briar waved his hand, sending his patrons retreating to their respective tables, and gave a great snort and snarl.

"Good!" Jarlaxle remarked, slapping his leg. "My reputation is saved from the rash actions of my impetuous friend. Now, if you would be so kind as to fetch me a fine and delicate drink, Gentleman Briar," he instructed, pulling forth his purse, which was bulging with coins.

"I'm servin' no damned drow in me tavern," Briar insisted, crossing his thin but muscled arms over his chest.

"Then I will gladly serve myself," Jarlaxle answered without hesitation, and he politely tipped his great plumed hat. "Of course, that will mean fewer coins for you."

Briar stared at him hard.

Jarlaxle ignored him and stared instead at the fairly wide selection of bottles on the shelves behind the bar. He tapped a delicate finger against his lip, scrutinizing the colors, and the words of the few that were actually marked.

"Suggestions?" he asked Entreri.

"Something to drink," the assassin replied.

Jarlaxle pointed to one bottle, uttered a simple magical command, and snapped his finger back, and the bottle flew from the shelf to his waiting grasp. Two more points and commands had a pair of glasses sitting upon the bar before the companions.

Jarlaxle reached for the bottle. The stunned and angry Briar snapped his hand out to grab the dark elf's arm.

He never got close.

Faster than Briar could possibly react, faster than he could think to react, Entreri snapped his hand on the barkeep's reaching arm, slamming it down to the bar and holding it fast. In the same fluid motion, the assassin's other hand came, holding the jeweled dagger, and Entreri plunged it hard into the wooden shelf right between Gentleman Briar's fingers. The blood drained from the man's ruddy face.

"If you persist, there will be little left of your tavern," Entreri promised in the coldest, most threatening voice Gentleman Briar had ever heard. "Enough to build a proper box to bury you in, perhaps."

"Doubtful," said Jarlaxle.

The drow was perfectly at ease, hardly paying attention, seeming as though he had expected Entreri's intervention all along. He poured the two drinks and eased himself back, sniffing, and sipping his liquor.

Entreri let the man go, glanced around to make sure that none of the others were moving, and slid his dagger back into its sheath on his belt.

"Good sir," Jarlaxle said. "I tell you one more time that we have no argument with you, nor do we wish one. Our road behind us has been long and dry, and the road before us will no doubt prove equally harsh. Thus we have entered your fair tavern in this fair village. Why would you think to deny us?"

"The better question is, why would you wish to be killed?" Entreri put in.

Gentleman Briar looked from one to the other and threw up his hands in defeat. "To the Nine Hells with both of ye," he growled, spinning away.

Entreri looked to Jarlaxle, who merely shrugged and said, "I have already been there. Hardly worth a return visit." He took up his glass and the bottle and walked away. Entreri, with his own glass, followed him across the room to the one free table in the small place.

Of course, the two tables near that one soon became empty as well, when the patrons took up their glasses and other items and scurried away from the dark elf.

"It will always be like this," Entreri said to his companion a short while later.

"It had not been so for Drizzt Do'Urden of late, so my spies indicated," the drow answered. "His reputation, in those lands where he was known, outshone the color of his skin in the eyes of even the small-minded men. So, soon, will my own."

"A reputation for heroic deeds?" Entreri asked with a doubting laugh. "Are you to become a hero for the land, then?"

"That, or a reputation for leaving burned-out villages behind me," Jarlaxle replied. "Either way, I care little."

That brought a smile to Entreri's face, and he dared to hope then that he and his companion would get along famously.

Kimmuriel and Rai-guy stared at the mirror enchanted for divining, watching the procession of nearly a score of ratmen, all in their human guise, trotting into the village.

"It is already tense," Kimmuriel observed. "If Gord Abrix plays correctly, the townsfolk will join with him against Entreri and Jarlaxle. Thirty-to-two. Fine odds."

Rai-guy gave a derisive snort. "Strong enough odds, perhaps, so that Jarlaxle and Entreri will be a bit weary before we go in to finish the task," he said.

Kimmuriel looked to his friend but, thinking about it, merely shrugged and grinned. He wasn't about to mourn the loss of Gord Abrix and a bunch of flea-infested wererats.

"If they do get in and get lucky," Kimmuriel remarked, "we must be quick. The Crystal Shard is in there."

"Crenshinibon is not calling to Gord Abrix and his fools," Rai-guy replied, his dark eyes gleaming with anticipation. "It is calling to me, even now. It knows we are close and knows how much greater it will be when I am the wielder."

Kimmuriel said nothing, but studied his friend intently, suspecting that if Rai-guy achieved his goal, he and Crenshinibon would likely soon be at odds with Kimmuriel.

⊷⊶

"How many does the tiny village hold?" Jarlaxle asked when the tavern doors opened and a group of men walked in.

Entreri started to answer flippantly, but held the thought and scrutinized the new group a bit more closely. "Not that many," he answered, shaking his head.

Jarlaxle followed the assassin's lead, studying the movements of the new arrivals, studying their weapons—swords mostly, and more ornate than anything the villagers were carrying.

Entreri's head snapped to the side as he noted other forms moving about the two small windows. He knew then, beyond any doubt.

These are not villagers, Jarlaxle silently agreed, using the intricate sign language of the dark elves, but moving his fingers much more slowly than normal in deference to Entreri's rudimentary understanding of the form.

"Ratmen," the assassin whispered in reply.

"You hear the shard calling to them?"

"I smell them," Entreri corrected. He paused a moment to consider whether the Crystal Shard might indeed be calling out to the group, a beacon for his enemies, but he just dismissed the thought, for it hardly mattered.

"Sewage on their shoes," Jarlaxle noted.

"Vermin in their blood," the assassin spat. He got up from his seat and took a step out from the table. "Let us begone," he said to Jarlaxle, loudly enough for the closest of the dozen ratmen who had entered the tavern to hear.

Entreri took a step toward the door, and a second, aware that all eyes were upon him and his flamboyant companion, who was just then rising from his seat. Entreri took a third step, then . . . he leaped to the side, driving his dagger into the heart of the closest ratman before it could begin to draw its sword.

"Murderers!" someone yelled, but Entreri hardly heard, leaping forward and drawing forth Charon's Claw.

Metal rang out loudly as he brutally parried the swinging sword of the next closest wererat, hitting the blade so hard that he sent it flying out wide. A quick reversal sent Entreri's sword slashing out to catch the ratman across the face, and it fell back, clutching its torn eyes.

Entreri had no time to pursue, for all the place was in motion then. A trio of ratmen, swords slashing the air before them, were closing fast. He waved Charon's Claw, creating a wall of ash, and leaped to the side, rolling under a table. The ratmen reacted, turning to pursue, but by the time they had their bearings, Entreri came up hard, bringing the table with him, launching it into their faces. Now he cut down low, taking a pair out at the knees, the fine blade cleanly severing one leg and nearly a second.

Ratmen bore down on him, but a rain of daggers came whipping past the assassin, driving them back.

Entreri waved his sword wildly, making a long and wavy vision-blocking wall. He managed a glance back at his companion to see Jarlaxle's arm furiously pumping, sending dagger after dagger soaring at an enemy. One group of ratmen, though, hoisted a table, as had Entreri, and used it as a shield. Several daggers thumped into it, catching fast. Bolstered by the impromptu shield, the group charged hard at the drow.

Too occupied suddenly with more enemies of his own, including a couple of townsfolk, Entreri turned his attention back to his own situation. He brought his sword up parallel to the floor, intercepting the blade of one villager and lifting it high. Entreri started to tilt the blade point up, the expected parry, which would bring the man's sword out wide. As the farmer pushed back against the block, Entreri fooled him by bringing up the hilt instead, turning the blade down and forcing the man's sword across his body. Faster than the man could react with any backhand move, Entreri snapped his hand, his weapon's skull-capped pommel, into the man's face, laying him low.

Back across came Charon's Claw, a mighty cut to intercept the sword of another, a ratman, and to slide through the parry and take the tip from another farmer's pitchfork. The assassin followed powerfully, stepping into his two foes, his sword working hard and furiously against the ratman's blade, driving it back, back, and to the side, forcing openings.

The jeweled dagger worked fast as well, with Entreri making circular motions over the broken pitchfork shaft, turning it one way and another and keeping the inexperienced farmer stumbling forward and off his balance. He would have been an easy kill, but Entreri had other ideas.

"Do you not understand the nature of your new allies?" he cried at the man, and as he spoke, he worked his sword even harder, slapping the blade against the wererat's sword to bat it slightly out of angle, and slapping the flat of the blade against the wererat's head. He didn't want to kill the creature, just to tempt the anger out of it. Again and again, the assassin's sword slapped at the wererat, bruising, taunting, stinging.

Entreri noted the creature's twitch and knew what was coming.

He drove the wererat back with a sudden but shortened stab, and went fully at the farmer, looping his dagger over and around the pitchfork, forcing it down at an angle. He went in one step toward the farmer, drove the wooden shaft down farther, forcing the man at an awkward angle that had him leaning on the assassin. Entreri broke away suddenly.

The farmer stumbled forward helplessly and Entreri had him in a lock, looping his sword arm around the man and turning him as he came on so that he was then facing the twitching, changing wererat.

The man gave a slight gasp, thinking his life was at its end, but caught fully in Entreri's grasp, a dagger at his back but not plunging in, he calmed enough to take in the spectacle.

His scream at the horrid transformation, as the wererat's face broke apart, twisted and wrenched, reforming into the head of a giant rodent, rent the air and brought all attention to the sight.

Entreri shoved the farmer toward the wrenching, changing ratman. To his satisfaction, he saw the farmer drive the broken pitchfork shaft through the beast's gut.

Entreri spun away with many more enemies still to fight. The farmers were standing perplexed, not knowing which side to take. The assassin knew enough about the shape-changers to understand that he had started a chain reaction here, that the enraged and excited wererats would look upon their transformed kin and likewise revert to their more primal form.

He took a moment to glance Jarlaxle's way then and saw the drow up in the air, levitating and turning circles, daggers flying from his pumping arm. Following their paths, Entreri saw one wererat, and another, stumble backward under the assault. A farmer grabbed at his calf, a blade deeply embedded there.

Jarlaxle purposely hadn't killed the human, Entreri noted, though he surely could have.

Entreri winced suddenly as a barrage of missiles soared back up at Jarlaxle, but the drow anticipated it and let go his levitation, dropping lightly and gracefully to the floor. He drew out two daggers as a host of opponents rushed in at him, grabbing them from hidden scabbards on his belt and not his enchanted bracer in a cross-armed maneuver. As he brought his arms back to their respective sides, Jarlaxle snapped his wrists and muttered something under his breath. The daggers elongated into fine, gleaming swords.

The drow planted his feet wide and exploded into motion, his arms pumping, his swords cutting fast circles, over and under, at his sides, chopping the air with popping, whipping sounds. He brought one across his chest, then the next, spinning them wildly, then went up high with one, turning his hand to put the blade over his head and parallel with the floor.

Entreri's expression soured. He had expected better of his drow companion. He had seen this fighting style many times, particularly among the pirates who frequented the seas off Calimport. It was called "swashbuckling," a deceptive, and deceptively easy, fighting technique that was more show than substance. The swashbuckler relied on the hesitance and fear of his opponents to afford him opportunities for better strikes. While often effective against weaker opponents, Entreri found the style ridiculous against any of true talent. He had killed several swashbucklers in his day—two in one fight when they had inadvertently tied each other up with their whirling blades—and had never found them to be particularly challenging.

The group of wererats coming in at Jarlaxle at that moment apparently didn't have much respect for the technique either. They quickly rushed around the drow, forming a box, and came in at him alternately, forcing him to turn, turn, and turn some more.

Jarlaxle was more than up to the task, keeping his spinning swords in perfect harmony as he countered every testing thrust or charge.

"They will tire him," Entreri whispered under his breath as he worked away from his newest opponents. He was trying to pick a path that would bring him to his drow friend that he might get Jarlaxle out of his predicament. He glanced back at the drow then, hoping he might get there in time, but honestly wondering if the disappointing Jarlaxle was still worth the trouble.

He gasped, first in confusion, and then in admiration.

Jarlaxle did a sudden back flip, twisting as he somersaulted so that he landed facing the opponent who had been at his back. The wererat stumbled away, hit twice by shortened stabs—shortened because Jarlaxle had other targets in mind.

The drow rolled around, falling into a crouch, and exploded out of it with a devastating double thrust at the wererat opposite. The creature leaped back, throwing its hips behind it and slapping its blade down in a desperate parry.

Before he could even think about it, Entreri cried out, thinking his friend doomed, for one sword-wielding wererat charged from Jarlaxle's direct left, another from behind and to the right, leaving the drow no room to skitter away.

"They reveal themselves," Kimmuriel said with a laugh. He, Rai-guy, and Berg'inyon watched the action through a dimensional portal that in effect put them in the thick of the fighting.

Berg'inyon thought the spectacle of the changing wererats equally amusing. He leaped forward, then, catching one farmer who was inadvertently stumbling through the portal, stabbing the man once in the side, and shoving him back through and to the tavern floor.

More forms rushed by, more cries came in at them, with Kimmuriel and Berg'inyon watching attentively and Rai-guy behind them, his eyes closed as he prepared his spells—a process that was taking the drow wizard longer because of the continuing, eager call of the imprisoned Crystal Shard.

Gord Abrix flashed by the door.

"Catch him!" Kimmuriel cried, and the agile Berg'inyon leaped through the doorway, grabbed Gord Abrix in a debilitating lock, and dived back through with the wererat in tow. He kept Gord Abrix held firmly out of the way, the wererat crying protests at Kimmuriel.

But the drow psionicist wasn't listening, for he was focused fully on his wizard companion. His timing in closing the door had to be perfect.

———⬥———

Jarlaxle didn't even try to get out of there, and Entreri realized, he had expected the attacks all along, had baited them.

Down low, his left leg far in front of his right, both arms and blades fully extended before him, Jarlaxle somehow managed to reverse his grip, and in a sudden and perfectly balanced momentum shift, the drow came back up straight. His left arm and blade stabbed out to the left. The sword in his right hand was flipped over in his hand so that when Jarlaxle turned his fist down, the tip was facing behind him, cocking straight back.

Both charging wererats halted suddenly, their chests ripped open by the perfect stabs.

Jarlaxle retracted the blades, put them back into their respective spins, and turned left, the whirling blades drawing lines of bright blood all over the wounded wererat there, and completing the turn, slashing the wererat behind him repeatedly and finishing with a powerful crossing backhand maneuver that took the creature's head from its shoulders.

Thus disintegrating Entreri's ideas about the weakness of the swashbuckling technique.

The drow rushed past into the path of the first wererat he had struck, his spinning swords intercepting his opponent's, and bringing it into the spin with them. In a moment, all three blades were in the air, turning circles, and only two of them, Jarlaxle's, were still being held. The third was kept aloft by the slapping and sliding of the other two.

Jarlaxle hooked the hilt of that sword with the blade of one of his own, angled it out to the side and launched it into the chest of another attacker, knocking him back and to the floor.

He went ahead suddenly and brutally, blades whirling with perfect precision, to take the wererat's arm, then drop the other arm limply to its side with a well-placed blow to the collarbone, then slash its face, then its throat.

Up came Jarlaxle's foot, planting against the staggered wererat's chest, and he kicked out, knocking the creature to its back and running over it.

Entreri had meant to get to Jarlaxle's side, but instead, the drow came rushing up to Entreri's side, uttering a command under his breath that retracted one of his swords to dagger size. He quickly slid the weapon back to its sheath, and with his free hand grabbed Entreri by the shoulder and pulled him along.

The puzzled assassin glanced at his companion. More wererats were piling into the tavern, through the windows, through the door, but those remaining farmers were falling back now, moving into purely defensive positions. Though more than a dozen wererats remained, Entreri did not believe that he and this amazingly skilled drow warrior would have any trouble at all tearing them apart.

Furthermore and even more puzzling, Jarlaxle had their run angled for the closest wall. While putting a solid barrier at their backs might be effective in some cases against so many opponents, Entreri thought this ridiculous, given Jarlaxle's flamboyant, room-requiring style.

Jarlaxle let go of Entreri then and reached up to the top of his huge hat.

From somewhere unseen in the strange hat, he brought forth a black disk made of some fabric Entreri did not know and sent it spinning at the wall. It elongated as it went, turning flat side to the wooden wall, then it hit . . . and stuck.

And it was no longer a disk of fabric, but rather a hole—a real hole—in the wall.

Jarlaxle pushed Entreri through, dived through right behind him, and paused only long enough to pull the magical hole out behind him, leaving the wall solid once more.

"Run!" the dark elf cried, sprinting away, with Entreri right on his heels.

Before Entreri could even ask what the drow knew that he did not, the building exploded into a huge and consuming fireball that took the tavern, took all of those wererats still scrambling about the entrances and exits, and took the horses, including Entreri's and Jarlaxle's, tethered anywhere near to the place.

The pair went flying to the ground but got right back up, running full speed out of the village and back into the shadows of the surrounding hills and woodlands.

They didn't even speak for many, many minutes, just ran on, until Jarlaxle finally pulled up behind one bluff and fell against the grassy hill, huffing and puffing.

"I had grown fond of my mount," he said. "A pity."

"I did not see the spellcaster," Entreri remarked.

"He was not in the room," Jarlaxle explained, "not physically, at least."

"Then how did you sense him?" Entreri started to ask, but he paused and considered the logic that had led Jarlaxle to his saving conclusion. "Because Kimmuriel and Rai-guy would never take the chance that Gord Abrix and his cronies would get the Crystal Shard," he reasoned. "Nor would they ever expect the wretched wererats ever to be able to take the thing from us in the first place."

"I have already explained to you that it is a common tactic for the two," Jarlaxle reminded. "They send their fodder in to engage their enemies, and Kimmuriel opens a window through which Rai-guy throws his potent magic."

Entreri looked back in the direction of the village, at the plume of black smoke drifting into the air. "Well thought," he congratulated. "You saved us both."

"Well, you at least," Jarlaxle replied, and Entreri looked back at him curiously, to see the drow waggling the fingers of one hand against his cheek, showing off a reddish-gold ring that Entreri had not noticed before.

"It was just a fireball," Jarlaxle said with a grin.

Entreri nodded and returned that grin, wondering if there was anything, anything at all, that Jarlaxle was not prepared for.

CHAPTER

BALANCING PRUDENCE AND DESIRE

20

Gord Abrix gasped and fell over as the small globe of fire soared past him, through the doorway, and into the tavern. As soon as it went through, Kimmuriel dropped the dimensional door. Gord Abrix had seen fireballs cast before and could well imagine the devastation back in the tavern. He knew he had just lost nearly a score of his loyal wererat soldiers.

He came up unsteadily, glancing around at his three dark elf companions, unsure, as he always seemed to be with this group, of what they might do next.

"You and your soldiers performed admirably," Rai-guy remarked.

"You killed them," Gord Abrix dared to say, though certainly not in any accusatory tone.

"A necessary sacrifice," Rai-guy replied. "You did not believe that they would have any chance of defeating Artemis Entreri and Jarlaxle, did you?"

"Then why send them?" the frustrated wererat leader started to ask, but his voice died away as the question left his mouth, the reasoning dissipated by his own internal reminders of who these creatures truly were. Gord Abrix and his henchmen had been sent in for just the diversion they provided, to occupy Entreri and Jarlaxle while Rai-guy and Kimmuriel prepared their little finish.

Kimmuriel opened the dimensional door then, showing the

devastated tavern, charred bodies laying all about and not a creature stirring. The drow's lip curled up in a wicked smile as he surveyed the grisly scene, and a shudder coursed Gord Abrix's spine as he realized the fate he had only barely escaped.

Berg'inyon Baenre went through the door, into what remained of the tavern room, which was more outdoors than indoors now, and returned a moment later.

"A couple of wererats still stir but barely," the drow warrior informed his companions.

"What of our friends?" Rai-guy asked.

Berg'inyon shrugged. "I saw neither Jarlaxle nor Entreri," he explained. "They could be among the wreckage or could be burned beyond immediate recognition."

Rai-guy considered it for a moment, and motioned for Berg'inyon and Gord Abrix to go back to the tavern and snoop around.

"What of my soldiers?" the wererat asked.

"If they can be saved, pull them back through," Rai-guy replied. "Lady Lolth will grant me the power to healing them . . . should I choose to do so."

Gord Abrix started for the dimensional doorway, and paused and glanced back curiously at the obscure and dangerous drow, not sure how to sort through the wizard-cleric's words.

"Do you believe our prey are still in there?" Kimmuriel asked Rai-guy, using the drow tongue to exclude the wererat leader.

Berg'inyon answered from the doorway. "They are not," he said with confidence, though it was obvious he hadn't found the time yet to scour the ruins. "It would take more than a diversion and a simple wizard's spell to bring down that pair."

Rai-guy's eyes narrowed at the affront to his spellcasting, but in truth, he couldn't really disagree with the assessment. He had been hoping he could catch his prey easily and tidily, but he knew better in his heart, knew that Jarlaxle would prove a difficult and cagey quarry.

"Search quickly," Kimmuriel ordered.

Berg'inyon and Gord Abrix ran off, poking through the smoldering ruins.

"They are not in there," Rai-guy said to his psionicist friend a moment later.

"You agree with Berg'inyon's reasoning?" Kimmuriel asked.

"I hear the call of the Crystal Shard," Rai-guy explained with a snarl, for he did indeed hear the renewed call of the artifact, the prisoner of stubborn Artemis Entreri. "That call comes not from the tavern."

"Then where?" Kimmuriel asked.

Rai-guy could only shake his head in frustration. Where indeed. He heard the pleas, but there was no location attached to them, just an insistent call.

"Bring our henchmen back to us," the wizard instructed, and Kimmuriel went through the doorway, returning a moment later with Berg'inyon, Gord Abrix, and a pair of horribly burned, but still very much alive, wererats.

"Help them," Gord Abrix pleaded, dragging his torched friends to Rai-guy. "This is Poweeno, a close advisor and friend."

Rai-guy closed his eyes and began to chant, and opened his eyes and held his hand out toward the prone and squirming Poweeno. He finished his spell by waggling his fingers and uttering another line of arcane words, and a sharp spark crackled from his fingertips, jolting the unfortunate wererat. The creature cried out and jerked spasmodically, howling in agony as smoking blood and gore began to ooze from its layers of horrible wounds.

A few moments later, Poweeno lay very still, quite dead.

"What . . . what have you done?" Gord Abrix demanded of Rai-guy, the wizard already into spellcasting once more.

When Rai-guy didn't answer, Gord Abrix made a move toward him, or at least tried to. He found his feet stuck to the floor, as if he was standing in some powerful glue. He glanced about, his gaze settling on Kimmuriel. He recognized from the drow's satisfied expression that it was indeed the psionicist holding him fast in place.

"You failed me," Rai-guy explained opening his eyes and holding one hand out toward the other wounded wererat.

"You just said we performed admirably," Gord Abrix protested.

"That was before I knew that Jarlaxle and Artemis Entreri had escaped," Rai-guy explained.

He finished his spell, releasing a tremendous bolt of lightning into the other wounded wererat. The creature flipped over weirdly, then rolling into a fetal position, fast following its companion to the grave.

Gord Abrix howled and drew forth his sword, but Berg'inyon was there, smashing the blade away with his own, fine drow weapon. The warrior looked to his two drow companions. On a nod from Rai-guy, he slashed Gord Abrix across the throat.

The wererat, his feet still stuck fast, sank to the floor, staring helplessly and pleadingly at Rai-guy.

"I do not accept failure," the drow wizard said coldly.

* * *

"King Elbereth has sent the word out wide to our scouts," the elf Shayleigh assured Ivan and Pikel when the two dwarven emissaries arrived in Shilmista Forest to the west of the Snowflake Mountains. Cadderly had sent the dwarves straight out to their elf friends, confident that anyone approaching would surely be noticed by King Elbereth's wide network of scouts.

Pikel gave a sound then, which seemed to Ivan to be more one of trepidation than of hope, though Shayleigh had just given them the assurances they had come here to get.

Or had she?

Ivan Bouldershoulder studied the elf maiden carefully. With her violet eyes and thick golden hair hanging far below her shoulders, she was undeniably beautiful, even to the thinking of a dwarf whose tastes usually ran to shorter, thicker, and more heavily bearded females. There was something else about Shayleigh's posture and attitude, though, about the subtle undertone of her melodious voice.

"Ye're not to kill 'em, ye know," Ivan remarked bluntly.

Shayleigh's posture did not change very much. "You yourself have named them as ultimately dangerous," she replied, "an assassin and a drow."

Ivan noted that the ominous flavor of her voice increased when she named the dark elf, as if the creature's mere race offended her more than the profession of his traveling companion.

"Cadderly's needin' to talk to 'em," Ivan grumbled.

"Can he not speak to the dead?"

"Ooo," said Pikel and he hopped away suddenly, disappearing briefly into the underbrush, and reemerging with one hand behind his back. He hopped up to stand before Shayleigh, a disarming grin on his face. "Drizzit," he reminded, and he pulled his hand around, revealing a delicate flower he had just picked for her.

Shayleigh could hardly hold her stern demeanor against that emotional assault. She smiled and took the wildflower, bringing it to her nose that she could smell its beautiful fragrance. "There is often a flower among the weeds," she said, catching on to Pikel's meaning. "As there may be a druid among a clan of dwarves. That does not mean there are others."

"Hope," said Pikel.

Shayleigh gave a helpless chuckle.

"Ye get yer heart in the right place," Ivan warned, "so says Cadderly, else the Crystal Shard'll find yer heart and twist it to its own needs. It's a big bit o' hope he's puttin' on ye, elf."

Shayleigh's sincere smile was all the assurance he needed.

"Brother Chaunticleer has outlined a grand scheme for keeping the children busy," Danica said to Cadderly. "I will be ready to leave as soon as the artifact arrives."

Cadderly's expression hardly seemed to support that notion.

"You did not think I would let you go visit an ancient dragon without me beside you, did you?" Danica asked, sincerely wounded.

Cadderly blew a sigh.

"We've met one before and would have had no trouble at all with it if we had not brought it along with us across the mountains," the woman reminded.

"This time may be more difficult," Cadderly explained. "I will be expending energy merely in controlling the Crystal Shard at the same time I am dealing with the beast. Worse, the artifact will also be speaking to the dragon, I am sure. What better wielder for an instrument of chaos and destruction than a mighty red dragon?"

"How strong is your magic?" Danica asked.

"Not that strong, I fear," Cadderly replied.

"All the more reason that I, and Ivan and Pikel, must be with you," Danica remarked.

"Without the aid of Deneir, do you give any of us a chance of battling such a wyrm?" the priest asked sincerely.

"If Deneir is not with you, you will need us to drag you out of there and quickly," the woman said with a wide smile. "Is that not what your friends are supposed to do?"

Cadderly started to respond, but he really couldn't say much against the look of determination, and of something even more than that—of serenity—stamped across Danica's fair face. Of course she meant to go with him, and he knew he couldn't possibly prevent that unless he left magically and with great deception. Of course, Ivan and Pikel would travel with him as well, though he had to wince when he considered the would-be druid, Pikel, facing a red dragon. They did not want to disturb the great beast any more than to borrow its fiery breath for a single burst of fire. Pikel, so dedicated to the natural, might not be so willing to walk away from a dragon, which was perhaps the greatest perversion of nature in all the world.

Danica cupped her hand under Cadderly's chin then and tilted his head back up so that he was eyeing her directly as she moved very close to him.

"We will finish this and to our satisfaction," she said, and she kissed him gently on the lips. "We have battled worse, my love."

Cadderly didn't begin to deny her words, or her presence, or her determination to go along on this important and dangerous journey. He brought her closer and kissed her again and again.

⊸━━⊷

"We are too busy elsewhere," Sharlotta Vespers tried to explain to Kimmuriel and Rai-guy. The pair were not pleased to learn that Dallabad had somehow been infiltrated by spies of great warlords from Memnon.

The dark elves exchanged concerned looks. Sharlotta had insisted repeatedly that every spy had been caught and killed, but what if she were wrong? What if even one spy had escaped to tell the warlords in Memnon the truth about the change at Dallabad? Or what if other spies had now discerned the real power behind the overthrow of House Basadoni?

"Every danger that Jarlaxle has sown may soon come to harvest," Kimmuriel said to his companion in the drow tongue.

While Sharlotta understood the words well enough, she surely didn't catch the subtleties of the common drow saying, one that referred to revenge taken on a drow house for crimes against another house. Kimmuriel's words were a stern warning, a reminder that Jarlaxle's involvement with Crenshinibon may have left them all vulnerable, no matter what remedial steps they now took.

Rai-guy nodded and stroked his chin, whispering something under his breath that the others could not catch. He stepped forward suddenly to stand right before Sharlotta, bringing his hands up in front of him, thumb-to-thumb. He uttered another word, and a gout of flame burst forth, engulfing the surprised woman's head. She slapped at the fire and screamed, running around the room, and dived to the floor, rolling.

"Make sure that all others who know too much are similarly uninformed," Rai-guy said coldly, as Sharlotta finally died on the floor at his feet.

Kimmuriel nodded, his expression grim, though a hint of an eager grin did turn up the edges of his thin lips.

"I will open the portal back to Menzoberranzan," the wizard explained. "I hold no love for this place and know now, as do you, that our potential gains here do not outweigh the risk to Bregan D'aerthe. I do not even consider it a pity that Jarlaxle foolishly overstepped the bounds of rational caution."

"Better that he did," Kimmuriel agreed. "That we can be on our way to the caverns where we truly belong." He glanced down at Sharlotta, her head blackened and smoking, and smiled once more. He bowed to his companion, his friend of like mind, and left the room, eager to begin the debriefing of others.

Rai-guy also left the room, though through another door, one that led him to the staircase to the basement of House Basadoni, where he could relax more privately in secure chambers. His words of retreat to Kimmuriel followed his every step.

Logical words. Words of survival in a place grown too dangerous.

But still . . . there remained a call in his head, an insistent intrusion, a plea for help.

A promise of greatness beyond his comprehension.

Rai-guy settled into a comfortable chair in his private room, reminding himself continually that a return to Menzoberranzan was the correct move for Bregan D'aerthe, that the risk of remaining on the surface, even in pursuit of the powerful artifact, was too great for the potential gains.

Soon after, the exhausted drow fell into a sort of reverie, as close to true sleep as a dark elf might know.

And in that "sleep," the call of Crenshinibon came again to Rai-guy, a plea for help, for rescue, and a promise of great gain in return.

That predictable call was soon magnified a hundred times over, with even greater promises of glory and power, with images not of magnificent crystalline towers on the deserts of Calimshan, but of a tower of the purest opal set in the center of Menzoberranzan, a black structure gleaming with inner heat and energy.

Rai-guy's reminders of prudence could not hold against that image, against the parade of Matron Mothers, the hated Triel Baenre among them, coming to the tower to pay homage to him.

The dark elf's eyes popped open wide. He collected his thoughts and sprang from the chair, moving quickly to locate Kimmuriel, to alter the psionisict's instructions. Yes, he would open the gate back to Menzoberranzan, and yes, much of Bregan D'aerthe would return to their home.

But Rai-guy and Kimmuriel were not finished here just yet. They would remain with a strike force until the Crystal Shard had found a proper wielder, a dark elf wizard-cleric who would bring to the artifact its greatest level of power, and who would take from it the same.

In a dark chamber far under Dallabad Oasis, Yharaskrik silently congratulated himself on altering the promises of the Crystal Shard more greatly to entice Rai-guy. Kimmuriel had informed Yharaskrik of the change in Bregan D'aerthe's plans, but though

Yharaskrik had outwardly accepted that change, the illithid was not willing to let the artifact go running off unchecked just yet. Through great concentration and mind control, Yharaskrik had been able to catch the subtle notes of the artifact's quiet call, but the illithid had not been able to begin to backtrack that call to the source.

Yharaskrik needed Bregan D'aerthe a bit longer, though the illithid recognized that once the drow band had fulfilled its purpose in locating the Crystal Shard, he and Rai-guy would likely be on opposite sides of the inevitable battle.

Let that be as it may, Yharaskrik realized. Kimmuriel Oblodra, a fellow psionicist who understood the deeper truths about Crenshinibon's shortcomings, would surely stand on his side of the battlefield.

CHAPTER

21

"Why would you live in a desert, when such beauty is so near?" Jarlaxle asked Entreri.

The pair had moved quickly in the days after the disaster at Gentleman Briar's tavern, with Entreri even enlisting one wizard they found in an out-of-the-way tower magically to transport them many miles closer to their goal of the Spirit Soaring and the priest, Cadderly.

It didn't hurt, of course, that Jarlaxle seemed to have an inexhaustible supply of gold coins.

Now the Snowflake Mountains were in clear sight, towering before them. Summer was on the wane, and the wind blew chill, but Entreri could hardly argue Jarlaxle's assessment of the landscape. It surprised the assassin that a drow would find beauty in such a surface environment. They looked down on a canopy of great and ancient trees that filled a long, wide vale nestled right up against the Snowflake's westernmost slopes. Even Entreri, who seemed to spend most of his time denying beauty, could not deny the majesty of the mountains themselves, tall and jagged, capped with bright snow gleaming brilliantly in the daylight.

"Calimport is where I make my living," Entreri answered after a while.

Jarlaxle snorted at the thought. "With your skills, you could make your home anywhere in the world," he said. "In Waterdeep or in Luskan, in Icewind Dale or even here. Few would deny the value of a powerful warrior in cities large and villages small. None would evict Artemis Entreri—unless, of course, they knew the man as I know him."

That brought a narrow-eyed gaze from the assassin, but it was all in jest, both knew—or perhaps it wasn't. Even in that case, there was too much truth to Jarlaxle's statement for Entreri rationally to take offense.

"We must swing around the mountains to the south to get to Carradoon, and the trails leading us to the Spirit Soaring," Entreri explained. "A few days should have us standing before Cadderly, if we make all haste."

"All haste, then," said Jarlaxle. "Let us be rid of the artifact, and . . ." He paused and looked curiously at Entreri.

Then what?

That question hung palpably in the air between them, though it had not been spoken. Ever since they had fled the crystalline tower in Dallabad, the pair had run with purpose and direction—to the Spirit Soaring to be rid of the dangerous artifact—but what, indeed, awaited them after that? Was Jarlaxle to return to Calimport to resume his command of Bregan D'aerthe? both wondered. Entreri knew at once as he pondered the possibility that he would not follow his dark elf companion in that case. Even if Jarlaxle could somehow overcome the seeds of change sown by Rai-guy and Kimmuriel, Entreri had no desire to be with the drow band again. He had no desire to measure his every step in light of the knowledge that the vast majority of his supposed allies would prefer it if he were dead.

Where would they go? Together or apart? Both were contemplating that question when a voice, strong yet melodic, resonant with power, drifted across the field to them.

"Halt and yield!" it said.

Entreri and Jarlaxle glanced over as one to see a solitary figure, a female elf, beautiful and graceful. She was approaching them openly, a finely crafted sword at her side.

"Yield?" Jarlaxle muttered. "Must everyone expect us to yield? And halt? Why, we were not even moving!"

Entreri was hardly listening, was focusing his senses on the trees around them. The elf maiden's gait told him much, and he confirmed his suspicions almost immediately, spotting one, and another, elf archer among the boughs, bows trained upon him and his companion.

"She is not alone," the assassin whispered to Jarlaxle, though he tried to keep the smile on his face as he spoke, an inviting expression for the approaching warrior.

"Elves rarely are," Jarlaxle replied quietly. "Particularly when they are confronting drow."

Entreri couldn't hold his smile, facing that simple truth. He expected the arrows to begin raining down upon them at any moment.

"Greetings!" Jarlaxle called loudly. He swept off his hat, making a point to show his heritage openly.

Entreri noted that the elf maiden did wince and slow briefly at the revelation, for even from her distance—and she was still thirty strides away—Jarlaxle, without the visually overwhelming hat, was obviously drow.

She came a bit closer, her expression holding perfectly calm and steady, revealing nothing. It occurred to Entreri then that this was no chance meeting. He took a moment to listen for the silent call of Crenshinibon, to try to determine if the Crystal Shard had brought in more opponents to free it from Entreri's grasp.

He sensed nothing unusual, no contact at all between the artifact and this elf.

"There are a hundred warriors about you," the elf maiden said, stopping some twenty paces from the pair. "They would like nothing better than to pierce your tiny drow heart with their arrows, but we have not come here for that—unless you so desire it."

"Preposterous!" Jarlaxle said, quite animatedly. "Why would I desire such a thing, fair elf? I am Drizzt Do'Urden of Icewind Dale, a ranger, and of heart not unlike your own, I am sure!"

The elf's lips grew very thin.

"She does not know of you, my friend," Entreri offered.

"Shayleigh of Shilmista Forest knows of Drizzt Do'Urden," Shayleigh assured them both. "And she knows of Jarlaxle of Bregan D'aerthe, and of Artemis Entreri, most vile of assassins."

That made the pair blink more than a few times. "Must be the Crystal Shard telling her," Jarlaxle whispered to his companion.

Entreri didn't deny that, but neither did he believe it. He closed his eyes, trying to sense some connection between the artifact and the elf maiden again, and again he found nothing. Nothing at all.

But how else could she know?

"And you are Shayleigh of Shilmista?" Jarlaxle asked politely. "Or were you, perchance, speaking of another?"

"I am Shayleigh," the elf announced. "I, and my friends gathered in the trees all around you, were sent out here to find you, Jarlaxle of Bregan D'aerthe. You carry an item of great importance to us."

"Not I," the drow said, feigning confusion and glad that he could further mask that confusion by speaking truthful words.

"The Crystal Shard is in the possession of Jarlaxle and Artemis Entreri," Shayleigh stated definitively. "I care not which of you carries it, only that you have it."

"They will strike fast," Jarlaxle whispered to Entreri. "The shard coaxes them in. No parlay here, I fear."

Entreri didn't get that feeling, not at all. The Crystal Shard was not calling to Shayleigh, nor to any of the other elves. If it had been, that call had undoubtedly been completely denied.

The assassin saw Jarlaxle making some subtle motions then—the movements of a spell, he figured—and he put a hand on the dark elf's arm, holding him still.

"We do indeed possess the item you claim," Entreri said to Shayleigh, stepping up ahead of Jarlaxle. He was playing a hunch here, and nothing more. "We are bringing it to Cadderly of the Spirit Soaring."

"For what purpose?" Shayleigh asked.

"That he may rid the world of it," Entreri answered boldly. "You say that you know of Drizzt Do'Urden. If that is true, and if you know Cadderly of the Spirit Soaring as well—which I believe you do—then you likely know that Drizzt was bringing this very artifact to Cadderly."

"Until it was stolen from him by a dark elf posing as Cadderly," Shayleigh said determinedly and in a leading tone. In truth, that was about as much as Cadderly had told her about how this particular pair had come to acquire the artifact.

"There are reasons for things that a casual observer might not understand," Jarlaxle interjected. "Be satisfied with the knowledge that we have the Crystal Shard and are delivering it, rightfully so, to Cadderly of the Spirit Soaring, that he might rid the world of the menace that is Crenshinibon."

Shayleigh motioned to the trees, and her companions walked out from the shadows. There were dozens of grim-faced elves, warriors all, armed with crafted bows and wearing fine weapons and gleaming, supple armor.

"I was instructed to deliver you to the Spirit Soaring," Shayleigh explained. "It was not clear whether or not you had to be alive. Walk swiftly and silently, make no movements that indicate any hostility, and perhaps you will live to see the great doors of the cathedral, though I assure you that I hope you do not."

She turned then and started away. The elves began to close in on the dark elf and his assassin companion, with their bows still in hand and arrows aimed for the kill.

"This is going better than I expected," Jarlaxle said dryly.

"You are an eternal optimist, then," Entreri replied in the same tone. He searched all around for some weakness in the ring of elves, but he saw only swift, inescapable death stamped on every fair face.

Jarlaxle saw it, too, even more clearly. "We are caught," he remarked.

"And if they know all the details of our encounter with Drizzt Do'Urden. . . ." Entreri said ominously, letting the words hang in the air.

Jarlaxle held his wry smile until Entreri had turned away, hoping that he wouldn't be forced to reveal the truth of that encounter to his companion. He didn't want to tell Entreri that Drizzt was still alive. While Jarlaxle believed Entreri had gone beyond that destructive obsession with Drizzt, if he was wrong and Entreri learned the truth, he would likely be fighting for his life against the skilled warrior.

Jarlaxle glanced around at the many grim-faced elves and decided he already had enough problems.

As the meeting at the Spirit Soaring wore on, Cadderly fired back a testy remark concerning the feelings between the drow and the surface elves when Jarlaxle implied that he and his companion really couldn't trust anyone who brought them in under a guard of a score of angry elves.

"But you have already said that this is not about us," Jarlaxle reasoned. He glanced over at Entreri, but the assassin wasn't offering any support, wasn't offering anything at all.

Entreri hadn't spoken a word since they'd arrived, and neither had Cadderly's second at the meeting, a confident woman named Danica. Indeed, she and Entreri seemed cut of similar stuff—and neither of them seemed to like that fact. They had been staring, glowering at each other for nearly the entire time, as if there was some hidden agenda between them, some personal feud.

"True enough," Cadderly finally admitted. "In another situation,

I would have many questions to ask of you, Jarlaxle of Menzoberranzan, and most of them far from complimentary toward your apparent actions."

"A trial?" the dark elf asked with a snort. "Is that your place, then, Magistrate Cadderly?"

The yellow-bearded dwarf behind the priest, obviously the more serious of the two dwarves, grumbled and shifted uncomfortably. His green-bearded brother just held his stupid, naive smile. To Jarlaxle's way of thinking, where he was always searching for layers under lies, that smile marked the green-bearded dwarf as the more dangerous of the two.

Cadderly eyed Jarlaxle without blinking. "We must all answer for our actions," he said.

"But to whom?" the drow countered. "Do you even begin to believe that you can understand the life I have lived, judgmental priest? How might you fare in the darkness of Menzoberranzan, I wonder?"

He meant to continue, but both Entreri and Danica broke their silence then, saying in unison, "Enough of this!"

"Ooo," mumbled the green-bearded dwarf, for the room went perfectly silent. Entreri and Danica were as surprised as the others at the coordination of their remarks. They stared hard at each other, seeming on the verge of battle.

"Let us conclude this," Cadderly said. "Give over the Crystal Shard and go on your way. Let your past haunt your own consciences then, and I will be concerned only with that which you do in the future. If you remain near to the Spirit Soaring, then know that your actions are indeed my province, and know that I will be watching."

"I tremble at the thought," Entreri said, before Jarlaxle could utter a similar, though less blunt, reply. "Unfortunately, for all of us, our time together has only just begun. I need you to destroy the wretched artifact, and you need me because I carry it."

"Give it over," Danica said, eyeing the man coldly.

Entreri smirked at her. "No."

"I am sworn to destroy it," Cadderly argued.

"I have heard such words before," Entreri replied. "Thus far, I am the only one who has been able to ignore the temptation of the artifact, and therefore, it remains with me until it is destroyed." He felt an inner twinge at that, a combination of a plea, a threat, and the purest rage he had ever known, all emanating from the imprisoned Crystal Shard.

Danica scoffed as if his claim was purely preposterous, but Cadderly held her in check.

"There is no need for such heroics from you," the priest assured Entreri. "You do not need to do this."

"I do," Entreri replied, though when he looked to Jarlaxle, it seemed to him as if his drow companion was siding with Cadderly.

Entreri could certainly see that point of view. Powerful enemies pursued them, and the Crystal Shard itself was not likely to be destroyed without a terrific battle. Still, Entreri knew in his heart that he had to see this through. He hated the artifact profoundly. He needed to see this controlling, awful item be utterly obliterated. He didn't know why he felt so strongly, but he did, plain and simple, and he wasn't giving over the artifact not to Cadderly or to Danica, not to Rai-guy and Kimmuriel, not to anyone while he still had breath in his body.

"I will finish this," Cadderly remarked.

"So you say," the assassin answered sarcastically and without hesitation.

"I am a priest of Deneir," Cadderly started to protest.

"I name supposedly goodly priests among the least trustworthy of all creatures," Entreri interrupted coldly. "They are on my scale just below troglodytes and green slime, the greatest hypocrites and liars in all the world."

"Please, my friend, do not temper your feelings," Jarlaxle said dryly.

"I would have thought that such a distinction would belong to assassins, murderers, and thieves," Danica remarked, her tone and expression making her hatred for Artemis Entreri quite evident.

"Dear girl, Artemis Entreri is no thief," Jarlaxle said with a grin, hoping to diffuse some of the mounting tension before it exploded—and he and his companion found themselves squared off against the formidable array within this room and without, where scores of priests and a group of elves were no doubt discussing the arrival of the two less-than-exemplary characters with more than a passing concern.

Cadderly put a hand on Danica's arm, calming her, and took a deep breath and started to reason it all out again.

Again Entreri cut him short. "However you wish to parse your words, the simple truth is that I possess the Crystal Shard, and that I, above all others who have tried, have shown the control necessary to hold its call in check.

"If you wish to take the artifact from me," Entreri continued, "then try, but know that I'll not give it over easily—and that I will even utilize the powers of the artifact against you. I wish it destroyed—you wish it destroyed, so you say. Thus, we do it together."

Cadderly paused for a long while, glanced over at Danica a couple of times, and to Jarlaxle, and neither offered him any answers. With a shrug, the priest looked back at Entreri.

"As you wish," he agreed. "The artifact must be engulfed in magical darkness and breathed upon by an ancient and huge red dragon."

Jarlaxle nodded, but then stopped, his dark eyes going wide. "Give it to him," he said to his companion.

Artemis Entreri, though he had no desire to face a red dragon of any size or age, feared more the consequence of Crenshinibon's becoming free to wield its power once more. He knew how to destroy it now—they all did—and the Crystal Shard would never suffer them to live, unless that life was as its servant.

That possibility Artemis Entreri loathed most of all.

Jarlaxle thought to mention that Drizzt Do'Urden had shown equal control, but he held the thought silent, not wanting to bring up the drow ranger in any context. Given Cadderly's understanding of the situation, it seemed obvious to Jarlaxle that the priest knew the truth of his encounter with Drizzt, and Jarlaxle did not want Entreri to discover that his nemesis was still alive—not now, at least, with so many other pressing issues before him.

Jarlaxle considered blurting it all out, on a sudden thought that speaking the truth plainly would heighten Entreri's willingness to be done with all of this, to give over the shard that he and Jarlaxle could pursue a more important matter—that of finding the drow ranger.

Jarlaxle held it back, and smiled, recognizing the source of the inspiration as a subtle telepathic ruse by the imprisoned artifact.

"Clever," he whispered, and merely smiled as all eyes turned to regard him.

Soon after, while Cadderly and his friends made preparations for the journey to the lair of some dragon Cadderly knew of, Entreri and Jarlaxle walked the grounds outside of the magnificent Spirit Soaring, well aware, of course, that many watchful eyes were upon their every move.

"It is undeniably beautiful, do you not agree?" Jarlaxle asked, looking back at the soaring cathedral, with its tall spires, flying buttresses, and great, colored windows.

"The mask of a god," Entreri replied sourly.

"The mask or the face?" asked the always-surprising Jarlaxle.

Entreri stared hard at his companion, and back at the towering cathedral. "The mask," he said, "or perhaps the illusion, concocted by those who seek to elevate themselves above all others and have not the skills to do so."

Jarlaxle looked at him curiously.

"A man inferior with the blade or with his thoughts can still so elevate himself," Entreri explained curtly, "if he can impart the belief that some god or other speaks through him. It is the greatest deception in all the world, and one embraced by kings and lords, while minor lying thieves on the streets of Calimport and other cities lose their tongues for so attempting to coax the purses of others."

That struck Jarlaxle as the most poignant and revealing insight he had yet pried from the mouth of the elusive Artemis Entreri, a great clue as to who this man truly was.

Up to that point, Jarlaxle had been trying to figure out a way that he could wait behind while Entreri, Cadderly, and whomever Cadderly chose to bring along went to face the dragon and destroy the artifact.

Now, because of this seemingly unrelated glimpse into the heart of Artemis Entreri, Jarlaxle realized he had to go along.

CHAPTER

22

The great beast lay at rest, but even in slumber did the dragon seem a terrible and wrathful thing. It curled catlike, its long tail running up past its head, its huge, scaly back rising like a giant wave and sinking in a great exhalation that sent plumes of gray smoke from its nostrils and injected a vibrating rumble throughout the stone of the cavern floor. There was no light in the rocky chamber, save the glow of the dragon itself, a reddish-gold hue—a hot light, as if the beast were too full of energy and savage fires to hold it all in with mere scales.

On the other end of the scrying mirror, the six unlikely companions—Cadderly, Danica, Ivan, Pikel, Entreri, and Jarlaxle—watched the dragon with a mixture of awe and dread.

"We could use Shayleigh and her archers," Danica remarked, but of course, that was not possible, since the elves had absolutely refused to work alongside the dark elf for any purpose whatsoever and had returned to their forest home in Shilmista.

"We could use King Elbereth's entire army," Cadderly added.

"Ooo," said Pikel, who seemed truly mesmerized by the beast, a great wyrm at least as large and horrific as old Fyrentennimar.

"There is the dragon," Cadderly said, turning to Entreri. "Are you certain you still wish to accompany me?" His question ended weakly, though, given the eager glow in Artemis Entreri's eyes.

The assassin reached into his pouch and brought forth the Crystal Shard.

"Witness your doom," he whispered to the artifact. He felt the shard reaching out desperately and powerfully—Cadderly felt those sensations as well. It called to Jarlaxle first, and indeed, the opportunistic drow did begin physically to reach for it, but he resisted.

"Put it away," Danica whispered harshly, looking from the green-glowing shard to the shifting beast. "It will awaken the dragon!"

"My dear, do you expect to coax the fiery breath from a dragon that remains asleep?" Jarlaxle reminded her, but Danica turned an angry glare at him.

Entreri, hearing the Crystal Shard's call clearly and recognizing its attempt, understood that the woman spoke wisely, though, for while they would indeed have to wake the beast, they would be far better served if it did not know why. The assassin looked at the artifact and gave a confident, cocky grin, and dropped it back into his pouch and nodded for Cadderly to disenchant the scrying mirror.

"When do we go?" the assassin asked Cadderly, and his tone made it perfectly clear that he wasn't shaken in the least by the sight of the monstrous dragon, made it clear that he was eager to be done with the destruction of the vile artifact.

"I have to prepare the proper spells," Cadderly replied. "It will not be long."

The priest motioned for Danica and his other friends to escort their two undesirable companions away then, though he only dropped the image from the scrying mirror temporarily. As soon as he was alone, he called up the dragon cave again, after placing another spell upon himself that allowed him to see in the dark. He sent the roving eye of the scrying mirror all around the large, intricate lair.

There were many great cracks in the floor, he noted, and when he followed one down, he came to recognize that a maze of tunnels and chambers lay beneath the sleeping wyrm. Furthermore, Cadderly wasn't convinced that the dragon's cave was very secure structurally. Not at all.

He'd have to keep that well in mind while choosing the spells he would bring with him to the home of this great beast known as Hephaestus.

⊕══⊕

Rai-guy, deep in concentration, his eyes closed, allowed the calls of Crenshinibon to invade his thoughts fully. He caught only flashes of anger and despair, the pleas for help, the promises of ultimate glory.

He saw some other images, as well, particularly one of a great curled red dragon, and he heard a word, a name echoing in his head: Hephaestus.

Rai-guy knew he had to act quickly. He settled back in his private chamber beneath House Basadoni and prayed with all his heart to his Lady Lolth, telling her of the Crystal Shard, and of the glorious chaos the artifact might allow him to bring to the world.

For hours, Rai-guy stayed alone, praying, sending away any who knocked at his door—Berg'inyon and Kimmuriel among them—with a gruff and definitive retort.

Then, when he believed he'd caught the attention of his dark Spider Queen, or at least the ear of one of her minions, the wizard fell into powerful spellcasting, opening an extra-planar gate.

As always with such a spell, Rai-guy had to take care that no unwanted or overly powerful planar denizens walked through that gate. His suspicions were correct, though, and indeed, the creature that came through the portal was one of the yochlol. These were the handmaidens of Lolth, beasts that more resembled half-melted candles with longer appendages than the Spider Queen herself.

Rai-guy held his breath, wondering suddenly and fearfully if he had erred in letting on about the artifact. Might Lolth desire the artifact herself and instruct Rai-guy to deliver it to her?

"You have called for help from the Lady," the yochlol said, its voice watery and guttural all at once, a dual-toned and horrible sound.

"I wish to return to Menzoberranzan," Rai-guy admitted, "and yet I cannot at this time. An instrument of chaos is about to be destroyed . . ."

"Lady Lolth knows of the artifact, Crenshinibon, Rai-guy of House Teyachumet," the yochlol replied, and the title the creature bestowed upon him surprised the drow wizard-cleric.

He had indeed been a son of House Teyachumet—but that house of Ched Nasad had been obliterated more than a century before. A subtle reminder, the drow realized, that the memory of Lolth and her minions was long indeed.

And a warning, perhaps, that he should take great care about how he planned to put the mighty artifact to use in the city of Lolth's greatest priestesses.

Rai-guy saw his dreams of domination over Menzoberranzan melt then and there.

"Where will you retrieve this item?" the handmaiden asked.

Rai-guy stammered a reply, his thoughts elsewhere for the moment. "Hephaestus's lair . . . a red dragon," he said. "I know not where . . ."

"Your answer will be given," the handmaiden promised.

It turned around and walked through Rai-guy's gate, and the portal closed immediately, though the drow wizard had done nothing to dispel it.

Had Lolth herself been watching the exchange? Rai-guy had to wonder and to fear. Again he understood the futility of his dreams of conquest over Menzoberranzan. The Crystal Shard was powerful indeed, perhaps powerful enough for Rai-guy to manipulate or otherwise unseat enough of the Matron Mothers for him to achieve a position of tremendous power, but something about the way the yochlol had spoken his full name told him he should be careful indeed. Lady Lolth would not permit such a change in the balance of Menzoberranzan's power structure.

For just a brief moment, Rai-guy considered abandoning his quest to retrieve the Crystal Shard, considered taking his remaining allies and his gains and retreating to Menzoberranzan as the coleader, along with his friend, Kimmuriel, of Bregan D'aerthe.

A brief moment it was, for the call of the Crystal Shard came rushing back to him then, whispering its promises of power and glory, showing Rai-guy that the surface was not so forbidding a place as he believed. With Crenshinibon, the dark elf could carry on Jarlaxle's designs, but in more appropriate regions—a mountainous area teeming with goblins, perhaps—and build a magnificent and undyingly loyal legion of minions, of slaves.

The drow wizard rubbed his slender black fingers together, waiting anxiously for the answer the yochlol had promised him.

<hr />

"You cannot deny the beauty," Jarlaxle remarked, he and Entreri again sitting outside of the cathedral, relaxing before their journey. Both were well aware that many wary gazes were focused upon them from many vantage points.

"Its very purpose denies that beauty," Entreri replied, his tone showing that he had little desire to replay this conversation yet again.

Jarlaxle studied the man closely, as if hoping that physical scrutiny alone would unlock this apparently dark episode in Artemis Entreri's past. The drow wasn't surprised by Entreri's dislike of "hypocritical" priests. In many ways, Jarlaxle agreed with him. The dark elf had been alive for a long, long time, and had often ventured out of Menzoberranzan—and had known the movements of practically every visitor to that dark city—and he had seen enough of the many varied religious sects of Toril to understand the hypocritical nature of many so-called priests. There was something far deeper than that looming here within Artemis Entreri, though, something visceral. It had to be an event in Entreri's past, a deeply disturbing episode involving a priest. Perhaps he had been wrongly accused of some crime and tortured by a priest, who often served as jailers for the smaller communities of the surface. Perhaps he had known love once, and that woman had been stolen from him or had been murdered by a priest.

Whatever it was, Jarlaxle could clearly see the hatred in Entreri's dark eyes as the man looked upon the magnificent—and it was magnificent, by any standards—Spirit Soaring. Even for Jarlaxle, a creature of the Underdark, the place lived up to its name, for when he gazed upon those soaring towers, his very soul was lifted, his spirit enlightened and elevated.

Not so for his companion, obviously, and yet another mystery of Artemis Entreri for Jarlaxle to unravel. He did indeed find this man interesting.

"Where will you go after the artifact is destroyed?" Entreri asked unexpectedly.

Jarlaxle had to pause, both fully to digest the question and to consider his answer—for in truth, he really had no answer. "*If* we destroy it, you mean," he corrected. "Have you ever dealt with the likes of a red dragon, my friend?"

"Cadderly has, as I'm sure have you," Entreri replied.

"Only once, and I truly have little desire ever to speak with such a beast again," Jarlaxle said. "One cannot reason with a red dragon beyond a certain level, because they are not creatures with any definitive goals for personal gain. They see, they destroy, and take what is left over. A simple existence, really, and one that makes them all the more dangerous."

"Then let it see the Crystal Shard and destroy it," Entreri remarked, and he felt a twinge then as Crenshinibon cried out.

"Why?" Jarlaxle asked suddenly, and Entreri recognized that his ever-opportunistic friend had heard that silent call.

"Why?" the assassin echoed, turning to regard Jarlaxle fully.

"Perhaps we are being premature in our planning," Jarlaxle explained. "We know how to destroy the Crystal Shard now—likely that will be enough for us to use against the artifact to bend it continually to our will."

Entreri started to laugh.

"There is truth in what I say, and a gain to be had in following my reasoning," Jarlaxle insisted. "Crenshinibon began to manipulate me, no doubt, but now that we have determined that you, and not the artifact, are truly the master of your relationship, why must we rush ahead to destroy it? Why not determine first if you might control the item enough for our own gain?"

"Because if you know, beyond doubt, that you can destroy it, and the Crystal Shard knows that, as well, there may well be no need to destroy it," Entreri played along.

"Exactly!" said the now-excited dark elf.

"Because if you know you can destroy the crystalline tower, then there is no possible way that you will wind up with two crystalline towers," Entreri replied sarcastically, and the eager grin disappeared from Jarlaxle's black-skinned face in the blink of an astonished eye.

"It did it again," the drow remarked dryly.

"Same bait on the hook, and the Jarlaxle fish chomps even harder," Entreri replied.

"The cathedral is beautiful, I say," Jarlaxle remarked, looking away and pointedly changing the subject.

Entreri laughed again.

⊷══⊶

Delay him, then, Yharaskrik imparted to Kimmuriel when the drow told the illithid the plan to intercept Jarlaxle, Entreri, and the priest Cadderly and his friends at the lair of Hephaestus the red dragon.

Rai-guy will not be deterred in any way short of open battle, Kimmuriel explained. *He will have the Crystal Shard at all costs.*

Because the Crystal Shard so instructs him, Yharaskrik replied.

Yet it seems as if he has freed himself, partially at least, from its grasp, Kimmuriel argued. *He dismissed many of the drow soldiers back to our warren in Menzoberranzan and has systematically relinquished our holdings here on the surface.*

True enough, the illithid admitted, *but you are fooling yourself if you believe that the Crystal Shard will allow Rai-guy to take it to the lightless depths of the Underdark. It is a relic that derives its power from the light of the sun.*

Rai-guy believes that a few crystalline towers on the surface will allow the artifact to channel that sunlight power back to Menzoberranzan, Kimmuriel explained, for indeed, the drow wizard had told him of that very possibility—a possibility that Crenshinibon itself had imparted to Rai-guy.

Rai-guy has come to see many possibilities, Yharaskrik's thoughts imparted, and there was a measure of doubt, translated into sarcasm, in the illithid's response. *The source of those varied and marvelous possibilities is always the same.*

It was a point on which Kimmuriel Oblodra, who now found himself caught in the middle of five dangerous adversaries—Rai-guy, Yharaskrik, Jarlaxle, Artemis Entreri, and the Crystal Shard itself—did not wish to dwell. There was little he could do to alter the approaching events. He would not go against Rai-guy, out of respect for the wizard-cleric's prowess and intelligence, and also because of his deep relationship with the drow. Of his potential enemies, Kimmuriel feared Yharaskrik least of all. With Rai-guy at his side, he knew the illithid could not win. Kimmuriel could neutralize Yharaskrik's mental weaponry long enough for Rai-guy to obliterate the creature.

While he held respect for the manipulative powers of the Crystal Shard and knew that the mighty artifact would not be pleased with any psionicist, Kimmuriel was honestly beginning to believe that the artifact was indeed a fine match for Rai-guy, a joining that would be of mutual benefit. Jarlaxle hadn't been able to control the artifact, but Jarlaxle had not been properly forewarned about its manipulative powers. Kimmuriel doubted that Rai-guy would make that same mistake.

Still, the psionicist believed that all would be simpler and cleaner if the Crystal Shard were indeed destroyed, but he wasn't about to go against Rai-guy to ensure that event.

He looked at the illithid and realized that he already had gone against his friend, to some extent, merely by informing this bulbous-headed creature, who was certainly an enemy of Rai-guy, that Rai-guy meant to enter an alliance with the Crystal Shard.

Kimmuriel bowed to Yharaskrik out of respect, and floated away on psionic winds, back to House Basadoni and his private chambers. Not far down the hall, he knew, Rai-guy was awaiting his answer from the yochlol and plotting his strike against Jarlaxle and the fallen leader's newfound companions.

Kimmuriel had no idea where he was going to fit into all of this.

CHAPTER

THE FACE OF DISASTER

23

Artemis Entreri eyed the priest of Deneir with obvious mistrust as Cadderly walked up before him and began a slow chant. Cadderly had already cast prepared defensive spells upon himself, Danica, Ivan, and Pikel, but it occurred to Entreri that the priest might use this opportunity to get rid of him. What better way to destroy Entreri than to have him face the breath of a dragon errantly thinking he had proper magical defenses against such a firestorm?

The assassin glanced over at Jarlaxle, who had refused Cadderly's aid, claiming he had his own methods. The dark elf nodded to him and waggled his fingers, silently assuring Entreri that Cadderly had indeed placed the antifire enchantment upon him.

When he was done, Cadderly stepped back and inspected the group. "I still believe that I can do this better alone," he remarked, drawing a scowl from both Danica and Entreri.

"If it was as simple as erecting a fire barrier and tossing out the artifact for the dragon to breathe upon, I would agree," Jarlaxle replied. "You may need to goad the beast to breathe, I fear. Wyrms are not quick to use their most powerful weapon."

"When it sees us all, it will more likely loose its breath," Danica reasoned.

"Poof!" agreed Pikel.

"Contingencies, my dear Cadderly," said Jarlaxle. "We must allow for every contingency, must prepare for every eventuality and turn in the game. With an ancient and intelligent wyrm, no variable is unlikely."

Their conversation ended as they both noted Pikel hopping about his brother, sprinkling some powder over the protesting and slapping Ivan, while singing a whimsical song. He finished with a wide smile, and hopped up and whispered into Ivan's ear.

"Says he got a spell of his own to add," the yellow-bearded dwarf remarked. "Put one on meself and on himself, and's wondering which o' ye others'll be wantin' one."

"What type of spell?"

"Another fire protection," Ivan explained. "Says doo-dads can do that."

That brought a laugh to Jarlaxle—not because he didn't believe the dwarf's every word, but because he found the entire spectacle of a dwarven druid quite charming. He bowed to Pikel and accepted the dwarf's next spellcasting. The others followed suit.

"We will be as quick as possible," Cadderly explained, moving them all to the large window at the back of the room on a high floor in one of the Spirit Soaring's towering spires. "Our goal is to destroy the item and nothing more. We are not to battle the beast, not to raise its ire, and," he looked at Entreri and Jarlaxle as he finished, "surely not to attempt to steal anything from mighty Hephaestus.

"Remember," the priest added, "the enchantments upon you may diminish one blast of Hephaestus's fire, perhaps two, but not much more than that."

"One will be enough," Entreri replied.

"Too much," muttered Jarlaxle.

"Does everyone know his or her role and position when we enter the dragon's main chamber?" Danica asked, ignoring the grumbling drow.

No questions came back at her. Taking that as an affirmative answer, Cadderly began casting yet again, a wind-walking spell that soon carried them out of the cathedral and across the miles to the south and east to the caverns of mighty Hephaestus. The priest didn't magically walk them in the front door, but rather soared along deeper chambers, the understructure of the cavern complex, coming into a large antechamber to the dragon's main lair.

When he broke the spell, depositing their material forms in the cavern, they could hear the great sighing sound of the sleeping wyrm, the huge intake and smoky exhalation.

Jarlaxle put a finger to pursed lips and inched ahead, as silent as could be. He disappeared around an outcropping of stone, and came right back in, actually clutching the wall to steady himself. He looked at the others and nodded grimly, though there could be no doubt he had seen the beast simply from the expression on his normally confident face.

Cadderly and Entreri led the way, Danica and Jarlaxle followed, with the Bouldershoulder brothers behind. The tunnel behind the outcropping wound only for a short distance, and opened up widely into a huge cavern, its floor crisscrossed by many cracks and crevices.

The companions hardly noticed the physical features of that room, though, for there before them, looming like a mountain of doom, lay Hephaestus, its red-gold scales gleaming from its own inner heat. The beast was huge, even curled as it was, its size alone mocking them and making every one of them want to fall to his knees and pay homage.

That was one of the traps in dealing with dragons, that awe-inspiring aura of sheer power, that emanation of helplessness to all who would look upon their horrible splendor.

These were not novice warriors, though, trying to make a quick stab at great fame. These were seasoned veterans, every one. Each, with the exception of Artemis Entreri, had faced a beast such as Hephaestus before. Despite his inexperience in this particular arena, nothing in all the world—not a dragon, not an arch-devil, not a demon lord—could take the heart from Artemis Entreri.

The wyrm's eye, seeming more like that of a cat than a lizard, with a green iris and a slitted pupil that quickly widened to adjust to the dim light, popped open as soon as the group entered. Hephaestus watched their every movement.

"Did you think to catch me sleeping?" the dragon said quietly, which still made its voice sound like an avalanche to the companions.

Cadderly called out a cueing word to his companions, and snapped his fingers, bringing forth a magical light that filled all the chamber.

Up snapped Hephaestus's great horned head, the pupils of its eyes fast thinning. It turned as it rose, to face the impertinent priest directly.

To the side, Entreri eased the Crystal Shard out of his pouch, ready to throw it before the beast as soon as Hephaestus seemed about to loose its fiery breath. Jarlaxle, too, was ready, for his job in this was to use his innate dark elf powers to bring forth a globe of darkness over the artifact as the flames consumed it.

"*Thieves!*" the dragon roared. Its voice shook the chamber and sent shudders through the floor—a poignant reminder to Cadderly of the instability of this place. "You have come to steal the treasure of Hephaestus. You have prepared your proper spells and wear items of magic that you consider powerful, but are you truly prepared? Can any mere mortal truly be prepared to face the awful splendor that is Hephaestus?"

Cadderly tuned out the words and fell into the song of Deneir, seeking some powerful spell, some type of mighty magical chaos, perhaps, as he had once used against Fyrentennimar, that he could trick the beast and be done with this. His best spells against the previous dragon had been of reverse aging, lessening the beast with mighty spellcasting, but he could not use those this time, for so doing would diminish the dragon's breath as well, and defeat their very purpose in being there. He had other magic at his disposal, though, and the Song of Deneir rang triumphantly in his head. Along with that song, though, the priest heard the calls of Crenshinibon, discordant notes in the melody and surely a distraction.

"Something is amiss," Jarlaxle whispered to Entreri. "The beast expected us and anticipates our movements. It should have risen with attacks, not words."

Entreri glanced at him, and back at Hephaestus, the great head swaying back and forth, back and forth. He glanced down at the Crystal Shard, wondering if it had betrayed them to the beast.

⸻

Indeed, Crenshinibon was sending forth its plea at that time, to the beast and against Cadderly's spellcasting, but it had not been the Crystal Shard that had warned Hephaestus of intruders. No, that distinction fell to a certain dark elf wizard-cleric, hiding in a tunnel across the way along with a handful of drow companions. Right before Cadderly and the others had wind-walked into the lair, Rai-guy had sent a magical whisper to Hephaestus, a warning of intruders and a suggestion that these thieves had come with magic designed to use the creature's own breath against it.

Now Rai-guy waited for the appearance of the Crystal Shard, for the moment when he and his companions, including Kimmuriel, could strike hard and begone, their prize in hand.

⸻

"Thieves we are, and we'll have your treasure!" shouted Jarlaxle. He used a language that none of the others, save Hephaestus, understood, a tongue of the red dragons, and one that the great wyrms believed that few others could begin to master. Jarlaxle, using a whistle that he kept on a chain around his neck, spoke it with perfect inflection. Hephaestus's head snapped down in line with him, the wyrm's eyes going wide.

Entreri dived aside in a roll, coming right back to his feet.

"What did you say?" the assassin asked.

Jarlaxle's fingers worked furiously. *He thinks that I am another red dragon.*

There seemed a long, long moment of absolute quiet, of a gigantic hush before a more gigantic storm. Then everything exploded into motion, beginning with Cadderly's leap forward, his arm extended, finger pointing accusingly at the beast.

"Hephaestus!" the priest roared at the appropriate moment of spellcasting. "Burn me if you can!"

It was more than a dare, more than a challenge, and more than a threat. It was a magical compulsion, launched through a powerful spell. Though forewarned by some vague suggestions against the action, Hephaestus sucked in its tremendous breath, the force of the intake drawing Cadderly's curly brown locks forward onto his face.

Entreri dived ahead and pulled forth Crenshinibon, tossing it to the floor before the priest. Jarlaxle, even as Hephaestus tilted back its head, came forward with the great exhalation and produced his globe of darkness.

No! Crenshinibon screamed in Entreri's head, so powerful and angry a call that the assassin grabbed at his ears and stumbled aside, dazed.

The artifact's call was abruptly cut off.

Hephaestus's head came forward, a great line of fire roaring down, mocking Jarlaxle's globe, mocking Cadderly and all his spells.

⊶═══⊷

Even as the globe of darkness came up over the Crystal Shard, Rai-guy grabbed at it with a spell of telekinesis, a sudden and power-ful burst of snatching power that sent the item flying fast across the way, past Hephaestus, who was seemingly oblivious to it, and down the corridor to the hiding wizard-cleric's waiting hand.

Rai-guy's red-glowing eyes narrowed as he turned to regard Kimmuriel, for it had been Kimmuriel's task to so snatch the item—a task the psionicist had apparently neglected.

I was not fast enough, the psionicist's fingers waggled at his companion.

But Rai-guy knew better, and so did Crenshinibon, for the powers of the mind were among the quickest of magic to enact. Still staring hard at his companion, Rai-guy began spellcasting once more, aiming for the great chamber.

⊕══════⊕

On and on went the fiery maelstrom, and in the middle of it stood Cadderly, his arms out wide, praying to Deneir to see him through.

Danica, Ivan, and Pikel stared at him intently, praying as well, but Jarlaxle was more concerned with his darkness, and Entreri was looking more to Jarlaxle.

"I hear not the continuing call of Crenshinibon!" Entreri cried hopefully above the fiery roar.

Jarlaxle was shaking his head. "The darkness should have been consumed by the artifact's destruction," he cried back, sensing that something was terribly, terribly wrong.

The fires ended, leaving a seething Hephaestus still staring at the unharmed priest of Deneir. The dragon's eyes narrowed to threatening slits.

Jarlaxle dispelled his darkness globe, and there remained no sign of Crenshinibon among the bubbling, molten stone.

"We done it!" Ivan cried.

"Home!" Pikel pleaded.

"No," insisted Jarlaxle.

Before he could explain, a low humming sound filled the chamber, a noise the dark elf had heard before and one that didn't strike him as overly pleasant at that dangerous moment.

"A magical dispel!" the dark elf warned. "Our enchantments are threatened!"

This left them, they all realized, in a room with an outraged, ancient, huge red dragon without many of their protections in place.

"What d' we do?" Ivan growled, slapping the handle of his battle axe across his open palm.

"Wee!" Pikel answered.

"Wee?" the perplexed yellow-bearded dwarf echoed, his face screwed up as he stared at his green-haired brother.

"Wee!" Pikel said again, and to accentuate his point, he grabbed Ivan by the collar and ran him a short distance to the side, to the edge of a crevice, and leaped off, taking Ivan on the dive with him.

Hephaestus's great wings beat the air, lifting the huge wyrm's front half high above the floor. Its hind legs clawed at the floor, digging deep gullies in the stone.

"Run away!" Cadderly cried, agreeing wholeheartedly with Pikel's choice. "All of you!"

Danica rushed forward, as did Jarlaxle, the woman rolling into a ready crouch before the wyrm. Hephaestus wasted not a second in snapping its great maw down at her. She scrambled aside, coming up from her roll in a crouch again, taunting the beast.

Cadderly couldn't watch it, reminding himself that he simply had to trust in her. She was buying him precious moments, he knew, that he might launch another magical attack or defensive spell, perhaps, at Hephaestus. He fell into the song of Deneir again and heard its notes more clearly this time, as he sorted through an array of spells to launch.

He heard a scream, Danica's scream, and he looked up to see Hephaestus's fiery breath drive down upon her, striking the stone floor and spraying up in an inverted fan of fires.

Cadderly, too, cried out, and reached desperately into the song of Deneir for the first spell he could find that would alter that horrible scene, the first enchantment he could think of to stop it.

He brought forth an earthquake.

Even as it started—a violent shudder and rumbling, like waves on a pond, lifting and rolling the floor—Jarlaxle drew the dragon's attention his way by hitting the beast with a stream of stinging daggers.

Entreri, too, moved—and surprised himself by going ahead instead of back, toward the spot where Hephaestus had just breathed.

There, too, there was only bubbling stone.

Cadderly called out for Danica, desperately, but his voice fell away as the floor collapsed beneath him.

"Let us begone, and quickly," Kimmuriel remarked, "before the great wyrm recognizes that there were more than those six intruders in its lair this day."

He and the other drow had already moved some distance down the tunnel, away from the main chamber. Leaving altogether seemed a prudent suggestion, one that had Berg'inyon Baenre and the other five drow soldiers nodding eagerly, but one that, for some reason, did not seem acceptable to the stern Rai-guy.

"No," he said firmly. "They must all die, here and now."

"As the dragon will likely kill them," Berg'inyon agreed, but Rai-guy was shaking his head, indicating that such a probability simply wasn't good enough for him.

Rai-guy and Crenshinibon were already fully into their bonding by then. The Crystal Shard demanded that Cadderly and the others, these infidels who understood the secret to its destruction, be killed immediately. It demanded that nothing concerning the group be left to chance. Besides, it telepathically coaxed Rai-guy, would not a red dragon be an enormous asset to add to Bregan D'aerthe?

"Find them and kill them, every one!" Rai-guy demanded emphatically.

Berg'inyon considered the command, and broke his soldiers into two groups and ran off with one group, the other heading a different direction. Kimmuriel spent a longer time staring hard at Rai-guy, seeming less than pleased. He, too, disappeared eventually, seemed simply to fall through the floor.

Leaving Rai-guy alone with his newest and most beloved ally.

In an alcove off to the side of the tunnel where Rai-guy stood, Yharaskrik's less-than-corporeal form slid through the stone and materialized, the illithid's Crenshinibon-defeating lantern in its hand.

CHAPTER

C H A O S

24

With skills honed to absolute perfection, Danica had avoided the flames by a short distance, close enough so that her skin was bright red on the left side of her face. No magic would aid Danica now, she knew, only her thousands and thousands of hours of difficult training, those many years she had spent perfecting her style of fighting and, more importantly, dodging. Danica had no intention of battling the great wyrm, of striking out in any offensive manner against a beast she doubted she could even hurt, let alone slay. All her abilities, all her energy and concentration, was solely on the defensive now, her posture a balanced crouch that would allow her to skitter out to either side, ahead, or back.

Hephaestus's fang-filled jaws snapped down at her with a tremendous clapping noise, but the dragon hit only air as the monk dived out to the right. A claw followed, a swipe that surely would have cut Danica into pieces, except that she altered the momentum of her roll to go straight back in a sudden retreat.

Then came the breath, another burst of fire that seemed to go on and on forever.

Danica had to dive and roll a couple of times to put out the flames on the back side of her clothing. Sensing that Hephaestus had noted her escape and would adjust the line of fiery breath, she cut a fast corner around a jag in the wall, throwing herself flat against the stone behind the protective rock.

She noted two figures then. Artemis Entreri was running her way, but leaping short of her position into a wide crevice that had opened with Cadderly's earthquake. The strange dark elf, Jarlaxle, skittered behind the dragon, and to Danica's astonishment, launched a spell Hephaestus's way. A sudden arc of lightning caught the dragon's attention and gave Danica a moment of freedom. She didn't waste it.

Danica ran flat out, leaping even as the spinning Hephaestus swept its great tail around to squash her. She disappeared into the same crevice as had Artemis Entreri.

She knew as soon as she crossed the lip of the crack that she was in trouble—but still far less trouble, she supposed, than she would have found back in the dragon's lair. The descent twisted and turned, lined with broken and often sharp-edged, stone. Again Danica's training came into play, her hands and legs working furiously to buffer the blows and slow her descent. Some distance down, the crack opened into a chamber, and Danica had nothing to hold onto for the last twenty feet of her drop. Still, she coordinated her movements so that she landed feet first, but with her legs turned slightly, propelling her into a sidelong somersault. She tumbled over and over again, her roll absorbing the momentum of the fall.

She came up to her feet a few moments later, and there before her, leaning on a wall looking bruised but hardly battered, stood Artemis Entreri. He was staring at her intently and held a lit torch in his hand but tossed it aside as soon as Danica took note of him.

"I had thought you consumed by the first of Hephaestus's fires," the assassin remarked, coming away from the wall and drawing both sword and dagger, the smaller blade glowing with a white, fiery light.

"One cannot always get what one most wants," the woman answered coldly.

"You have hated me since the moment you saw me," the assassin remarked, ending with a chuckle to show that he hardly cared.

"Long before that, Artemis Entreri," Danica replied coldly, and she advanced a step, eyeing the assassin's weapons intently.

"We know not what enemies we will find down here," Entreri explained, but he knew even as he said the words, as he looked upon Danica's mask of hatred, that no explanation would suffice, that anything short of his surrender to her would invite her wrath. Artemis Entreri had little desire to battle the woman, to do any unnecessary fighting down here, but neither would he shy from any fight.

"Indeed," was all that Danica answered. She continued coming forward.

This had been coming for some time, both knew, and despite the fact that they were both separated from their respective companions, despite the fact that an angry dragon was barely fifty feet above their heads, and all of it in a cavern that seemed on the verge of complete collapse, Danica saw this encounter as more than an opportunity but a necessity.

For all his logic and common sense, Artemis Entreri really wasn't disappointed by her feelings.

⊕━━━⊕

As soon as Hephaestus began its stunningly fast spin, Jarlaxle had to question the wisdom of his distracting lightning bolt. Still, the drow had reacted as any ally would, taking the beast's attention so that both Entreri and the woman might escape.

In truth, after the initial shock of seeing an outraged red dragon turning at him, Jarlaxle wasn't overly worried. Despite the powerful dispel that had saturated the room—too powerful a spell for any dragon to cast, the mercenary leader recognized—Jarlaxle remained confident that he possessed enough tricks to get away from this one.

Hephaestus's great jaws snapped down at the drow, who was

standing perfectly still and seemed an easy target. The magic of Jarlaxle's cloak forced the wyrm to miss, and Hephaestus roared all the louder when its head slammed into a solid wall.

Next, predictably, came the fiery breath, but even as Hephaestus began its great exhale, Jarlaxle waggled a ringed finger, opening a dimension door that brought him behind the dragon. He could have simply skittered away then, but he wanted to hold the beast at bay a little bit longer. Out came a wand, one of several the drow carried, and it spewed a gob of greenish semiliquid at the very tip of Hephaestus's twitching tail.

"Now you are caught!" Jarlaxle proclaimed loudly as the fiery breath at last ceased.

Hephaestus spun around again, and indeed, the wyrm's tail looped about, its end stuck fast by the temporary but incredibly effective goo.

Jarlaxle let fly another wad from the wand, this one smacking the dragon in the face.

Of course, then Jarlaxle remembered why he had never wanted to face such a beast as this again, for Hephaestus went into a terrific frenzy, issuing growls through its clamped mouth that resonated through the very stones of the cavern. It thrashed about so wildly its tail tore the stone from the floor.

With a tip of his wide-brimmed hat, the mercenary drow called upon his magical ring again, one of the last portal-enacting enchantments it could offer, and disappeared back behind the wyrm, a bit further along the wall than he had been before his first dimension door. There was another exit from the room back there, one that Jarlaxle suspected would bring him to some old friends.

Some old friends who likely had the Crystal Shard, he knew, for certainly it had not been destroyed by Hephaestus's first breath, certainly it had been magically stolen away right before the powerful magic-defeating spell had filled the room.

The last thing Jarlaxle wanted was for Rai-guy and Kimmuriel to get their hands on the Crystal Shard and, undoubtedly, come looking for him once more.

He was out of the cavern a moment later, the thunderous sounds of Hephaestus's thrashing thankfully left behind. He reached up into his marvelous hat and brought forth a piece of black cloth in the shape of a small bat. He whispered a few magical words and tossed it into the air. The cloth swatch transformed into a living, breathing creature, a servant of its creator that fluttered back to Jarlaxle's shoulder. The drow whispered some instructions into its ear and tossed it up before him again, and his little scout flew off into the gloom.

⬥

"We will take Hephaestus as our own," Rai-guy whispered to the Crystal Shard, the drow considering all the great gains that might be made this day. Logically, the dark elf knew he should be well on his way out of the place, for could Kimmuriel and the others really defeat Jarlaxle and the powerful companions he had brought to the dragon's lair?

Rai-guy smiled, hardly afraid, for how could he be fearful with Crenshinibon in his possession? Soon, very soon, he knew, he would be allied with a great wyrm. He turned and started down the wide tunnel toward the main chamber of Hephaestus's lair.

He noticed some movement off to the side, in an alcove, and Crenshinibon screamed a warning in his head.

Yharaskrik stepped out, not ten paces away. The tentacles around the illithid's mouth were waving menacingly.

"Kimmuriel's friend, no doubt," the dark elf remarked, "who betrayed Kohrin Soulez."

Betrayal implies alliance, Yharaskrik telepathically answered. *There was no betrayal.*

"If you were to venture here with us, then why not do so openly?" the drow asked.

I came for you, not with you, the ever-confident illithid answered.

Rai-guy understood well what was going on, for the Crystal Shard was making its abject hatred of the creature quite apparent in his thoughts.

"The drow and your race have been allied many times in the past," Rai-guy remarked, "and rarely have we found reason to do battle. So it should be now."

The wizard wasn't trying to talk the illithid out of any rash actions out of fear—far from it. He was thinking he might have, perhaps, made another powerful connection here, one that could be exploited.

The screaming in his mind, Crenshinibon's absolute hatred of the mind flayer, made that alliance seem less likely.

And even less likely a moment later, when Yharaskrik lit the magical lantern and aimed its glow Crenshinibon's way. The protests in the drow wizard's mind faded far, far away.

The artifact will be brought back before the dragon, came Yharaskrik's telepathic call. It was a psionically enhanced command, and one that had Rai-guy involuntarily taking a step toward the main chamber once more.

The cunning dark elf had survived more than a century in the hostile territory of his own homeland, and he was no novice to any type of battle. He fought back against the compelling suggestion and rooted his feet to the floor, turning back to regard the octopus-headed creature, his red-glowing eyes narrowing threateningly.

"Release the Crystal Shard and perhaps we will let you live," Rai-guy said.

It must be destroyed! Yharaskrik screamed into his mind. *It is an item of no gain, of loss to all, even to itself.* As the creature finished, it held the lantern up even higher and advanced a step, its tentacles wriggling out, reaching for Rai-guy hungrily though the drow was still too far away for any physical attack, but not out of range for psionic attacks, the drow found out a split second later, even as he began casting his own spell.

A blast of stunning and confusing energy washed over him, reached into him, and scrambled his mind. He felt himself falling over backward, watched almost helplessly as his line of vision rolled up the wall, and to the high ceiling.

He called for Crenshinibon, but it was too far away, lost in the swirl of the magical lantern's glow. He thought of the illithid, of those horrid tentacles burrowing under his skin, reaching for his brain.

Rai-guy steadied himself and fought desperately, finally regaining his balance and glancing back to see Yharaskrik very close—too close, those tentacles almost touching him.

He nearly exploded into the motion of yet another spellcasting, but he recognized that he had to be more subtle here, that he had to make the creature believe he was defeated. That was the secret of battling illithids, as many drow had been trained. Play upon their arrogance. Yharaskrik, like all of its kind, would hardly be able to comprehend that an inferior creature like a drow had somehow resisted its psionic attacks.

Rai-guy worked a simple spell, with subtle movements, and all the while feigning helplessness.

It must be done! the illithid screamed in his thoughts. The tentacles moved toward Rai-guy's face, and Yharaskrik's hand reached for the Crystal Shard.

Rai-guy released his spell. It was not a devastating blast, not a rumble of some great explosion, not a bolt of lightning nor a gout of fire. A simple gust of wind came from the drow's hand, a sharp and surprising burst that snapped Yharaskrik's tentacles back across its ugly face, that blew the creature's robes back behind it and forced it to retreat a step.

That blew out the lantern.

Yharaskrik glanced down, thought to summon some psionic energy to relight the lantern, and looked up and thought to strike Rai-guy with another psionic blast of scrambling energy, fearing some second spellcasting.

As quickly as the illithid could begin to do either of those things, a wave of crushing emotions washed over it, a Crenshinibon-imparted flood of despair and hopelessness, and, paradoxically of hope, with subtle promises that all could be put right, with greater glory gained for all.

Yharaskrik's psionic defenses came up almost immediately, dulling the Crystal Shard's demanding call.

A jolt of energy, the shocking grasp of Rai-guy, caught the illithid on the chest, lifted it from the ground, and sent it sprawling backward to the floor.

"Fool!" Rai-guy growled. "Do you think I need Crenshinibon to destroy the likes of you?"

Indeed, when Yharaskrik looked back at the drow wizard, thinking to attack mentally, he stared at the end of a small black wand. The illithid let go the blast anyway, and indeed it staggered Rai-guy backward, but the drow had already enacted the power of the wand. It was a wand similar to the one Jarlaxle had used to pin down Hephaestus's tail and momentarily clamp the dragon's mouth shut.

It took Rai-guy a long moment to fight through this burst of scrambling energy, but when he did stand straight again, he laughed aloud at the spectacle of the illithid splayed out on the floor, held in place by a viscid green glob.

The mental domination from Crenshinibon began on the creature anew, wearing at its resolve. Rai-guy walked to tower over Yharaskrik, to look the helpless mind flayer in the bulbous eye, letting it know in no uncertain terms that this fight was at its end.

⊶━━⊷

She had no apparent weapon, but Entreri knew better than to ask for her surrender, knew well enough what this skilled warrior was capable of. He had battled fighting monks before, though not often, and had always found them full of surprises. He could see the honed muscles of Danica's legs twitching eagerly, the woman wanting badly to come at him.

"Why do you hate me so?" the assassin asked with a wry grin, halting his advance a mere three strides from Danica. "Or is it, perhaps, that you simply fear me and are afraid to show it? For you should fear me, you understand."

Danica stared at him hard. She did indeed hate this man, and had heard much about him from Drizzt Do'Urden, and even more—and even more damning—testimony from Catti-brie. Everything about him assaulted her sensibilities. To Danica, finding Artemis Entreri in the company of dark elves seemed more an indictment of the dark elves.

"But perhaps we would do better to settle our differences when we are far, far from this place," Entreri offered. "Though our fight is inevitable in your eyes, is it not?"

"Logic would so dictate to both," Danica replied. As she finished the sentence, she came forward in a rush, slid down to the floor beneath Entreri's extending blade, and swept him from his feet. "But neither of us is a slave to wise thinking, are we, foul assassin?"

Entreri accepted the trip without resistance, indeed, even helped the flow of Danica's leg along by tumbling backward, throwing himself into a roll, and lifting his feet up high to get them over her swinging leg. He didn't quite get all the way back to his feet before reversing momentum, planting his toes, and throwing himself forward in a sudden, devastating rush.

Danica, still prone, angled herself to put her feet in line with the charging Entreri, then rolled back suddenly and with perfect timing to get one foot against the assassin's inner thigh as he fell over her, his sword reaching for her gut. With precision born of desperation, Danica rolled back up onto her shoulders, every muscle in her torso and legs working in perfect coordination to drive Entreri away, to keep that awful sword back.

He went up and over, flying past Danica and dipping his head at the last moment to go into a forward roll. He came back to his feet with a spin, facing the monk, who was up and charging, and stopping cold in her tracks as she faced again the deadly sword and its dagger companion.

Entreri felt the adrenaline coursing through his body, the rush of a true challenge. As much as he realized the foolishness of it all, he was enjoying this.

So was the woman.

The sound of a voice came from the side, the melodious call of a dark elf. "Do slay each other and save us the trouble," Berg'inyon Baenre explained, entering the small area along with a pair of dark elf companions. All three of them carried twin swords that gleamed with powerful enchantments.

Coughing and bleeding from a dozen scrapes, Cadderly pulled himself out of the rockslide and stumbled across a small corridor. He fished in a pouch to bring forth his light tube, a cylindrical object with a continual light spell cast into it, the enchantment focused into an adjustable beam out one end. He had to find Danica. He had to see her again. That last image of her, the dragon's fiery breath falling over her, had him dizzy with fear.

What would his life be without Danica? What would he say to the children? Everything about the life of Cadderly Bonaduce was wrapped inextricably around that wonderful and capable woman.

Yes, capable, he pointedly told himself again and again, as he staggered along in the dusty corridor, pausing only once to cast a minor spell of healing upon a particularly deep cut on one shoulder. He bent over and coughed again, and spat out some dirt that had gotten into his throat.

He shook his head, muttered again that he had to find her, and stood straight, pointing his light ahead—pointing his light so that it reflected off of the black skin of a drow.

That beam stung Kimmuriel Oblodra's sensitive eyes, but he was not caught unawares by it.

It all fell into place quickly for the intelligent priest. He had learned much of Jarlaxle in speaking with the drow and his assassin companion and had deduced much more with information gleaned from denizens of the lower planes. He was indeed surprised to see another dark elf—who could not be?—but he was far from overwhelmed.

The drow and Cadderly stood ten paces apart, staring at each other, sizing each other up. Kimmuriel reached for the priest's mind with psionic energy—enough energy to crush the willpower of a normal man.

But Cadderly Bonaduce was no normal human. The manner in which he accessed his god, the flowing song of Deneir, was somewhat akin to the powers of psionics. It was a method of the purest mental discipline.

Cadderly could not lash out with his mind, as Kimmuriel had just done, but he could surely defend against such an attack, and furthermore, he surely recognized the attack for what it was.

He thought of the Crystal Shard then, of all he knew about it, of its mannerisms and its powers.

The drow psionicist waved a hand, breaking the mental connection, and drew out a gleaming sword. He enacted another psionic power, one that would physically enhance him for the coming fight.

Cadderly did no similar preparations. He just stood staring at Kimmuriel and grinning knowingly. He cast one simple spell of translation.

The drow regarded him curiously, inviting an explanation.

"You wish Crenshinibon destroyed as much as I," the priest remarked, his magic translating the words as they came out of his mouth. "You are a psionicist, the bane of the Crystal Shard, its most hated enemy."

Kimmuriel paused and stared hard, with his physical and his mental eye. "What do you know, foolish human?" he asked.

"The Crystal Shard will not suffer you to live for long," Cadderly said, "and you know it."

"You believe I would help a human against Rai-guy?" Kimmuriel asked incredulously.

Cadderly didn't know who this Rai-guy might be, but Kimmuriel's question made it obvious that he was a dark elf of some power and importance.

"Save yourself, then, and leave," Cadderly offered, and he said it with such calm and confidence that Kimmuriel narrowed his eyes and regarded him even more closely.

Again came the psionic intrusions. This time Cadderly let the drow in somewhat, guided his probing mind's eye to the song of Deneir, let him see the truth of the power of the harmonious flow, let him see the truth of his doom should he persist in this battle.

The psionic connection again went away, and Kimmuriel stood up straight, staring hard at Cadderly.

"I am not normally this generous, dark elf," Cadderly said, "but I have greater problems before me. You hold no love for Crenshinibon and wish it destroyed perhaps more passionately than do I. If it is not, if your companion, this Rai-guy you spoke of, is allowed to possess it, it will be the end of you. So help me if you will in destroying the Crystal Shard. If you and your kin intend to return to your lightless home, I will in no way interfere."

Kimmuriel held his impassive pose for a short while, and smiled and shook his head. "You will find Rai-guy a formidable foe," he promised, "especially with Crenshinibon in his possession."

Before Cadderly could begin to respond, Kimmuriel waved his hand and became something less than corporeal. That transparent form turned and simply walked through the stone wall.

Cadderly waited a long moment and breathed a huge sigh of relief. How he had improvised there and bluffed. The spells he had prepared this day were for dealing with dragons, not dark elves, and the power of that one was substantial indeed. He had felt that keenly with the psionic intrusions.

Now he had a name, Rai-guy, and now his fears about the truth of Hephaestus's breathing had been confirmed. Cadderly, like Jarlaxle, understood enough about the mighty relic to know that if the breath had destroyed Crenshinibon, everyone in the area would have known it in no uncertain terms. Now Cadderly could guess easily enough where and how the Crystal Shard had gone. Knowing that there were other dark elves about, compounding the problem of one very angry red dragon, didn't make him feel any better about the prospects for his three missing friends.

He started away as fast as he dared, and fell again into the song of Deneir, praying for guidance to Danica's side.

"Always I seem doomed to protect those I most despise," Entreri whispered to Danica, motioning with his hand for the woman to shift over to the side.

The dark elves broke ranks. One moved to square off against Danica, and Berg'inyon and one other headed for the assassin. Berg'inyon waved his companion aside.

"Kill the woman, and quickly," he said in the drow tongue. "I wish to try this one alone."

Entreri glanced over at Danica and held up two fingers, pointing to the two that would go for her, and pointing to her. The woman gave a quick nod, and a great deal passed between them in that instant. She would try to keep the two dark elves busy, but both understood that Entreri would have to be done with the third quickly.

"I have often wondered how I would fare against Drizzt Do'Urden," Berg'inyon said to the assassin. "Now that I will apparently never get the chance, I will settle for you, Drizzt's equal by all accounts."

Entreri bowed. "It is good to know that I serve some value for you, cowardly son of House Baenre," he said.

He knew as he came back up that Berg'inyon wouldn't hesitate in the face of those words. Still, the sheer ferocity of the drow's attack nearly had Entreri beaten before the fight ever really began. He leaped back, staying up on his heels, skittering away as the two swords came in hard, side by side down low, then low again, then high, then at his belly. He jumped back once, twice, thrice, then managed to bat his sword across those of Berg'inyon on the fourth double-thrust, hoping to drive the blades down low. This was no farmer he faced, and no orc or wererat, but a skilled, veteran drow warrior. Berg'inyon kept his left-handed sword pressing up against the assassin's blade, but dropped his right into a quick circle, then came up and over hard.

The jeweled dagger hooked it and turned it aside at the last second. Entreri rolled his other hand over, the tip of his own sword going toward Berg'inyon. He didn't follow through with the thrust, though, but continued the roll, bringing his blade down and around under the drow's, and stabbing straight ahead.

Berg'inyon quickly turned his left-hand blade across his body and down, disengaged his right from the dagger and brought it across over the left, further driving Entreri's sword down. In the same fluid motion, the skilled drow rolled his right-hand blade up and over his crossing left, the blade going forward at the assassin's head, a brilliant move that Berg'inyon knew would be the end of Artemis Entreri.

Across the way, Danica fared no better. Her fight was a mixture of pure chaos and lightning fast, almost violent movement. The woman crouched and dropped, sprang up hard, and rushed side to side, avoiding slash after slash of drow blades. These two were nowhere near as good as the one across the way battling her companion, but they were dark elves after all, and even the weakest of drow warriors was skilled by surface standards. Furthermore, they knew each other well and complemented each other's movements with deadly precision, preventing Danica from getting any real counterattacks. Every time one came ahead in a rush that seemed to offer the woman some hope of rolling past his double-thrusting blades, or even skittering in under them and kicking at a knee, the companion drow beat her to the potential attack zone, two gleaming swords holding her at bay.

With those long blades and precise movements, they were working her to exhaustion. She had to react, to overreact even, to every thrust and slash. She had to leap away from a blade sent across by a mere flick of a drow wrist.

She looked over at Entreri and the other drow, their blades ringing in a wild song and with the dark elf seeming, if anything, to be gaining an advantage. She knew she had to try something dangerous, even desperate.

Danica came ahead in a rush, and cut left suddenly, bursting out to the side though she had only three strides to the wall. Seeing her apparently caught, the closest dark elf cut fast in pursuit, stabbing at . . . nothing.

Danica ran right up the wall, turning over as she went and kicking out into a backward somersault that brought her down and to the side of the pursuing dark elf. She fell low as she landed and spun around viciously, one leg extended to kick out the dark elf's legs.

She would have had him, but there was his companion, swords extended, blade driving deeply into Danica's thigh. She howled and scrambled back, kicking futilely at the pursuing dark elves.

A globe of darkness fell over her. She slammed her back against the stone and had nowhere left to go.

He ran along, with the less-than-corporeal Kimmuriel Oblodra following close behind.

"You seek an exit?" the drow psionicist asked with a voice that seemed impossibly thin.

"I seek my friends," Cadderly replied.

"They are out of the mountain, likely," Kimmuriel remarked, and that slowed the priest considerably.

For indeed, would not Danica and the dwarves search for a way out of the mountain—and there were many easy exits from the lower tunnels, Cadderly knew from his searching of the place before this journey. Dozens of corridors crisscrossed down there, but a quiet pause and a lifted and wetted finger would show the drafts of air. Certainly Ivan and Pikel would have little trouble in finding their way out of the underground maze, but what of Danica?

"Something comes this way," Kimmuriel warned, and Cadderly turned to see the drow shrink back against the wall, and stand perfectly still, seeming simply to disappear.

Cadderly knew the drow wouldn't aid him in any fight and would likely even join in if the approaching footsteps were those of Kimmuriel's dark elf companions.

They were not, Cadderly knew almost as soon as that worry cropped up, for these were not the steps of any stealthy creature.

"Ye stupid doo-dad!" came the roar of a familiar voice. "Droppin' me in a hole, and one full o' rocks!"

"Ooo oi!" Pikel replied as they came bounding around the bend in the tunnel, right into the path of Cadderly's light beam.

Ivan shrieked and started to charge, but Pikel grabbed him and pulled him down, whispering into his ear.

"Hey, ye're right," the yellow-bearded dwarf admitted. "Damned drows don't use light."

Cadderly came up beside them. "Where is Danica?"

Any relief the two dwarves had felt at the sight of their friend disappeared immediately.

"Help me find her!" Cadderly said to the dwarves and to Kimmuriel, as he spun around.

Kimmuriel Oblodra, apparently fearing that Cadderly and his companions would not be safe traveling company, was already long gone.

His smile, a wicked grin indeed, widened as one of his blades came up over the other, for he knew that Entreri had nothing left with which to parry. Out went Berg'inyon's killing stab.

But the assassin was not there!

Berg'inyon's thoughts whirled frantically. Where had he gone? How were his weapons still in place with the previous parries? He knew Entreri could not have moved far, and yet, he was not there.

The angle of the sudden disengage clued Berg'inyon in to the truth, told the drow that in the same moment Berg'inyon had executed the roll, Entreri had also come forward, but down low, using Berg'inyon's own blade as the visual block.

The dark elf silently congratulated the cunning human, this man rumored to be the equal of Drizzt Do'Urden, even as he felt the jeweled dagger sliding into his back, reaching for his heart.

"You should have kept one of your lackeys with you," Entreri whispered in the drow's ear, easing the dying Berg'inyon Baenre to the floor. "He could have died beside you."

The assassin pulled free his dagger and turned around to consider the woman. He saw her get slashed, saw her skitter away, saw the globe fall over her.

Entreri winced as the two dark elves—too far away for him to offer any timely assistance—rolled out in opposite directions, flanking the woman and rushing into that darkness, swords before them.

Just a split second before the darkness fell, the dark elf standing before Danica to the right began to execute a roll farther that way, spinning a circle to bring him around quickly and with momentum, the only clue for Danica.

The other one, she guessed, was moving to her left, but both were surely coming in at a tight enough angle to prevent her from rushing straight ahead between them. Those three options: left, right, and ahead, were unavailable, as was moving back, for the stone of the wall was solid indeed.

She sensed their movements, not specifically, but enough to realize that they were coming in fast for the kill.

One option presented itself. One alone.

Danica leaped straight up, tucking her legs under her, so full of desperation that she hardly felt the burn of the wound in her thigh.

She couldn't see the double-thrust low attack of the drow to her right, nor the double-thrust high attack from the one on the left, but she felt the disturbance below her as she cleared both sets of blades. She came up high in a tuck, and kicked out to both sides with a sudden and devastating spreading snap of her legs.

She connected on both sides, driving a foot into the forehead of the drow on her right, and another into the throat of the drow on her left. She pressed through to complete extension, sending both dark elves flying away. She landed in perfect balance and burst ahead three running steps. A forward dive brought her rolling out of the darkness. She came up and around—to see the dark elf now on her left, and the one she had kicked on the forehead, still staggering backward out of the darkness globe and into the waiting grasp of Artemis Entreri.

The drow jerked suddenly, violently, and Entreri's fine sword exploded through his chest. The assassin held it there for a moment, let Charon's Claw work its demonic power, and the dark elf's face began to smolder, burn, and roll back from his skull.

Danica looked away, focusing on the darkness, waiting for the

357

other dark elf to come rushing out. Blood was pouring from her wounded leg, and her strength was fast receding.

She was too lightheaded a moment later to hear the final gurgling of the drow dying in the darkness globe, its throat too crushed to bring in anymore air, but even if she had heard that reassuring sound, it would have done little to bolster her hopes.

She could not hold her footing, she knew, or her consciousness.

Artemis Entreri, surely no ally, was still very much alive, and very, very close.

Yharaskrik was overwhelmed. The combination of Rai-guy's magic and the continuing mental attack of the Crystal Shard had the illithid completely overmatched. Yharaskrik couldn't even focus its mental energies enough at that moment to melt away through the stone, away from the imprisoning goo.

"Surrender!" the drow wizard-cleric demanded. "You cannot escape us. We will take your word that you will promise fealty to us," the drow explained, oblivious to the shadowy form that darted out behind him to retrieve an item. "Crenshinibon will know if you lie, but if you speak of honest fealty, you will be rewarded!"

Indeed, as the dark elf proclaimed those words, Crenshinibon echoed them deep in Yharaskrik's mind. The thought of servitude to Crenshinibon, one of the most hated artifacts for all of the mind flayers, surely repulsed the bulbous-headed creature, but so, too, did the thought of obliteration. That was precisely what Yharaskrik faced. The illithid could not win, could not escape. Crenshinibon would melt its mind even as Rai-guy blasted its body.

I yield, the illithid telepathically communicated to both of its attackers.

Rai-guy relented his magic and considered Crenshinibon. The artifact informed him that Yharaskrik had truthfully surrendered.

"Wisely done," the drow said to the illithid. "What a waste your death would be when you might bolster my army, when you might serve me as liaison to your powerful people."

"My people hate Crenshinibon and will not hear those calls," Yharaskrik said in its watery voice.

"But you understand differently," said the drow. He spoke a quick spell, dissolving the goo around the illithid. "You see the value of it now."

"A value above that of death, yes," Yharaskrik admitted, climbing back to its feet.

"Well, well, my traitorous lieutenant," came a voice from the side. Both Rai-guy and Yharaskrik turned to see Jarlaxle perched a bit higher on the wall, tucked into an alcove.

Rai-guy growled and called upon Crenshinibon mentally to crush his former master. Even as he started that silent call, up came the magical lantern. Its glow fell over the artifact, defeating its powers.

Rai-guy growled again. "You need do more than defeat the artifact!" he roared and swept his arm out toward Yharaskrik. "Have you met my new friend?"

"Indeed, and formidable," Jarlaxle admitted, tipping his wide-brimmed hat in deference to the powerful illithid. "Have you met mine?" As he finished, his gaze aimed to the side, further along the wide tunnel.

Rai-guy swallowed hard, knowing the truth before he even turned that way. He began waving his arms wildly, trying to bring up some defensive magic.

Using his innate drow abilities, Jarlaxle dropped a globe of darkness over the wizard and the mind flayer, a split second before Hephaestus's fiery breath fell over them, immolating them in a terrible blast of devastation.

Jarlaxle leaned back and shielded his eyes from the glow of the fire, the reddish-orange line that so disappeared into the blackness.

Then there came a sudden sizzling noise, and the darkness was no more. The tunnel reverted to its normal blackness, lightened somewhat by the glow of the dragon. That light intensified a hundred times over, a thousand times over, into a brilliant glow, as if the sun itself had fallen upon them.

Crenshinibon, Jarlaxle realized. The dragon's breath had done its work, and the binding energy of the artifact had been breached. In the moment before the glare became too great, Jarlaxle saw the surprised look on the reptilian face of the great wyrm, saw the charred corpse of his former lieutenant, and saw a weird image of Yharaskrik, for the illithid had begun to melt into the stone when Hephaestus had breathed. The retreat had done little good, since Hephaestus's breath had bubbled the stone.

It was soon too bright for the eyes of the drow. "Well fired . . . er, breathed," he said to Hephaestus.

Jarlaxle spun around, slipped through a crack at the back of the alcove, and sprinted away not a moment too soon. Hephaestus's terrible breath came forth yet again, melting the stone in the alcove, chasing Jarlaxle down the tunnel, and singeing the seat of his trousers.

He ran and ran in the still-brightening light. Crenshinibon's releasing power filled every crack in every stone. Soon Jarlaxle knew he was near the outside wall, and so he utilized his magical hole again, throwing it against the wall and crawling through into the twilight of the outside beyond.

That area, too, brightened immediately and considerably, seeming as if the sun had risen. The light poured through Jarlaxle's magical hole. With a snap of his wrist, the drow took the magic item away, closing the portal and dimming the area to natural light again—except for the myriad beams shooting out of the glowing mountain in other places.

"Danica!" came Cadderly's frantic call behind him. "Where is Danica?"

Jarlaxle turned to see the priest and the two bumbling dwarves—

an odd pair of brothers if ever the drow had seen one—running toward him.

"She went down the hole after Artemis Entreri," Jarlaxle said in a comforting tone. "A fine and resourceful ally."

"Boom!" said Pikel Bouldershoulder.

"What's the light about?" Ivan added.

Jarlaxle looked back to the mountain and shrugged. "It would seem that your formula for defeating the Crystal Shard was correct after all," the drow said to Cadderly.

He turned with a smile, but that look was not reflected on the face of the priest. He was staring back at the mountain with horror, wondering and worrying about his dear wife.

CHAPTER

25

Hephaestus was an intelligent dragon, smart enough to master many powerful spells, to speak the tongues of a dozen races, to defeat all of the many, many foes who had come against it. The dragon had lived for centuries, gaining wisdom as dragons do, and in that depth of wisdom, Hephaestus recognized that it should not be staring at the brilliance of the Crystal Shard's released energy.

But the dragon could not turn away from the brilliance, from the sheerest and brightest, the purest power it had ever seen.

The wyrm marveled as a skeletal shadow rolled out of the brilliantly glowing object, then another, and a third, and so on, until the specters of seven long-consumed liches danced about the destroyed Crystal Shard, as they had danced around the object during its dark creation.

Then, one by one, they dissipated into nothingness.

The dragon stared incredulously, feeling the honest emotions as clearly as if it were empathically bound to the next form that flowed out of the artifact, the shadow of a man, hunched and broken with sadness. The stolen soul of the long-dead sheik sat on the floor, staring at the stone forlornly, an aura so devastated flowing out from the shadow that Hephaestus the Merciless felt a twinge in its cold heart.

That last specter, too, thinned to nothingness, and, finally, the light of the Crystal Shard dimmed.

Only then did Hephaestus recognize the depth of its mistake. Only then did the ancient red dragon realize that it was now totally blind, its eyes utterly destroyed by the pureness of the power released.

The dragon roared—how it roared! The greatest scream of anger, of rage, that ever-angry Hephaestus had ever issued. In that roar, too, was a measure of fear, of regret, of the realization that the wyrm could not dare go forth from its lair to pursue the intruders who had brought this cursed item before it, could not go out from the confines to the open world where it would need its eyes as well as those other keen senses to truly thrive, indeed to survive.

Hephaestus's olfactory senses told the wyrm that it had at least destroyed the drow and the illithid that had been standing in the corridor a few moments before. Taking that satisfaction in the realization that it was likely the only satisfaction Hephaestus could hope to find this day, the wyrm retreated to the large chamber secretly and magically concealed behind its main sleeping hall, the chamber where there was only one possible entrance, and the one where the dragon kept its piled hoard of gold, gems, jewels, and trinkets.

There the outraged but defeated wyrm curled up again, desiring sleep, peaceful slumber among its hoarded riches, hoping that the passing years would cure its burned eyes. It would dream, yes it would, of consuming those intruders, and it would set its great intelligent mind to work at solving the problem of blindness if the slumber did not bring the desired cure.

Cadderly nearly leaped for joy when the form came rushing out of the tunnels, but when he recognized the running man for who he was, Artemis Entreri, and noted that the woman slung across his shoulders was hardly moving and was covered in blood, his heart sank fast.

"What'd ye do to her?" Ivan roared, starting forward, but he found that he was moving slowly, as if in a dream. He looked to Pikel and found that his brother, too, was moving with unnatural sluggishness.

"Be at ease," Jarlaxle said to them. "Danica's wounds are not of Entreri's doing."

"How can ye know?" Ivan demanded.

"He would have left her dead in the darkness," the drow reasoned, and the simple logic of it did indeed calm the volatile brothers a bit.

Cadderly, though, ran on. As he was beyond the parameters of Jarlaxle's spell when it was cast, he was not slowed in the least. He rushed up to Entreri, who, upon seeing his approach, had stopped and turned one shoulder down, moving Danica to a standing, or at least leaning, position.

"Drow blade," the assassin said as soon as Cadderly got close enough to see the wound—and the feeble attempt at tying it off the assassin had made.

The priest went to work at once, falling into the song of Deneir, bringing forth all the healing energies he could find. Indeed, he discovered to his absolute relief that his love's wounds were not so critical, that she would certainly mend and quickly enough.

By the time he finished, the Bouldershoulders and Jarlaxle had arrived. Cadderly looked up at the dwarves and smiled and nodded, and turned a puzzled expression on the assassin.

"Her actions saved me in the tunnels," Entreri said sourly. "I do not enjoy being in anyone's debt." That said, he walked away, not once looking back.

Cadderly and his companions, including Danica, caught up to Entreri and Jarlaxle later on that day, after it became apparent, to everyone's relief, that Hephaestus would not be coming out of its lair in pursuit.

"We are returning to the Spirit Soaring with the same spell that brought us here," the priest announced. "It would be impolite, at least, if I did not offer you magical transport for the journey back."

Jarlaxle looked at him curiously.

"No tricks," Cadderly assured the cagey drow. "I hold no trials over either of you, for your actions have been no less than honorable since you came to my domain. I do warn you both, however, that I will tolerate no—"

"Why would we wish to return with you?" Artemis Entreri cut him short. "What in your hole of falsehood is for our gain?"

Cadderly started to respond—in many directions all at once. He wanted to yell at the man, to coerce the man, to convert the man, to destroy the man—anything he could do against that sudden wall of negativism. In the end, he said not a word, for indeed, what at the Spirit Soaring would be for the benefit of these two?

Much, he supposed, if they desired to mend their souls and their ways. Entreri's actions with Danica did hint that there might indeed be a possibility of that in the future. On a whim, the priest entered Deneir's song and brought forth a minor spell, one that revealed the general weal of those he surveyed.

A quick look at Entreri and Jarlaxle was all he needed to confirm that the Spirit Soaring, Carradoon, Shilmista Forest, and all the region about that section of the Snowflake Mountains would be better off if these two went in the opposite direction.

"Farewell, then," he said with a tip of his hat. "At least you found the opportunity to do one noble act in your wretched existence, Artemis Entreri." He walked by the pair, Ivan and Pikel in tow.

Danica took her time, though, eyeing Entreri with every step. "I am not ungrateful for what you did when my wound overcame me," she admitted, "but neither would I shy from finishing that which we started in the tunnels below Hephaestus's lair."

Entreri started to say, "To what end?" but changed his mind before the first word had escaped his lips. He merely shrugged, smiled, and let the woman pass.

"A new rival for Entreri?" Jarlaxle remarked when the four had gone. "A replacement for Drizzt, perhaps?"

"Hardly," Entreri replied.

"She is not worthy, then?"

The assassin only shrugged, not caring enough to try to determine whether she was or not.

Jarlaxle's laugh brought him from his contemplation.

"Growth," the drow remarked.

"I warn you that I'll tolerate little of your judgments," Entreri replied.

Jarlaxle laughed all the harder. "Then you plan to remain with me."

Entreri looked at him hard, stealing the mirth, considering a question that he could not immediately answer.

"Very well, then," Jarlaxle said lightheartedly, as if he took the silence as confirmation. "But I warn you, if you cross me, I will have to kill you."

"That will be difficult to do from beyond the grave," Entreri promised.

Jarlaxle laughed once more. "When I was young," he began, "a friend of mine, a weapon master whose ultimate frustration was that he believed I was the better fighter—though in truth, the one time I bested him was more good fortune than superior skill—remarked to me that at last he had found one who would grow to be at least my equal, and perhaps my superior, a child, really, who showed more promise as a warrior than any before.

"That weapon master's name was Zaknafein—you may have heard of him," Jarlaxle went on.

Entreri shook his head.

"The young warrior he spoke of was none other than Drizzt Do'Urden," Jarlaxle explained with a grin.

Entreri tried hard to show no emotion, but his inner feelings at the surprise betrayed him a tiny bit, and certainly enough for Jarlaxle to note it. "And did the prophecy of Zaknafein come true?" Entreri asked.

"If it did, does that hold any revelation for Artemis Entreri?" Jarlaxle asked slyly. "For would discovering the relative strength of Drizzt and Jarlaxle tell Entreri anything pertinent? How does Artemis Entreri believe he measures up against Drizzt Do'Urden?" Then the critical question: "Does Entreri believe he truly defeated Drizzt?"

Entreri looked at Jarlaxle long and hard, but as he stared, his expression inevitably softened. "Does it matter?" he answered, and that indeed was the answer that Jarlaxle most wanted to hear from his new, and, to his way of thinking, long-term companion.

"We are not yet done here," Jarlaxle announced then, changing the subject abruptly. "There is one group lingering about, fearful and angry. Their leader has decided that he cannot leave yet, not with things as they stand."

Entreri didn't ask, but just followed Jarlaxle as the dark elf made his way around the outcroppings of mountain stone. The assassin fell back a few steps when he saw the group Jarlaxle had spoken of: four dark elves led by a dangerous psionicist. Entreri put his hands immediately to the hilt of his deadly dagger and sword. A short distance away, Jarlaxle and Kimmuriel spoke in the drow tongue, but Entreri could make out most of their words.

"Do we battle now?" Kimmuriel Oblodra asked when Jarlaxle neared.

"Rai-guy is dead, the Crystal Shard destroyed," Jarlaxle replied. "What would be the purpose?"

Entreri noted that Kimmuriel did not wince at either proclamation.

"Ah, but I guess that you have tasted the sweetness of power, yes?" Jarlaxle asked with a chuckle. "You are seated at the head of Bregan D'aerthe now, it would seem, and you suppose all by yourself. You have little desire to relinquish your garnered position?"

Kimmuriel started to shake his head—it was obvious to Entreri that he was about to try to make peace here with Jarlaxle—but the surprising Jarlaxle cut short Kimmuriel's response. "Very well then!" Jarlaxle said dramatically. "I have little desire for yet another fight, Kimmuriel, and I accept and understand that my actions of late have likely earned me too many enemies within the ranks of Bregan D'aerthe for my return as leader."

"You are surrendering?" Kimmuriel asked doubtfully, and he seemed even more on his guard then, as did the foot-soldiers standing behind him.

"Hardly," Jarlaxle replied with another chuckle. "And I warn you, if you continue to do battle with me, or even to pursue me and track my whereabouts, I will indeed challenge you for the position you have rightly earned."

Entreri listened intently, shaking his head, certain that he must be getting some of the words, at least, very wrong.

Kimmuriel started to respond, but stuttered over a few words, and just gave up with a great sigh.

"Do well with Bregan D'aerthe," Jarlaxle warned. "I will rejoin you one day and will demand of you that we share the leadership. I expect to find a band of mercenaries as strong as the one I now willingly leave behind." He looked to the other three. "Serve him with honor."

"Any reunion between us will not be in Calimport," Kimmuriel assured him, "nor anywhere else on the cursed surface. I am bound for home, Jarlaxle, back to the caverns that are our true domain."

Jarlaxle nodded, as did the three foot-soldiers.

"And you?" Kimmuriel asked.

The former mercenary leader only shrugged and smiled again. "I cannot know where I most wish to be because I have not seen all that there is."

Again, Kimmuriel could only stare at his former leader curiously.

In the end, he merely nodded and, with a snap of his fingers and a thought, opened a dimensional portal through which he and his three minions passed.

"Why?" Entreri asked, moving up beside his unexpected companion.

"Why?" Jarlaxle echoed.

"You could have returned with them," the assassin clarified, "though I'd have never gone with you. You chose not to go, not to resume control of your band. Why would you give that up to remain out here, to remain beside me?"

Jarlaxle thought it over for a few moments. Then, using words that Entreri himself had used before, he said with a laugh, "Perhaps I hate drow more than I hate humans."

In that instant, Artemis Entreri could have been blown over by a gentle breeze. He didn't even want to know how Jarlaxle had known to say that.

EPILOGUE

For days, Entreri and Jarlaxle wandered the region, at last happening upon a town where the folk had heard of Drizzt Do'Urden and seemed, at least, to accept the imposter Jarlaxle's presence.

In the nondescript and ramshackle little common house that served as a tavern, Artemis Entreri discovered a posting that he found, in light of his present situation, somewhat promising.

"Bounty hunters?" Jarlaxle asked with surprise when Entreri presented the posting to him. The drow was sitting in a corner, sipping wine and with his back to the corner. "A call by the forces of justice for bounty hunters?"

"A call by someone," Entreri corrected, sliding into a chair across the table. "Whether it begets justice or not seems of little consequence."

Jarlaxle looked at him with a wry grin. "Does it?" he said, seeming less than convinced. "And what gain did you derive, then, from carrying Danica from the tunnels?"

"The gain of keeping a powerful priest from becoming an enemy," the pragmatic Entreri answered coldly.

"Or perhaps there was more," said Jarlaxle. "Perhaps Artemis Entreri had not the heart to let the woman die alone in the darkness."

Entreri shrugged as if it did not matter.

"How many of Artemis Entreri's victims would be surprised?" Jarlaxle asked, pressing the point.

"How many of Artemis Entreri's victims deserved better than they found?" the assassin retorted.

There it was, Jarlaxle knew, the justification for a life lived in the shadows. To a degree, the drow, who had survived among shadows darker than anything Entreri had ever known, couldn't rightfully disagree. Perhaps, in that context, there was more to the measure of Artemis Entreri. Still, the transformation of this killer to the side of justice seemed a curious and odd occurrence.

"Artemis the Compassionate?" he had to ask.

Entreri sat perfectly still for a moment, digesting the words. "Perhaps," he said with a nod. "And perhaps if you keep saying foolish things, I will show you some compassion and kill you quickly. Then again, perhaps not."

Jarlaxle enjoyed a great laugh at that, at the absurdity of it all, of the newfound life that loomed before him. He understood Entreri well enough to take the man's threats seriously, but in truth, the dark elf trusted Entreri the way he would trust one of his own brothers.

However, Jarlaxle Baenre, the third son of Matron Baenre, once sacrificed to Lady Lolth by his mother and his siblings, knew better than to trust his own brother.

LISA SMEDMAN

The New York Times best-selling author of *Extinction* follows up on the War of the Spider Queen with a new trilogy that brings the Chosen of Lolth out of the Demonweb Pits and on a bloody rampage across Faerûn.

THE LADY PENITENT

BOOK I
SACRIFICE OF THE WIDOW

Halisstra Melarn has been a priestess of Lolth, a repentant follower of Eilistraee, and a would-be killer of gods, but now she's been transformed into the monstrous Lady Penitent, and those she once called friends will feel the sting of her venom.

February 2007

BOOK II
STORM OF THE DEAD

As the followers of Eilistraee fall one by one to Halisstra's wrath, Lolth turns her attention to the other gods.

September 2007

BOOK III
ASCENDANCY OF THE LAST

The dark elves of Faerûn must finally choose between a goddess that offers redemption and peace, or a goddess that demands sacrifice and blood. We know what a human would choose, but what about a drow?

June 2008

RICHARD LEE BYERS

The author of *Dissolution* and The Year of Rogue Dragons sets his
sights on the realm of Thay in a new trilogy that no
FORGOTTEN REALMS fan can afford to miss.

THE HAUNTED LAND

BOOK I
UNCLEAN

Szass Tam has never been content to be one of the many powerful wizards who hold
Thay in their control, and when a necromancer who is himself a lich goes to war, it
will be at the head of an army of undead.

April 2007

BOOK II
UNDEAD

The dead walk in Thay, and as the rest of Faerûn looks on in stunned horror, the very
nature of this mysterious, dangerous realm begins to change.

March 2008

BOOK III
UNHOLY

Forces undreamed of even by Szass Tam have brought havoc and death to Thay, but
the lich's true intentions remain a mystery—a mystery that could spell doom for the
entire world.

Early 2009

Anthology
REALMS OF THE DEAD

A collection of new short stories by some of the Realms' most popular authors sheds
new light on the horrible nature of the undead of Faerûn. Prepare yourself for the
terror of the *Realms of the Dead*.

Early 2010

THOMAS M. REID

The author of *Insurrection* and The Scions of Arrabar Trilogy
rescues Aliisza and Kaanyr Vhok from the tattered remnants
of their assault on Menzoberranzan, and sends them off on
a quest across the multiverse that will leave
FORGOTTEN REALMS fans reeling!

THE EMPYREAN ODYSSEY

BOOK I
THE GOSSAMER PLAIN

Kaanyr Vhok, fresh from his defeat against the drow, turns to hated Sundabar for the
victory his demonic forces demand, but there's more to his ambitions than just one
human city. In his quest for arcane power, he sends the alu-fiend Aliisza on a mission
that will challenge her in ways she never dreamed of.

May 2007

BOOK II
THE FRACTURED SKY

A demon surrounded by angels in a universe of righteousness? How did that
become Aliisza's life?

November 2008

BOOK III
THE CRYSTAL MOUNTAIN

What Aliisza has witnessed has changed her forever, but that's nothing compared
to what has happened to the multiverse itself. The startling climax will change the
nature of the cosmos forever.

Mid-2009

*"Reid is proving himself to be one of the best up and coming authors
in the FORGOTTEN REALMS universe."*
—fantasy-fan.org

FORGOTTEN REALMS®

PAUL S. KEMP

"I would rank Kemp among WotC's most talented authors, past and present, such as R. A. Salvatore, Elaine Cunningham, and Troy Denning."
—Fantasy Hotlist

The New York Times best-selling author of *Resurrection* and The Erevis Cale Trilogy plunges ever deeper into the shadows that surround the FORGOTTEN REALMS world in this Realms-shaking new trilogy.

THE TWILIGHT WAR

BOOK I
SHADOWBRED
It takes a shade to know a shade, but will take more than a shade to stand against the Twelve Princes of Shade Enclave. All of the realm of Sembia may not be enough.

BOOK II
SHADOWSTORM
Civil war rends Sembia, and the ancient archwizards of Shade offer to help. But with friends like these . . .

September 2007

BOOK III
SHADOWREALM
No longer content to stay within the bounds of their magnificent floating city, the Shadovar promise a new era, and a new empire, for the future of Faerûn.

May 2008

ANTHOLOGY
REALMS OF WAR
A collection of all new stories by your favorite FORGOTTEN REALMS authors digs deep into the bloody history of Faerûn.

January 2008

FORGOTTEN REALMS®

THE KNIGHTS OF MYTH DRANNOR

A brand new trilogy by master storyteller
ED GREENWOOD

Join the creator of the FORGOTTEN REALMS® world as he explores the early adventures of his original and most celebrated characters from the moment they earn the name "Swords of Eveningstar" to the day they prove themselves worthy of it.

BOOK I
SWORDS OF EVENINGSTAR

Florin Falconhand has always dreamed of adventure. When he saves the life of the king of Cormyr, his dream comes true and he earns an adventuring charter for himself and his friends. Unfortunately for Florin, he has also earned the enmity of several nobles and the attention of some of Cormyr's most dangerous denizens.

BOOK II
SWORDS OF DRAGONFIRE

Victory never comes without sacrifice. Florin Falconhand and the Swords of Eveningstar have lost friends in their adventures, but in true heroic fashion, they press on. Unfortunately, there are those who would see the Swords of Eveningstar pay for lives lost and damage wrecked, regardless of where the true blame lies.

August 2007

BOOK III
THE SWORD NEVER SLEEPS

Fame has found the Swords of Eveningstar, but with fame comes danger. Nefarious forces have dark designs on these adventurers who seem to overturn the most clever of plots. And if the Swords will not be made into their tools, they will be destroyed.

August 2008

FORGOTTEN REALMS®

You cannot escape them, you cannot conquer them,
you can only hope to survive . . .

THE DUNGEONS

DEPTHS OF MADNESS
Erik Scott de Bie

Twilight awakes in the dungeon of a deranged wizard surrounded by strangers as
lost as she is. Twisted magic and deadly traps stand between her and escape, and
threaten to drive Twilight mad—if she lives long enough. . . .

March 2007

THE HOWLING DELVE
Jaleigh Johnson

Meisha returns to find her former master insane, and sealed in his dungeon home
by Shadow Thieves. She must escape, but her survival isn't enough: she must also
rescue the mentor she left behind.

July 2007

STARDEEP
Bruce R. Cordell

The seals that imprison an eldritch wizard within his prison are breaking
down, and the elves scramble to find the reason before the wizard's
nightmarish revolution begins.

November 2007

CRYPT OF THE MOANING DIAMOND
Rosemary Jones

When an avalanche of stone traps siegebreakers undermining the walls of a
captured city, their only hope lies deep within the tunnels. With water rising around
them, and an occupying army waiting above them, will they be able to escape alive?

December 2007

During the Last War, Gaven was an
adventurer, searching the darkest reaches
of the underworld. But an encounter with
a powerful artifact forever changed him,
breaking his mind and landing him in the
deepest cell of the darkest prison in
all the world.

THE DRACONIC PROPHECIES

BOOK I

When war looms on the horizon, some see it as more
than renewed hostilities between nations. Some see the
fulfillment of an ancient prophecy—one that promises
both the doom and salvation of the world. And Gaven may
be the key to it all.

THE STORM DRAGON

The first EBERRON hardcover by veteran game designer and
the author of *In the Claws of the Tiger*:

James Wyatt

SEPTEMBER 2007